Hello, dear Reader~

We offer you an advance reading copy (ARC) of Tripsy South's
Darlington, which will be published in trade paperback on 01
November 2019.

It's a clever and gripping thriller for those who love the taste and
smell of Old Florida, and who can never get enough of these
unforgettable tough guys with thinking minds and powerful hearts:

-John D. MacDonald's Travis McGee (*The Deep Blue Goodbye*)
-Randy Wayne White's Doc Ford (*Tampa Burn*)
-Robert B. Parker's Jesse Stone (*Stone Cold*)
-James W. Hall's Thorn (*Tropical Freeze*)
-Robert Crais's Elvis Cole (*The Monkey's Raincoat*)
-Elmore Leonard (*Rum Punch*)
-Dennis Lehane (*A Drink Before the War*)

Please note that this ARC is not in its final edited form and should
not be quoted without permission.

We thank you kindly for taking the time to consider *Darlington*.

Katharine Petersen
Publisher

Katharine.Petersen@adagiopress.com

DARLINGTON

TRIPSY SOUTH

ADAGIO

AN INDEPENDENT PUBLISHING CRUISE
est. January 1, 2001

Katharine L. Petersen
Publisher
William Garner
Editor

Copyright © 2007-∞ Tripsy South LLC
All worldwide rights reserved

Published in America by Adagio Press

Adagio and colophon are Trademarks of Adagio Press

Library of Congress Control Number: 2019946577

ISBN: 9781944855208

Cover and interior design: Dino Garner

This book is a work of fiction,
inspired by a thousand true stories.

P19591126
First Impression ~ 26 November 2019

for Kouda ~
Enjoy the wild ride
through Old Florida w/
Tommy Darlington ~

Tripsy

The exquisite violence coloring these pages
is dedicated to those assholes who fuckn shot me.
Three times.
You know who you are.
See you again, motherfuckers.

"Ye remnant of the brave!
Who charge when the pipes are heard;
Don't think, my lads, that you fight for your own,
'Tis but for the good of the land."

—Mackenzie MacBride
in *The History of the Highland Clearances*
Alexander MacKenzie

BLOODSMOKE

"*Darlington.* This guy the best we have?" The Old Man filled two glasses with 150-year-old whisky. Had its own otherworldly glow, a spirit of crimson hues on the verge of wildfire. He handed one to Alfred.

Slowly and imperceptibly, the Old Man's skin unfurled into a rictus, the furrows of his brow growing deeper, ploughed by years of violence and sinful thought. He sneered at Alfred's dark-gray, hand-stitched Brioni suit. *Fresh outta some pizza oven*, he thought.

Ran his huge sausage fingers through a shock of rich bimetallic hair that seemed to wave and slither of its own accord.

Alfred took the glass, couldn't summon the required single nerve to meet his boss's glare. "No, but he does things quietly and to standard, leaves no mess for someone else to clean up, or for a curious detective to discover."

Skin around the Old Man's mouth drew in slightly, straining under something that tried to claw its way out. Unbuttoned another snap of his fifty-year-old Stetson shirt, sat back in the overstuffed club chair, exhaling the unspoken comment he wanted to loose on Alfred. "Sounds like the best to me."

"He's small time," Alfred said, dismissing the Old Man outright. He absently loosened his tie, unbuttoned the top mother-of-pearl of his crisp white shirt, thought better about adjusting anything else and getting comfortable.

"What are you looking to have in your stable? Some high-end killer in bespoke Armani and Prada? A Hollywood version of the real thing?" Eyes yawed in Alfred's direction, locked on their target.

The two men sat in front of an ancient fireplace, built during the reign of Andrew Jackson. Dutifully burned day and night with old-forest oak that cracked and popped its presence every now and then. House was secluded in a forest of a thousand trees and deadfall from a hundred years of come and go, all cycles of weather, sun and the celestia. The heavy stone walls and triple-tiled roof kept the interior chilled down to 70 degrees, even in the dead of a Florida summer.

No living soul within 20 miles.

"He's not what I expected in a fixer, that's all. But he gets things done." As an afterthought, Alfred mumbled, "Sir," its three small letters falling harmlessly to the floor, noticed only by the dust bunnies.

"Family?" The Old Man drew harder on the whisky, threw a lasso around a few words that tried to escape. Poured himself another; didn't offer one to Alfred.

"High school sweetheart or something. Novelist. Not bad at all. Couple of hit books maintain them in cash, so they live comfortably. Little condo out on North Longboat Key."

"His work for us, all this gratis?" Filled his lungs with whisky that diffused up and burned into an evil countenance.

"Near as we can tell, she doesn't know a thing about his little side business."

"What else he do?"

"Paints."

The Old Man took careful aim at Alfred's eyes: "Houses or *Picasso*?"

"More like Picasso. Actually, he's excellent but won't get out there in the market. Keeps a very low profile."

His glare pulling off Alfred, it softened as it aimed somewhere up in the vaulted rough-hewn rafters: "Smart boy."

"Yes, but it'd be good for him to do something other than drive his own taxi. He needs a creative outlet."

"Drives a cab?"

"TommyTaxi, if you can believe that."

Both men snorted what may have been a laugh. Alfred's was a derisive one. The Old Man was genuinely amused.

"Did well on that last job. How'd it end?" The Old Man knew the answer.

A corner of Alfred's mouth rose imperceptibly. Was it pride? "Local law enforcement called it a suicide."

"Good frame-up?"

"It'll work, yes."

The Old Man turned and leaned into Alfred: "Not like last time with that . . . *sicario* you brought in from downtown Puerto Rico. Disaster."

Not turning to his boss: "Unfortunately, these types are all pretty much the same."

The Old Man's mouth pitched up slightly: "You're a snob, Alfred. A high-bred, white-collar snob. Bet you've never even been in a fist fight your entire life."

Alfred looked nervously over at the man who gave him all his marching orders, remained smartly silent.

"And I'll bet this Tom guy's never been over to your house, has he? Hell, you don't even thank the kid for a job well done, do you?" The Old Man laughed at his underling, reached over with a grizzly paw and patted him on his arm, cutting the tension a bit, but knowingly adding a whole new level: "Don't worry, I've been in this business too long just like you, so I'm a bit of one, too."

That was a lie: the Old Man came from nothing, sweat blood in bust-ass blue-collar shitwork, crawled up the ranks and over every warm body in his way, even buried the bodies himself.

No response from Alfred. Looked straight ahead. "Tom will do right by us, Viktor. And then we'll give him another job. And another. And he'll keep doing well . . . until you have him, ah, accidentally—" Alfred regretted that last statement before the finish.

The Old Man's head turned slowly, eyes narrowed. Patted him on the arm again, claws out this time.

Alfred flinched noticeably.

"You need a vacation, son."

Alfred recoiled again, knowing what the Old Man meant: he would be shuttled out of the office for an indefinite period, while they found a younger replacement, someone maybe not so uptight and snobbish with the hired help.

"Alfred, your problem is simple: you're an asshole wound up too tight. Your strings are thinned in places that make you vulnerable to snapping at an inopportune moment. Can't have that, can we?"

No response from Alfred.

"Darlington sounds like good people to me. Keep him around. What do you think?" Didn't give a damn about Alfred's reply. Took a long sip of his drink, held the glass in front of him, watching the flames meld with the ancient whisky and dance wildly through the flutes, reminding him of that bouncy little redhead. *Teeth, tits and ass on a stick of dynamite, that one*, he thought.

"I think he should show his paintings somewhere, get his face out there." Alfred felt his entire body quiver.

"The kid needs to be brought along slowly."

Alfred's small voice: "I hear Malaysia is considering new artists for government installations. Maybe we could make some calls." Quivering, and now a painful itch inside his shoes: traumatic neuropathy.

"Just make sure he stays on the payroll, son."

Another whisky.

"I'll see if we can't get some of his work out there, maybe use a different name for Tom. Be good for him." Now shaking, Alfred tried desperately to maintain a small measure of control.

"Bring up one of the girls, Alfred. The little blonde thing this time."

"It's only a matter of time before Tom—ah, Mr. Darlington's artwork is discovered, then he's off to Paris." He leaked slightly into his silken underwear.

"Make it two: blondie and Tina. She's still with us, eh? The redhead?" The Old Man put a firm hand on Alfred's arm, stilled his shaking.

Through an all-body shudder, he felt the Old Man's grip tighten up up up over his chest and farther up around his throat, cutting off blood to his next thought.

Alfred dropped the glass.

Cell phones suck. They annoy me more'n no-see-ums and pimps.

The one on the night stand next to my head buzzed and vibrated. Thought it was a mosquito so I slapped at it 'til I figured out it wasn't the State Bird of Florida.

It was Alfred: "Tommy. We have a job for you. Trail Motel, room 204 in the back. Single occupant, male. One seventy-five. Expedite."

He went on for another minute, filling me in on my next bull's-eye and where I'd pick up my cash, then the usual: no goodbye and a cut connection. Hell, at least the guy paid on time and in untraceable bills any Sarasota bank would kill to have on deposit.

Drove to the motel in between fares, since there weren't many calls I felt like taking. They were all local gigs out to SRQ, the airport between Sarasota and Bradenton. Tried not to hate a place that ferried people on their way to their dreams, while I was stuck in this hellish paradise.

Did a coupla 360s around the parking area and neighborhood, parked about half a mile off Martin Luther King, Jr. Blvd.

Why is it that every town in the US with a sizable Black presence had a Martin Luther King, Jr. Boulevard . . . in a rundown section of town? Could you imagine that—Beverly Hills with a Martin Luther King, Jr. Boulevard?

Sarasota was no different, but the town's power council ensured it was well away from the good upstandin' white folk on the ocean side of the tracks.

I disliked the name on several levels, not the least because it was too long to pronounce and use in everyday conversation, it was a screaming insult to The Man Hisself, and it was saddening that no one had made an effort to find a suitable diminutive, kinda like a nickname.

Me? To honor the man, I called it King.

Simple.

Parked somewhere along The Boulevard Dedicated To The Man Hisself and walked back to the motel, passing a few street prostitutes who, even at a freshly harvested fourteen looked a haggard fifty. At least I knew what they'd look like in thirty years, if they survived that long: much the same, except gray in the skin and low in everything else.

Sadder still was knowing a typical streeter's half-life was about five years on the long side, six months if they were really unlucky.

Their pimp was their handler, mentor and slave-owner, and he was the one who determined the early or late grave. I came to know every pimp in Sarasota and Manatee Counties by name, face and demeanor. There was always only one type: rotten-mean shitheads who devalued girls into a very short life of pussy for profit, then sold them for a short stack of 100s to some john or cop or local state representative who put three or four of them up in a small house north of town for $500 a month, and visited them a few times a week in blessed conjugation, then returned home to their Catholic lives in upmarket Osprey or on South Longboat Key.

Every full moon or so, my fangs and claws popped out and I made one of those pimpins my little pet, especially when I couldn't sleep, got tired of watching *Banshee* or *Bloodline*, or when Rachel and I were a few degrees out of phase. Many a pimp spent the last minutes of his beautiful life wondering what 5'10" and 180 lbs. of cruel fate had dumped him inside the gaping maw of a Dumpster, with thirty fast-burning seconds left on his game clock.

Everyone I knew said I had a calming demeanor and was pleasant to be around, so at least those pimpins received a sympathetic send-off and a one-gun salute en route to their next port of call, on the coast of kingdom come.

Cell again. Rachel. I let it go to voicemail, then listened in: "Tommy, you better be making some money, you loser. I'm writing my ass off today and I wanna celebrate in Margaritaville next month, so get off your lazy—"

Enough was enough: I folded my sweet Rachel, stuffed her back in my pocket, hoping to stamp out her little brushfire before she scorched my Levi's.

"Great sex revives the dead," she once told me.

Wished I'd come up with that one, but at least I could implement the thought later on when I got home and sexed her into little submissive sighs.

Room 204 was at the back of the building and it faced a stretch of King that had a long line of 60-foot palm trees and six-foot-high bushes along the street. I moseyed through an opening in the bushes and up to the motel where several partiers were laughing and pissing in the pool. Looked inviting enough to most tourists and weekenders escaping their duties and responsibilities, especially since they were all girls, about 19 or 20 years old, and obviously not from here.

In less than two notes, I guessed they were all from some holler up in Kentucky. The thick fertile air of Florida this time of year made it easy to make out the scent of a few molecules of Jack Daniels coming off the girls.

Once again focused on my primary, I moved upstairs and walked past 200 . . . 202 . . . and 204, stopping the briefest of moments to sense what was up across the two inches of sun-dead stucco, cheap laminated wood, and toxic Chinese drywall. Curtains were open a crack:

One man sitting on the bed . . .

Watching *Guardians of the Galaxy, Vol. 2* on the flatscreen . . .

Drinking a Golden Monkey IPA . . .

Freshly showered, wearing a towel around waist . . .

Smoking a cigarette . . .

Several lines of pink blow on a small pocket mirror just to his right . . .

A/C struggling on max at 68 degrees . . .

Warm exhaust streaming under the window, betraying a recent meal: Little Caesar's Meat Mania, lotsa crushed peppers. . . .

Didn't notice me go by.

At the end of the walkway, I stopped in front of a door, room 212, looked back toward 204. He wasn't curious enough to step outside and look up and down the walkway.

Down the stairs at the other end, then underneath the walkway, back to the other side and up again. Slowly this time.

Got to his room and stopped in front of his door, waited. Nothing. The tv was still on and he was still sitting on the bed, the coke field now down to forgotten dust particles.

My presence there didn't register.

Most people stumbled over the obvious in their mundane lives and kept right on walking into the next moment. I noticed everything, even surveyed the air molecules in front of me over and over as they floated past on journeys to who-knows-where. We all have this enigmatic affair, the subconscious, which is the quantum motor behind everything we do in life. Mine was abuzz full throttle here inside my skull, a mushy tangle of gray and black matter.

Rachel fancied herself the clever one, but she really had no clue what drove her own behavior. I smiled at that and reminded myself to mention it to her sometime.

The guy was oblivious to my presence, so I just stood there in front of his door: he got up from the bed and dropped his empty Monkey in the trash can outside the bathroom, got another one from the reefer, sat back down again in the same spot as before, not one inch to the left or right.

Creature of habit.

All I needed to know for today.

Ever seen air flash-freeze between a man and a woman?

I blinked once, taking a snapshot of her expression.

Eight seconds passed as she hovered there in front of me, all those once-soulful dancers of air now forming a solid block of ice between both of us.

The love of my life and me.

Blink two.

Another eight seconds.

Blink three.

Then she drifted closer to me, right in my face: "Fuck you, Tommy."

Rachel was my only real pain in the ass at the moment, although I could name a few pimps who gave me a dirty itch, the kind you wanted to scratch off with a cheese grater. If only this woman knew what I *really* did for a living.

Past girlfriends had little problem sharing emotions, and that's why I did whatever I could to keep them in my closet world, the unadulterated Tommy I kept hidden from soiled humanity. Each girl with her characteristic slap, kick, jab. One with a solar-plexus punch that rolled and bounced my eyes like ball bearings across a marble floor.

Each as different as the palette of an artist's protovision, my women defined my entire miserable life . . . guiding me down paths I never would've listed on my To-Dos, running the errands of love.

Since high school, Rachel had methodically experimented with every offensive maneuver on the map, 'til she came up with what worked best against me: the stinging verbal assault. Her simple little fuck-yous were hollow-point bullets, machine-gunned so fast at the center of my face that I only had time to react to my own pathetic response to her volley, never once addressing my actual intended target: each painful dismissal.

Even if I actually had the necessary reaction time, I wouldn't know what to do with it: how to execute a low-flying missile that always evaded my operational radar and managed to obliterate its target—me.

Mine was always just a wide-eyed look of shock, mashed up with despair and heartbreak. Too busy wrestling with fright to be angry at her, by the time I got around to where I was supposed to be pissed,

I'd melted again.

The fear of losing her. The lust of having her.

All rushing to gain first tracks, my emotions kept missing their designated mark. Stunted and bruised growth in many ways. Over the years, I struggled to redefine each feeling. Anger was no longer anger. Hurt was something altogether different, a welcomed misery. When I felt what I thought was madness, I dismissed it as something else entirely. I did feel and deal with things. In an unexpected and seemingly surgical way. In my job, I wasn't permitted the luxury of normal feelings, you might say.

Heart on a hard, I pressed on.

Rachel, someday I'm gonna tell you a little story. "I'm sorry, Rach. It wasn't my fau—"

"You were snoozing during coming of age, Tommy—"

"Got it the first time you said it, Rach. Like, years ago."

This girl had no problem sexing me twice a day, but when her thunderbolts unleashed on me, I was still the little kid from down the block, the guy she used to laugh and thumb her nose at, while she dated guys four and five years older. I was the little brother figure she toyed with, yet still loved in some odd way that haunted me for many years. And defined those paths into the wretched unknown.

Who could blame her? She was intelligent and thinking, 5'7" and then some, about 125 firm pounds, sexy banana-blonde curls, and richly sculpted Italian slash Russian features.

Clean and untouched, even by a single probing finger, until she was 23. I know this fact because I'm the man who unzipped her Levi's and released her from virginal chains and all that Jesuit chastity her mother preached like Matthew from the age of 18 months on. She'd been programmed like a PlayStation, but somewhere along the way had hijacked her mother-written code and reworked it into her own vision, something even she struggled to define.

Rachel wasn't simply the love of my young life, she was my life, long before old age set in, washing away other, mostly insignificant, childhood memories and the little horrors of adolescence and puberty.

"If you got it years ago, then why are you such a fuck-up, TommyBoy? TommyTaxi. What a joke. You're a Disney cartoon,

Tommy."

Like I've been trying to tell you for a while, Rachel, there's a little more to me than you'll ever want to know. "Cartoon."

Her insults were always delivered piping hot, with an ironic smile that said maybe she was half-kidding. Or not. The enigmatic smirk said it could go both ways but I secretly knew which way it usually played out.

"I wasn't destined to make old bones with anyone, Rach."

"Don't go there." Her head rotated slowly toward me, eyes scanning my face for just one sign of weakness.

"We're there, Rachel."

"You always do this." Still trying to find a chink in my paper armor.

"No, only lately." This time I looked her dead on. "You're looking for excuses. Again."

"Always putting the blame on me, Tommy."

That's when she backed away a foot or so, turned her head to the wall, seemed to continue the conversation there instead of with me, soon as she saw that look slide over my face, a look that said, *Don't do this now, Rachel.*

Regret was a constant companion these days: out of fear and anxiety from my real job, the one I tucked away from Rachel. I often said or did something to piss her off, then I'd get just a little defensive and that hidden monster clawed ever so closer to the surface.

"I don't know you anymore, Tommy."

My dry smile said it all. I mumbled something to my own distant wall: "You have no clue, MyLove."

With that, she slipped away and all I could do was watch, my heart dropping farther down my chest, desperate to return to its rightful place upstairs.

She came back down and shot a paper airplane at me. Smacked me in the center of my forehead and crashed to the floor.

Bent down and unfolded it. A poem I had recently written for her, somewhat of a promise that so far had gone unfulfilled.

I had titled it *Cycles* after all the endless iterations of good and bad with Rachel:

Loaded with chains and sorrows,

I step into many uncertain tomorrows
While storms and tempests convulse the sea,
and sweep away trackless paths that bring you safely to me
I am thus wrecked against the breakers of an unfortunate life,
and relegated to traverse all terraqueous ground in tearful strife
I consult the withered hags of my destiny,
they fail to treasure up aphorisms and maxims of ecstasy
Now deeply tinctured with false beliefs,
I go forth bravely, my heart heavy with griefs
Hoping that planetary influences oppose my fate,
and continue to keep me from my beloved mate
I hold out for smiles abundant and frowns a-few,
and many a year at home, my love, with you
But my future is assigned by a distant celestial orb,
whose grievous infidelity I cannot accept, let alone absorb
I take comfort that centuries will roll over the meanest of my history,
and flatten it into a beautiful truth of mystery
My dreams now a-glimmer on a distant horizon,
I set sail again, all the more wizened
Now filled with the pleasures of a voluptuous court,
my beliefs never again will I abort
No longer am I filled with the repetition of evil thought,
nor the acidic residue of all that is naught
The great planets, sitting in judgment over me,
lay me to sleep in a field of unfractured glee
I then hum incantations of the ancient and new,
that once again bring me safely home to you

I hate nice guys who do stupid things. Really stupid things.

Something sooo stupid that yanks them outta that Nice Guy category and stuffs 'em into Bad Guy territory, a dark place where unforgiving men with silent billions and a dark-adapted soul make one call that trickles down to my cell phone and wakes me up at some odd hour, that doggone mosquito buzzing in my ear.

Nice guys don't deserve what I have to give them. But someone out there thinks they do so I carry on and try not to think too much about it. Nice guys don't always finish last, but they almost never finish first, usually a distant second at best.

Room 204 had won the lotto, though, inventing some software that could hijack a person's computer, sit there like an invisible glacier, undetected by virus hunters, and continually suck up all the data on a hard drive or any external drive attached to the computer, directly or wirelessly. Whatever software and hardware lived on 1s and 0s, this program could swallow it all and surreptitiously stream it over to servers in India, Pakistan or some Fill-In-The-Blank-istan.

He'd rented a midsize at the airport, left it parked out back by the pool, nothing inside except the smell of new used rental car. This guy was conservative, though, and even had a bottle of ammonium cleaning solution and some paper towels in the back seat. Clean freak? Probably not, just someone who knew he could get MRSA or Ebola from touching a contaminated steering wheel. Or arrested for having cocaine dust on the dashboard.

"You coming in or not!?" One of the daisy-brain bikini-teens by the pool.

Even behind the anonymity of oversized Dollar Store sunglasses, her sparkling blues zeroed in on my muscled forearms and did a slow finger-walk all the way down to my crotch.

Looked over at her and nodded imperceptibly, and kept on walking.

"Be here all day, mister," she said in a lower Kentucky drawl, a little sultry spiced in. Didn't work well on her, but the effect was cute. Made a note of it: the cute, not the girl. Wasn't into 19-year-old kids. These girls couldn't touch the love of my life on any level—except maybe in kindness—so I never gave them a second look. In my line of work, I hoped they would do me the same courtesy. For her sake, I prayed she hadn't read too much into that little nod.

He was still on the bed, watching an old episode of *Californication*: Hank Moody was sitting in Dean Koontz's office, doing his impression of Popeye.

Probably hadn't moved all night. New lines of coke on the little mirror. If Hank had been there, this guy's coke woulda been hoovered up yesterday.

In my old flips, I padded up the stairs near his room and again stopped in front of his door. This time, though, I knocked four times.

The door opened and he peeked out and said, "Hey, what's up? You the pizza guy?"

Dayum, he was even smiling. A nice guy, no cares at all, like he was just in town for a few days on business, not sampling the stale bikinis downstairs. Just a nice guy. Who did a very bad thing to a whole lot of bad folks.

His coming-out party was sliding into servers at InstaSomething and ripping off every square nanometer of data over a month, and then presenting tidbits of it to the Board of Directors at their annual meeting, which he also crashed as a waiter carrying around bottles of champagne. When he managed to squeeze his way to the head table, he dropped small gift-wrapped flash drives in front of each director. If he'd done his own due diligence, he would've discovered that the majority of the directors all worked in the intelligence community, mostly for the CIA and Mossad.

By the time he reached the loading dock, alarm bells and klaxons were sounding throughout the Agency, not to mention a hundred other intelligence and security firms across the globe. Hitting InstaWhatever was only a distraction from the real job: stealing data from every single entity in the Department of Defense, plus hundreds of other clandestine organizations, departments and sections, and private companies and firms.

He could've created a website that made WikiLeaks look like a grade-school kid's blog, but his motive was entirely different: he wanted the recognition and he wanted a very high-paying job in the security industry without having to gain asylum in Russia or Peru.

While he'd correctly calculated his escape route, he had inaccurately estimated the power and depth of the world's intelligence and security apparatus, which was led at the very top by men in dimly lit offices somewhere over there in Europe and spread throughout every government and transnational corporation across the globe. Or so I heard.

And now here he was, holed up in a medium-rent hotel room, good cable and firm bed, plenty of Golden Monkey in the reefer, and some young sex at the pool if he so chose. Slice of heaven to most nice guys from outta town.

"Stewart Parrish?"

"Not the pizza guy, are you?" Clearly resigned, he opened the door all the way, let me in.

Broke my heart I had to do this. Wanted to wag my finger in front of his nose and lecture him. "You weren't very careful."

"H-h-how did you find me?" Sitting on the bed again, in his favorite spot, staring at Hank, now uncharacteristically mute, he absently grabbed an empty beer can and upended it like it was full.

"Someone got a call, they called a someone, that someone called me."

"So really you—"

"Your last option."

He looked perked up, looked at me. "Option?"

A nice guy who didn't just pull the tiger's tail, he had the CO Jones to tie a ball of fire to it. Nice guy who thought he would get off easy, get paid for having invented something cool and useful to a large organization, retire to Belize or Costa Rica, work from some designer hut on the beach. All the while never once considering the domino effect his route would have.

His was a dream world and my job was to shatter that world.

Nice guys always thought they had a plan, a way out. Stewart was no different and, like Rachel, never once considered the consequences of selfish action. If only they had some degree of introspection, but they subconsciously feared what lurked beneath so they buried it deep and away from prying eyes and thoughtful minds.

If we look hard enough, we can see the end of something, maybe a goal or wish or dream, but we never even think to see the means to get there, all the sacrifices and pains and collateral damage. If we could just understand the paths that get us to the end.

Uh-huh, if only. . . .

"Look, man, I can make you rich beyond anything you ever imagined," he told me, his voice now an octave well into the ceiling.

Just looked at him.

"Don't kill me. Please don't kill me. I'm only 23. I'm a fuckin' kid, man. A kid. I know what I did was wrong, but—" then some invisible hand pulled him away, and a grin slowly spread across his entire face. A wide, fatuous smile.

Pride.

Satisfaction.

Disbelief at having kicked all their asses, made them look bad, forced some higher-ups into retirement. To a McMansion on Bird Key, probably.

Just stood there for a moment, not answering him, then: "Stewart, you're a sweet kid, but you messed with all the wrong people. And if you can't see this, then you're sweet ... and stupid."

Each nice guy, regardless of how stupid he was, when he saw a break, a way in or out, made the mistake of jumping at it without thinking, a monkey blindly swinging in the dark from one golden branch to the next, taking for granted it would be there at his call.

"See? I told you, man! I can get you wealthy quick. Just let me go, dude. Please."

I wasn't heartless, especially with nice guys. I felt sorry for them. They were the ones who got picked on in school, shunned in college, ignored by the beautiful women at those big corporations they slaved at. They attracted flies like honey does, like shit does. Nice was worse than shit because everyone wanted to be nice but couldn't because they were all wired to be shitheads. So when nice came around, people crapped all over it, tore it down to its basic elements, and rebuilt it in their own image: shit.

Little voice in some deep recess of my subconscious reminded me that sometimes nice wasn't so nice and it had to be junked. That justification stirred up all the butterflies in my stomach, because I had always focused my energy on bad guys. Not like I had some special creed like Dexter. My Code of Deathics was altogether different. I enjoyed taking out the trash. Good people were not trash.

But hey, I didn't always get what I wanted in life and sometimes my choices weren't really my own. They were made by the men who paid me to do a job. Someday I would get to rewrite their rules, but not on this beautiful day in Sarasota, Florida, US of A, Incorporated.

When I left the room, I made sure the tv was tuned to HBO, which had non-stop movies; ensured I'd cleaned all horizontal surfaces with ammonium and paper towels, after brushing down the walls with a broom. Freshly sloughed-off skin cells can stick to walls as easily as any horizontal surface. I wasn't gonna leave behind even a strand of my DNA. If so, it would be lost forever in the putrid fibers of the hotel carpet.

At the pool, I smiled at the young lipgloss lolly in her thong bikini. She'd not only seen me but noticed me in a carnal way that wrote an indelible something in her reptilian brain stem. My careless nod cemented it in place.

Not cool at all, this loose end.

"Ready for me, are ya?" she said, that Kentucky twang a very wet, one-note Jew's harp.

As I walked away from NiceGuy's final resting place, moving toward his rental car, I hoped the loose end in the pink bikini would forget me.

Took a few more steps . . .

Turned around . . .

Soon as I saw the tall, gorgeous, young stud approach her, bend down and kiss her all sloppy-like, put his hand inside her bikini bottom and made her slither and twitch, I knew I was a distant memory that would blend and dissipate with the outgoing tide of her coming hangover.

Wondered if Rachel would see me this way sometime soon.

I could discern the edge of a whisper in combat or tell how many years a person had been drinking or smoking by listening to all the little harmonics in their voice. But I could not, for the life of me, figure out my girlfriend. And I hated that.

Some people wrote a novel after lengthy research and preparation, drawing on years of experiential experience and wisdom, and planning to the nth degree. Maybe a 100-page outline before they even started writing the book itself. By that time, the book was 25% done, which was a breeze to write.

"Just fill in the gaping holes with sweet bullshit," Rachel would say.

She sat in front of her overpriced MacBook Pro, a gift from me last Christmas, and banged out chapter after chapter without a moment of forethought. And the end result was always a seamless blend of mystery and passion and . . . murder of some kind. Obsessed with death and violence, Rach would sketch out details of grisly killings that scared the holy hell out of all the butterflies in my gut.

I wondered if she'd invaded my subconscious and ripped off pages from my own horror stories.

So it was no surprise that her latest story concerned me a bit: a young art student by day/taxi driver by night is found dead in a flat he shared with his novelist girlfriend. Was I reading into that one too much or—?

"Relax, pinhead, just blowing off steam," she told me in such a casual fashion I thought she was reciting a recipe for a bacon-and-cheese quiche.

"At what point in the literary process do you change the guy's name from Tommy to—"

"It's just a placeholder 'til I find his real name."

"And how do you—"

"His voice comes to me when it comes to me, Tommy."

"Then you just take dictation, write it down in place of my—"

"Something like that."

Most men would scream a hissy fit if their significant other cut their sentences short of any checkered flag, but I was happy with it: never had to say much around Rachel. She always thought she knew what I was thinking and felt the need to say it for me rather than painfully watch as I tried to do it all on my own. It must've been unbearable for her to witness my shredding the Modern English lexicon, desperately trying to find just the right words appropriate for her level of communication.

"Cool."

That always pissed her off, too: my single-word replies, ambiguous if not give-a-fuck. Maybe a last-ditch effort at getting her attention—something positive, I hoped, even though subconsciously I knew it was the wrong approach. My simple scripts gave her nowhere to go. So she burned a path and threw me down it, however long and tortuous and painful. I had always been a slave to her path-building. Thing is, each of her prescribed routes for me seemed better than I could've conjured myself so—subconsciously, at least—I went with whatever she gifted me.

"Naming characters is like naming your baby. It's marked for life so you best get it perfect at birth or it'll haunt you for decades," she explained, not looking at me.

18

"Or the kid."

Turned her head slightly: "Fuck you, Tommy."

Rachel's passion could go from warm pastels to cold blues in an eye blink, depending on the celestial alignment at that moment. Or whether she'd just charged herself with that secret sauce. She had a collection of old Mason jars on a shelf in the living room, told me once that's where she kept the acidic residue of summer storms. During a downpour, she'd walk outside and steal the darkest storm clouds in the sky, stuff them into the jars, let 'em ferment.

I swear she used it like some kinda ancient balm.

Reached under her shirt and ran my hands over the sides of her breasts, feeling the sweet descending curves that ended in pebbles topped with the thinnest film of soft, pliable flesh. Reminded me of those candy-coated peanuts in Cracker Jacks. I nibbled on them a bit, calming her down to a Category 1, and worked my hands into her cut-off Levi's. No complaints, insults or fuck-yous so I pressed on. When she was humming herself to sleep, I slipped out and hopped in TommyTaxi and merrily skipped off to my little moonlight hobby.

The more predictable I thought she was, the more mysterious she became.

Soon as I walked in the door after a long night on the town, knew exactly where she was. Rachel measured solar and lunar cycles with precision timepieces that put her in the same position this time yesterday and the day before, doing the same thing as yesterday and the day before.

Call me simple: I kept time by the passage of tears, headaches and empty beer bottles, and I still managed to get wherever I needed to be ... usually five minutes early, even to dental appointments.

I'd gotten in a little earlier than expected, having left one job unfinished. Didn't wanna think about that one.

Headphones on, listening to whatever dirge or funeral march was appropriate to the scene she was writing at the moment. Was a foot away from her and she was clueless, absorbed in her own sandbox fantasy of mystery and intrigue.

Backed away and went to the kitchen, looked around at all the junk we'd accumulated over the years: toaster oven we used like, four times in the last year . . . brand-new microwave convection oven . . . counter-top icemaker. Now there was a useful machine, a contraption that dispensed chewable ice. I prayed to the icemaker every day, enjoyed a chew whenever I passed it, stole little tidbits in the middle of the night and felt drunk afterward. In Florida, an icemaker that dispensed chewable ice was as essential as central air conditioning that ran at 68 degrees every second of every day in this miserable drippy oven.

Rachel was here and loved Sarasota, so I was here and I learned to tolerate the place. Truth? My roots could never quite gain the purchase necessary to call it home. Imaginary or not, they dragged under me with each step, every now and again putting out a feeler that probed the ground for signs of hope. To me, that was the ultimate in blind faith: always trying to find something that would never be found. My root-seeking apparatus was always on, forever hopeful, and forever failing, at least in Sarasota.

I was homesick for my own paradise that was so close yet still impossibly far off. Wondered if I would I get down to Costa Rica. Once I got there, what would I do? Sit around on the dock all day and fish?

"You're back early." She pillared in front of her office, arms crossed, no smile but, then again, no smirk either.

"Slow day." Grabbed a handful of ice, popped it in my mouth, chewed loudly. An excuse not to engage her and eventually say something that would set off all the firecrackers in her heart.

"Get my message?" She wasn't looking at me.

Pulled out my cell, unfolded it, pretended to scroll through the hundred or so messages I'd not gotten today, folded it back and said, "Nope. So tell me now."

"Asshole." Brushing past me noticeably, stealing my built-up static electricity, she went to the bathroom and took a long shower, leaving me alone with the icemaker and my now-depleted reservoir of combat electrons.

Used to add flavoring to the ice before eating it, but found it more refreshing to chew naked ice off the tap. Flavoring was a distraction from the wonder that was the crunchy coldness and refreshment of plain ice. The simplicity of bare ice was still a wonder to me, like water was a mystery.

Rachel was like that: a single drop of water.

The most enigmatic molecule in the known universe, water could be a solid, liquid, gas or crystal all at once.

How could one possibly deal with an entity like that?

Cold one instant, scorching the next, she could evaporate in front of your eyes into the ether and then form behind you or above you a moment later.

She could diffuse into the smallest of your chinks and cracks, ones you didn't even know you had, and then cool down to freezing, slowly expanding and pushing outward in all directions, and then fracturing what you thought was an impenetrable chunk of rock or block of iron that comprised your whole being, your flawless male essence.

"A massage would be nice."

Looked over at her as she fragranced her way to the bedroom, still dripping from her shower.

How does one accurately describe a woman's body?

A truly beautiful body. Rachel was so perfect in every way, not just every man's dream girl, but every woman's dream girl. No other woman I'd known was like her, getting both men and women all wet and teen-stupid. But Rachel did that to humanity, walked through life a complete mystery to all. A mirage, an elusive drop of water on a horizon that seemed so close yet forever far off. The closer you got, the more diffuse the image, until the last possible moment you realized it had been nothing at all. Or still a mile down that road.

"You coming, Tommy?"

Already at the door, watching her unfold her curves onto the mattress, dance slowly to a tune I couldn't discern. Eyes closed, she slow-waved a finger at me.

Dropped my clothes and stopped at the foot of the bed, admiring her. Beauty is one thing, but beauty in motion—in slow motion—is something to behold. It's like a thousand stunning images of the same scene, each somehow different and moving to the soul. She knew I loved to watch her dance and move slowly, very slowly, to capture each scene in my mind, savor it for as long as I could before moving onto the next one. Each transition from one scene to the next was sadness at having left one behind and eagerness to experience the next one.

It was like being perpetually aroused, only slightly falling from the orgasm, then being brought up up up again and again to that a sensation that was always and forever asymptotic to the grandest of sensations, a continuous sine wave on the universal graph of pleasure, with the dips and descents and hollows never ever going below the zero or neutral point where one could actually detumesce even for an instant in time, and recover from overindulging in the candy of the lotus.

There was no hot, steamy sex between us, where we ripped our clothes off and dived into each other's passions. That was for B movies and 13 year olds. Our lovemaking was the slowest possible level of touching and tasting each other's kisswater, feeling the textured deliciousness of the upper tongues in old-style deep-kissing, tasting the aroma and scent and deep-space chemistry of the flesh.

From her head, I ran my fingers over her scalp and through each bundle of wet and silky hair, now cool in the breeze of the overhead fan. Slow movements, sometimes firm, sometimes softer, all over her head and face. "Mmmmm" was her only response.

Moved down beside her, running my hand over her hips and waist, up around her chest, then to her tummy and that perfect, elongated and very deep navel. My tongue fit nicely inside it and that's where I spent considerable time when she was asleep. It was a tiny vagina to me, and I lamented over not being able to. . . .

As I consumed her entire body well into the evening, little spikes from my subconscious shot into my bliss, distracting me from Rachel and our lovemaking.

Pissed me off that I hadn't contained them, those otherworldly demons.

Feeling rushed, I rolled her over onto her back and pleasured myself into short, explosive bursts that left me with little white sparkling lights in front of my eyes, tightly closed, trying to push back those other little spikes that reminded me of something I had to finish up soon.

Didn't want to, but had to.

With Rachel, I tried to pretend that everything was okay.

Everything was not okay.

The best you could hope for in this life was that some small component of the machine that was your entire day would run smoothly for a few minutes, maybe hours, without derailing and causing a chemical spill or mass evacuation.

Seven pm: same sweet stuff with this woman, served with a twist.

"I work all day to earn enough money for both of us, Tommy, and what do you do? Go out and drive a fucking cab up and down the Trail for a few bucks a trip!"

"TommyTaxi works for me, Rachel. Writing works for—"

"Yeah, it works for you, but it doesn't pay you shit."

Oh, Rachel, if only you knew. My last gig paid $175,000. Add that to the $3.45M I'd stashed away the past few years and you had a nice starter account, something to retire on. Heck, I didn't even know what retirement meant, let alone knew what to do with it if I ever found myself swimming in it or stroking a putt over it.

Besides, there would always be the odd side job that kept me in the game of taking out the trash. The real trash in this town. And when I cleaned up here, well, there was always the fine State of Georgia.

With all these extracurricular activities, I had yet to build my little home down in Costa Rica, the only semblance of paradise left in the tropics. All my life I'd dreamed of having a peaceful place on the water, down there in the mountains or on the beach. The money I had stashed away would get me there, but the timing wasn't right; never was. Add to that, didn't know whether I could really trust Rachel. One day I wanted to tell her everything, the next . . . let's just say I didn't wanna share a thing.

"C'mon, Rachel, what's wrong with—"

"What's wrong with it? I'll tell you: balance, asshole. Equality. Uniformity. Sharing in everything."

Rachel was anything but balanced, although she professed to be a Libra. I guess she was one, at least according to her astrological chart, but on the inside she struggled with demons that tipped the scales more toward the corrosive and she tried to undermine and ultimately destroy every relationship she'd been in. While we'd known each other since potty training, and dated and played on and off, we'd actually only been together for a few years, still trying to figure it all out. And still floundering because of my demons that fought for the same purchase over my heart as Rachel and because of her own inability to self-monitor her caustic thoughts and behaviors.

Nowhere to go, I decided to drag a six-pack and a bucket of ice to the bedroom.

Mistake: she followed me like a fly on . . . shit.

"I'm not gonna do this with you, Rachel. Not now. I just got off my shift and I'm tired and I need a few beers. I'd like to—"

"Fuck you, Tommy!"

"Okay, Rach, please back off."

She opened her mouth to say something and I raised my hands in front of my face, closed my eyes and tried to say . . . something. How pathetic I looked in that moment.

For the first time in a long time, she sunk a little inward, like my display of helplessness had sucked the air from the only sail on her little glass boat. Made her look small and insignificant, a little less beautiful. Pitiful even, her feeling sorry for me like that.

Guilt and sadness rushed over me because I knew she really tried to make this work and she busted her beautiful ass at her own work to earn what she could for us. Her uncommon beauty radiated so much more: pride, satisfaction, and a self-confidence born of having found success even though she started with next to nothing.

Although she never spoke it, she was very proud that she was supporting both of us during such troubled economic times. We were very comfortable, living out here on North Longboat Key, and it could've been even better if I'd dipped into some of my own cash.

Some hidden voice told me not to. Not yet.

Why?

I wanted to tell her everything but in a selfish way sensed I would lose everything I had worked so hard for all these years. Hell, even with all that money, I wouldn't get down to Costa Rica anytime soon. And I hated knowing that.

Not wanting to admit it, I was now stuck in a relationship with the love of my life, who was hating me a little more each day, and getting caught up in a dirty business that would likely consume me and destroy both of us. Any move I made, any route I took was dangerous.

"I guess I've always wanted to know the real you, Tom. The man I've been madly in love with since forever. The man I saved myself for. The man who's always been my hero."

"You've never called me Tom before."

Small smile. "You are a Tom. A good one."

"You've never said I was your hero, Rachel."

Bitter tears formed in her eyes, fell in silver pearled strings down her cheeks to her t-shirt, grew into dark wet circles at her fraying collar, dissolving it a little more.

This was the most vulnerable I'd ever seen her and I had no idea what to do, what to say to her, how to react in any way. Worse, I was on that same path, not knowing where I was, where I was going. Whatever choice I made, I knew it would lead to disaster.

All my emotions, thoughts and feelings converged into some slushy amorphous thing, a volatile chemical soup.

I want you to know everything about me. "You don't wanna know me, Rachel. Not the real me."

Eyes opened just a little wider. Mouth dissolved from pain to something at least neutral. It spread across her face, muscle by muscle, dragging the overlying skin with it into something she needed more than I did: hope. She looked like Stewart in Room 204: pitifully hopeful that he had a chance. That he would survive me.

I'm not just a taxi driver. "I'm just a taxi driver. That's all I'll ever be."

"That's not true, Tom. You're an artist. You—"

"Paint? When was the last time you actually saw me pick up a brush?"

Inside voices told me to tell her, maybe just a little, something to keep her interest, keep her there with me, if only for a moment. If I lost her now, it would be forever. Rachel was looking for that golden branch, maybe just a small one, a tiny word not even fully formed.

"Okay, so I do it now and then. So what?"

Even though she didn't move, her eyes, her face, her whole body tried to pull away from me.

I reached out to her, expecting her to withdraw but she didn't. She let me come closer and wrap my arms around her, gently kiss her wet face, reassuring her that even though all may not be well right now, at least we listened and responded to each other in ways we never had before.

Led her to our bed, pushed her back onto the mattress and pleasured her once more in a desperate effort to push back all those monsters that lurked within the mirror of my delicate surface.

I love watching a beautiful woman sleep.

Sat back and stared at Rachel for hours, wondering what life would be like with her down in the fairytale land of Costa Rica. If the past were any indication, it'd be chaotic at best, even though the Universe moved toward organization and willful assembly. Something said to me that Rachel and I would somehow defy those Universal laws of physics and end up splitting some atoms.

Fueled by that thought, I hopped up and started a little project....

She was finally awake.

Blinked several times, not trusting her eyes. Rubbing the sleep away, she pulled herself up on an elbow, blinked again. The mountain of cash was spread out over the entire king comforter and all over the floor. More than three million dollars in 50s and 20s in 1,262 individual bundles.

Morning sunlight and a gentle breeze filtered through the white sheers and reflected off the bounty, throwing a light shade of green that shimmered across the walls, an ethereal effect in a room quickly filling with something other than what I had intended.

"Tommy?" She slowly pulled away from the sight, all that cash a giant cobra, swaying directly in front of her. Slower now, then sliding off the bed, backing away, eyes never leaving it, reaching around behind her for the wall, then the bathroom door, then: "Tommy!? What the fuck?"

Out of nowhere, I appeared, touched her shoulder. "Hi."

She jumped: "Shit! Asshole! What the fuck is this? What did you do!?"

Big smile.

"Answer me!" She punched my chest. Hard.

"Hey, relax."

"Don't tell me to—"

"Fine, then come into the kitchen and lemme make you breakfast and 'splain ya a few things."

"What the f—"

Held a hand in front of her face. She froze.

"You want an explanation, you'll get one. You want to know the real me, you will. Question is, dear Rachel, is that what you really want?"

"You're scaring me, Tommy." She tried to back away, but I held her arm, nudged her into the kitchen.

"Sit down."

Under my power, she sat uncomfortably on a bar stool, her eyes following me, also looking for a good escape route. At the moment, there wasn't one.

Rachel, I kill bad people for a living. And occasionally good people who do really stupid things. And I do the bidding of some billionaire assholes in Sarasota. "Rachel, I . . ." Then just blurted it out: "Sold a few paintings."

Explosive sigh, then: "What!? Sold a few paintings!? Which ones!? When!? Where!?"

"Calm down, Rachel."

"How can I be calm, Tommy—"

That hand again, stopping her midstream.

"Just a few paintings to some investors in Singapore and Hong Kong. I dunno who. That lady in LA, the one who asked me for a portfolio last year? She called and said she made a few huge sales."

"How much is in the bedroom, Tommy?"

Looked down the hall in theatrical fashion, straining to see into the bedroom beyond the corner and the door. "Uhhh, I dunno. Few mil."

"Million dollars!? You got paid in cash!?" Her face morphed into a rictus. "Who pays artists in cash, Tommy!?"

I started to move my hand in front of her face, she quieted down a bit.

"Rachel, you and I are gonna be just fine." I knew she didn't buy that explanation, but it was better to have a small form of mutual knowledge without my giving her all the details, at least all at once.

Continued preparing breakfast while she sat in mute protest, watching my every move, and ever so gradually a smile formed and spread from one end of her face to the other, a new sunrise that filled the room with a light never before seen or felt in our home. Diffusing into the bedroom, our new light washed over the pastel green emanating from the cash, softening the edges and slowly dissolving the giant cobra.

While I was surprised at her softening up quickly, I was disturbed that it was over such vulgar material wealth. I was seeing a different side to Rachel, one I did not like.

Costa Rica was retreating further and further away.

Some days with Rachel were a blur of pastels.

Don't even recall if we talked to each other. Yeah we did. We must have. About what?

Nothing was said about the cash, which I eventually mopped and hoovered up and tossed in the various holes and stashes safe from curiosity.

She wanted answers but not the ones she didn't want to hear, so I gave her a safe one: I'd sold some paintings. Maybe that's what I'd planned to tell her all along.

That was a lie and we both knew it.

I wanted to share the truth. About everything.

But something held me back.

What the hell was it!?

How do you tell someone who's never accepted responsibility for any wrong she'd ever done that she was indeed the cause of it all?

It's not that she skated through life blaming others. Not at all. Any shit that fell on her rolled off and stuck to someone else. Some people can do that, and it makes for a lighter load walking from one experience to another. Repression of certain memories. Suppression of thoughts. Didn't matter to her, long as the added weight of unwanted shit wasn't her burden.

My search for answers always brought me back to the same place I'd started, and so I did what I always did: left it at that and pressed on. In a way, I was like Rachel: I left a lot of dead weight in my shadow for someone else to carry. In my case, my own porter.

"Eggs?"

No response, but she sort of nodded in my general direction, stared out over the Gulf and setting sun. Normally she would've made a crack about having breakfast for dinner.

She pulled herself from the view outside and watched intently, my hands sliding the spatula across the pan, tilting the mass over, scraping some more, folding that, finally adding her favorite cheeses and spices.

Small smile on her sculpted Italian slash Russian front. Cocked her head sideways, all puppy-like. "Those, ah, paintings." Again, she looked out over the Gulf, a giant body of water she called Key Ocean.

"Mmmm?" One last fold and then slid them out of the skillet onto a plate, served with a glass of milk.

"You haven't sold any paintings."

Popped a few chunks of ice in my mouth, crunched loudly. "Ice cream follows eggs. Cookies and cream or plain vanilla?"

"The money."

More chewable ice. Wished it would've numbed my tongue enough for it to stop working. "And if you wish, m'lady, sprinkled with slivered almonds."

"With that kind of money, lots to think about."

"Midnight snack in the reefer: cannoli."

"All that accounting." Her hand reached out to me, ran over my arm and shoulder, massaging and kneading.

"Coffee afterward. New blend. You'll like it."

"Gotta be careful not to attract attention, though."

"Bon appetit."

"Need to keep it all in a safe place."

It went on like that for an hour, an antiparallel conversation: her with the money and me with this evening's menu, traveling side by side in opposite directions but still eerily consonant.

Up from her chair, stretched her bones like a kitten after a long nap, climbed over and sat on my lap facing me, blocked my view of Key Ocean, breathed warm words over my face as she kissed me, little things I couldn't quite make out but somewhere deep inside my subconscious I understood them completely.

I hate snowbirds. These guys who came down from Canada and

polluted Florida with bogus quarters and foul air pissed me off. How easy it was to go into s omeone else's backyard, drop your crap and then leave without as much as a thank-you. I hate those Canadians. Guess I'm prejudiced against all foreigners, having seen their destructive force on us, especially down under, the land of alligator, mosquito and sinkhole.

Nah, it was simpler than that: I was just pissed off, period. I needed a new bull's-eye, was all.

Alfred called again.

Voice and tone different this time. Said he had an urgent need and made sure I understood him accurately. Hard not to when he's yelling in my ear, offering next to nothing in pay. So I aimed the business end of my grump at him, told him to fuck himself.

Later in the afternoon. That's when the Old Man rang me.

I'd heard of him over the years, more like rumors of a certain presence well above Alfred and his condescending babble. This guy, though, he was old school. He'd grown up in the sticks like I had, knew his way around a job site. How he came to be the Chairman of the Board was beyond me, all those wealthy men who answered to him and never talked back. At least that's what I heard.

"Alfred talks highly of you, Tommy."

I knew it wasn't a lie. "Thank you, sir."

"Let's have a sit-down, you and I. A car will pick you up at noon tomorrow, SRQ, main entrance."

He didn't have to tell me not to be late. Every syllable and intonation in his backwoods drawl commanded it.

It's easy for a day to pass when you flip on autopilot and just get to it to the fun.

This was unfun.

The hours after the Old Man's call went by second by painful second. I'd already done many jobs for these men, just about every type on all terrain in all weather. And I never made an error. Was always prepared for stuff to get out of hand, and when it did, I was steps ahead, armed with plenty of viable options and a cool box of tools.

They never knew of these errors, didn't need to. All they had on me was that I was good at my job, never complained about anything or anyone. And was 100% reliable.

Even though I'd not formally met any other tech they used, I knew I was near the top of their current list, because I was often called in to clean up the messes left by others, and it sometimes included cleaning up the techs themselves.

That was the dirty irony, knowing that if I ever crossed them, these powerful men would kill me too.

Driving in Florida in the dead of summer. I was surprised that anything wanted to survive in this drippy oven but there they were, a legion of pretty real-estate agents, pushing easy buys, flocks of skeeters hovering over small water sources, and those ever-present gators, lying in wait. Anything that ancient, still around after millions of years without a make-up change, gave me a cold shiver, even under ninety-eight degrees and humidity points.

More I thought about it, Rachel was kinda like all of 'em: real-estate agents, skeeters and gators. Maybe that's why I hadn't told her about the money before. Or about my plans to head on down the road someday to Costa Rica.

Took a long theatrical glance down at my left wrist where a watch should've been. It was time, Tommy.

Made it out to SRQ in nice slow time, enjoying the a/c full blast, watching the mosquitoes super-glue their little bodies and hypodermics to my windshield, and seeing fewer pimps than usual out in the Newtown jungle. At least until a new swarm of wannabes popped up in their place.

Hey, more pimpins, more bull's-eyes for Tommy.

I wondered why the Old Man's guy had to pick me up at SRQ and then drive all the way out to the sticks, but didn't question it much. I'd learned that, with these wealthy and powerful men, you could get dead right quick asking too many questions. 'Sides, the answers to those stupid questions never made any difference anyway.

Still. . . .

"Good you could make it, Tommy," the Old Man grumbled. As ancient as those gators, he had a bone-crushing handshake that made me wince and he took delight in it. His leathery skin was as distressed as my boots, which shrunk in his presence.

"Yessir." At 5'10" and 180, I wasn't a wimp, but even at 80 years or so he made me look underfed.

"You know, Tommy, a man gets to old age and looks back, wonders all the things went wrong, tries to right 'em all, realizes he's doing all the wrong things." Looked over at me. "Follow me?"

Thought for a sec about acting all cool-like, but he'd seen it all before. Stared straight ahead: "Nossir, not at all."

He snorted. "Anyone else would've just agreed, but you're smart, Tommy. You're your own man. I like that." He slapped me on my back, kept one eye on me to see the effect.

Tried not to let on that he'd just knocked all the air outta my lungs, broke a coupla ribs, and now I needed a few deep breaths and a month of rehab to catch up. Wondered what he'd been like at 30. A brawler, probably. Wrestled gators for fun, then skinned 'em up and ate them whole—redneck-cracker sushi.

"Comes a time in a man's life he takes stock. I'm doin' that right now, son. And as I survey my field, examine the herd, I'm downright disappointed."

"Yessir." I slid away from him about six inches so he couldn't slap the wind out of me again. At worst, he'd take off my shoulder.

He noticed my having shifted to his left. "See that man out there, Tommy?"

The condescending asshole I'd listened to on the phone over the years half-floated in the center of a small lake, maybe about a hundred yards diameter at its widest point and obviously deep near the middle. He was tied up to a floating wooden platform, his head twisting right left, right left, not fully understanding his current predicament. Blood flowed down his face and neck, his sudden torquey movements tie-dyeing his once-white shirt. Clearly he'd been beaten.

"That there's a bad seed, Tommy. Done me wrong more'n once."

"Been pretty good to me." I knew it was the wrong thing to say.

Thought about snapping the Old Man's bull neck then and

there, jumping in the suv and skidding down the road to safety. But someone'd find me. Worse, they'd find Rachel.

His eyes burned into me: "Thunder down, boy." Looked away again. "That man I raised like a son, Tommy. And for the past seventeen years, been stealin' from me, a little here, little there. Thought we wouldn't notice the small changes in numbers on various handwritten ledgers, in the computer programs." He shook his head, lowered it for effect, raised an arm and twirled his hand in the air a few times, a signal for the show to start.

I knew it was just a little demo for me to see how he dealt with employees who got outta hand. If I bothered to ask why, the Old Man would say it was just business.

Alfred screamed something unholy.

Water at the edge of the lake, in about ten different places along it, slapped and splashed and churned, and then I noticed a dozen large alligators break free from invisible bonds and stroke out for the middle of the lake.

Bile rose in my throat. I knew exactly what I would see, how it would all go down, and still my eyes wouldn't pull from the unfolding scene.

"Man's gotta do things he don't wanna do, Tommy." Looked in my direction, sizing up my reaction again.

There wasn't one. Hell, I was just happy he couldn't slap me on the back again to punctuate his silly point.

I was a stone in that patch of pine forest out there in the middle of Florida fuckin' nowhere. Palmettos and sappy trees. A hellhole. Jumping up and down inside myself, I steeled my skin and bones to the sight that broke next.

Alfred loosed a loud bellowing sigh and went under for a brief instant, then came up with a guttural yelp and then a staccato shriek that drove all the wildlife from the trees, scattered the small birds and ground critters from the palmettos. His head thrashed side to side as one gator tore into an arm and death-rolled it off his torso in one rotation.

Shrieks and cries and sighs sounded from different directions, all those echoes throwing noise back and forth, back and forth, until it all converged right in my face.

Others moved on whatever patch of the one-armed prey they could get into, tore off more flesh until Alfred stopped screaming and gave one last wide-eyed look in our direction, his other arm seemingly slapping at my face in punctuation before going under the growing circle of crimson and Old Testament damnation.

"Real shame, Tommy." The Old Man turned away and leisured back to the truck, a retiree coming off two grueling holes of golf.

Without a word or reaction, I followed him into the next unknown, trying not to wonder who was in charge of putting those fuckin' dinosaurs back in their lairs.

Remember, Tommy, those answers didn't matter a damn.

Behind us, dark-red water diffused out in all directions and, under the high sizzling sun, drew swirly convection and eddy currents where Alfred once stood, a ghost of blood and smoke that marked the beginning of something I would never quite comprehend in these moneyed assholes, Sarasota's silent billions who flaunted their casual disregard for human life.

Not at all the way I operated but, then again, those I had dispatched over the years might've argued the point.

"We can't stay here, Rachel."

Good thing I had so few material things to my name, because it made it easy to throw some last-minute extras into my go-bag, which was always prepped and standing in a corner of the spare bedroom. Just add adrenaline.

"Tommy, what the hell?" She just stood there, defiant as always.

"Can't explain now, Rach. Pack only what you absolutely need. We're leaving this place now."

"What's going on?" Still not moving, and puffing herself up to look two sizes bigger.

Two long strides and I was in her face, drove my hand in front it, said, "Get your shit packed now. I'll answer all your questions when we're outta here, Rachel."

My sense of urgency finally caught fire and she started moving. "Okay, okay!"

In four hours, we were halfway to Key West, never once looking in the rearview. Said almost nothing on the way down, except when she had to stop and pee. Summer in the Keys was almost as miserable as summer on North Longboat Key or anywhere else in Florida, except one little detail: the view was stunning on all sides and it made you forget about whatever misery you were carrying at the moment.

At eight pm, the sun was just dipping into Key Ocean off to our right, with the great Atlantic on our left side, still trying to paint the beautiful dark turquoise with its battleship-gray hues. And failing with every wavy stroke of its dirty brush.

More hours flashed by as we rolled over the last bridge and onto the Key, slowing down to a crawl at Roosevelt Boulevard. Too much to say in one sentence, I just called it Rosy, trying to simplify my life even further. A right at Rosy, then about three and a half miles to Sunset Pier.

Nice to sit down for a bit and see the last few photons jet across the sky, a mushy and tranquil painting I needed to capture someday, maybe put it to canvas. Even though I'd seen this type of painting hundreds of times before, I finally saw the message: mine was a dangerous world of smeared strokes and slashes, a life that could never be defined by any well-defined straight or gently curving lines. Life for Tommy was just too abstract.

Rachel sat in silence, staring into the growing darkness, blind to the splendor in front of us. She sometimes zeroed in on the misery.

"So tell me now," she said, not demanding. Too exhausted to be afraid.

"That three mil?"

She nodded and nudged my shoulder with her chin, tired eyes eager for an answer.

"Didn't sell any paintings."

"Fuckin-duh." She pulled back and punched my arm. Hard.

"Before we got together, Rach, I worked for these assholes . . . guys you don't wanna know."

She looked at me intently, not saying anything, and expecting everything. After all, I'd promised.

"After the Army, met this guy who put me in touch with them. Little jobs at first, testing me out, but I had a knack for the dirt, never complained about anything, and always did things to spec. It impressed them."

Couldn't look at her right then, because I'd lied about what I'd done after I left Ranger Bat. "Rach, there're people out there who are just plain bad and they do evil things, and sometimes good people just get in the way of someone's business interests, and the people I've been working for send me in to shake things up so it doesn't happen again, so they can go on making billions. And I get paid a lot of cash to make that happen."

Our beers arrived. She took hers and sucked it down, asked for another before the waitress left our table.

Leaning into me, brushing my mouth with hers: "You mean you kill people, Tommy."

A brief look at her to say yes, then I looked out toward Cancun, 350 miles off to my left, wondered if some guy out there, looking over at me sitting here, was about to get his ass whooped by his girlfriend because he'd put many a life underground. Probably not, but I felt that distant camaraderie, nonetheless.

Me: a proverbial monkey on a black night, reaching for and expecting the next branch that wasn't there. That poor soul in room 204 at the motel had more faith in his invisible golden branch than I had in my entire repertoire of bullshit wishes and dreams.

Rachel could be a drama queen when she wanted, but in the shit she was oddly centered, like the eye of the worst hurricane, handled rough company better than most, bad news without crying a torrent, and hearing that the love of her life was a trained killer sitting on more than three and a half million dollars without punching him out in public and rolling his eyes down the boardwalk. Or screaming to the cops.

"You're gonna stay here for a day, then boat over to Cancun for a coupla weeks. I'll meet you there."

"My man kills assholes for a living. TommyTaxi." She smacked me again, whispered, "You should open up a new biz, Tommy: The North Longboat Sunshine Disposal Factory," then downed the second beer like water. "And what about you, Tommy? What will you do when I'm sunning nude on the beach down in . . . Canfuckincun?"

Still not looking at her: "I can't let them know I've left. I know he knows about you."

"Who?"

"The Old Man who hires me. Viktor something. I'll drive back up, let them see nothing's changed, do another job if necessary."

"How do you know they don't already know about our being down here? How do you know you didn't fuck this up, too, Tommy? Maybe you already killed both of us."

Long pause.

Looked back at Canfuckincun, hoping for a sign. A strong, positive one. Nothing but angry rain clouds in the distance, occasional little slivers of white light cutting the ocean surface.

Aftershocks of thunder punched the atmosphere, a dozen exclamation marks.

There was a message in there somewhere.

Had to be. . . .

"He's gone, sir. Left early last night with the girl."

"He'll be back," the Old Man said, a knowing smile that held so much more.

"The Canter job, sir."

The Old Man threw back a whisky. "Give it to Tommy."

"That's risky, sir. Do we want to do that, given what we now know?"

Alfred's replacement was twenty years younger but had more weight than his predecessor ever did. Ballsy enough to question his boss and smart enough not to come to work in a $5,000 Brioni suit. His was off-the-rack Men's Wearhouse, with a few handmade wrinkles on the sleeves for effect.

The Old Man respected him. "Let's see how he handles it. Then I want you personally to see to the loose ends. Understood?"

"Clearly, sir." Poured his boss another whisky, handed it to him. Ballsy enough to offer his glass as a toast . . . more than just to a new position under the Old Man. "I'll be sad to see this one go, sir. He's been very effective for us."

The Old Man turned to his subordinate: "No loose ends."

"And the girl?"

"No . . . loose . . . ends." He bristled at his subordinate's insistence, then dismissed it as diligence. He needed someone like this ambitious shit on his team. Alfred had been too weak and flinching. This new

37

guy was at the opposite end of a short spectrum, but at least he could be trusted to do whatever was necessary.

"Sir, just so you know: I have the Coles standing by in Key West to assist."

A sardonic look fell over the Old Man. "The Coles. Excellent. They'll look after the girl." He upended the glass, absently held it out for a refill.

Florida at summer noon: a crockpot that dissolves everything to the bone. What's left slow-bakes down to a powdery stick-figure of calcium and phosphorous this-and-that.

If I had disliked things before this day, I now wanted them in my rearview, driving into the lair of an Old Florida dragon, one I knew I could never slay. Too much power and old money, all spitting an otherworldly fire.

I never asked questions before; too busy killing assholes who needed to get gone. Now, a flood of who-what-when-where-why poured outta my head, so it seems my subconscious had been questioning things the whole time, storing them up for the right moment for me to do something about it. Our safety on my mind, this was definitely not the right moment.

With Rachel ensconced in Key West, I still felt uneasy and my anxiety kicked up a gear. The medicine cabinet still held my prescription bottles of that special pharmaceutical, and it called to me but I knew it might take the edge off. I'd ignored being an anxiety-depressive far too long, and now my carelessness was slowly haunting me, dulling my only remaining resources.

As I walked through the place, I wished I'd set up security cams with a 24/7 DVR to record any movement. At least I could've seen if anyone entered after we'd left. Preoccupied with my bratty Rachel, I missed a few little things like installing the cams.

I dismissed what I couldn't control and simply stopped and sensed the air.

A faint odor that blended in well with the background noise. Something earthy. Citrus undertones. Manly. Unfamiliar.

Left that mystery to my subconscious while I got a few beers from the reefer and sat out on the balcony, knowing there wasn't much to do for now, and I needed to appear normal. At least if anyone happened to be watching me, even from a comfortable distance, I'd be seen as the guy who came back to the house, casually drank a few beers in plain sight of the occasional passerby on our secluded beach, not a care in the world.

That's what an outside observer would've seen, maybe recorded to show the Old Man. On the inside, I was a roil of nerves, all twisting about each other in a new pattern, pinching in a thousand places and sending shooting pains up and down my already shaky core.

After the third beer, they unwound a little, found their rightful place somewhere along my main line, allowing me to settle in for a long night in a chair under a high silver moon, one of those things to howl at on a restless night in the hell I'd created for myself.

For my dear Rachel.

"We only need one crew member. Interested?" The young couple sat on the dock next to their newly purchased motor yacht, a fifty-two-footer with less than 100 hours in blue water.

Wearing her hiking pack, Rachel stood in front of the pair, listening to their bullshit, sensing they were amateur sailors. There was something more and it raised small tingles on her arms, scratching their way down to her fingers where it turned painful.

"C'mon, all expenses paid. How often do you get an offer like that?" The man guilted her, flashing teeth whiter than the hull of his mint-condition baby yacht.

"Let me think about it. I'll give you a call this afternoon." Rachel shook hands with Brad and Lydia Cole, took his cell and sat-phone numbers, then sent a quick SMS to Tommy:

Found a ride to Cancun. Quirky couple. Horny but harmless. See you there.

As she left, the woman's eyes followed her until Rachel disappeared beyond the security gate. "She's perfect, you know? You'd love her." Nudged her husband with a sharp elbow.

"A little old, don'tcha think?"

"Hell, no. See those tits on her? High and firm. I'd love to—"

"Watch me do her for a few hours, then you can have her."

"Not like the last one, baby." Her hands pushed up her breasts.

"We said we weren't going to talk about her again." His hands found her perfect DDs, undid her sports bra.

"That perfect round ass, though. Never forget that one, and I don't care what we agreed on. I'd love to find another one like her, husband. She said she needed to get there in a few days. No other boats or cruises running to Cancun all week, all these storms approaching. The girl has no choice." Gave her pretty husband a grim look: "Besides, Viktor wants this one looked after."

The woman turned back to the last spot where she saw Rachel. "She'll be back."

"Guaranteed."

Her eyes now back on him, pulled her top off, threw it at him: "Take me below and fuck me."

A perfect smile spread over his perfect face, and she wondered if it were in anticipation of pleasing his super-sexy wife . . . or indulging in sweet, delish Rachel and her exquisite jewels. . . .

My dad used to love a hangover because it was the only time he could feel anything. Sometimes I inherited his habit.

As I tangled with the sheet, a nagging dream looped over and over for my viewing pleasure:

Walking on a sidewalk at Disneyland . . .

Mickey and his oversized plastic smile offer me a boiling Budweiser . . .

I reach out to accept . . .

Fall into an endless pit . . .

Crash through rock bottom and the scene before me is a whole new kinda hell . . .

I am being alligated by a twelve-foot-long, single mother of six little dinosaurs and they all nibble at me for twenty-five years until only my tongue, lips and eyeballs remain.

After all, I needed to be able to share my sweet horror with Rachel.

At dawn, the sky burned dark angry reds and grays that signaled new storms over the Gulf, an eerie reminder of the scene with Alfred and the gators.

Awakened on the balcony in the same position as I last recalled, about midnight or so. Stiff and creaky, and still reeling from my nightmare about mama gator and her babies, I rose and showered for nearly an hour under hot water and steam that washed away the last few days' anxiety and tension. Soon as I emerged, it all hit me again with the same magnitude-six rocker.

Shit.

Rachel's only commo to me was the brief SMS, but she still hadn't answered her cell in twelve hours, so I left six voicemails. It wasn't unusual for her not to pick up. She rarely answered, preferring to let it go to voicemail, like I usually did with her calls. Was she punishing me? No, she was okay with the new intel I'd shared with her. Wouldn't play any petty games now.

Not to panic. This was vintage bratty Rachel. Nothing wrong here. All was well and good, except for that SMS: no "Hi, Tommy" or "I love you, Tommy!"

The call came at eleven am. The Old Man's new bitch boy had given me my bull's-eye: some guy named Canter, small-time businessman with a lot of money and a big mouth that had just cost someone a lot of their precious millions, according to BitchBoy.

Plan was simple: follow Canter out to Arcadia this evening around 7:00 pm, and ensure he didn't reach his destination.

Simple.

My thought was, if someone else says it's simple, it's not.

I left early to get out to State Road 70 by six. There was only one area to park so I could see the man's car, an older Mercedes, black.

He did not disappoint: the man rolled onto 70 at around 7:25 and I fell in about half a mile behind him.

No traffic at this time. Not even the usual speed traps. State Police were completing shift changes, and this was the quietest time of the year so no one was eager to sit alone all night waiting for the single odd motorist riding into Arcadia, Middle of Sticks, Florida.

I ran behind the man for an hour, then crept up slowly 'til I was about 400 yards back. At a long stretch coming up, with a 60-degree turn to the left. Turned off my headlights soon as I saw him disappear ahead. Ran full black until I was about fifty yards on his six. There was nothing but swamp and palmettos for the next dozen miles, perfect place to run off and not be seen for weeks, if at all.

41

Welcome to the original Jurassic Park.

No oncoming traffic.

Forty yards back.

His stereo blasted through his open windows and I could see him jamming to the beat, his left arm slamming the outer door of the car. Giddyup, hoss!

Twenty yards.

If he'd been observant, he would've detected the reflection of his rear lights on my hood.

If he'd been observant.

Five yards.

At about 10 feet, I gunned it and pulled alongside him, raised my .45 and looked over at him. Stunned, he threw his head to his left and looked directly at me, mouth agape, and I fired two shots directly in front of his right eye, missing it by an inch maybe, each bullet exiting through the opening of his passenger window and out into the dead of air.

His right hand had been on the steering wheel, with his left arm hanging outside the car, banging out that beat.

Upon seeing the blasts from my pistol, and surely hearing both over the ruckus of the music, he reacted as I had hoped: crapped his pants and jerked the wheel to the right, and his beautiful Mercedes careened off the road so smoothly one might've thought it had been his intended direction all along.

In painful irony, his headlights illuminated his final path: a sandy section of palmettos with who-knows-what in the shadowy beyond.

My car followed slowly off the road, pulled well off and into the palmettos, and I walked over to where the Mercedes now lay in a horseshoe, the driver's side wrapped nicely around a 65-foot pine deep into the woods, lights still aglow. How he had managed to miss all those other pines and pick one 100 yards into the forest was lost on me. For sure a moment of boondocks comedy. From the looks of it, he had tried to avoid the tree with a hard right turn, but the Laws of Physics objected and sentenced him to a split-second of inertia and a chance meeting with a seven-ton stop sign.

Reached inside carefully, my hand and arm inside a plastic garbage bag, and turned off his lights, checked his head to ensure I'd not shot him, said a final goodbye to the man, and retreated to my Nissan piece of crap, stolen earlier from a small, closed-up warehouse off I-75, the owner out of town for a good while, judging from the sheen of dust all over the body.

The drive back to North Longboat was uneventful and I almost said fuck it and stole down to Key West again.

Bad idea, riding down wide open road in a stolen vehicle.

Dumped the Nissan and retrieved my taxi, cruised back and popped a couple of Stellas, sat out again and flipped open my cell, tried Rachel but again no joy. Not even a text message. Nothing unusual.

Tell that to the thousand butterflies with razor-wings zipping around my insides.

I was able to reach my contact and give him a quick sitrep: man sleeping well. He told me where the money was, but I wasn't eager to pick it up tonight. Since it was in a poorly trafficked area of town, I knew I could retrieve it any time. His voice had been so casual, the Old Man's BitchBoy. Made me even more uneasy.

Everything's great 'til something goes wrong. . . .

The next morning, I grabbed a few extras and stuffed them into my go-bag and walked around the block, trying to spot anything out of the ordinary. When you have an excellent subconscious that's on 24/7, you can spot anything that doesn't fit. All you need do is pay attention and then act on that valuable intel. Of course, when you're a lifelong anxiety-depressive under severe stress, things may fall through the cracks.

Seeing and sensing nothing unusual, took a SCAT bus down to Venice and checked into a motel well away from the craziness of downtown and the water. Practically empty, the place was quiet, well lit, with a few vagrants shuffling around outside. No concern there.

Tried Rachel again.

No answer.

No voicemails.

No texts.

Ignoring gravity, an acid dragon began a steady ascent from a deep pit way down beyond my boots, and burned my chest and throat in achingly slow pulses. Each beat of my dying heart pushed the demon further up up up into an already crowded space. Something had to give.

Downed a gallon of water and ate some crackers over the hours, but that damn dragon kept clawing its way up.

Day later, rented a car with my Mississippi driver's license, an assumed name from my past, and headed down to Ft. Myers, to the Key West Express. Got in just before the initial boarding at seven am, found a choice seat in the main cabin, air conditioned and relatively quiet, and took a long nap, still fighting that dragon. Long as I remained calm, the beast remained still.

Almost four hours later, we arrived at the ferry terminal, now hopping with tourists, mopeds and rickshaws.

Called Rachel four times.

No answer.

Walked to our agreed-upon meeting spots.

No joy.

The acid demons moved in fast and claimed new territories inside my lungs and sinuses. Went to Mallory Square, found a seat at the nearest bar, and downed four beers in earnest. The place was packed with tourons doing as I was doing, so no one noticed my modest binge.

Overheard a conversation about a motor yacht that braved the trip over to Cancun, so I sided up to the trio of sailors, struck up small talk.

"Yeah, couple of lookers with that guy," one man offered. "All those tits and nipples and just one pretty yachtie boy. Lucky fucker."

I knew one of them was Rachel. I asked them to describe the women and they confirmed Rachel's looks and clothing, her old backpack with the straps shoved off to both sides of her impressive chest.

Now in even worse shape from the acid beers, I moved away from the conversation and sat on a nearby bench, hyperventilated for five minutes, managed to calm myself enough to call her again, knowing she was already well out to sea. She'd been gone for nearly 24 hours, which put the motor yacht about one-third of the way there, unless they'd met a nasty counter-current. Regardless, I couldn't reach her.

A spear of hot acid shot up into my jaw, flames radiating out in all directions. I doubled over and fought it, slamming my eyes shut and forcing my thoughts and sensations out of that long, dark tunnel. I hoped no one saw the anxiety attack, and looked around for confirmation. Each of the hundreds of tourons, alcoholics and drug addicts was lost in his own world of fake fun in a paradise that could be rent by a hurricane at any moment.

They couldn't possibly have noticed my fit of misery, which seemed to blend in well.

After a quick recovery, the best I could do was sit back and wait for her to call.

That acid again.

Fuck that.

Threw myself off the bench and ran down to the Coast Guard Station, asked about any reports of vessel boardings around Cuba.

No.

One guy behind a desk stood up and looked over at me, waited for his superior officer to leave the front desk, said that a motor yacht with a US vessel number had been reported stranded about 65 miles west of Bahia Honda, and the Cuban authorities had dispatched a cutter.

"Taking on water," he told me, while looking through faxed reports from US Navy Guantanamo Bay. "Hold on, sir . . . here's a report of intercepted messages to/from the vessel, a 52-foot Meridian motor yacht out of Key West: boat taking on water . . . two passengers safe . . . provisions for one week. That's it, sir. Sorry."

Two passengers safe.

Rachel had departed with a couple, presumably a man and woman.

"Any way to ID those two?"

He searched through more messages, deciding on whether to share them with a stranger, clearly against reg's. "No, sir. I could call someone . . . stand by, sir." He picked up a phone, speed-dialed a number. "Sir, Petty Officer Randall, Coast Guard Sector Key West. Any further traffic on that stranded US motor yacht out of Key West, sir?"

I tried to listen to the words from the guy on the other end. Sounded like: "Two passengers . . . husband/wife . . . Cole. Returning to Key West."

Randall looked at me, wrote down the names of the two passengers: Brad and Lydia Cole.

Where the hell was Rachel?

"Sorry, sir, nothing more than this so far. You said there were three passengers on the vessel?"

By the time he turned around, I was half a block away.

My only option, shitty as it was: I had to wait until the Coles returned from Cuba, and that would take about a week, depending on how long they were detained by Cuban authorities.

What if they had harmed Rachel?

I'd already shown my face at the Coast Guard Station, so questioning the Coles was not an option, especially if it came down to using a violent tactic to get intel from them.

And if I had to disappear the Coles, I'd be the first suspect.

Even if I ran, word would get back to the Old Man.

Rachel was fucked.

I was fucked any way you looked at it.

All that careful planning, quickly dissolving into the already saturated Florida air that flamed the burning tingles and itches under my skin.

The acid spear loosed itself again and shot out of my mouth in long, painful convulsions. . . .

Get used to it, Tommy: the pain is here to stay.

Woke up the next morning to a stiff tropical wind, the advance party of a huge storm headed our way. I'd left the windows open in my hotel room, praying to a thousand pagan gods that Rachel would call to me, let me know where she was, how she was.

And then I felt it, a terrible and painful itch deep inside my gut— all those butterflies had morphed fangs and claws. The room began to spin so I sat down on the edge of the bed, dropped my head between my knees.

For the first time in my adult life, I *cried*.

Little whimpers at first, then a rush of hot tears.

Stumbled to the shower and stood under the hottest I could take, hoping no one outside my room would hear my cries to Rachel.

I've never been a pessimist, but I'd also been on enough overseas and stateside missions to know how this all ended. Rachel had been kidnapped by two people who were probably experienced at this, done it many times before. It was a shitty case of bad luck and Rachel had made that choice. A very bad one, with considerable assistance from me.

Out of blind optimism, I called Petty Officer Randall again, hoping yesterday's news was only a nightmare I'd conjured up in my fitful sleep last night.

A frothy mix of anger and excitement: "You left before I could tell you more, sir!"

"What do you mean?"

The longest pause hung before Randall on one end and me on the other, like that block of ice between Rachel and me during an argument, and I could only watch it get larger and larger, filling up the space between us, consuming all the oxygen . . . and any sense of hope I'd cultivated, one small speck at a time.

"A third passenger was found . . . sir, really sorry for the interruption, got an emergency call. I'll get back to you ASAP." The line went dead.

How far can a heart reach up into one's throat?

I couldn't manage a grunt, let alone an appropriate response, like "Who's the third passenger? Is it Rachel? Is she alive? Injured? What are her injuries? When will she be transported back here?"

My mind went through a thousand different scenarios about what had happened to my Rachel: pleasure cruise gone bad . . . kidnapped and raped and murdered . . . molested and thrown overboard . . . taken by sharks. . . .

Even armed with a working map, compass and a true azimuth, sometimes I was just plain stupid.

I'd been careless on this trip. Hell, I should've seen it as a *real-world mission*. Rachel was my PC, my precious cargo, and I should've treated her like it but I was too casual in my thinking and planning, trying to spar with her and boss her around, telling her to meet me in Cancun in a few days, without taking proper steps to ensure her safety.

I'd never done this on an op, so why with her?

I wanted to believe in her, trust her like I trusted myself.

That was it: I needed her to be just like me.

But she wasn't like me.

Rachel was a wannabe tough guy who prided herself in being able to handle rough company, and I bought into it this time. I depended on her good judgment in a dangerous situation, one where she was out of her element, and now I regretted it.

Like all the other civilians, especially women, in my life, she overestimated her personal power at the very moments she was pissing off those with the real power. Pulling that tiger's tail, treating it like a stuffed Disney character. Women in today's society were trained to yell and scream at powerful men they'd cornered in some high-end DC restaurant. That was all Hollywood and Disneyland. These same women were woefully out-gunned in the real world. They had been set up by years of propaganda and mind control.

Rachel was one of those fools. And I was a bigger fool for buying into her blustering.

Now I wondered where else I'd been careless lately. The Canter job. Had I left a bullet in his car somewhere? Was my DNA on his car or body? What about the two at the motel? The smitten bikini I left at the pool, the computer brainiac?

How else had I screwed up so badly?

The Old Man surely was onto me now. They would send several teams to grab me, tie me up to that platform on the lake, watch me get picked apart by those fuckin' dinosaurs. They'd take Rachel, too.

I'd killed us twice.

Fucking fool.

In the throes of self-flagellation, I heard the phone shriek.

Randall! This time I was armed with all the right questions. Took a few deep breaths.

Soon as I sensed him on the line, I steeled myself not to react. Still those butterflies did dogfights up and down my main line.

"Haven't picked up your paycheck, Tommy."

The Old Man.

His tone was dark, voice slow and deliberate: "I hear Rachel will be repatriated soon. Good to hear. Gimme a ring when you two get back into town now, y'hear?"

He hung up the phone before I could say something stupid.

Instead of words, only a gaping hole in the lower center of my face, dripping acid onto the carpet.

Rachel will be repatriated soon.

"Yessir, she's alive." Petty Officer Randall snapped into the phone.

Overwhelmed, I fell to my knees, curled up on the rug, crying whatever else was left inside me. Tears were like shit: fulla stuff your head didn't need, so it dumped 'em in one big whoosh.

My Rachel was alive.

Squeaky voice down at my feet.

Pulled the phone to my ear, listened, tried to talk but couldn't, cried some more, gave him my information in burst transmissions, still using my false ID from Mississippi. Told him I was Rachel's brother and wanted to see her as soon as possible.

"She'll be arriving at NAS Key West tomorrow noon, sir. You can check in the main gate, see security about an escort, unless you have military ID."

"Noon. Tomorrow. Main gate. See security," I parroted, not at all embarrassed for sounding like a blubbering idiot. Good cover, actually, acting like Rachel's wimpy, distraught brother.

No one would suspect I disappeared people in my profession.

In my current state of mind, not even me.

In the chaos of trying to find intel on Rachel, I'd repressed that remark from the Old Man: "Rachel will be repatriated soon." He already knew more about her than I did, and that chilled me to the core.

Who did he know and where, in what organizations? Man that old and in that line of work made some very powerful friends in strange and dangerous places, especially as Chairman of the Board of some powerful underground organization of wealthy men.

The Old Man's tentacles most likely stretched out to places I couldn't imagine. The more I learned about these powerful men, the more I saw they were everywhere I looked. A cancer you could never excise. If you cut out one part, the rest grew back tenfold.

And the Old Man, what was he really like? Cruel, but only in the way predators are cruel: capturing, dismembering and killing their prey. Killing for survival.

Not a psychopath who tortured people slowly with some hidden purpose, the sheer enjoyment of it.

Nope, the Old Man got right to it: fed them to his alligators and didn't bother to stay back and share in their suffering, short as it was. He didn't need to worry about dead bodies because he had a recycling facility in his own backyard, certified by the Florida Department of Environmental Protection.

A real-life *Crawl*.

Yeah, I tried to convince myself of all that crap, then played back the last conversation we had: "I hear Rachel will be repatriated soon."

What kinda predator toys with his prey like that?

A week in Key West is always a Margaritaville cruise. Until it's not.

Rachel had suffered hypothermia and second-degree sunburn, mostly on her head and face, severe dehydration and, worst of all, psychological trauma, courtesy of Brad and Lydia Cole.

Randall from the Coast Guard stopped in to check on her, left an envelope for me with the ICU charge nurse.

"Sir?" the charge nurse called to me as I walked to Rachel's room.

Still in a world of haze and fog, I looked over at her, saw her mouth moving, hand me the envelope.

Flashed back to that nightmare: Mickey holding out a boiling Budweiser, I start to take it . . . then I fall into that fuckin' hole. . . .

Just stared at Nurse Mickey for a minute, absently took it from her, shoved it in a cargo pocket and looked back at Rachel.

There was no way to accurately describe what I saw, or what I knew and what I sensed had happened. And what lay ahead for her.

Tubes and electrodes fell in rivulets from her face, arms and groin. Pulled back the sheet to see the extent of the damage.

Rush of hot tears . . .

Burning itch cascading down down down.

What the cruel sea hadn't done to her the Coles surely had. Deep cuts along her legs and arms, black bruises inside her thighs and stomach and breasts, swollen and torn genitals.

"Sir? Did you read the note from the Coast Guard?" The nurse was standing next to me the whole time, watching as I examined Rachel and wept as I moved a hand over her torn and battered body. She'd even handed me a wet hand towel to put on Rachel's forehead to cool her down, and I'd not noticed anything.

Except Rachel.

"Thanks," I whispered.

"Randall is a friend of mine, sir. A good friend." She moved closer to me. "He told me about what happened. Said you might want to look at his note sooner than later. Not sure what he meant, but he had a sense of urgency in his voice. And if I know Randy, he meant now, sir."

My focus still on Rachel, I reached down and pulled out the envelope, tore it open, pulled the note up to my face. One eye on her, one on the boiling Budweiser, I took in as much as I could, put it back I my pocket.

One last look at Rachel, a kiss on her shredded cheek, and I was off.

I would never see paradise the same way again.

The drive to Anna Maria Island was the slowest and most painful haul ever. All rights, the Island should've been a Lonely Planet travel destination, not a mission.

Randall had put out feelers to his underground buddies, all from Army and Navy Intelligence, and they tracked the Coles from the moment they were picked up by the Coast Guard in international waters.

Why he went that far for me was beyond reason, and I didn't question his gift. Maybe I should have. Did he know who I really was? He'd mentioned his buddies in Army Intel. Had they revealed something about me? There had to have been some kind of information exchange, because guys like Randall didn't hand out information so casually to a shaggy-haired nobody with a driver's license from some Mississippi backwater. What was his motive? Questions best left for another day.

"Look, anything happens to them and you're a prime suspect." Randall was adamant.

"I have only one shot at this. I back off now, and I'll never get this chance again."

"Rachel's still in ICU."

"I know. She'll be safe there."

"You said this guy knows she's there."

"The Old Man, yeah. She's not a threat to him."

"But you are. And that means she's in his crosshairs, too."

My judgment was off now. Just shook my head.

"Never underestimate an old pissed-off Florida rattler. They've got a long memory, brother."

That voice underneath my subconscious said he was right and I knew it, even on a conscious level, that day-to-day surface where a proverbial taxi driver took me everywhere I needed to go but couldn't think a simple thought like what to eat for breakfast.

Breakfast.

I'd not eaten in two days. IHOP was two blocks down. Decided to walk before it got too hot. The place was hopping with regulars, their big rigs parked in the ample lot across the street, waitresses scurrying about like puppies, balancing three hefty plates on each arm and delivering each with cushioned accuracy.

Took a spot in the back by the bathrooms. Quiet. Away from the din of hurry-up-and-eat, shovel it down, get out the door and back on the road. A mentality I could easily understand: it reflected nearly every walking drone in the United States of America, Inc.

My cell rang and vibrated in my shirt pocket. Slapped at it, fumbled with it, dropped it on the table.

Randall.

"Look, I know you wanna protect Rachel now, but I wanted to give you the latest intel: they're still on the Island. Bed and breakfast. Gulf and Coconut. Secluded. Faces the Gulf. Checked in for a week. That was six days ago."

Folded the cell, made a note of each of the bullets he'd just shot me with. Knew exactly where they were. Problem was, they may be gone in less than a day. I had no time to plan or prepare. Fighting on the run wasn't just risky, it was gambling your life away. Too many things unaccounted for.

My nerves were being eaten away by those demon-butterflies.

In the seconds it took me to reach the parking lot, my mind shot over the immediate options:

Rachel. Couldn't leave her now.

Money.

Cancun now.

Belize or Costa Rica later.

A dirty blur of probabilities and I was clueless in which direction to move.

When in doubt, pick any direction. You could course-correct at any time en route to hell. . . .

The house was Old Florida: tin roof, Bahama shutters, many shade palms all around the space and pool. Nice, even. Something I could see myself enjoying down in Costa Rica someday, sitting out back overlooking the mountains and beach.

No foot traffic out this way, even on the beach. A few bicyclists every half hour, but that was about it. No cars parked on the street like in every other neighborhood in the real world. Not here in Old Florida. Nope. Each house a fortress unto itself, dropped right next to its neighbors, maybe a few feet of grass separating them.

Best bet I had was to park in their lot, walk right in like I was a guest.

"I'm sorry, sir, we don't have a reservation for you." She was as ancient as Old Florida, probably deeded with the land back in the day.

"I heard a couple of folks might be leaving soon."

"Where did you hear that?"

"Small island."

"Yes. Yes, it is." She looked at the register, then took a painfully long look on her computer—first generation, just like her.

"That old thing still work, ma'am?"

"Course it does, young man. When I go, it goes." Back to her search.

"Yes, okay. Ummm. All right, the Coles leave here later this afternoon. Checkout is usually noon, but they asked for four pm. I could ring you if you like."

As she looked up from her spot behind the desk, I was out the door.

The beach grounds were well kept, yard maintained, heated saltwater pool immaculate. Hundred-foot-tall Australian pines dotted the beach area, with stainless-steel barbecues at four stations in the picnic area. Wish I'd known about this place before we'd stolen down to the Keys.

The Coles were in the cottage closest to the beach. The hand-painted wooden sign read: #1 Tavernier. Nice two-bedroom suite. From the path, I could see the pair standing in the kitchen, laughing it up, sharing old war stories of rape and murder, torture and dismemberment.

How Rachel could ever have chosen to go with this pair was beyond me at this point. Rachel had no idea what real danger was. To her, it was still a stuffed, plush Disney character.

Focus, Tommy.

No time to prepare for anything safe and effective, I made the best of a hellacious situation. Armed with a folding blade and dull wit, made my way to the back bedroom area, looked for a way in.

Nothing.

They'd locked up each window tight, screwed bolts into the frames.

Shit.

Could see through the guest bedroom and out into the living room: two suitcases with wimp wheels, a small carry-on.

They were already packed and ready to leave.

Something eerie, some small entity, disturbed the air around me. I sensed the molecular displacement, was preparing to act, then—

"Something I can help you with, friend?"

A lightning bolt of acid shot through my body . . .

Jumped a good foot straight up, turned around mid-air . . .

Fell to the ground . . .

My hand outstretched, holding an imaginary pistol.

Didn't have to imagine how I looked.

Her explosive laughter said it all.

Soon as she caught her breath, said, "You okay?" Curious but not threatened by my odd presence.

This girl was clearly a predator, armed with a semi-automatic smile and a full clip of bullshit.

"Yeah. I think so. The old lady in the office said you guys might be leaving soon so I was just looking around, checking out the site." Pulled myself up, dusted off the sand, embarrassed that the slamming in my chest sounded like an earthshaking GONG!

"Lydia." She thrust out a manly Nordic hand like a sword, a tool that had clearly done some damage a thousand years ago.

Was she the one who'd beaten and tortured Rachel?

Those hands said fuck, yes. Like the Old Man's, hers was a bone-crusher. She looked directly into my eyes, searching for the same effect. I gave her nothing.

"Chris. Pleased to meet you." My Mississippi ID.

Behind me, I heard her husband creep up on me. I let him so I could sense his small predatorial advance.

Sometimes it was best to allow a predator to make a move or two, just so you could feel their movements.

"Listen, I'm really sorry about all this. I best be heading on down the road." I tried to act all casual, but my clumsy entrance killed that effect.

Lydia pulled her husband to her, wrapped those killer hands around his arm. "This is my man, Bradley Cole the Third." She wasn't just proud, she was full of an arrogance well beyond the simple happiness one feels after accomplishing something. Lydia Cole had painted a grotesque fantasy of herself and that pretty Bradley Cole the Third.

Those blindingly white teeth. I was sure he brushed them with Bic's Wite-Out, followed by a thorough washing with hydrogen peroxide, not less than 10%.

"Listen, since you'll be renting the place, why don't you come on in? We're doing the last of our Margaritaville before we head home."

Margaritaville.

Rachel used to love telling me that's where she wanted to party when we celebrated finishing her latest novel.

"Where's home?" I blurted out. Dumb schoolkid.

They looked at each other, a knowing exchange between hyenas. She said, "We're bicoastal. LA and New York. You?"

"One coast is too much for me: North Longboat Key."

"Ah, but in places it's narrow enough to have two, ah, coasts, only a hundred yards apart, yes?"

Clever, gleaming pearly whites Bradley.

Lydia came back with a margarita. Tequila fumes preceded the real thing by seconds and filled my nostrils with 200-proof shit-to-come.

Was this how they started with Rachel?

Killer tequila, playful banter, lots of laughs, slow removal of unnecessary clothing, one of them accidentally trips over the stool and onto the couch . . . My, what big, cozy boobs you have, Rachel!

Hand on the knife, slowly unfolding it, stretching it out as far as it would go, wishing it were a six-foot-long Claymore, a battle sword to slice these two Spaghetti-Os into a dozen nothings.

Cell phone buzzed and vibrated.

Had a fuckin' heart attack.

"Interesting ring, Chris. That a downloadable ringtone I can get somewhere?" Lydia asked, moving closer to me.

Too close.

"Sorry, guys, I should take this."

Lydia was already well into her accidental trip onto my lap when I jumped up from the couch and smartly moved to the door, closing it behind me, the cell phone pressed to my ear.

"Get back here now!" Randall, my new best friend. "She's gone."

Just as I had felt some small return to neutral, that ever-elusive zero point where things calmed down long enough allowing some sort of recovery, I was ripped away from it again, straight up the y-axis marked amplitude, the end point of which was hell.

A hot, burning soup pushed its way out of my mouth in a projectile vomit, an acid snake that choked me into a coughing fit.

Hands broke out in a flood of perspiration, rivered with the mix of the rising acid, heat and humidity.

"Tell me again. What the hell happened?" I barked.

"Her grandfather came down and had her discharged into his care."

The Old Man.

I love killing assholes. It's more than just a public service. That's what I preached to myself every night, although it is not what I practiced every day.

The Coles were right in front of me, not three feet away from feeling my blade all the way to the hilt.

Right in fuckin' front of me.

There was no plan.

Didn't need one.

So I stopped all thought, pushed back all the demons that had surfaced these past few days way back under the scorching Florida sand.

Shot off the couch and took down WhiteTeethBrad with one slice deep into his heart, ripped it around a few strokes as he spat out his last words in bright-red blood, his nicely manicured hands gently pushing back against me, fighting like the wimp he was.

Elbowed Lydia's surgeon-enhanced face, and she toppled over the wooden rocking chair. In one step, I was on her, bladed her from one ear to the other. Through the gaping wound, that animal screamed something at my face, defiant to her last spasm.

"Fuck you!" was it?

Both amateurs, the Coles had been so innocuous that no one had seen through their veil of evil. Each of their destinations was an ecotour of murder.

If any half-cop had bothered to do even a little research, they would've found these two, connected enough dots of circumstantial evidence, put them away in deep holes for a lifetime.

But that didn't happen, fuck me.

Those vivid images of dicing up the Coles faded with each passing mile down 789 to North Longboat.

When I ran out of their cottage to the truck I'd ripped off, they were right out there, waving sweet and smiling goodbyes, Lydia telling me to visit them in Belize sometime, and hey, we'll do Thanksgiving together!

The Old Man.

In my cloud of anxiety and depression, something I'd continually fought to suppress all these years, I'd underestimated him and his shrewd depth.

Again.

Bashed the dashboard and screamed something unintelligible, a deep, guttural wolf-like howl and a flood of oversalted tears that blinded me with hot needles.

In that moment, I was a runaway train with no uphills to slow me down, no barriers to brake me.

It would all end sadly and I knew this.

Rachel was the biggest pain in the ass, always had been.

She was also the ruler of my lines and the compass in my rucksack, always had been.

And I'd selfishly pulled her into my fucked-up world to comfort me and make me feel safe and loved. It was beyond the self-serving ego. I didn't do what I should've done to protect my precious cargo.

I'd killed my Rachel, my other self, many times unknowingly, yet there was so much I could've done to prevent those deaths.

The Old Man knew I would be coming, so when I got back to the house and dug up my big guns, they weren't there. His men had already searched the place, found all my secret holes and stashes, but not the ones with my cash. They weren't on the property.

Fuckin' cell phone on the passenger side buzzed and hopped across the seat. Knew who it was. Reached over and snatched it, that nasty old Florida rattler promising another lethal bite.

Fingered the window button, it slid down a few inches.

Threw out the phone.

Stole a look in the rearview: it shattered into a hundred black rattlers, the Old Man still hissing and snarling, slithering to catch up to me.

Alone and unarmed, I drove out to his place deep in that lonely pine forest of Florida fuckin' nowhere, getting sucked into a growing vortex designed, built and maintained by a group of men whose power I could not fathom.

And still I followed. . . .

Rachel was already dead.

That agonizing thought pulled me along the highways and roads all the way out to the Old Man's spread.

Nah, he'd leave her alive long enough for me to watch the death-struggle of this now-broken woman.

His cruelty ran that deep, and since I'd crossed him he would stick around to watch the entire episode, even join in at the rap party, slap me on my back again just to be sure I was awake 'til last call.

The Old Man would have his men all around, back in the woods and bushes, out of sight, waiting to pounce on me soon as I entered the compound.

And I'd go willingly, now beaten down to roadkill.

He knew it and I knew it.

I was now low-grade Winn-Dixie meat for his barbecuing pleasure.

Parked the truck a mile south of his place, after doing a wide box around his impressive property. The sun would set to my left as I approached, throwing any shadows to my right. None of his scouts would be looking in that direction. They'd expect me to be coming from the north. At least that's what any reasonable idiot might think.

The Old Man had been anything but a moron, but I was too wasted to come up with a better plan now. Running on past experience and spent luck, I was operating in the blind and on the cheap.

The Coles were now boarding their flight to Belize or Costa Wherever, and I imagined their bright sunny smiles, laughing it up with the flight attendants in first class, getting the royal treatment of champagne, 12-ounce mixed drinks, warm pillows and microwaved hand towels.

A small camouflaged shed off to my left. Storage. The Old Man owned every piece of dirt for 30 miles in every direction, so it wasn't unusual or out of place, but is was reasonably hidden.

Low-crawled up to it, stopped for 10 minutes among the palmettos, just waited.

Listened, tasted the hot moist air.

Moved to the double doors, snapped open the cheap lock, pulled the doors fully open.

Holy crap.

These guys thought they were being smart, hiding in plain sight, assuming that no one would dare set foot on the Old Man's property.

Boots without brains, you ask me.

Complacent, careless and stupid also came to mind.

In front of me was a small arsenal of pistols, shotguns, and rifles, all of various caliber, ammunition in military canisters, cleaning supplies and maintenance tools, all encased in heavy waterproofed plastic bins with transparent covers, probably stored out here well away from all the fire hazards in and around the main cabin.

Hiding in plain sight, because they thought no one would ever think of setting foot on the Old Man's property.

No one that stupid.

Or arrogant.

Sometimes the best security was anonymity. Then again, not with someone like me, a guy who could see through it . . . or just go on walkabout in the woods and blindly stumble onto it.

No time to think about that one.

Relied on old habits and previous training. As Rangers, we always trained like we fought, and fought like we trained. In the shit, we sometimes retreated to the basics, so a long time ago I'd ensured that mine was the best-equipped box of killing tools anywhere. I didn't simply train to the bottom rung of my ability like all the others, I trained to be the best Ranger I could possibly be. And more.

Simple.

Two minutes had passed and I was loaded with a nice balance of weapons, bullets and a fluid plan that wasn't actually a plan. More like a big Christmas wish.

Quietly closed up the shed, double-checked my gear, squirted heavy doses of light oil into the moving parts of the two .45 pistols and single M4 rifle, drained and wiped off the excess, and headed deeper into trouble, stopping a moment to check the wind direction: blowing slightly north to south and pushing the aroma of fresh gun oil well away from the old man's house.

In a fight, sometimes the enemy didn't have to see or hear you. With the right breeze, your spearmint breath or preshit vapors assaulted them from a hundred yards off, making you an easy kill.

A sudden shock of needles rocketed across my chest.

Couldn't breathe or even summon the next heartbeat.

Along the edge of the lake, I could see Rachel, now tied up to the same little platform in the center as Alfred had been during his ceremonial retirement from the organization.

Her hair was somehow darker, a rich red . . . all that blood.

Focus, Tommy.

Control your breathing.

Scan your sectors.

From this point, also saw most of the various alligator nests, each with a caged front likely controlled electronically from the house.

She looked even more fragile than before, her head slumped down, then moving slowly right left, right left again, and looking up briefly in my direction. Wailed something unintelligible but my subconscious got a solid lock on her signal.

Had to slam my eyes shut and swallow hard to stop my heart from climbing up into my neck.

Normally, I would've walked the entire perimeter, noting any and all obstacles, personnel, and anything that was tactically important to my work.

All I could see and think of was Rachel and all the stupid and careless things I'd done to put her in the middle of that lake.

I should've been out there, not Rachel.

Had no idea how many men the Old Man had out here, where they may've been, what kind of weapons and capabilities they had. I doubted that the little shed I just raided was their only source of arms and ammo. It was merely a secondary storage shed, hiding in plain sight.

I knew absolutely nothing about my enemy, except that the Old Man was indeed cruel and sadistic, and probably got off on seeing his victims die horribly and without granted dignity.

I had severely underestimated that level of inhumanity in him.

Sun Tzu would've said something pithy about a guy in my boots: Know your enemy and know yourself, and you'll win every battle.

You're royally fucked, WhiteBoy.

A smart man would've moved about the grounds slowly and meticulously, even though his chances of getting out alive were less than that of Hurricane Tommy rolling across a junkyard and then spitting out a buncha shiny new Cadillacs.

A careless soldier outta time and without a plan would've done what I did: fired two shots at each of the cages at lake's edge, letting the preternatural beasts know they were no longer the alpha predators on the lake.

Sudden movements in front of me and to my right: two soldiers with pistols. They were scanning the woods for the threat.

As they wasted precious milliseconds, my M4 rose in one fast movement, taking down each man with a head and neck shot.

Four men spilled from the main cabin, the Old Man bellowing orders and directions.

Sounded like, "Release . . . gators!"

Shit!

If I faced off with these soldiers, I'd probably take down a few more, then get careless or overwhelmed, and take a bullet.

Rachel would die.

If I made my way carefully to her, swam the 30 or so yards out to the middle and freed her from the platform, the soldiers would take me down.

I would die, leaving Rachel to the creatures.

My whole life quickly distilled down to this very moment. . . .

Firefights were always a blur of hot and wet darkness, demonic shadows, nonstop action, unpredictable spherical balls of lightning all around you.

Even though your adrenaline-kick opened up more memory storage in each neuron and recruited thousands more, you still couldn't possibly take in the entire horror show, let alone act on each movement and action.

Everything was supposed to be in slow motion, but still some things zipped by like little comets and meteors.

The Old Man had emerged from the house, hefting a SuperSix grenade launcher, firing very fucking large 40-mm bullets in my general direction, and sweeping the entire area like a flame-thrower.

Florida felt hot to the touch.

So did the shrapnel and kicked-up sand and pine splinters that zipped through my skin and muscles, arresting me in place for a few agonizing seconds.

Only two soldiers remained, the others having fallen under the Old Man's fire, carelessly shooting in all directions as I dashed from one firing position to the next.

He may have thought himself capable, but his actions were those of an 80-year-old brawler: sluggish and largely ineffectual. Except when he got lucky.

Still a smear of fuzz and smoke, I was right next to him as he held a small black box in his bloody hand, the SuperSix lying inert at his boots.

Resigned to his fate, he didn't bother to look at me, just grunted through a tunnel of hot gravel: "Took some balls comin' out here, Tommy."

"All it took was a GPS . . . asshole."

His face now awash in resignation as he pressed a few buttons on the black box: "Comes a time, Tommy. . . ."

Nothing I could do because all was a blur and I had no idea where to run to or how far it was or when I'd get there, so I followed the path of an old Code of Deathics: shot the last few syllables out of the Old Man's mouth, watched in slow motion as his weathered face tore off and frisbeed across the porch.

The gruesome carnival mask stared up at me in mute protest as I sprinted past.

Running down to the lake now, water churning from all sides, my weapon firing at the bow waves along the lake's periphery where the gators had been freed and were tail-stroking out to the platform.

Now at the edge, finding moving targets, shooting them through the dark, roiling liquid.

Screams seemed to come from different directions, a whirl of confusion and despair.

Through the din of the fight, I also felt the high-pitched oscillations of the last two sensations a warrior wanted to face: abject pain and fear.

Rachel's cries once again disarming me . . .

Jumping into the lake, shooting here, over there, farther over there still, not seeing targets any longer, because the giant monsters had submerged . . .

Rachel shrieked my name again . . .

Rifle now spent, pistols in both hands, bumping into a target, shooting its belly and head . . .

Rushing to the center of the lake where all the noise and screams and otherworldly rips and tears and bone-breaking pops could be seen, heard and felt . . .

Rachel . . .

Atavistic screams in the fading light, coming from all directions, it seemed, because my head was on fire, spinning and stopping then shooting, spinning and stopping then shooting again . . .

Above the surface, bullets cutting the air in long golden spears that found their mark . . .

Alligators rolling over and over near the platform, chunks of bloody humanity suspended in their jaws . . .

I fired until the heavy metallic CLICKS! of empty weapons finally registered . . .

Knife now slicing and cutting into the rough hide of one of the beasts that whipped its head and slammed into my back and jetted for the safety of a cage, the remaining beasts retreating in its wake . . .

"Rachel!!!"

The screams battering my ears had been my own.

She was already long gone . . . now in bits of flesh and shattered bone . . . sinking to the bottom of the transparent lake.

I dropped the knife and went under the water, a dozen feet deep around the platform, and fell in a mix of acid resignation and numbed senses with what remained of the love of my life. . . .

The silver light of an early moon splintered through the tops of the pines, a legion of swords cutting through the lake surface.

As I sank below, looked up and saw it: a slowly diffusing and curling vision, a ghostly canvas that moved in a million individual scenes, each new scene more visceral than the previous.

I struggled with each one, hesitant to let go of the hypnotic engagement, knowing it would be the last I would see of her.

Thrust into the next frame, an acid-speed shutter more horrifying in its metamorphosis of reality.

All of me awash in it . . .

Tasting it . . .

Breathing it . . .

Drinking it. . . .

My beloved Rachel, now little more than bloodsmoke against a fractured darkness that would haunt me every hour, as I drifted into exile from this cruel world.

I was true to her when I said that I'd never grow old bones with her.

Thing is, I always figured she would be the one who outlasted me, the underground rebel who took the lives of the unjust, sent them to untold depths.

That very rebel was the undoing of my love, my Rachel.

No recovery from such a loss, I sank even lower beneath the bloody mud, until my lungs screamed for air.

Any air would do, even the scorching moisture of this Florida fuckin' furnace.

With very few places to run or hide, I shot to the surface, bellowed something inhuman and chanted an ancient call to arms that sent waves across the lake, rocked the dense forest of oak, pine, palmetto and death, and even awoke the recently dead soldiers who did the Old Man's bidding.

The post-traumatic moments of combat are burned into a man's mind in fire and ice. Nothing eroded those seconds of sheer terror and pleasure.

The horror of losing dear friends.

The rush of killing and dispatching the enemy, destroying what he holds true to him.

Looked up at the Old Man's house.

Another full-on wave of adrenaline raged over me.

This time I felt every cut and slice of the relentless onslaught, a searing megadose of fire and itching powder.

I was a wide-awake drunk as I looked all around me and took a series of snapshots of the battlefield, then felt pulled back to the Old Man's cabin.

I blinked once . . .

Through smoky cataracts, saw a tall nude figure stumble across the threshold of the open door . . .

Me: blink two . . .

The figure fell to the deck in a heap . . .

Long blonde locks, matted together in sweat and blood, in a lazy freefall . . .

Frozen from battle, adrenalized legs barely carried me up to the house where I fell at the crumpled form . . .

All the anguish of the day's events came and went in a whoosh—anger, fear, frustration, desperation, loss—all soon replaced by a whole new set of feelings I thought I'd never see or feel . . .

Hope . . .

Faith . . .

Stroked her hair, pulling it from that familiar look . . .

Kissed her bloody head, her torn face, her beautiful swollen mouth and whatever I could lock onto . . .

Felt for injuries . . . some here, more there.

Too many. If I'd taken the time to examine each one, I would've spun outta control . . .

Closed my eyes as tight as I could, took short breaths. The rush gradually subsided . . .

Triaged what I could, then held her to me . . .

Cried in small short bursts at first then, as she awakened and called to me, mourned and celebrated all at once in a long wail that vaporized any frozen air between us . . .

It created a small vacuum that quickly sucked us together in a painful embrace that rent torn and bloody skin, fractured tender bones . . .

For once, we were in whole agreement, even if it were a broken yes . . .

In a raspy voice, stained with old love: "Fuck you, Tommy . . . all your fault."

We both cried in bitter laughter, painful and strained as it was, struggling with the emotions we needed to shed, words we desperately wanted to share in torrents and little hurricanes.

Thousands of scenes zipped across my mind, each one a question to be addressed well beyond the aftershock.

Not right now, the inner voice of my subconscious told me.

Pulled away from her mouth, said, "I thought you were—"

She tried to punch me. "Not me . . . fucking asshole." Then held me tighter than ever.

"The girl."

"Drifter. Guy had a stable of them but they're all gone except for her."

I couldn't tell her about the lake. "Her name?"

"Tina."

Held her as close to me as I could, realizing that Rachel, and not the innocent drifter, could've been the forsaken figure in the Old Man's lake of horror.

She crawled deeper into my bloody shirt. "Tina. Where is sh—"

"Gone . . . I'm so sorry . . . I tried—"

It was like that for hours, the horrible pain of injuries old and recent setting in as the numbing rush of adrenaline subsided, an outgoing tide of comfort and protection that now left us vulnerable, confused and spent.

The rising sun clawed its way through the dense pines and veil of ground fog, and shot tiny golden sparkles over her face, illuminating a wrecked beauty.

Kissed her and promised I would take care of her, knowing I was in no shape to promise anything to anyone.

Picked her up ever so gently in my arms, stole the Old Man's truck, and absently stumbled back to civilization.

You have two choices in life: give in or persevere.

Rachel was a fighter. She'd shown it all along and I'd missed the better part of that strength, mistaking it for some bratty overconfidence because I was blinded by my own arrogance and carelessness, gifts from a life of anxiety and depression.

She slept fitfully on the drive back, then drifted off into a painful slumber, still holding my hand in a puzzle-fit of flesh like never before.

Sitting beside her in the ICU at Sarasota Memorial.

Seemed like we hadn't left this place, after her miraculous return from Havana.

New tubes and wires poured off her head, face and chest.

Fresh bandages and stitches.

Rising bruises and contusions and welts.

More high-tech machinery in red, blue, green and orange lights, beeping, buzzing and flashing with news not good, a future uncertain.

I wanted to wake her and tell her all about my day, hear what she'd written in her latest novel, share drinks in "Margaritaville, you asshole," and laugh into the early hours of a better tomorrow.

Held her hand and lay my head next to her, my other hand touching her face, fingering her soft, curly banana-locks. Her breathing labored, mine soon fell in synch with it.

Too tired to fight the legion of demons—hers and mine—I let them take me under, down down down to the bottom of that murky abyss beyond rock bottom.

A moondance of silver swords cuts the darkness all around me, the searing vision of bloodsmoke forever in my mind's eye.

DEADLIGHT

I needed to murder something. . . .

Day by day, Rachel pulled further away from me, back into that forever abyss of horror and bloodsmoke. In our typical antiparallel fashion, I successfully escaped and survived the ordeal at old man Viktor's backwoods cabin, and she was drawn back to it under a mild yet inexorable magnetic hand that tugged ever so gently at her deepest fears. As usual, there was little I could do except try to convince her that all was okay and would be better soon.

According to the nadir of her heart, the world remained flat as ever.

Running a short errand one day, I rolled back home and saw her packing up the last of her things and tossing them in the back of a Jeep.

Not hers.

Some guy I didn't know was at the wheel, lighting a blunt and flipping back his long dirty-blonde locks and checking his pretty reflection in the rear-view.

Didn't look very Uber-driver to me, a low-level threat in anyone's book, but here he was, taking her just as Viktor had. Not under an atmosphere of violence, but his was even worse: it was under the illusion of a promised something beyond the bleak horizon Rachel insisted I had painted for us.

I sat there and watched this guy's new girlfriend load her stuff in his little beat-ass surfer-boy Jeep, not once offering to help. Guess it was age-appropriate. Maybe she liked that, having to raise a jungle kid who knew no rules or order. A fuckin' slob, you ask me, but I guess Rachel wanted this: simple, uncomplicated. And if Rachel wanted it, so did I.

By default.

Didn't move from my spot off the side of the road. Rachel looked over once, spotted me, didn't wave or acknowledge me in any way, grabbed the blunt from SurferBoy and dragged on it, blowing the exhaust in a dark cloud my way. Her eyes still on me, flicked the joint toward the house, trying to detonate the emotional dynamite she'd left behind, then turned back to her new horizon.

Although it felt like an hour, she and SurferBoy were off in minutes. As he pulled north onto 789, not even bothering to check the cross-traffic, Rachel locked eyes with me again.

Not a sadness.

A resignation of some kind.

We both knew time had run out for us, leaving an uncertain space with no definition. It wasn't the kind of vacuum that had sucked us back in together in front of Viktor's cabin months back, holding each other in painful vise-like grips and crying spent tears. Nope, this was something that defied the laws of physics. It just stayed empty, that vacuum, right there between us, and expanded as the Jeep grew smaller in my ever-narrowing field of view.

Skin began to tingle and leak its brand of toxic tears.

Breaths came in short bursts, parching my mouth.

Veins bulged and pulsed with acid that flooded every cell, each threatening to pop like a fragile party balloon and burn through everything around me.

Before the flood of tears unleashed, I raised my arms like swords and jerked my head upward, a mute scream of anguish loosing up up up into the blue heights.

A crush of demons shot from me, and in its wake a dark lust instantly filled what Rachel's outgoing wave had abandoned.

My last image of Rachel shriveled down to a single quantum of deadlight, blinding me to all that was good in my life.

I fuckin' needed to murder something. . . .

The first punch jerked her head fully to the left. All that thick, tar-black hair, winging out in every direction, torqueing her head and entire body in a painful rotation into the side of the building.

He loomed over the inert figure, surveyed the damage.

Obviously not enough, so his size-12 Mark Nason Bayard punted into her ribcage.

One shot.

Two.

Then a couple to her ruined face.

Took a step back and rolled his head to the side, smile fulla gold and silver glitter, not less than $5K of 18-carat gold injected into the top four teeth of his pitbull jaw. The two canines each got a dose of pure platinum. When he smiled in the dark, if there was just the right moonshine or starlight, his mouth glowed a shiny bear trap.

Just across the street, I lit up a cigarette.

The girl hit the building with a high-pitch SLAP!

In seconds, all thirteen of Popeye's patrons spilled outside.

Held the match up to my eyes and watched the dim flame of the strike-anywhere burn all the way down to my thumb and forefinger, the gruesome scene with the girl playing out in full focus in the background.

Tyreese was screaming at the small bundle on the ground: bitch this, bitch that.

A sharp pinprick from the dying flame left a black spot on my digits. In seconds, they blistered and I wanted to pop them. Thought better of it when I recalled how Mr. Muppets, Jim Henson, died some years back: got a simple bacterial infection, ignored it for a few weeks because Kermit and Miss Piggy were in therapy so they wouldn't kill each other on the set. Yup, he ignored that little infection right up to the moment it took his beautiful life.

Knowing how diligent I was about my work, I'd get caught up in kicking Tyreese all the way down the road to Miami, forget my little infections, and get eaten alive by microbugs from the inside out.

Finger and thumb blistered up some more, reminding me of the sourdough loaves Rachel used to bake us. Popped both of them.

I wanted to project my pain exponentially onto Tyreese.

Patience, Tommy.

Looked up again at the massive pimp standing over the girl, the small crowd shuffling into negotiated positions around the scene. Each of the thirteen rubbernecks had a gallon-size Coke under one arm and a bucket o' fried chicken under the other.

CinnamonSkin, the ugly little thing in a double-wide muumuu, said, "Hey, Tyreese, little white girl got blood on them pretty boots of yours. Whatcha gonna do about it, homeboy?" She then stuffed two wings into her maw, crunching on bones, feathers and all.

Tyreese took one step in her direction.

"Lissen, honey, this muumuu come wit eighteen wheels and air brakes standard. You sure you wanna mess wit dat?"

Imperceptible smile on the big man. Looked back at his work in progress.

Another woman bent over and pulled off the girl's scarf, her only real possession, a goodbye present from her mama before she'd split Fayetteville for points south only six weeks back.

The big man dragged the girl back to his '78 El Dorado, something tricked and pimped by a guy up in Tampa. Guy had been on a reality tv show last month and had been earning good cash lately. When he demanded payment for the El Dorado job, Tyreese shot him and stuffed him in a barrel, took his tv earnings.

I'd heard about the story from another pimp up the Trail, minutes before I turned off his lights and laid him to rest inside a Dumpster. Yup, he'd told me a lot about Tyreese that night under a billion stars and galaxies far far away.

The bright yellow floodlights from the end of the building threw a long shadow behind the girl. The grim silhouette possessed a pathetic Walmart dignity, stumbling and struggling over every crack and bump in the sidewalk, yet somehow keeping up with the girl.

Walked a few yards past Popeye's and saw Tyreese leaning over and trying to kiss his girl so everyone could see she was okay and all was right with her beautiful life.

He was kissing a corpse.

All I needed to know for now.

Turned around and headed back across the tracks to my TommyTaxi, hoping sixty-six degrees of a/c was still waiting for me. In heat like this, even at midnight, I left the car running and locked it, a reliable shelter to run to when things got unbearable in this drippy oven.

Tyreese.

My skin burned and tingled, a small itch that started in the middle of my back, a place where the demons inside me knew I couldn't reach. Rubbed my back up against the seat, trying to put out the fire.

Shit.

Gave up and looked in my rearview, just as Tyreese and his now-dead streeter pulled onto Tamiami Trail heading deeper into the Newtown jungle. Off on their honeymoon.

Small wave of nausea shot out from my gut.
Face flushed and still felt cold to the touch.
A burning cold.
A frozen burn.
Choose one. There was no wrong answer.

After two fares out to SRQ, my fave party destination in Sarasota, my head ached and my eyes swam in little bright sparkling lights that shot around like pissed-off photons.

The woman in the red Armani dress up waaay past her hips sweet-talked me all the way to the airport, shoving her business cards—six of them—down the front of my shirt, her long, soft fingers loitering on my chest. Guess she hadn't followed the news lately, all those women leveling sexual assault charges against moneyed men. She was a local real estate attorney, so maybe she was above the law.

Take it from me, down here in the sticks, it worked both ways.

Each time I glanced in the rearview, Tyreese flashed his fangs at me, said, "Keep watchin', whiteboy. Can't nothin' touch Tyreese, fucka."

Even the fare from Des Moines, a young doctor, white like notebook paper and skinny as dried spaghetti, chatted me up and down about how excited he was, landing that internship at Sarasota Memorial Hospital. This Doogie was a surgeon. Kind of a cute, high whine for a laugh that ordinarily would have shot me full of giggles. I enjoyed a smart, thinking person who knew stuff, had a unique set of tools that helped people . . . things other than what I carried with me in my tackle box of mayhem.

But Tyreese was right there in the back seat, cackling and spitting venom: "Whiteboy, I take you out back by the woodpile, chop you down to dog food."

"Sir!? Hey, Mr. Darlington!"

Hit the brakes and pulled off just in time to avoid swatting the neon-green VW Bug stopped at the light.

"You missed the turnoff to the airport," Doogie said.

Loud cackle from the ghost of Tyreese: "Man, I all up inside your head, whiteboy. You doooooomed."

Doogie got a free ride and a short apology. He reminded me to take it easy in paradise, not let all the sunshine and tropical fumes seduce me. Left me with a $20 tip just 'cuz. I'm certain it was for not killing the young mom and her baby in the VW.

Long drive down 41 toward Ringling Bridge. I wasn't looking forward to getting back home 'cos there was nothing there. SurferBoy had driven right up to my doorstep and ripped off the only precious thing that mattered in my life. And I hadn't done a damn thing about it.

Why?

At 10th street, could no longer ignore the growing burn making its way up to my neck, so I did a u-turn and pounded back up 41 into the jungle. I wanted to study this pimp a little more, see the extent of his business, maybe even where he got his girls so I could pay the import/export dude a visit some night at zero-three.

That stupid burning itch in the middle of my back.

Didn't bother putting out that flame. Just went with it.

The closer I got to Tyreese, the more my skin crept closer to meltdown. By the time I turned onto 22nd from Palmadelia, the whole taxi was on fire, even with the a/c blasting at sixty-six degrees. And it was only one am.

His house was 150 yards down and I inched along slowly as I could, feeling the heavy motor of TommyTaxi punch the asphalt. I wanted him to feel my sledgehammer roll into his 'hood, down into his lair, and right up into his evil bear-trap grin.

Didn't want him to feel any fear.

Or run for his life.

Huh-uh, when a man fears you, his body is shot with mind-numbing chemicals that roadblock all pain highways, stopping those outlaw signals from reaching the brain and letting him know he's about to get dumped into a meat grinder.

Fuck fear.

I wanted Tyreese "DaddyBoy" Glover to fully and completely feel, sense and experience each hammer-punch, elbow, stab and slice, and the thousand ripples of aftereffects and post-traumatic shocks and tremblors.

My final wish to the Universe was that every cylinder in his one-byte brain would be firing at 100% factory efficiency, so he could wholly focus on the full-on suffering, torture and punishment I was about to gift his sorry ass.

If the city of Sarasota only knew the public service I performed, they'd give me a fat tax break and the key to the banks.

Or send me up to Raiford for a long spell.

Elise Campbell's mom bawled into the phone and it made me angry, her cold reptilian tears.

I told her about how her daughter had died.

"I will kill that bastard," she said. "He took my baby, my sweet little girl. My—"

Something in her voice didn't vibe, so I cut her off: "It's been taken care of, ma'am. I'm so sorry for your loss."

Knew I shouldn't have told her that—it's been taken care of. Just slipped out. What the hell, my subconscious knew she wouldn't reveal it to anyone. My sub was never wrong. The only time things went wrong was when I ignored my subconscious.

For long minutes, she insisted paying me "a little something" for it. Besides, it would come out of the funeral expenses and insurance. She'd taken a small policy out on her daughter's life, knowing that this would probably happen sooner or later, her baby working the streets like she did.

"Hey, did you get my scarf back?" she asked. "It was a present from—"

Enough of this bullshit.

Cut the connection, dropped the oversized cell in my shirt pocket, although I wanted to pitch it out the window and watch another $800 Samsung Galaxy S-Something bounce down the road and shatter into 800 one-dollar bills like the one I'd pitched onto I-75 last weekend on my way back from a midnight recon up to St. Pete Beach.

In that dark moment, I wondered who the bad guy was here: Tyreese for beating young Elise to death. Me for ripping up Tyreese in his longest, most-splendid final hour. Or Elise's mom for. . . .

Ah, hell, I didn't understand this messed-up world, let alone what powered the malevolent entropy. After all, I was born and bred in an

Everglades junkyard, surrounded by the rusting scum of Detroit's finest autos, guard dogs big as panthers but a whole lot meaner, baby bottles full of Tabasco, and a guard for a mom and a warden for a dad.

If you can't make sense of something, study it 'til you can . . . or press on.

Cruised to an empty home for a six-pack and what promised to be a scorchin' sunrise over the Gulf of Mexico. Woo-fuckin-hoo.

I was naïve to think Viktor's death would've been the end of this misadventure.

Far from it: when I went back to his spread in the sticks, it had been razed down to the dirt, the area steam-cleaned and spit-shined. The forest remained as before, but where the house and other structures had once been, there now stood the ghost of emptiness, greeting me with a sardonic smile and an outstretched bony hand, inviting me over for a look-see.

And I eagerly followed.

His hollow eye sockets were illuminated by a deadlight that made me rocket-vomit and cough in rolling spasms.

While I lay on the sand, the entire battle replayed before me:

Turned around and saw a mirage of Viktor's weapons shed, a previous iteration of myself low-crawling from the shed to the old man's house, seeing targets pop up like electronically controlled plastic Ivans on our old Army Ranger firing range back in the day, and casually dropping them just as I had as a Ranger private.

Train like you fight and fight like you train.

That got me through the battle that day and night on Viktor's homestead, on autopilot from second one to the last bullet. . . .

As I looked around more and more, the scenes unfolded in slow motion, revealing details I'd missed back then:

Two of the old man's soldiers had popped up from around the back of his house, two stealthy Ivans ready to gun me down, but the old man's carelessness felled both of them. 40-mm rounds from his Milkor South Africa SuperSix failed to arm properly at that close range, but punched through each man's torso and did high-speed somersaults into the surrounding pine trees, shattering on impact and spraying fine splinters in all directions.

At the time, I hadn't been aware that Viktor had murdered his own soldiers.

Under normal circumstances, we go through life seeing all images and scenes as a syncopated filmstrip where not every image is recorded. It would take too much organic juice to power a typical brain on full auto 24/7. We'd have to consume the equivalent of a Snickers bar every minute of the battle, and all that sugar would have to be converted to glucose in milliseconds and shot through the blood-brain barrier and into the neural furnace in gallon buckets.

Without all those high-energy Snickers, we'd pass out from exhaustion, steam literally coming off our scalp, a busted radiator gone meltdown. The human brain is programmed to take in only so much intel at a time, and is capable of allowing only small burst-transmissions of information under times of severe stress.

Adrenaline and other neurochemicals are awash over the human brain in combat, kicking neurons into high gear, waking up dormant brothers for the fight. Time slows to a crawl because our brain is coded to "see" time under normal conditions as it really is. One second in real time equals one second to the brain.

But under severe conditions, when the cortex comes alive in ways we never thought possible, time stretches out interminably, making everything we see appear much slower, with colors and textures and tones all greatly enhanced and supersaturated on all levels, allowing us to see every detail of the threat and react quickly and appropriately.

During those moments of what we call the mad adrenaline rush, one second of brain-time stretches out to seem like 10 seconds of real time because of all the hyper-information the brain receives when supercharged during those mad minutes.

In reality, the hopped-up brain in combat processes and stores more intel, allowing us to see more of the threat sooner, in glorious Technicolor and Dolby TrueHD high-definition surround sound. Didn't need a neurobiologist to explain any of this to me. I'd seen it and lived it on each of my missions.

Replaying the tapes over and over, I pieced together the entire battle and as before, felt spent in the end. I remember carrying Rachel to the old man's truck and driving through the forest of pine and palmetto, somehow finding the main road back to Sarasota and then onto Longboat Key.

But I'd dropped a few frames back then: on the hardball to Sarasota, squinting to see through the haze of post-traumatic stress, I'd hit a speed bump.

Speedbump in the sticks?

Slowed down and lit the rear roll-bar lamps and saw this fourteen-foot alligator dragging it's broke-ass tail into the bush and then looking over at me briefly, bellowing a small earthquake that rocked the truck. The beast seemed to say, "See you again, asshole . . . see you again. . . ."

I hate mirrors.

Any kinda reflective surface. They're never faithful or true. When I used to pass one and spy the image looking back at me, I never recognized it but somehow I knew it was familiar. Maybe a forgotten or repressed memory, one meant to be thrown away to make room for something meaningful. Or less traumatic.

Since Rachel left, the condo sat motionless, all the frenetic photons diffusing out the windows and French doors for sunnier spaces to light on fire. Some of the electrons, the really pissed-off ones, stuck around and buzzed around me at night, taunting me with painful itches and burns and pricks no amount of scratching or hydrocortisone or beer could cure.

So I just let those memories of pain nibble away at me, like every mosquito in Florida eventually did, taking away the last of my blood, now a thick sludge of dead cells and spent platelets. By the time they'd gotten down to the bones, I was passed out on the lounger outside, hoping to take in my last breath of warm, heavy Florida sky.

And not wake up again.

I hate alarm clocks more'n mirrors, mostly because they remind of responsibilities I don't want, people I have to take care of but would rather ignore. Slapped at every horizontal surface until I figured out the alarm was on my arm. Caleb's watch. He'd left it here the other night and told me to hold onto it 'cos it was a Father's Day present from his daughter. Wanted to throw it out off the balcony just to kill that stale, artificial BUZZZZZZZ, composed on an iPhone by some little Japanese kid for Casio. Coulda gone down to the corner market and gotten a replacement, but I said no, just pressed the oversized center button and rolled over and went back to my nightmare, let it take me up and away, over and down to the next inferno.

Out of the fire, she came to me same as always: drifting in from the balcony, seemingly floating across the floor, enigmatic smile on her perfectly sculpted Russian slash Italian façade, hands unfolding and fingers beckoning me. Such a sucker, I was, following that vision into the next dark unknown, like that stupid monkey reaching out in the dark for a golden branch that wasn't there.

Behind her, a hundred men, women, children spilled out of a shipping container, their faces melted away.

They all screamed at me in some invisible tongue.

But I did get it. And it burned into me, all at once a thousand mosquitoes.

BUZZZZZZZ.

Oookay, that was it.

Took off Caleb's watch and his stupid reminders, rolled outta bed and drowned it in the kitchen sink.

Held it down for a full minute 'til it stopped breathing and shaking.

One down.

Cortez called to me for some reason, but I ended up in Newtown. The drive out there was different today: it wasn't midnight and then some. Today's sunshine was a bitched-up whitewash, everything around me a bleak Antarctic winterscape. Needed sunglasses and an umbrella to repel the evil sun, but I'd left them at the condo. Nothing of substance in the trunk except a few pistols, a stubby double-tube shotgun, and boxes of big bullets. Any normal guy would've had emergency water and rations, extra petrol, blankets. Why bother with conventional supplies? In an emergency, I could always walk into anyone's house or store and—

Closed the trunk and walked up to the one-room structure, the only one in town with a 30-foot-tall white cross on the front lawn. It'd been the last pine tree on that old lot, and all the town's citizens asked the church not to chop it down. Instead, they all trimmed and groomed it and then converted it into a giant cross.

"Bless me, Father, for I have sinned!" he thundered, shaking the walls of his little church of God or whoever he was into these days.

Couldn't help but smile at him, extended my hand: "Father Chappy, aren't I supposed to say that?"

He slapped my hand out of the way, attacked me. Bear hugs are something I hate, 'cos they squeeze all life outta me and I can't do a goddamned thing about it, just wait for the next round of air to shoot back in.

"How the hell ya doin', Tommy!" He slapped me hard on the back, reminded of old man Viktor that day at his cabin in the sticks. Pulled me away from him so he could take it all in, then hugged me again.

Shit. "Hell, Father, I'm just peachy. How the holy hell are you?"

"Not gettin' any, that's what you're askin'!" He motioned me inside his tiny office that held two stiff wooden chairs, small table, and a tall dorm-style reefer filled with the coldest beer I'd ever tasted. "Damn women in this town all think a man of God don't like to fuck."

"Maybe you should write a sermon on that one, Father."

"What, like an invitation? And have the congregation pray all the pussy in Newtown walks through my doors and throws their panties at me?"

Silence.

Just sized each other up like we always did.

I looked him up and down, checking for pulses, tasting the chemistry, sniffing his pheromones and fight-flight-freeze molecules.

He just stared at my eyeballs like they were some special crystal that revealed all. But only to him.

His big head nodded knowingly. "Heard someone put the hurtin' to Tyreese Glover. Know anything about that, Tommy?"

"DNA . . . does—"

"Does not apply. I know what DNA means, smartass."

Just looked at him.

"Only one kinda animal coulda done that to Tyreese."

Still nothing from me.

"Look, man, I know you two went to high school together, played ball, wrestled at state." He stopped, got two beers from the reefer, handed me one.

It was a block of ice, that one. Popped the can, upended it. It froze the entire length of my esophagus and stomach, shooting lightning bolts every which way. Nearly doubled over. Instead, I just caught the buzz and let it take me.

The big man threw his head back and laughed something deep and guttural, came back and slapped my leg.

Dayum! Couldn't scootch my chair to avoid the next one, the room being so small. So I just stood up, grabbed another beer. Was gonna throw that one at him if he slapped me again. "Yeah, but Tyreese was the animal, Father. Not I. You remember what he did to that kid from St.Pete at the finals?"

Nodded his head. "Uh-huh. Flipped him over and bent him backwards, broke his back."

"And you're questioning me about . . . what, exactly? The good Lord may have proclaimed you all sinners, Father, but he gave me a sword and Code of Deathics. You know that."

He held up a giant paw. "I know, I know. I'm the one who passed those deathics onto you, son, so don't go preachin' to this holy man."

Got solemn a moment. "Tommy, there's folk in these parts don't take kindly to anyone whoopin' up on a Black man, even if he's meaner than he is Black. And they 'specially don't like some white dude like you doin' all the ass-whoopin'."

He sat back, chugged the whole beer. "Them same folk also praise Jesus for a white dude like you comin' in here and sendin' them scum-suckin' muthafuckas to some deep part o' Hell."

The thin walls of the tiny room vibrated like a bass drum with the punching booms of our laughter.

Went on for another coupla hours, him mostly doing the talking and I just sitting back and drinking all that frozen beer. I hate Budweiser but, in it's frozen state, it was passable. He told me about some new foreigners coming into town recently, scoping things out, not talking to anyone or asking questions like good people do. Nope, these guys were predators and no one liked them. Said they were Bulgarian or Romanian. Maybe old-school Russian.

First reaction: more foreigners coming in to dirty up my space.

Second thought: more targets when my supply of pimps started to run low.

Final thought: at least he stopped bustin' my ass about Tyreese. After all, he's the man who schooled me years back on putting pimps and other sordid detritus in Dumpsters.

"For the good of my people," he'd preached, as he blessed my struggling soul, then later baptized me in a cauldron of fire and ice.

Everything around me I could possibly see—the government, economy, life—started to unravel into mushy spaghetti.

Sadly, I started to see it in my own backyard.

South Longboat Key was insulated from the real world by BigMoney that fled Ft. Lauderdale when the Cubans and southerly Latinos started to invade the US in the late '70s. They propagated like amoeba and pushed all that money and so-called power up against a wall. BigMoney weren't fighters. Since they were outgunned, they fled to Sarasota. Lazy cowards.

There was no middle class on Longboat Key. Wealthy or broke as fuck were your two choices. Anyone who served the money was bused in from the ghettos of Bradenton and Venice, slaved for the unappreciative landlords, and went home to suffer quietly. If anyone wanted to see how the US would wind up in ten years, all they had to do was tour South and North Longboat Key and witness the ever-widening rift between the wealthy and the poor. The saddest part of the equation was that it was designed to be that way, both on Longboat and throughout the entire United States.

One eye on my sorry ass and the other always on the nearest exit, BigMoney saw me as some low-lifer looking for an angle, some way into their secret rentier paradise. Mostly because of my simple lifestyle, the way I dressed, the car I drove. None of it screamed status like their million-dollar Benz or Rolls, the Manhattan-style apartment on Gold Gate Point, the shopping sprees in Monaco and Paris.

I must've stolen mine or earned my money from illicit trade of arms, drugs or pussy, according to their narrow view. How ironic and hypocritical, though, as many of them earned theirs from illicit dealings. This one high-powered lawyer I'd run into years ago? Read somewhere she'd imploded, lost her business and the three million-dollar condos on The Point, and fled into hiding, mostly out of embarrassment. The moneyed people she thought were her friends blew her off in a New York minute.

On Longboat Key, if you weren't BigMoney, you were meat on the hoof.

No one really talked about them, the Money. Not because we feared them. We didn't talk BigMoney because they were irrelevant, too far removed from reality, living in some high-rise cocoon or severely gated estate that overlooked their section of a lukewarm Gulf.

They didn't contribute to any society we knew, only coalesced at moneyed functions and events in Sarasota, ensured that the dollars stayed within their purses, while everyone else opened up their shallow pockets and gave all they could, never once knowing where it actually wound up.

I hated BigMoney even more than I hated pimps, and I prayed they stayed well away from me, they in their high-end cars and me in my tangerine TommyTaxi. Deep down, though, I sensed we were on some destined collision course.

Put that thought outta my mind and got back to more important items.

Before work, took a long drive up 789 and finally wound up in Cortez. Like last time, when I'd rolled into Newtown to see Father Chappy, hadn't planned it. Something drew me there and my subconscious wasn't letting on why. If I questioned every order my subconscious handed down, I'd get stuck in Gorilla glue and never move.

"Haven't seen you around much, Tommy." Donny McCracken was old-school fisherman, mostly mullet. Ran a dive shop on Cortez, bought with fuck-you money from the '70s dope trade in southwest Florida. He and his daddy were the original Mary Jane Millionaires long before Jimmy Buffett rolled into Margaritaville. Donny escaped because his family was Florida Redneck Royalty, going all the way back to when Andrew Jackson raped the Seminoles and their land.

Donny's kin had filled one of the massive niches left behind when

Hurricane Jackson lighted for points north, and the Clan McCracken land-grabbed as much as they could along Florida's west coast.

Handed me a near-frozen beer. "How's Rachel?"

In some slob's bed. "Gone." Sipped the beer slowly, something unusual for me. A quick-buzz gulper, I was. Killed the symptoms of this disease that attacked me without warning: anxiety-depression.

Not a shred of emotion on this man. Any leftover feelings had already diffused up into the whispy tendrils of cigarettes and weed: "Sorry to hear," he said, racking some wetsuits. "Work slow?"

Donny kept a keen eye on everyone in town, knew the highest of the money and lowest of the smugglers and dealers. Neutral to most, he was a pastor of sorts, willing to hear many a confession from unlikely people. When strangers trusted you that much, you could learn anything. And if you were Donny, you had enough dirt on people to use when you needed a special favor, although I don't subscribe to that kinda leverage. It eventually backfired.

"Yeah, taking the summer off, pretty much." Sipped some, looked around the place: distressed in a kept way, clean floors and nautical décor, latest dive gear and jazzy bling. Made you feel at home.

"Wanna sell that taxi of yours?" Filled a bank of air tanks.

Pushed around some of the new t-shirts, loudly colored parrots and some mention of five o'clock somewhere. "You'd turn it into a rolling billboard." Downed my beer. "No, thanks."

Handed me another one, this time frozen at the neck. Donny never passed out beer so casually.

"Lookin' for work?" The filling hose cut loose and lassoed wildly about the filling station. Without looking, Donny casually reached out into empty space, grabbed the snake-hose by its head, refitted it.

"Dunno. What's up?"

He looked around the shop, took a step closer and leaned into me: "PI over in Sarasota needs some help with surveillance. Pays good, I hear."

Sensed some bigger message coming on, wrapped in another frozen beer, even though I didn't need it.

He didn't disappoint: "With big money comes big responsibility."

BigMoney: I wondered if he meant it the same disparaging way as I did.

"Sounds like there's more to good money than I thought." Warmed up the bottle neck just enough to open up a channel. The beer jumped out as I tipped the bottle, shot into my throat, a mild burn. Felt good. The buzz and the burn.

He went back to the air tanks, looked at me: "Known this guy all my life, Tommy."

That meant the guy had run drugs and arms and other things I didn't want to think about. Some of the people who had hired me over the years were probably into the same shady stuff, but I never asked questions. Tried not to think too much about it.

"An opportunist." His hands looked for something else to control. "On the other side of the law these days."

"Private investigator?"

"Yeah, but he's also been deputized by the Feds, so has access to things."

"Things." The only private guys who could possibly get "deputized" as a Fed are already way up the flagpole. Goosebumps popped up all over my forearms and a small shudder ran through my trunk. All around me, it was a melt-worthy ninety degrees.

"Stuff you don't want to hear, Tommy. Look, man, no offense but you're kinda small time. These guys? They're big leagues and they play hard." His hands now fully into his work. "Like I said, big money, big responsibility."

I love *Old Florida*. While Sarasota and the surrounds weren't exactly Old Florida, they had just enough spice to keep me here. For now. It's a small-time town on the west coast, about 55 miles south of Tampa. Too close to Tampa, you ask me, but there was large body of water that separated us just enough to calm me down a notch.

When I moved up here years ago, the atmosphere was pleasant and inviting, save the dive-bombing mosquitoes. Over the years, I noticed things changed gradually . . . and not in the right direction. I loved small-time. It suited me.

What I didn't like about Sarasota: many multi-millionaires and billionaires have "second" homes here. You'd never know it, though. It's not like they shop every day at Kmart or Publix. Most don't even mix with the moneyed locals. Their homes were tucked away far from Tamiami Trail and the prying eyes of the public.

As with Longboat Key, racial refugees from Ft. Lauderdale and Miami flooded in during the late '80s and set up shop on Golden Gate Point, an exclusive high-rise jungle on the bay, plus parts of downtown and all along the waterfront down to sleepy Siesta Key. They're the ones who made my town a wannabe, turning a good thing—my home—into their own image: shit.

The drive over to Sarasota was pleasant enough. Donny's old friend was set up in a high-rise office building on the Trail near the marina, an all-glass structure melting dark-gray tears when the sun struck twelve o'clock high.

"Donny speaks highly of you." He attacked my hand and shook it three times, dropped it and ran around his desk, fell into a high-back.

Speaks highly of you. A bit stilted, you ask me.

Donny was right: this old friend of his had distanced himself from the old crowd, gone uptown. Even though I was a few inches taller than him, he looked down on me from his high-altitude elevator boots.

"Donny's a friend." Pulled up a chair in front of his desk, eased into it.

"Looking for work?"

"Depends." Looked around the office, all autographed photos of him with plastic people wearing toothy smiles.

He studied me for a few seconds. "I'll get to the point, Tommy: you're ex-spec ops with a cool bag of tricks. You get things done. On time and to spec. Never complain or criticize the hand that feeds you. All good traits in this business."

How did this guy know about me?

Slowly and painfully, it came to me: old man Viktor.

If this guy knew about me from that bastard, what else did he know? That I wasted Viktor and his soldiers? Was this the guy who put a new coat of paint on his spread in the sticks, erased all trace of Hurricane Tommy? Was he now setting me up for something? Guys like him always had an elaborate, sometimes long-term plan to erase their enemies. Their dogged patience and persistence made me wary.

Those goosebumps again, reminding me of a Corsican adage:

"If you want revenge and take action in twenty years, you're being impatient."

In the middle of meeting with this yahoo, thoughts pulled me back to my sweet Rachel. Why now? Something in my upper periphery caught my eye: a picture of this guy at one of Rachel's book signings, standing right behind her. What the hell was he doing there? Tried not to stare at my Rachel.

"What business is that?" I asked absently. Found another interesting shot of him and some buddies, high on a bookshelf, focused in on it.

"Donny didn't tell you?"

Shook my head as I recognized the contents of the picture: he wore freshly pressed BDUs and a boonie cap, held an AR-15. His buddies around him wore the drawn look of seasoned warriors, while this guy smiled the day away. Fresh meat in the jungle he saw as Disneyland. Or the unit's comic relief. Or neither.

Couldn't tell, but his current attitude suggested something far deeper. Sinister. What bothered me about that picture, those men? And the other one with Rachel? That was something else to look into, but not today.

"This is a private investigations firm. We cater to high-end clients with special needs. Understand?"

Yeah, jackass, I understand BigMoney all too well. "High-end clients, special needs."

My sarcasm wasn't lost on him: "Look, ah, Tommy, we're looking for someone who can support our on-going operations on several levels. The pay is excellent and the bennies aren't too bad, either."

"This job comes with benefits." It wasn't a question. I wanted to poke him some.

The guy shook it off: "Company car or truck, whatever you prefer. And an assistant."

"Assistant." That meant one thing: not a bitch boy but a handler, someone who reported my progress up the ladder, made sure I didn't step outta line.

"Yes. We like to think of it as an insurance policy. I'm sure you understand." Flashed me lotsa white teeth. Kinda the way a pit bull does when it smiles its fangs at you.

"I work alone for several reasons, not the least of which is that I trust myself, my training and my actions. Other people always get in the way. I don't do assistants." The truth was that I had lost an edge when Rachel took off. Maybe I could use some help. What a stupid thought, Tommy.

He held up a hand. "Tommy, this is non-negotiable. The assistant. Now, if you would like a black suv and not white, that's fine with us."

Us.

Did he openly acknowledge some higher power in his little universe?

This was the wrong thing to do and I knew it. A year from now, I'd be slapping myself for getting in bed with "Us." If I lived that long. I wasn't ready for anything new and my subconscious pounded at me. My heart was a prune from the day Rachel drove off with BluntBoy, leaving me that dark cloud to suck on.

"Sure, sounds good," I said, regretting it immediately and wanting to rewind the whole scene as fast as I could so I could tell him to fuck himself. Or just put my knife in his pretty smile.

He immediately stood, bent over his desk an inch maybe, threw out his hand. "Excellent. John is outside. He'll give you all the details. You can dictate to him your list of needs, Tommy." That same smile from the picture on his bookshelf.

What he meant was, I was now another head of cattle that just got sizzle-branded on the ass and slack-pastured for convenient use. And if I bitched about it, they'd drop me off at the special factory that cranked out those delicious Jimmy Dean sausages.

"Let's knock him down a few notches." Peter Jamison sat in his high-back, his flashy fangs directed at the man in front of his desk. "Viktor was a good man." Looked away, whispered, "A *friend.*"

"And he said good things about Mr. Darlington," his assistant replied.

Torn from his reverie, Jamison flashed the pointy teeth again: "Let's remember that this low-life singlehandedly killed Viktor and his entire organization at the lake three months ago." Turned away again, talking to the lines of traffic below: "I've spent considerable time and money cleaning up the mess he made. And now that he's our charge, I'm not letting him think a goddamned thing on his own. He'll do as we tell him, when we tell him, and we'll throw just enough money at him to keep him quiet."

"A few girls, too?"

Peter Jamison waved a hand dismissively: "Whatever. But he remains with us until the day he checks out. Understood?"

"Okay, boss. I'll stay on him." John rose and left the office.

Jamison speed-dialed a number: "Sir, the schedule is solid."

On speaker, another voice: "How'd you recover so fast, Peter?"

"Please allow me to handle things on my end. I promise you won't be disappointed."

"With you, I never am." The man cut the connection.

Jamison summoned his assistant: "John, have my car downstairs in two mikes."

John Jamison was a younger cousin, eager to please but strong and able to delegate and negotiate on his own. He buzzed the private valet downstairs.

In the marina area, it wasn't uncommon to see a Rolls or Bentley at any time of day or night. Jamison's Porsche blended in well with his uptown crowd, but was easy to spot by someone who was looking.

I fell in behind Jamison as he rolled over the scenic, two-mile Ringling Bridge and onto stylish but subdued Bird Key. An isolated little isle only 2,000 feet at its widest point and 4,000 at its longest, Bird Key was a floating Manhattan Beach, with most homes within arm's length each other, over-maximizing the small area and putting millions more into deep pockets already stuffed with cash.

From the air, Bird Key was a diamond-studded earring, artfully displayed on turquoise velvet. True to BigMoney, they had built an impressive fantasy island for wealthy tv personalities, rock stars and plain-vanilla rich folk.

Near Bird Key Drive and North Spoonbill, Jamison found the unassuming house, thirty years old and finished in Spanish double-tile on the long overhanging roof, and dotted with bushy oaks that cooled the place down by fifteen degrees. The left-side garage was opening as he pulled inside.

Interior garage door to the house was ajar. He followed the

breadcrumbs to the study, to an expansive library set in a dark medieval wood trimmed in rich purples and greens.

"You're making me nervous, Peter, all this clean-up you've been doing lately." Paul Jamison stood in the center of the library, holding two glasses of a blood-red vino, extended one to his brother.

"While it wasn't written into the original plan, we did expect some resistance." Peter took a seat at the massive fireplace, faced it more than he did his brother.

"You mean surprises."

"Paul, you sit here anonymously in your padded cockpit, well behind the rear lines of battle. Let me handle the operations."

His big brother stopped there. "How do we replace Viktor?"

An arm shot up in exasperation. "We don't."

Paul turned to him, pointed his glass like a sword: "You lose a major part of an organization and you tell me you're not—"

Peter rotated in his chair, spread his legs, both elbows on them for effect. "Relax. Fact is, we could never replace Viktor."

His chin punching the air between them, Paul said, "Fine. Tell me how we're proceeding."

"Thank you." Addressing the recently cut oak logs, in a slow crackling burn: "We lose a limb, we autotomize the appendage, move on. In this case, we already cut our losses when Viktor was lost. He outlived his usefulness anyway."

"You would have retired him soon, that it?"

Closed his eyes a moment, continued: "The operation is solid. We're funneling in the needed children, supplying our friends with the entertainment they pay us so well for. We're the talent scouts: we audition the prospects, identify those who can suck a dick without gagging or throwing up, and container them into Tampa for processing."

"Nothing runs this smoothly, Peter. Nothing. We're bound to attract the attention of someone we didn't consider. We'll be blindsided by someone we least expect."

"Again, relax. We're covered, remember."

A long silence between them.

"Oh, yes, by people we've never met. By people who take our money and permit us to stay in business, abiding by their laws and rules. That the cover you're talking about, Peter?"

"They don't take our money, brother. We pay them a percentage to operate. Cost of doing business. Been going on for two thousand years. Render unto Caesar, no?" Got up and paced around the room. "You're the accountant. Besides, we've been through this before, always arriving at the same result."

"And we'll go through it again. You do the operations, I do the accounting. There has to be a balance between us, Peter."

"Operations and Accounting . . . ne'er the twixt shall meet." His voice trailed off as he moved over to the twelve-foot ladder that led up to the second floor of the library stacks.

"Enough nostalgia." Paul clapped his hands, smiled at his brother, urging him to move on.

"Yes . . . you asked about Viktor: he and his team were taken out by someone we had suspected. That man is now working for us."

Paul now rose, followed his brother's footsteps to the ladder. "Do tell, brother."

"Coincidentally, Donny McCracken referred him to our PI firm. I interviewed him today. He's in line, although he doesn't know it."

"There are no coincidences. You summoned him, didn't you?"

No response from Peter.

Paul continued: "So, Donny McCracken." He lowered his head, replaying old tapes in his mind's eye. "Guy's come a long way from running dope across the southern straits in outboards, but he's still a shit farmer."

"Don't worry, he's not a threat to us. Besides he knows where our gold is. Never forget that."

"Just remember, brother, he's your friend, not mine. And if he ever becomes a threat, I don't care about that alleged gold. No one has a thousand bars of gold, not even the Chinese."

Peter dropped his head, closed his eyes: "It's as real as all the books in this library, brother. Soon we'll have word on its location. I sent a little message to Mr. McCracken."

"What kind of message?"

"He's doing a dive tour this week. Something tells me he'll visit the old wreck."

"The old—"

The massive main library door opened and an older woman in a maid's uniform entered, looking at Peter: "Sir, your two o'clock is on line two."

Paul Jamison looked over at his brother: "Sylvia's been with our family for twenty-seven years and still can't tell us apart."

The twins loosed a sardonic laugh.

Miss Sylvia, clearly uncomfortable, bowed her head in mock acknowledgment and departed quietly.

Reunions: you can never really go back. Not really.

"Look, Tommy, try it out for a few days, see if it fits. Besides, I need a reliable hand in blue water with these novice divers, six of 'em on the card." Donny: One hand on filling tanks, the other on the phone with me.

In old times I would've hung up on him, not wanting to get sucked into his dope biz. "I'll be there."

Dive shops are some of the sleaziest operations in the world of adventure entertainment. Before you can even get scuba certified at some location, you sign away 100% of your rights and that includes your right to live. Reason is, scuba diving is a dangerous activity. I hate to call it a sport, but dive operators in the '70s saw an opportunity to cash in on the sports craze sweeping the country after the Vietnam War, so they labeled their "death and danger" gig a sport.

Same as skydiving. There's nothing sporty about falling out of an airplane, your parachute not opening, and then making a wet hole in the ground at 120 miles an hour. You see that anywhere in baseball or football?

What crap.

If you can wade through the various forms you must sign in blood, you're on your way to losing your life. The US *Constitution* is a dead letter in every dive shop in the US and anywhere US dive-shop operators conduct business.

Why did I agree to do some grunt work with Donny? I dunno, maybe I was now in the habit of making a few more really bad life choices. Or maybe I was bored staying at home, taxiing around the odd customer, thinking about Rachel under someone else's sheets.

Having eyewitnessed the slob, I'd guess his sheets were at least three weeks old before they saw the inside of a washing machine.

Oh, yeah, and that pet hobby of mine, putting pimps in Dumpsters, was getting mighty old. Each time I dropped one, three more popped up. In Florida, just add water. Started wonderin' if I were actually doing more harm than good.

What the hell. All things considered, I needed a new rush. . . .

The *Mama Seata* pulled away from her berth on Cortez, swung left at the 684 bridge, motored a mile and a half down to the swinging doors of the Gulf of Mexico, and hung a right.

The edge of the Florida shelf was 175 miles due west, where the bottom dropped off into the abyss. From the island, water went from light shit-brown in the inland waterway to light green at the beach to turquoise just off shore to diaphanous blue twenty-five miles from home.

Today's dive profile included bottom time in shallow water with all the students forming a circle at about twenty feet, and each going through various emergency procedures and maneuvers.

What could possibly go wrong at twenty feet?

With six inexperienced divers trying to enter the water pretty much at the same time, Donny had his hands full settling them down and getting them to cooperate. Some of them were so excited about their first open-water dive, they didn't listen to Donny right off. That's when he invoked the old adage of the sea: when in doubt, scream like a klaxon.

Half an hour after chaos dropped to a simmer, we were all safely on the ocean floor in a small circle, some on their knees like Donny ordered, others on their butts trying to sit upright and rocking themselves to sleep. The scene was comical: half a dozen six year olds, all candidates for ADHD, playing musical chairs to a stop-and-go tune every two seconds, then finally planting their butts, all that energy and nothing to do with it.

The morning check-out sessions were a blur. Surprisingly, all went well and each student passed their certification test well ahead of Donny's expectations. Nervous at first, they all settled down and followed all orders and directions, and made the whole experience a pleasant one for me. Plus it was good to feel the warm ocean wrap her arms around me, infuse me with a new energy. Something told me I'd need it for my upcoming gigs with Mr. Peter Jamison and his crew.

At the end of the dive, Donny rewarded the students with a short bonus dive on the wreck of a WWII P-47 Thunderbolt that had gone down on a training hop in 1944.

In the '70s, Donny used to stash bales of marijuana at the wreck, because he and his runners were the only ones in southwest Florida who knew about it. Donny's granddad had been the pilot of the fighter and he and his admin buddies had destroyed every record of the crash, more out of embarrassment to him and his family, but maybe because Lieutenant McCracken had been running opium from a little-known route out of Mexico.

By one pm, we were in diaphanous blue water, swimming and paddling around the tail section of the plane, which was only fifty feet down. The entire aircraft was intact and resting comfortably on the sand bottom in full planform, surrounded by small mountains of elegant coral structures and rock that looked like the area had just been featured in *Architectural Digest*.

Donny and I floated on either side of the plane, keeping everyone in the rear area. The divers looked like colorful bees buzzing about, touching every part of the tail and stabilizers and trying to pry off anything that would look cool in a living room.

Fifteen minutes into the dive: "Donny, Donny, Donny. Diver six, 325, five-zero meters." I called on the intercom. Heading, 325 degrees, fifty meters away.

I'd done a lot of dives over the years, many recreational, and had seen my share of accidents that caused a panic among other divers. But I wasn't prepared for Diver 6 breaking away from the main group for a few minutes, off on her own near the nose of the plane, then shooting to the surface screaming out her last breath of air.

He was still at depth gathering up the other five divers. Luckily, they were all within a few meters of him and easily corralled.

As his head broke the surface, he immediately saw me and yelled, "She with you, Tommy!?"

I had her on deck, pulled off her wetsuit top and was doing chest compressions. "Come on, Maggie. Breathe, baby. Breath." Gently and forcefully pumped her chest a dozen times, stopping only to listen for breath signs, then continued over and over.

In minutes, Donny had the students safely on board and all sitting around the bow, well away from the stern where I was trying to revive Maggie.

Thoughts immediately flew me back to Rachel that night at Viktor's cabin in the sticks, holding her tightly to my face and chest so she had trouble breathing. Never wanting to let her go again.

SurferBoy's pretty face broke my reverie and screamed something garbled and broken, just as Maggie's eyes shot open and she coughed up a lungful of Gulf. I rolled her over on her side, encouraging her to come back to us so Donny wouldn't lose all those expensive licenses that kept him in business.

"Bodies! The bodies!" Still coughing violently and spitting up salt water.

Held her head and stroked her face, one I'd seen a thousand times before: my dear Rachel.

Frozen in the past, I missed her next words but Donny took over for me and helped her expel the last of the water she'd aspirated in her drowning. Thought I heard him tell me, "Pray there's no secondary drowning. I don't need this shit now, Tommy."

"There . . . were . . . bodies . . . down . . . there." Eyes closed, trying to drive off the sharp pain in her chest, she found a calm and settled into it. "I saw bodies. All tied up. Under propeller."

Donny gave me a knowing look, but I said nothing, not in front of the students, who were now all gathered around dear Maggie and snapping images of near-death on their smart phones and shooting them across Instagram, WhatsApp, Twitter and Facebook.

The ghost of emptiness drew me closer to some wretched unknown. . . .

Before Donny called in the report to the Coast Guard and Sheriff's Office, he and I descended on the wreck. In two dives, we found seven fresh bodies, each gagged with oily rags and bound with 100-mph tape and 550 cord. I didn't tell Donny about the parachute cord. Dunno why.

While he photographed the scene with a small underwater handheld, I noted how the cord was wrapped around each victim, and the knots used and how tight they'd been made. While 550 cord wasn't impossible to come by, most civilians would've just bought some twine or rope at a hardware store. They wouldn't go out of their way to buy a thousand-foot roll of MILSPEC parachute cord. Hell, they'd even fused the ends of each length of cord so the outer jacket and interior strands wouldn't fray.

Not just meticulous, these assholes. They were proud of their handiwork.

Or were they sending a message to someone?

The style of the knots had the flavor of seasoned military all over it. The over-tightness and depth of each tie and knot said this was somehow personal, or tied by someone really pissed off at each victim. Or maybe they were just being thorough. Something else was unmistakable, too: the victims were all young teens and kids.

On deck, we downloaded the images and took a quick look. All clear and in good focus, Donny made a copy to a flash drive, put it in a small zip-lock baggy, slipped it to me.

The students were busy consolidating their gear, putting on fresh clothes for the long ride back to the dive shop. Maggie had aspirated a lot of seawater and still had difficulty breathing at times, so we watched her as we went about our chores and duties in preparation for departure.

Donny pointed the nose roughly east and hit the gas. A few hours later, we entered the swinging doors to the inland waterway, motored left to the bridge and docked at the shop just as the sun was setting behind us. Everyone worked as a team, unloading all the tanks and equipment, and seeing to it that Maggie was as comfortable as we could make her until she could be loaded into the ambulance.

Donny talked with the paramedics, Coast Guard and Sheriff's Deputies, while I did my bit until done and then quietly slipped off the property before anyone with a badge could grill me with questions for the rest of the night.

The most polluted place on the planet is inside my own head. . . . Lay back in my empty bed, lingering over Rachel but running into the bodies of those kids at the wreck:

No shoes . . .

Tight non-cotton clothing . . .

Spandex or something . . .

Bright colors . . .

Knees bound . . .

Hands and feet tied behind them . . .

Skimpy bikini underwear on the girls . . .

Eyes plucked out by fish and crabs . . .

Tongues partially eaten by same . . .

Girls' breasts with unusual bruising . . .

Clear smooth skin otherwise. . . .

I'd seen that type of breast injury before.

Rachel.

Even without the pictures Donny had given me, I could see every square inch of the wreck and those kids. They'd all been tied in bundles, then dumped overboard onto the propeller where they settled just under it. Most likely, they fought violently once in the water and drowned on the way down, judging from the amount of scarring at the wrists, neck and ankles.

Death had fallen over these kids very slowly. But at least it came and ended all suffering. With their eyes taken and surrounding tissue eaten away, it was hard to figure out their nationality. At depth, the lighting was not good white light so I couldn't tell accurate skin tone, but when I saw Donny's shots, it was pretty clear: I'd say Latino boys and Eastern Euro girls.

Painful as it was, had to ask myself: who was famous for paying *special* attention to beautiful young kids like these?

Donny and I didn't talk for a week, then he called me out of the blue.

"Ready for another boat ride?" Clanking in the background, Donny was busy filling air tanks.

"They question you any further?"

"No, but they were real curious about how I knew about a 70-year old wreck out in the middle of the Gulf of Fuckin' Mexico."

"What'd you tell 'em?"

"Saw it in some chat room somewhere, long time ago."

"That work?"

"No further questions."

"Have a few of my own."

"Shoot." The background noise had stopped. Sounded like he dropped into a beach chair. "C'mon over, Tommy. Let's have a sit-down."

Helped myself to his near-frozen beer.

"What do you know about this wreck, other than what you told me? I mean, about your dad and all."

He hesitated. "My dad was into some heavy shit back in the day, Tommy, stuff my mom tried to hide from me but couldn't. I was always listening in on his conversations with buddies and strange characters that came around. Even stole a ride on one of his shrimp boats once when they went out to the Thunderbolt. Saw 'em hoisting up military-style metal lockers with something heavy in 'em."

"What was inside?"

Long pause, then: "Gold bars."

"You kidding me?"

"No, man, real gold bars. Looks like it went both ways with dad: he'd motor out to the wreck and drop the drugs or something for the next mule, and then later, maybe a week or so, go back out there and retrieve gold or cash. I saw gold that time, though."

"How do you know there was cash?"

"Saw him drag lockers of it from the boat at the dock and up to the shop. He opened 'em up once inside. That's when I got a good look at the cash in water-tight containers."

"Ever get caught?"

"Me? No. But dad probably knew I was there, 'cos he often said he was passing the business onto me and that he didn't have time to teach me everything so I would just have to get it by . . . I dunno."

"Osmosis."

"Yeah, but dad pro'ly meant stealing looks when I was doing my stealth missions."

"He should've tanned your hide, Donny."

We both laughed.

"Yeah, but he was always good to me, Tommy. Always loved me and had my back, taught me what I know now, left me something good to hang on to, pass on to my own son someday."

He cocked his head to me, paused a moment: "There's one question you haven't asked me, Tommy."

Downed my beer, got another one. "What's that?"

Looked down at his hands, rubbing over each other in a slow, continuous cycle.

"What question, Donny?"

The cycle broken, he looked up again, said, "How someone else knew about the wreck out there."

That had bothered me, yes, but I knew that secrets like that always found a way out, especially during the changing of the generational guard. A certain family member of his father's friends found out about it, told someone else in strict confidence. The original secret had been lost to time, now paraded around as an inflated war story or piece of "lost" family history, something embedded in a fireside tale at gatherings and reunions.

Donny added, "You're the only guy I've ever told about this, Tommy. And I don't know the other players anymore. All the fathers are dead, and the sons and daughters scattered across Florida and who-knows-where."

As Viktor still haunted me even on my best of days, so too did this "family secret" somehow follow Donny. The truth would emerge because someone always knew something. Even if it were insignificant and they were six feet under the hot dust and sand.

If more than one person knew about a secret, it probably wasn't safe.

Be careful what you wish for . . . you may just find it in an old book.

The Old Florida Historical Society, Inc. had its own building and archives on the Trail just north of downtown Sarasota. Bought and furnished by donations, the headquarters made me a little wary: why would anyone put that much money into something so seemingly insignificant?

I'd done research before in other libraries and archives when studying some of my bull's-eyes, my assigned targets, but this one surprised me. Fully air conditioned to 69 degrees and 50% humidity, the entire interior was a vault unto itself, with the archive on the lower floor and offices just above.

Gaining access was by appointment, so I had Donny call in a favor to get me in same day. He sounded like he wanted to tell me something on the phone, but held back. Didn't press him on it.

Watched under the scrupulous eye of a fussy little woman named Ginny, I was placed in a small conference room and forced to watch a short thirty-minute video about how to access research volumes in the archives, what to do, what not to do, don't touch this or that, and if you do this, you'll go to jail, do that and you're in prison for life. Stuff like that.

In time, she certified me "not a total idiot" and cut me loose at noon, so I wandered about the entire archives, noting everything and its place and position, where I would start my search, and how I would sneak out anything that I couldn't immediately copy or photograph. While they could surreptitiously place an RFID tag inside an old book, they couldn't very well tag every page or picture, and I had no compunction about ripping out good intel, folding it up and stuffing it in a cargo pocket or down my boxers.

Real estate records were not normally kept in historical archives unless they were more than fifty years old. The house Peter Jamison visited on Bird Key weeks back had to have been less than 30 years old, so there would've been no record of it at the Society.

But what about the land *under* the house?

Two hours later, I was sufficiently armed with new intel, so I thanked a cranky Ginny and strolled outside and walked around the entire building and grounds. No access other than the main door, which was heavy steel. The place reminded me of an underground bank vault.

Back in the parking lot, glimpsed a silver Porsche slipping out of the lot, some expensive suit trying to aim his iPhone cam in the general direction of my TommyTaxi.

"He visited the archives today, brother." Peter Jamison snapped into his cell phone.

Paul was trying to concentrate on his pet project, pruning a bonzai. He huffed at his brother: "We don't need this unwanted attention, especially at the family repositoire."

"Yes, I agree. We'll keep an eye on him, see what he's interested in, where he digs."

"When does he get his first work with us?" Paul held up the scalpel, imagined he was pruning Peter's ear so it would hear him better.

"Probably next week. I'll put him on something out of Tampa."

"Good idea, given he may've seen the broken package at the wreck site."

"We have to assume he did, and it doesn't matter. The package was damaged and no one can possibly trace its shipping path."

"Let alone provenance, which is good for the, ah, owner, I imagine, right?"

"Of course. Let's not pull Felix into things. He likes his distance and his anonymity."

Paul stabbed at the air in front of him, sighed. "Fine, brother." Went back to his work.

"Like I said before, Paul, we're keeping him under our thumb. He won't or can't do a thing without our permission or guidance. Besides, he has his little assistant to, shall we say, help him out."

"I know, but this guy Tommy worries me. He's got skills and he's curious."

"Don't worry, brother. I've got the operations end tied up. Yours is in—"

"I do not need to be reminded each time we discuss these things, Peter." Paul ended the call.

"Testy prick."

Peter immediately placed another call: "John, I want Tommy on the Tampa run for next week."

If you wanna learn about the rosy future, you need to dig up the weedy past.

Went back to the Historical Society and endured the silent wrath of Ginny the archivist. This time, though, I brought along a friend, Starbucks Brazil Nut Coffee ice cream. I'd seen an empty container in her trashcan in her office that first day.

"Mr. Darlington, we do not allow food or beverage in the archives."

Not wanting to challenge her, I said, "C'mon, Ginny, you've got three open containers of this stuff in your trash can at any one point during a day. Admit it, you're an addict."

At first, she was noticeably offended, but then like the residual ice cream in those empties, she melted. "Well, I guess I could make an exception, Mr. Darlington." She took the package, added, "And thank you for noticing my preference."

"My pleasure, ma'am."

"You must be a good researcher." She peeked into the bag, pulled out a single container held it to her nose, closed her eyes and savored it slowly.

"I'm an amateur, actually, so I could use your help with some things, if you don't mind."

Her eyes were still closed, taking in the cloyingly sweet aroma of the laboratory-grade ice cream. "Of course. What can I assist you with?"

"Are there any records of the land tracts on Bird Key?"

"Yes. Let me put this in a safe place and I'll be right with you." She was off before I could respond, and returned before I reached the archives.

She hefted several oversized volumes from a cart onto a large research table, pulled over a magnifying work light, opened one of the books.

"A hundred years ago, Bird Key was a tiny mosquito nest in Sarasota Bay, but it was developed by a couple of swindlers who wanted nothing more than to line their pockets."

"Ringling?"

"That would be one of the swindlers, yes. The other one built the Mira Mar and other areas on the bay, stole land from anyone who didn't sell, and murdered anyone who spoke out against him."

The victor usually wrote the history for the rest of us to read and study. "How did this information get out?"

She gave a small melancholy smile. "My grandfather was the postmaster back then, the man who replaced Abbe, who was murdered for being a lie, cheat and thief. Anyway, my grandfather kept very detailed diaries and notebooks about everything that went on in this town, especially under-the-table dealings."

Her smile grew expectant, even mischievous, as she pulled another large leather-bound volume from the cart.

"Word was, Bird Key had to be sanitized before they could build on it, so the powers that be, all those Yankees from New York, conspired with their cronies at Standard Oil and had the whole key sprayed with some petroleum oil that was discarded during the process of making gasoline."

"So they poisoned the entire island?"

"Hell, no, Mr. Darlington! They poisoned all of Sarasota Bay for more than ten years!"

"What happened?"

"Fishing was a bust all along the inland waterway from here up to Tampa and down to Venice. Today's horrible red tides are child's play compared to what happened back then. Even the Gulf beaches were a dead zone, with fish and crabs and dolphins washing up on shore each week for over a decade. Just a mess, I tell you!"

"How could something like this last ten years?"

"Did you hear me when I said Standard Oil?"

"Yes."

"Rockefeller carried a huge weight in New York, and gravity pulled that tonnage all the way down to Sarasota in the 1920s and '30s when those bastards started building up Bird Key." She looked through the book as she spoke: "Took them thirty years to get all done and tidied up, but they did it."

"Any complaints?"

She punched my arm lightly, then held it: "From the citizens? Hell, yes! My father told me about town hall meetings that broke out into brawls and shootings. But when Standard Oil sent in their goons, things turned against the citizens and we eventually lost the fight. They got their Bird Key and all those hundreds of new lots that sold for around $10,000 each fifty years ago. Not much in today's money, but it was a pretty penny then."

She adjusted the magnifier over the book and pointed to an entry for 1959.

"What's this?"

"The address you gave me. The 125th lot sold on Bird Key."

"The owner?"

"See for yourself." Her finger pointed to the entry.

Peered through the lighted lens.

The letters ballooned up 10 times in size and burst in my face.

No still means yes, even when someone tells you to piss off and don't ever come back.

The dive shop had been hopping since word got out about the wreck of the old P-47. Donny had to hire two new hands to help out, since I was no longer in the picture.

"You ran out on me, Tommy," he said, sort of kidding. "Gotta get these new tanks to the filling station."

We moved around to the back of the shop, deposited the new tanks in the water trough, and he did his thing.

"Sorry, things got a little out of hand there, Donny. With this Rachel thing on my mind, I didn't need the headache. I'm sorry."

"No worries. As you can see, we're doing okay."

"What about the wreck? The bodies?"

Slight twitch in his left eye. "No one's said anything else to me about it. Guess they solved the case." Looking impatient, he pushed me aside to grab two other tanks. "Anything else I can do for you, Tommy?"

"Tell me about the house on Bird Key, Donny."

This time he didn't just flinch. Turned around and looked at me full on: "Don't go stepping where you don't belong, Tommy. Remember what I told you: with big money comes big responsibility. And with big steps like you're taking come big risks."

Moved a little closer to him, gave him my full attention. "Mind telling me what that means, Donny?"

"All I'm saying is, don't go asking too many questions, Tommy."

"You're the one who put me onto that private investigations firm, remember?"

Gravity and embarrassment pulled his face to the floor. He mumbled at his feet, "They're not interested in any house on Bird Key, Tommy, I can tell you that."

Felt bad for the guy, but still got up in his face: "And how the *hell* would you know that, Donny?"

The drive back to the archives was the same as the drive out to Donny's: hot and miserable, even with air conditioning. It wasn't so much misery in the cockpit, but the misery outside all around me: people shuffling by slowly under the invisible weight of direct sunlight; heavy waves of heat shimmering and rising off the asphalt and concrete; buildings in the distance threatening to melt and paint the streets with a toxic glaze.

As I pulled into the Society's lot, Peter Jamison was just leaving, his gleaming Porsche stopping abruptly in front of me, just brushing my leg.

Rolled down a darkly tinted window: "Hello, Tommy, what brings you here today?"

"Research." I said, waving at him and walking to the front door, not bothering to let him look down on me from his low-slung car seat.

He yelled out the window, something that resembled: "Tommy, you be careful."

Inside, Ginny greeted me in the main hallway. "Good afternoon, Mr. Darlington. I'm sorry to inform you that your building privileges have been suspended indefinitely."

I already knew the answer: "On whose authority?"

"The managing director, I'm afraid." She wanted to say a lot more, held it all back.

"Sooo, Ginny, do you know of any freelance researchers in town who might be able to help me out with my work?"

"Does it pay?"

"Starbucks ice cream."

That impish smile returned to her face. "There might be someone in town who can help you, Mr. Darlington. I'll make some calls and get back to you. Meantime, I must ask you to leave immediately."

Before she cold react, I kissed her cheek and whispered a thank-you.

If you treat your job like a vacation, that makes it fun, unless you work for the US Postal Service or the IRS.

This one was a two-week gig up in Tampa. Almost sixty miles farther north, you'd think it would be a little cooler but it was worse. All that asphalt made it a heat island that shoved mercury into the red. The coastal area of the city wasn't so bad, long as a Gulf breeze pushed through. Rains in the summer came at around four or five, tried their hardest to chill the air but, lasting less than an hour, shaved off only a few degrees that quickly found their way back.

Dock workers were some of the toughest guys I'd ever dealt with, next to oil riggers and Army Rangers. The only difference among them was that Rangers operated under a strict code of discipline and respect.

At least until the five-o'clock whistle blew, then every commandment in the Ranger Creed was conveniently shoved aside until first call the next morning.

My orders were simple: watch the ships that rolled into the docks, look out for anything out of the ordinary.

Simple.

Thing is, I'd not hung around these docks much and I had no idea what ordinary was. My assistant had no clue, either, so he just sat in the air-conditioned suv and texted his girlfriend all night. We weren't even issued night-vision devices or weapons. Jamison had told John to tell me they weren't necessary on a surveillance operation.

Clearly, Jamison had never been on any op in his life, let alone a surveillance mission that required certain gear.

We had been hamstrung, plain and simple, and it made me wonder why and on whose ultimate authority. Took a secret stash of weapons and ammo. Didn't bother telling my trusty assistant.

Didn't argue the point, even though I should have. Just drove up there, sat around, walked around, looked through cheap-ass binos they'd given the assistant, and ate McDonald's and Wendy's. Nothing out of the ordinary except at least one fistfight each night, usually ending in the loser lying around for the better part of an hour before he picked himself up, dusted himself off and stumbled off to a local bar to get stinking drunk with the asshole who punched his lights out and left him for dead.

My assistant said little to nothing, only consumed my oxygen and a burger here and there. Put a stop to his thievery, though: smacked his hand with the binos. He looked over at me like he was going to cut my head off, until I dragged him outside the vehicle and slapped him silly, reminding him of a few unique skills I had acquired over the years, things he'd yet to learn and so far had only YouTubed on his iPad.

After that brief episode on Day Two, the assistant was obedient as a puppy, if not a sulking one. Wondered what he'd write in his report on me.

Plays well with others.

The Port of Tampa was a 5,000-acre operation that never stopped running. It operated 24/7 regardless of whether the sun showed up.

Ships from all over the world docked here, unloaded their precious cargo, and departed back into the quiet Gulf for points unknown. It would be impossible even for a battalion of well-trained operatives to monitor the thousands of goings-on at TPA, so I wondered why the fuck I, armed with toy binos from Target and cold cheeseburgers, had been singled out to stand post and be on the lookout for any suspicious characters coming into or leaving the port. Only one reason: I was being kept away from any main action by the very people who were probably involved in the main action. And that main action was back in Sarasota.

In two weeks, my assistant had made more than 150 cell phone calls, sent a thousand text messages, consumed half of my food and water, and generally annoyed me like a no-see-um, occasionally biting me on all the places on my body I couldn't reach in time or buzzing in my ear when I tried to drone off for a minute or two. I had put on six pounds of fat around my midsection, an unfortunate disease of the sedentary I called a "butterjacket." I wanted to slit my wrists the second I was off duty. Or kill my handler. I mean, assistant.

Donny had been accurate, though. The pay was indeed good: $55,000 for the fourteen days.

I was still in the dark about the second part of his warning— big responsibility. Something about that gig of boredom told me I'd soon discover exactly what Donny had tried to warn me about.

Forty-foot shipping containers hauled the majority of illicit goods across the globe.

Just ask all the imported "workers" from China who had to ride in one for two weeks with forty other hapless slaves. They could hold anything from Fruit Loops to bananas infested with Panamanian tarantulas.

KX-1236 was lifted off a freighter from Colombia by the gantry crane and placed onto a waiting big rig, its driver sweating even under the Arctic breeze of his cab's a/c. He called the dock boss twenty times in an hour, asking when he'd get his load. And when he got it, he called another dozen times to ask when he'd be permitted to exit the port and rubber the road.

The two container wranglers who'd supervised the lowering and docking of the container onto the truck noticed it first: a putrid smell coming from the container.

"What the fuck, Francisco. You gotta dirty ass, man. Betta get your old lady to clean that thing tonight."

Francisco had done this gig for twelve years, knew every type of container and, when it had a foodstuff, could tell you exactly what was in it, where it came from and where it was headed.

"Lissen, man, don't say shit about this one. Got me, homes?"

The other man was nervous and he tried to laugh at Francisco, but his smile faded when the black suv pulled up alongside the truck and a man in black BDUs exited, carrying a .45 pistol on each hip. He looked like a wild west gunslinger. Who'd just put on clean threads and a brand new hat.

"Hey, Francisco, what is this shit, man?"

They kept watching the container lower onto the bed of the truck, little by little finding the grooved edges of the bed.

"Shut up, you," he said in a loud whisper, looking around the entire container to ensure it had been properly seeded. "Let's go, homes, got the next one in three minutes."

The black-clad man suddenly appeared in front of Francisco and his coworker.

"You guys see anything unusual around here?"

Francisco had seen this one before: "No, sir. Good to go."

"Get moving," the spooky guy said.

Both dockers did a race-walk to the next truck, its container now being lowered.

Francisco grabbed his colleague, shook him by the collar. "You stupid motherfucker! You wanna get us killed!? You don't mess with those guys! Don't ask no questions. Don't say shit to no one. Just do as I tell you and we move on to the next fuckin' load, you got that, homes!?"

Visibly shaken, the younger man nodded a few times, held his hands out wide, said to his boss, "Sorry, boss, but what was that shit, Francisco? I know you smelled it, man. What the fuck?"

This one was curious. Francisco had seen a few in the last dozen years. His old supervisor had taught him many years back to handle these guys like the Catholic Church does its flock: feed them a little fact, mixed with a whole lotta bullshit, and call the whole thing the honest-to-God truth.

"Look, homes, it's just some overripe fruit from Colombia. Some organic farmers up north use it to make fertilizer, but they can only get it from the rich fields of Colombia so they ship it in and truck it up to their fields and call it organic. You dig now, homes?" He didn't wait around for an answer.

The Old Pour Bar off Channelside and York was hidden behind an ancient warehouse that looked abandoned from the street. Only those in the know could find the place and all the dockers at TPA knew about this one. An industrial-strength dive on the outside, the interior was a modern sports bar that allowed smoking. Only one in Tampa, far as I knew, save the deep underground BigMoney sex clubs that dotted the Sarasota penthouses.

I'd valet-parked at the Marriott on 12th and walked around the block twice to get the lay of the area. Dockers off shift flooded the streets and converged on Old Pour from the east.

Executives and business types stayed on the west side of 12th, somehow knowing that the Old Pour area didn't welcome their distinguished pedigree.

Once inside, I felt at home.

Wasn't the people, it was the atmosphere. Old blood. Field-hand musk. Wet leather. Like Old Florida to me. And damned fine beer from all over the planet, surreptitiously off-loaded right at the docks. The bars were set up like a traditional dock: one long main bar with a dozen offshoots.

When I thought about it, the place more resembled Bird Key: maximizing every square inch of space and bringing in a shitload of cash.

Looked around and saw what most guys were drinking, ordered one. Other dockers were sitting or standing alone, looking around so I did the same, trying not to look out of place. No eyes on me, so I was okay.

Then I spotted him: the guy who'd gotten his ass beaten the night before my last day at the TPA gig. Looked like someone had patched him up well, tied him up to the bar so he could nurse his wounds. I wondered if the man next to him, about ten years older, was the one who'd given him the beatdown.

Slowly made my way over to the men, found an empty place at the bar, and settled in for the night.

Over the roar of the crowd, caught a few bits of their conversation: "runaways . . . prostitutes . . . kids. . . ."

It went that way all night, guys coming and going, solitary dockers leaning back against the bars and sizing up the crowd. A few skanky girls wandered about, offering their services. No one approached me, though.

That concerned me.

Not my ego, but the possibility that I may've blown any cover I thought I'd walked in with.

Was my face too smooth?

Nope, I'd let it go for a few days of dark shadows.

My clothes?

Check.

The odor of soap or some other common chemical or substance I came in contact with each day, things you'd only find uptown?

Check.

What the hell was it?

Maybe nothing at all. Maybe no one wanted to have a chat with Tommy tonight, take him back to a dark room and sex him up the walls.

Since Rachel bailed, that was nothing new.

If it looks like a whore, walks like a whore, and quacks like a whore. . . .

As the thought of a blown cover zipped through my mind, a rather attractive girl, not of the skank genus, sided up next to me.

"Just get in?" Clinked her beer against my bottle.

"Yeah. You?"

"Sort of. New York and LA."

"So you're an out-of-towner, working the local docks?" It'd been a long time since I'd chatted up a dock ho, even one this pretty.

"Oh, you think I'm a traveling whore, do you?" She laughed and downed her beer.

I raised my bottle to a bartender on the run: "Two!" Turned back to her. "No, not at all."

"What, then?"

"Librarian. Maybe an author on a book tour."

She laughed. It wasn't genuine, though, but I didn't give a shit. "Librarian. Author. On the docks."

A space opened up next to the two men, my new targets. I moved around the girl and took up a place next to the man I heard was Francisco. He hadn't noticed my change of venue. After seven beers, I wasn't surprised.

She didn't miss a beat: "I'm not a librarian or—"

"Okay, I'm supposed to ask what you do for a living?"

"That would be nice." She gulped her beer, got two more.

"Hmmm, I'd say . . . journalist."

Clapped her hands and reached over and kissed me as close to my lips as she could. "Good guess, darlin'!" Upended her next beer and raised an eyebrow at the bartender. Two more showed up seconds later.

Francisco and his buddy were talking about rules of the road, regulations, how his subordinate was supposed to act around the docks, then all of a sudden things changed. His buddy blurted out, "That wasn't bad fruit or anything in that container, Francisco. It was shit, man. Human shit. And muerto. I know death, man. You think I fell off the back of some strawberry truck, don't you, man? I don't got community college like you, homes, but I know things. And I know the smell of human shit and dead people when I smell it, man!"

Francisco bristled. Took a long pull of his beer, set it down, leaned into his friend. "You got choices here, Hector, but only two: one, you do what I tell you on the job. Mmmm? Or two, I kill you for having a fuckin' big mouth. Mmmm? Which one you want, homes?"

As I processed their conversation, still looking at her lips move, I knew this could go on all night and I'd not learn anything new. "Gotta cruise."

Looked genuinely surprised, even a little put off, like I'd just ruined some plan of hers. "Why? Where you going?"

"Let me call you a cab." I almost slipped and told her I just happened to be driving one a few hours ago.

Pouting, she slurred, "Jus' gimme your number so I can call you one night. Maybe t'morrow, and tell you to come over and fuck me. Whadda ya say to tha', cowboy?"

Took her to the main entrance, called her a cab and waited for it to arrive. Francisco and his cohort would have to exit the same door, so it was no sweat waiting.

I was looking forward to sexing her. Maybe not tomorrow, but one night. Soon, I hoped, because my sweet Rachel was banging all kinds of pots and pans inside my head.

Good thing that my targets were headed my way, because it was sneaking up on four a.m. and I felt whooped. They walked over to a fairly new Ford F-150, climbed in and moved out of the enclosed parking lot and onto Channelside. Made their way north to Selmon Expressway then east to 22nd Avenue where Francisco turned north for a few blocks then went east on 5th Avenue to a bank of small houses, pulled into the third one. Both men exited the truck and staggered inside for the remainder of the morning.

Damn, and I was hoping to beat someone's ass.

"Take a vacation, Tommy. Relax in the sun for a while."

This coming from the guy whose boss, Peter Jamison, kept me on a short leash. I hung up on him before I could say something stupid.

There were several voicemails and emails on my cell, which I purposefully had not taken with me last night when tracking Francisco and his coworker, Hector.

Someone's always tracking you or listening or watching. Always.

Much as I hate to say it, there's no such thing as freedom in this country, let alone liberty. It's all an illusion, played out on an impressive theater stage at a junior high school.

Rachel: "Hi, Tommy. It's me. Just checking in to see how you are. Sooo, how are you?" She tried to sound cheerful but couldn't quite pull it off. Not the cheerful type.

"Mr. Darlington? This is Ginny. Ginny from the Society. Hope I'm not catching you at a bad time. Just letting you know I found someone. Call me when you get a chance."

Found someone.

She meant herself, of course. Thought that was cute. Made a note to get her something more than Starbucks next time. What do you get a lovely 50-year-old woman as a thank-you? Gift card to Starbucks?

The last voicemail: "Hey, docker. 'Member me? The journalist from New York and LA? Just thought I'd return your call from before. Oh, wait a sec! You forgot to call me. That's right. So I guess I'm calling you, huh? Gimme a ring sometime. See ya."

Immediately replayed the tapes in my head, trying to recall when I'd given her my cell. In the bar? Outside the bar? Just before I put her in the cab? No. No. No. How the fuck did she get my number? Good question, TommyBoy. Maybe you better reevaluate your surveillance methods.

Think, dummy.

How many beers did she drink that night and morning? Eight. I would be drunk at eight, unless I . . . went to the bathroom and threw up after three or four beers. Shit, then she rinsed her mouth out with more beer and came out and slobbered all over me. In the end, she would've consumed maybe the equivalent of at most two beers. Not even that.

This woman played me.

Why?

Did she know I'd been watching Francisco and Hector?

If so, she could be part of some organized crime thing or . . . an organized Fed thing.

A Fed.

If I had popped up on the Fed's radar, I was in deep shit. And if she thought she could work me somehow, I would be hers by week's end.

At this early point in her working me, she wouldn't have reported anything about me to her boss just yet. At best, I was a note or two on her cell phone or a laptop, maybe a Post-It note on her wall. She was good. But she was also flawed in a way I knew was the unraveling of many an operative: she believed all the praise from her boss and higher how good she really was, and that made her arrogant.

She'd lost her edge a long time ago, and that would be my in.

"You always answer on the first ring, don't you?" I asked her. That was another good sign about this mob girl or Fed girl: she was anxious.

"What? Oh, hey! How are ya? Didn't recognize you at first? Glad you called."

"I'm good. Hey, I'm free tonight. Drinks?"

The long pause was filled with what sounded like her waving someone off or away from her.

Couldn't be sure, but I'd seen enough pauses to know so.

"Okay, tonight's good."

"Your place okay? I'll bring the beer." Catching her off guard was making me laugh, since she was supposed to be a trained something or other.

"Uh, lemme think. . . ."

She was mouthing some words to someone in the background. This I could easily sense.

"Okay, yeah. I don't usually do this kinda thing, but yeah, why not?"

Despite the lack of rain, stupidity bloomed early this year.

Soon as she gave me the address, I had a PI buddy do a search so it wouldn't trace back to me. I knew the search itself might pop up on some Fed's computer, especially if she were working for them in some capacity, but I had no choice.

These days, it was practically impossible to do background checks and not get noticed by people who didn't want you to poking around in their illicit business. Yeah, those companies you get background checks from say it's all 100% private, your identity is secure, but don't believe it.

Her place belonged to someone no longer alive, so I assumed it was a throw-away house, something Feds bought up, maintained only minimally, and used for purposes like this: simple meet-and-greets or drug deals or maybe . . . kidnappings and killings.

Not my idea of a safe house.

What had troubled me most about this location was that this woman's Tampa address was so close to Francisco and Hector's place.

Too close.

When I see the occasional coincidence, I make a note of it, let my subconscious stew on it.

More than one is a pattern.

And when they start to add up too quickly, it's a conspiracy.

There are only two ways to prove it: one, the assholes came forward and admitted their deed. Yeah, right. Two, someone did good research, connected enough dots of circumstantial evidence, analyzed the results, and came up with a good sound hypothesis. With more and more hard evidence, it became a theory. And when the truth vibed right down to your DNA, it was 200 proof they were up to no good.

Someone told me that process once and I've found it to be true, so when I saw the makings of one, I started looking hard at the dots and possible connections. Usually, there were plenty. BigMoney was so confident no one would even care about their misdeeds that they developed this dark arrogance, something they rubbed in our faces, the rest of us.

More than ever, I sensed black clouds on the horizon, being blown toward me by an evil wind. What was I gonna do about it?

The house itself was run down on the outside, and only a little less so inside. She definitely didn't fit the place: clothes a little too nice, soap from Publix and not bottom-shelf Walmart. Things didn't add up.

And still I stayed.

Was this another bad decision in a long line of them, post-Rachel? My indifference concerned me, yet, still I stayed.

"Glad you could make it." She smiled and kissed me. On the mouth this time.

In the harsh light, she looked rougher than before, with dull blue eyes slightly sunken, skin a little pasty and dry, wrinkles around the mouth but not the eyes. That last observation told me something important: her smiles were all forgeries. Genuine smiles pull in the eyes and mouth, the whole face even. Hers were bottom-face smiles, forced and held there a little too long. For false effect.

"How long you lived here?" Stayed as close to the front door as I could, even as she retreated to the kitchen.

In a few minutes, she emerged with a ghetto cheese tray from Walmart and bottle openers for the beer and vino, set it all on the dingy coffee table. She opened the wine, sipped it. "A good year, this wine?"

I'd gotten the cheapest thing I could find, and she thought it a good vintage. *Right.* "For alcohol, yes, a very good year." A nice blend of pinot, cab sauv and hydrochloric acid.

She smirked. "Take a seat." That bottom-smile in full bloom, her blue eyes going gray, like she had seen this before and just wanted to cut to the good part, whatever that was.

Before I could follow orders and take a seat, she was shoving me onto the couch and pulling off her gauzy shirt with no bra. My hands found her lovely nipples and took each into my mouth where I licked and sucked and bit her lightly.

Her hands dropped into my pants and grabbed and tugged on me hard, sighed loudly, then started masturbating me before she attacked me with her cool mouth, all low-end-factory foreplay.

Deep guttural moans from her, lots of fast predatorial hands and mouth and teeth. A she-lion, this one. Still, all that forgery could give a twenty year old erectile dysfunction.

My cell phone vibrated in my pocket down around my ankles. I'd put it on the lowest setting. If it did, that meant that my night-eyes outside, a buddy who'd joined me on this little Operation Skank Tampa had spotted at least one person outside the house. And if it vibrated again in about thirty seconds, there was a second bad guy out there, too.

It vibrated again.

Her pants now unzipped and hanging off her hips.

Buzzed again.

Three times meant get the hell out. Or did that mean three guys outside? I didn't hesitate, pulled away from her snapping jaws: "Bathroom."

She dropped her head, looked annoyed, since I'd only just rolled in and let her jump me. "Uhhh, yeah, sure. Down the hall, right side," she said, wiping her mouth and gulping down more of that good vintage.

Truth? I wanted to fuck her. Not because she turned me on. She was a far cry from Rachel. I'd say Rachel's opposite: somewhat attractive, sexy in a feral way, but with a hard character that conveyed nonchalance on one hand and a feverish desire on the other. Plain and simple, this woman was pure psycho and I wanted to taste that demon chemistry.

Walls started to close in around me . . .

White-noise at 130-dB flooded my ears . . .

Pushed into low gear, then shifted up and up with each passing second.

Ah, shit.

Had she already drugged me?

How?

Hadn't drunk or eaten anything yet. I only touched the doorknob on the way in.

Anxiety rush?

No, couldn't be. My mind was on sexing this lioness, not reeling from some anxious moment.

The doorknob. Had she poisoned it?

Speed-dialed Caleb and pressed 2, a sign that I needed extraction behind the house at bathroom window.

A fellow Ranger, Caleb had done the sniper thing for ten years before moving up and out to start his own private military firm. He was the only man outside of myself I could trust, even though this week was first time I'd seen him and his daughter in years.

The window had been locked and nailed from the inside, so I turned on the water faucet full, broke the seal around the entire pane, jerked up the window and lifted myself over the pane and down the side of the dilapidated house.

In that moment, my head began to spin.

No, the world around me began to rotate in a slow merry-go-round, slowly overcoming unthinkable inertia.

She'd surely noticed the water running too long. Maybe even heard my breaking out, I dunno.

Tripped over a man's body.

Moly fuckin' hoses!

Didn't stop to see if he were alive. I knew Caleb had dropped him.

All at once, bullets sizzled and zoomed in all directions, so I picked a direction that looked a little less dangerous than all my other choices and I sprinted, a burst of wind not completely invisible but hopefully reasonably stealthy.

Out across the street to a vacant lot ...

Through a yard with two pit bulls I'd surprised in mid-sleep but they gave chase and caught my tennis shoe as I scaled a six-foot fence ...

Hard right down railroad tracks, praying it wasn't my night to stumble and fall ... or run into a train going in the opposite direction.

In combat when you had to run for your fuckin' life, especially away from bullets and rockets, the best thing to do was to run the fuck away from bullets and rockets and not look back. Reasoning went something like this: if something was gonna get you, it would get you, regardless of whether your eyes were pointing forward or backward. Best if you kept them forward so you didn't run smack into something solid and get KO'd.

Like a wall.

Or a train.

Train?

TRAAAAAIN!!!!!!

A series of open-ocean waves roared in my adrenalized ears.

The oncoming train, no headlight, screaming at me at thirty miles an hour.

My eyes had been distracted by the floodlights from the warehouse to my left, and left me momentarily blind.

Blind in my dominant left eye.

My shooting eye.

Blind to the shit around me and also in the middle of an ass-kick anxiety attack.

It hadn't been drugs on the fuckin' doorknob, idiot.

The train finally registered as it ran passed me at a mere forty-four feet per second. Doesn't sound like much until you consider something more than just velocity: stuff like momentum and inertia and a million-ton iron fist.

Without even really knowing, I'd thrown myself off the tracks and onto the gravel that cut into my hands and arms, punched my right hip and thigh into mush. Pain shot through me from all directions. Held back a scream.

At least the bullets and rockets stopped zoomin' my way. . . .

A heart never forgets it was once broken.

"We have to assume Jamison knows about this." Sipping a scotch, Caleb Silverthorn sat with me on my balcony, taking in the stunning Gulf view and looking down at his Casio I'd returned to him yesterday. "You do something snarky to my watch, son?"

Ignored him, trying to recall if the recent drowning I'd given that stupid watch had done any harm. C'mon, it was a Casio.

He fiddled with the watch, reset the alarm settings, shook a threatening finger at me.

Only hours ago, we'd pulled up from Tampa after the brief firefight with Whatshername and her Fed buddies. I'd served with Caleb at the 1st Ranger Battalion years back and then went through Ranger School where he was a Ranger Instructor in the Florida phase. He went on to help found an international private military firm.

"Puts me in a crappy situation, C-man, assuming Jamison is onto me about the old man and last night's op."

"My rule is always this, Ranger: everybody knows everything. So it becomes a cat-and-mouse game of tactics that you have to invent on the fly. Sun Tzu is your best friend."

The evening sun on North Longboat Key, far from the moneyed towers south of here, drifted away faster in the summer months. Rachel said it was a scientific fact, since it traveled fewer miles at the north end of the key, so it was best that we enjoyed it as long as we could.

What's a few seconds of less sun, I told her. Doesn't matter, idiot, she would say. Just go with the romance of the story, Tommy. Go with the romance. . . .

She had been right all along: I took every gram of romance I could find and broke it apart into its individual components so I could study it. Thing is, I could never put them back together again so they resembled something short of romantic.

Caleb could tell I was distracted, lost in the zippy sunset, lost in thoughts of Rachel, lost in last night's harrowing escape from hell in Tampa.

Tapes replayed in my head now: Caleb had stationed himself across 5th Street on top of the warehouse, and could see pretty much the entire yard except directly in the back. He'd shot the first guy on the side of the house, the dude I'd stepped on during my hasty ejection from the men's room.

Two and Three were out front, waiting for me to stumble out, and started shooting when they heard me fall out the bathroom window and onto the metal trashcans. He blasted them in place as I limped behind the house.

Whatshername popped out the front door, pistol in hand, looking around for signs of life—her guys—and seeing them both on the ground, started for the street, looking for viable targets.

That's when Caleb hit her in her pretty chest and left her in pre-rigor on the driveway.

"Yeah, nice work . . . I never got her name. But she wasn't a Fed."

"Nope." Big smile on Caleb's face. "You know what that means."

Long pause. "Okay, I give," I said, looking over at him.

"Means you need to leave town 'cos everybody seems to know all about you and since you dragged me into this spreading pile of sun-kissed dogshit, I'm on the run, too." He clinked his glass against my bottle. "Nice going." Smile still on his face.

I could only imagine the possibilities: no one knew anything and so I was in the clear . . . or as Caleb said, everyone knew everything and so I was a nice target. He was, too.

"Okay, so what?" I was on my third beer in only a coupla minutes.

"Go back to the beginning."

Paused a moment. "Rachel, the old man, seeing Donny again, learning about his father's previous occupation as a drug runner, Jamison the private investigator who was so eager to get me out of town, finding Donny's old house on Bird Key was now Jamison's new house on Bird Key, the Tampa gig at TPA, gunfight with Feds who weren't Feds."

"Any patterns yet?"

Thought about it some more. "All seem tied in somehow."

"Rachel, too?"

How could my love possibly be tied to this mob?

Tears slowly filled my eyes.

Not missing a thing, he lowered his head and shook it: "I'm puttin' you in for extended sick leave, son." Handed me a bowl of spicy trail mix.

I looked over at him, mumbled, "Dude, I didn't fight my way to the top of the food chain to eat nuts and twigs. Gimme a drumstick."

Look, Felix, we don't know who took out your people in Tampa." Peter Jamison paced his office, cell phone glued to his ear.

"You've never disappointed us before, Peter."

Jamison felt the sting of the threat. "I'll make this right, Felix. We will find out exactly what happened up there. Was the shipment compromised?"

"If you mean, did someone steal the package? No, of course not. No one steals from us."

"Then what's your concern?"

"That someone knew of the package and said something to someone else. It is a breach of our security. That's what concerns me, Peter."

"But, Felix—"

"Shush, Peter. We operate under a cloak of anonymity. Have for many years. That's how this operation has run so smoothly."

"And it will still run smoothly, Felix." Paced some more, lit up a cigarette, his first in months.

"Nothing runs smoothly with even the smallest of kinks. When we brought you in, we impressed upon you that it would be a closed-cell business, everyone on a need-to-know."

His reply was measured: "So what do you suggest, Felix?"

"Find the people responsible for this breach."

Jamison could feel Felix lean into his speakerphone.

"And *kill* them, Peter."

The dead connection punctuated his point.

And put a dent in Jamison's confidence.

He marched to the outer office and ripped the phone from John's ear. "We're going to the Key."

"To Paul's?"

Jamison was already in the elevator heading down.

I love creatures of habit: they make dazzling stationary targets, even when they're moving.

No one noticed me pull out behind Jamison's Porsche, John at the wheel.

"Do we want to put Tommy on the next job in Tampa?" John passed several tourists on the Ringling Bridge, swerved in and out of traffic all the way to Bird Key. Two cars were in the left turn lane to enter the Key. John pulled up ahead of both, cut off oncoming traffic and gunned it past the guardhouse, going airborne over the speed bumps and slamming his boss's head into the low ceiling.

"Slow down, idiot!"

"You said to—"

"I said to get us there yesterday, not call unwanted attention!"

Flashing lights in the rearview.

"Sorry, sir, we've got company." He slowed down and pulled to the right, stopped.

"Shit." Jamison jumped out of the car, waved at the Sheriff's deputy and walked toward him.

The deputy normally would've drawn his pistol and ordered the foolish citizen to stop and go back to his vehicle. He paused for a moment, letting the recognition set in. "Mr. Jamison. You okay, sir?"

"Yes, yes, we're fine. A small emergency. I'm sorry to be driving so fast. Couldn't be helped."

"Anything I can do? Need an escort?"

"No, no, we're fine. Just need to get going. That okay?" It wasn't a request.

"Yessir, have a good day." With that, the good deputy spun around and returned to his cruiser, did a 180 and rolled off to fight crime and terrorism among the rich and needy.

Jamison fell into the passenger's seat in a huff, looked at his protégé: "We have enough trouble for now, John."

"Understood, sir. I'm sorry," Not looking at his boss, pulled away slowly and made his way to the house.

"Don't tell me we're doing fine, Peter." Paul Jamison paced the grounds of the library, fidgeting. "And don't you dare invoke your silly separation of operations and accounting this time, either."

"Paul, let's focus." He stood in front of his brother, normally a calming presence.

"I thought that's what operations did, brother."

Two hours later, John pulled out of the garage and headed back to Sarasota.

I picked him up at Bob White Drive as the Porsche roared over the little bridge across the inland waterway, followed loosely back to Sarasota, noting that Peter Jamison was not with him.

An operational maxim: Regardless of where you are, even in the middle of the blazing Namib, someone's always watching, always listening.

Next morning, parked the car I had pinched from an underground garage in one of the high-rise condos, in a semicircular driveway a block away on Bob White Drive. Caleb had verified the owners were away for the summer.

He pulled up minutes later in a white Lexus suv, parked next to the white Mercedes I had driven and walked into the vacant house like he owned the place. Neighbors probably wouldn't give our presence a second look, as there were usually two white vehicles parked in the driveway.

I was setting up a remote listening device with a parabolic receiver, aimed it at the Jamison's across the canal. "So far, got two men in a room at the back of the house."

"Betcha they ain't talking Tampa Rays baseball," Caleb said, pulling out binos and directing them at the house.

"Gimme a sec. I should have them up ... here were go." I adjusted a few dials, stepped back.

Both of us listened intently.

"Don't tell me we're doing fine, Peter . . . and don't you dare invoke your silly separation of operations and accounting this time, either."

"Paul, let's focus."

"I thought that's what operations did, brother."

Caleb and I looked at each other, eyebrows rising ever so slowly. Our eyes then returned to the conversation being recorded on the digital device between us.

"Felix said we're a go for the next shipment."

"I seriously doubt Felix would allow another shipment to enter Tampa without first ensuring complete operational security, Peter."

Looked over at Caleb, whispered, "Okay, dunno who this guy is, but the other guy is my new boss, Peter Jamison." I pointed to a dancing waveform on the receiver, marked it in green. The waveform had a frenetic step to it—just like Peter Jamison.

"Felix is on board one hundred percent, Paul. Period."

I marked the waveform corresponding to Paul's voice in red, whispered to Caleb, "Okay, we now have Peter's brother . . . Paul."

"Bullshit! Felix doesn't make a move without complete control over everything. We don't have complete control over this operation, do we?"

"We will, brother. We will."

Caleb shut off the unit, looked over at me: "After listening to these yahoos, I need a dose o' Mitch Hedberg."

Always be careful where you dig . . . there might be a few bodies in that hole.

Ginny was waiting for me in the parking lot. I pulled into a parking space on the far end of the Society's building, well away from all street traffic.

"Hello, Tommy." She got in the stolen Mercedes. "You're moving up in life, I see."

"Don't ask, Ginny." My tone said I was serious.

A bit put off, she withdrew, then: "The Jamisons had two boys living with them until 1976. Evidently there was a boating accident in the bay and one of the boys drowned, his body was never recovered." She handed me a copy of the newspaper article.

"Names of the boys?" She looked at the article. "Says here . . .

Peter and Paul."

"So Paul allegedly drowned." The picture of the twins was odd in some way. One of the boys in a full-face grin, the other wearing a dead face that stretched right down to his boat shoes.

"Paul drowned, yes." She pointed to the picture in the article. "That's Peter."

Big smile on Peter, same as the one I saw in that photograph high atop his bookshelf in his skyscraper office.

"Any further news about the family after the accident?"

"No, couldn't find anything. The family moved back to New York."

"Where were they living at the time?"

"Records I have say Tampa, on the Davis Islands. That's it."

"So this kid drowned in Tampa Bay?"

"Correct."

"What's the family's connection to Sarasota?"

"Evidently, the father was in business with someone. It's here somewhere . . . I thought I'd made a note of it . . . oh, yes . . . the McCrackens. He married the youngest daughter of Donald Jr."

The Physics of Love: it applies to you and governs everything you do, but your girlfriend is immune to it.

Handed Caleb the article.

He hummed his way through it. "Donny McCracken and the Jamisons are cousins. Linked by blood."

"These guys keep everything in the family."

"Like Old Italy—the Borgias and Orsinis."

"Yup."

"They intermarried and kept all the secrets and jewels for themselves. If there was someone in the family who needed to be leashed, they gave him a shit job in a remote place where they could control him so he didn't stir up too much crap."

"Sorta like Jamison did to me by putting me in Tampa?" I said.

"You're thinking too romantically into this, no pun intended."

"Pun?"

"Romance. Romans. Whatevs. Look at it this way, somehow you managed to get your ass-end tied to all this, at least in their book. Makes me nervous."

"Suggestions," I said, even though I had a list hanging in front of my eyes.

"We already know Paul is somehow important to overall operations. We don't know why the family chose to fake his death, if that's what they did."

"He was being groomed for something higher in the future, maybe in case something happened to Peter. Like having a—"

"Hitler clone," he said.

We were both silent for a moment.

I left and came back with four beers, sat down again. "So, back to the original question: why am I involved?"

"First, we ask how and not why. Why's too philosophical. How gets into the mechanics of the shitstorm, sees the moving parts." Took a long pull, sat back. "Did you go to Donny or did Donny come to you?"

Had to think about it. "I went to him at first and he mentioned the job."

"He wanted you to make you think that." Familiar knowing smile on Caleb.

"So he conned me, too." More of the link-up with Donny floated in front of my eyes, revealing details I'd missed.

He tapped my arm with his bottle. "You are a rockodon, fresh off a break-up from the love of your crappy life. Lemme tell you something else, too: there's this thing called hysteresis. It's when you apply a magnetic field to an object and all the little things inside the object line up a certain way to follow the orders of the field. You following me?"

No. "Uh-huh."

"When you take away that magnetic field, all the little things inside that object fall back to their original positions like good little soldiers. Except for a few. Those rockodons who don't line back up right stand out like, well, sore thumbs. That's hysteresis."

"And this means?"

"You're not the same with Rachel gone. She was your magnetic field. When she split, all those little iron atoms in your heart didn't line back up all normal-like. Makes you a nice pop-up target."

He wasn't far from the truth. I'd lost an edge when Rachel left, and had since been blind to certain things around me. I knew I hadn't been ready for any jobs, but something unusual drew me to Donny's that day, sucked me into crewing for him on a dive out to his grandfather's wrecked P-47.

"Why would Donny all of a sudden reveal the P-47 wreck?"

"Maybe someone ordered him to do it," he said, leaning back more, that smile growing wider. "Guy like Donny? Keeps that shit to himself. Nope, I say the people pullin' Donny's strings set him up."

Looked off into the Gulf, mumbled absently, "Donny needs our good company right about now."

Revenge is the worst heart condition.

If Donny didn't have his hands all over a scuba tank, it was repairing or refurbishing a regulator, testing a dive computer, or running one of his boats. Not one to sit down for too long, he kept himself busy every waking moment, not allowing the past to creep onto one of his front burners.

When I arrived, he was in his office, a small room with stacks of papers, books, manuals, and unopened letters.

"How about a chat, Donny."

He was paging through a sheaf of legal papers, didn't answer or look up.

"Once again—and I want the truth this time—tell me about the house on Bird Key."

Rose his head about an inch, still not answering.

Found a clear spot, sat down, drilled my eyes into his forehead. "Peter and Paul Jamison."

"With big money comes big responsibility, Tommy."

"You said that before, Donny. Now tell me what it means."

Not looking up, he said, "Bad lot, that family. Real bad lot."

Hoped my silence would encourage him.

"Guess you're wonderin' about the plane."

I'd only asked about the Jamisons and the house on Bird Key. The plane was a bonus.

"Pull up a chair, Tommy." That's when he looked up, saw me sitting across from him. "Okay, then." Handed me the papers.

Skimmed through them: a house deed.

"To keep 'em off my back, I gave 'em the house."

"But the deed's right here, Donny."

"Like I said, I gave 'em the house, so they took it. Told 'em I didn't know where the deed was, so Paul said no matter, they'll just take it anyway. I pay all taxes, keep it in my name. Didn't make sense 'til I realized the big picture."

I just sat there, listened.

"Somehow they found out about granddad's drug running, the plane, whatever. Said they'd take over the family business for me, I wouldn't have to lift a finger, just keep up appearances on the house."

"But they didn't want a paper trail with the deed back to them?"

"Something like that."

"Okay."

"They muscled me out of the business my granddad started, first with opium, then later marijuana before it was known around these parts." He was staring off into the past, trying to claw his way forward. "Dad was doing real well, had everyone in his pocket, kept 'em all in plenty of cash to keep the chatter down to a low hum. Until that family came back, wanting all that—"

"That what?" Sounded like he said *gold*.

"Nothin'."

Didn't push it. "But you're related to that family, Donny."

He looked up at me, disgust forming on his mouth, spreading to the eyes. "Blood don't make a family, Tommy." Looked back down again, then out the window, twirling a pen in each hand. "They'd planned this all along, taking over the drug running and all. Their old man tried to take it from my dad way back, but pop was too sly for them. That man had a machine going in this town, Tommy. No one could touch him for miles. Those Jamisons got to him, though, drove him to an early trip to Potter's Field."

"They killed your dad."

"Yup. Right out there at the wreck, just after he showed 'em the whole operation. They run him down 'til he talked. Didn't do it direct and all. All behind the scenes, slowly threatening everyone pop knew, scaring 'em all off like jackrabbits. Soon as the business went to shit, they forced pop to unload all the details, then they just moved in like it'd been theirs all along."

"What happened to your dad, Donny?"

Took in a deep breath, exhaled his story: "One night they took pop out to the wreck. He said there was a shipment of dope coming in, and they wanted to see how it all went down. Soon as the other boat came on the wreck, the Jamisons and their goons shot everybody, scuttled the boat, took all the cash and dope. And that was the start of their little empire."

"Your dad?"

"On the bottom of the other boat when it went down."

"How do you know?"

"I stole away that night on pop's boat, the one with the Jamisons and two goons."

"You saw the whole thing."

"Heard it, saw it, kept it right here for 45 years, Tommy." He pointed to his heart.

"So Peter and Paul Jamison's father killed your dad, took over his shady business, and built a legitimate one for himself and his sons. But what about the all the booty your grandfather and father had found."

He wasn't listening. "They coulda included me, you know."

Again, didn't push the gold issue. "What happened after that?"

"I never knew if they knew I'd been on the boat that night. Still don't to this day. But old man Jamison closed down the shop for a few years, using it as a tool shed mostly, 'til I got old enough. That's when he fixed it up, turned it into a small dive shop, handed it over to me."

"So they did know about you."

"Now that I tell it to you, Tommy, maybe they did."

"Why not just kill you, too?" I knew the answer to that one: they wanted the gold, but knew they couldn't threaten or hurt Donny to get it. They would be patient—years, even—and wait until the right time to get the location out of him.

He looked at me full on. It was the first time I'd seen a grown man tear up like that, all that pain slowly bubbling up: "I was their blood. Said I was now part of their family and needed some structure and all. Gave me the business, but I know it was just to keep me quiet. Like a throwaway bastard son."

"Why'd you reveal the wreck?"

He was now crying, his face buried in his hands. Looked up long enough to blurt it out to me: " 'Cos fuck them, Tommy! Fuck those assholes. Killed my pop! And for what!? Money!" His voiced became small, trailed off to a whisper: "Shit, man, those people deserve something worse than death. But they'll never find that gold, I tell ya. Never. Right under their feet." His voice trailed off.

They'll never find that gold . . . right under their feet.

"What now, Donny?"

Looked up at me again, wiping his face with a dirty towel. "I know everything." That's when he smiled something awful, full of decades of pain, built on shaky sand and gravel, a smile that wasn't a smile at all.

Payback time.

If you subscribe to Occam's Razor, the simplest explanation is usually the right one . . . unless there's a hidden hand in there somewhere, polluting the narrative.

By the time I shared the entire story with Caleb, it was two a.m. He didn't stop me to get a beer or take a piss, just listened to the whole saga, some thriller you couldn't put down.

"Why the hell would the Jamisons want me involved in their operation? I'm important to all this somehow."

Caleb slapped me on the back, almost as hard as the old man once did out at the lake. "Don't you go getting all sappy on me now."

"I'm here for a reason, Caleb."

"Tommy, lemme learn ya a little: when this is all done and gone, those soft-touches in that tower downtown Sarasota aren't saying thank you and giving you a gold watch."

I snorted what I thought was a laugh, didn't notice he'd gone to the kitchen.

"Drink this. In fact, there's a whole case of this homeopathic medicine I want you to drink. Time to drown those romantic notions you got inside that brick head of yours about your being tied to these people in some way. Near as I can see it, they know you did something bad. Thing is, we just gotta figure out how to get you some protection."

"Or kill the whole lot."

"That's the smartest thing you've said all night." Clinked his bottle against my empty, handed me another cold one. "You up for a little mission this morning?" He was already standing up, ready for the door.

"Thought you wanted me to drown my self-indulgent bullshit."

"Don't tell me you can't do two things at once."

The first gift my dad ever gave me was a hangover. When I was nine. The second was a hooker. What I recall, I wasn't even eleven. Before I hit my teens, I had already gotten thoroughly drunk and expertly laid.

He put me on an old air mattress in the bed of the truck, my head propped up just enough to see it: the moon off the surface of the Gulf, a silver pearl that hovered and shimmered in the offshore breezes and light surface waves. He didn't know it, but it kept me from throwing up.

Caleb drove the five miles up from my place on 789 to Donny's dive shop on Cortez. We should've seen the illuminated building, parking lot and dock area from half a mile away. This morning, it was dark, only the moon throwing its silver daggers across the lot. Caleb knocked on the rear window, alerting me.

We parked just off the road and walked slowly to the shop. Caleb walked; I stumbled at first, found my sea legs and straightened up a bit.

I took in the whole scene: Donny's truck was parked in its usual spot at the back of the lot near the dock . . . no lights anywhere except a few small blue and green LEDs from computers inside the office . . . rear door between shop and tool shed was open . . . otherwise, nothing out of the ordinary.

Caleb was already inside, scanning the main dive shop and each room. He knew I was useless as a backup, so he pressed on without me.

"Tommy." His voice was so flat, without the usual sparkle or twinkle of mischief.

I knew it even before I stepped into the tool shed. "Shit."

"Don't bother. Been gone a while now. Few hours, my guess." He looked around the shed for signs, anything that might help us piece this together.

Donny was sitting in a chair, gagged with a grimy towel, hands and feet trussed up with 550 cord, his head slumped over to the right, a foot-long gash around his neck.

"Looks like a someone sent Donny a message." Caleb shook his head. "For giving up the wreck, betcha."

"Now they're sending someone else a message." I was still trying to sober up and get in the game. "Who, though?"

He looked up at me, disappointed that I'd not seen the obvious. "Lissen, rockodon, wake up in a day, gimme a ring and I'll learn ya a thing or two."

"Is there anything around here . . . evidence?"

Caleb looked at me again. "Well, let's see: one dead dude, throat slashed, signs of torture." Looked up at me again. "Nope, no evidence, Ranger. Take a knee, face outward and hydrate, Tommy. Now would be good because you are disturbing my process of analysis."

Caleb had said that to me in Ranger School. When an RI told you to face out and take a knee, it meant to rest up a bit because right at the moment you were pretty useless and could walk off the trail at any moment and that meant some RI like Caleb would have to go a-lookin' for you and probably get his BDUs dirty in the process, then come back and smoke your bags for making him have to do extra laundry when he got off his shift.

Caleb took a knee, too. "Man, this is just getting more fun by the minute. I might have to cancel all other appointments the next coupla days and hang out with you. Most fun I've had in a while."

Took another look at Donny, that thick red ear-to-ear clown-grin on his face, and threw up a week of beer and anxiety, scattering Caleb and the cockroaches to the four corners of the shed.

Bad news didn't always travel fast. Sometimes it traveled in stupid little envelopes via the US Postal Service, and this one came two days later. I'd left it on the table out on the deck, still unopened. Dunno why I didn't at least look at it. Maybe I already knew the contents.

Later in the evening, Caleb rolled in, let himself in like mi casa was his casa, found me out back, three beers into a sixer for the evening.

"Tommy, you just don't learn the first time, do you?" Put two cold-ass Heinekens in my lap.

"Isn't the first time." Stared at the envelope.

"Trying to burn a hole in it?"

"Dunno what I'm doing."

"Who's it from?"

"Donny."

Smirked at me, reached for the envelope, sliced it open with a folding blade that came out of nowhere, dropped the contents on the table. The blade disappeared back into its secret hold.

Something about the papers was familiar: the deed to Donny's house on Bird Key. "You gotta be kidding me."

"Son, I think the proper words are 'ya gotta be shittin' me.' What is it?"

"Donny left me the deed to his house."

"Uppity Bird Key-kinda house?"

Nodded my head, pulled on the Heineken. Handed the deed to him.

"Even in death, this man amazes me." He read the few pages, handed them back to me.

"What could I possibly do with a thirty-year-old deed to a dead man's house?"

For once, Caleb didn't crack a wise one. He knew I liked Donny. So did he.

"I'd say there's a lot you can do, Tommy. On the strictly legal side, you can road march down to the Clerk of the Court and show it to them, tell them you'd like to re-establish a new deed in your name and see about evicting the squatters who've been there for the past 30 years. That might be a good start. Or you and I might drive over to your new house, knock on the door and when one of those evil twins answers, do some face-smashin' and home-wreckin'."

Sometimes it's good just to get the fuck on the road. No planning, no map, just light out for any point. Didn't matter where, pick one. That's the way it felt the night Caleb and I drove out to Bird Key, to the Jamison's cute little home. Oh, my bad: *my* new little home.

I loaded up two .45s, both suppressed, cross-mounted on my chest. Caleb packed his usual .38 on each hip. We didn't figure on another firefight, so we left behind extra ammo.

After all my training downrange, if I couldn't shoot a man in the face with a .45 and drop him for a standing eight-count, then I probably deserved a good butt-kicking.

What's the difference between a psychopath and a normal? Everything.

"Don't even think of parking 400 yards out, then humping in," I told him.

"Bud, we now have the keys to the castle. Your castle. So I say we roll right on into the living room, toot the horn."

We both laughed, something we'd not done in a while.

"Un-ass the vehicle, Ranger," Caleb said.

Got out like we owned the place. At least I did. Knocked on the door.

The maid stood at the entrance. "We've been expecting you both. Please come in."

If ever my nerves got all tied up at once over a few simple words, it was right then.

We've been expecting you both.

It was not lost on Caleb, either.

Waited until Caleb stood next to me, then he tapped my shoulder like he'd been waiting for me to be the first target inside the lair of the two-headed dragon.

What the hell: I stepped in, Caleb followed, hands on both hips.

Spartan interior. Not a speck of dust to be found, even around the few inches right in front of my face.

The maid had backed into the foyer. "I'll tell Mr. Jamison you're here, gentlemen."

Not a minute later, Peter Jamison appeared from his cave, a darkened and deep-set room filled with books. What should've smelled like a library wasn't at all. I'd recognized it from many a trip to a morgue.

He ushered us into a grand living room, the first place I'd gut when I moved in. Caleb was off to my right and slightly behind me.

That was his idea of having my back, using me as a shield against Jamison.

Something about Peter Jamison tugged at the hairs on the back of my neck . . . Peter Jamison wasn't Peter Jamison.

Paul, I presume.

More nerves tangled themselves all around me, a climbing vine from jungle-hell. I could sense Caleb was feeling it, too.

"So, Tommy, how's the work going?"

Waited for him to introduce himself as Paul.

"John said you did well on the Tampa gig. Glad to hear. You'll excuse me if I'm not myself today. Been under the weather, all this flu going around."

The advertisements for flu season wouldn't officially commence for a few more months.

He floated into a shiny leather club chair. "We're very happy you're here, Tommy." He looked over at Caleb. "Your, ah, friend, as well."

This version of Jamison lacked the energy of the other one, the oily signature smile nowhere to be found.

I handed him the original deed to the land and house.

"What's this?" He scanned the papers, no expression on his face other than the bored, white-bread executive face he probably wore 24/7. "Ah, a deed." Handed the papers back to me and smiled for the first time. A small sardonic grin one might find on a cat. One of the big ones.

Caleb broke the silence: "This house and the land under it belong to this man here."

I think Caleb and I expected some kind of response, maybe a "fuck you, now leave."

Looking at Caleb, he said, "I'm afraid this deed is null and void, Tommy."

"How you figure that?" Caleb asked.

"This house has been in my family for more than thirty years. Simple as that. And any challenge to our claim is ridiculous." He rose and smiled that little big-cat smile again.

I wanted to shoot it off his face. Like I'd done with Viktor at his cabin in the sticks. Could only imagine what Caleb wanted to do to him.

"If there's nothing else, Tommy, I'm late for a meeting." He held his arm out, pointing it toward the front door.

"Why'd you kill Donny McCracken?" Caleb was often subtle in his approach with assholes.

Jamison's expression remained as before: "Tommy, I find your friend here a bit rude." He started walking away, spoke to the walls: "You may call on John for your next assignment."

If things aren't going the way you want and you need to stir things up, crouch down behind a heavy wall and watch while someone else does it.

"Not like you didn't piss the guy off or anything, Gatewood."

On the road back to North Longboat.

"Sometimes, Tommy, when things aren't moving like you want, you need to shake things up a little."

"Pull the tiger's tail is more like it." I pressed it further.

Reminded me of someone else who enjoyed doing that, pulling the tiger's tail and pressing issues: Rachel.

"That gets people to do one of two things—"

"Or something stupid," I blurted out.

"These guys may've been in business longer than me, but I'll tell you one thing: they ain't rocket wizards."

"What'll be their next move, you think?" I already knew.

"Ask me, I say things are just starting to heat up to boiling. The Jamisons know more about you than they let on."

"The maid said they were expecting both of us."

"Don't read into that too much."

As we passed Donny's dive shop, saw a flood of trucks and Mexicans, moving everything out of the buildings, off the dock.

Caleb said, "Don't stop. We'll find out later what's going on. Be good not to show our faces, attract attention."

"Haven't we sort of done that already?"

"Second thought, pull in over there away from the crowd."

No one paid us mind, just kept loading up the trucks with everything Donny had built for himself and his family over the years. It was sad to see it all tossed and jammed into boxes, disappear into a fleet of rented vehicles.

"We've been expecting you two." John Jamison.

How the hell was it that every bad guy in the good State of Florida was expecting us today?

Without missing a beat, I said, "Peter said you have my next gig for me. Gotta few minutes now to fill me in?"

"Stop by the office tomorrow morning. Just you, Tommy." He turned and walked away.

Caleb looked at me, made a moue, pushed into the crowd, looked around, saw a few familiar faces in the main dive shop. Or what was left of it. "Sheriff, what brings you guys out here today?"

Sarasota County Sheriff Bill Kershaw never left his air-conditioned office if he could help it. His 450-man tactical force of deputies allowed for this. You could find him in full dress uniform at high-end social functions, though. "Sir, what's on your mind? Got some news of a crime in my backyard?"

"Sorry, Sheriff. I'm fresh out of news on crimes in this county. It's squeaky clean, you ask me."

"Then get the fuck out. Now." Kershaw nodded at two oversized deputies, a couple of retired WWF wrestlers, the cartoon variety Sarasota liked to hire.

Caleb stood there for a moment, then thought better of pressing it, tapped me on the chest and pointed to the exit.

We both left quietly, Deputy Goons One and Two in close tow.

If the weather report predicted an atmosphere of musk and tension, you best prepare for war.

Peter Jamison's office was a full house, no one I recognized, no one I wanted to know. That much, I knew.

Musk and tension.

Caleb was sitting in his air-conditioned suv, listening in on the conversation. He'd placed three tiny microphones, two above my belt and one below. "Hopefully," he said, "we might pick up some good stuff. And don't scratch your balls."

"Tommy, have a seat over here, will you." Peter Jamison—the actual Peter Jamison—stood behind the seat, hands on both arms of the chair.

The gesture alone spoke volumes, not the least of which was, *we own you.*

I could imagine Caleb's reaction downstairs, wanting to snap the man's neck.

Took my seat as ordered, looking around the room once again, mostly for all available exits, even the windows. If I had to, I'd consider throwing a chair out one of the large picture windows, with Peter Jamison in it.

Behind me, I felt the predators converge on me, and I wondered whether I'd lower myself and actually call for Caleb to climb the tower and rescue poor Tommy. Reality was, he wouldn't arrive on the scene until well after the slaughter. Comforting thought that refocused my attention on Peter Jamison and his kingly speech.

"Tommy, as you know, we run a tight operation here. So when things don't go as planned, all of us feel it right away and it makes us a tad nervous."

Think what he meant was, it made his boss nervous, which scared the shit out of him. And we all know that shit rolls downhill. Fear was a great motivator that often got people killed, and not those who should've been in fear to begin with. Usually, it was the idiots who followed their orders.

"We see that you've been involved with Mr. McCracken and his, ahhh, business." He waited patiently for a reply.

Got nothing from me.

"I see . . . Donny worked for us, Tommy."

Still no reply. I was holding out for something better than this amateur parlor game.

"Like his father before him."

Peter Jamison would have to wait quite some time before he shook me up.

A voice from behind me, to the left a few feet: "Mr. Darlington, we're aware of your actions against one of our colleagues, Viktor Krinski."

Didn't sound like a question to me. Caleb was probably yelling into the recorder, "Just say yes!"

"Viktor was a friend of mine, and so I took his death quite personally."

I may have made a small smile in Peter Jamison's direction.

Regardless of who spoke, I kept my eyes on Jamison. The others I could discern from noticeable smirks and snorts, or their distinct heat signature and thousand-dollar cologne.

"And the little fiasco in Tampa recently," he continued. "That was also you and your friend. Of course, you're not obligated to speak on your own behalf, Mr. Darlington. This isn't an inquisition. Merely a meeting to understand each other better."

A *tad* better, I guessed.

He moved to the left side of Jamison's desk, leaned his hip on the edge.

"The way we see things here, you have two options: one, you continue your work with us and discontinue your—how to put it?—extracurricular activities. Or two, we retire you immediately." This one also waited for a reaction from me.

Didn't get it.

So he continued: "With a generous severance package, of course."

Read: they would disconnect my head from my body. Same with Caleb.

My silence and indifference to his threat made him nervous. This much was evident. These weren't seasoned killers who did this for a living. These assholes were the guys who hired seasoned killers who did this for a living. And got away with it.

"Peter, why don't we show Mr. Darlington just how generous we can be?" The man barely turned around to address Jamison. "I think then he will understand we wish to be his friends."

Someone else from rear of the pack stepped forward and placed a briefcase on Jamison's desk.

The asshole leaning against Jamison's desk continued: "Please accept this advance as a display of our commitment to your continued success with our organization, Mr. Darlington."

My eyes didn't leave Jamison.

"Go ahead, Mr. Darlington, open it."

Doubtless, Caleb was jumping up and down inside the suv, having a heart attack and a stroke, and probably shitting himself.

I stood and opened the briefcase, my eyes still on Jamison. Looked down for a second, then back at Jamison. "An advance for what?"

"Ahhh, he speaks," said the man who was obviously at least one rung above Peter Jamison on their corporate ladder.

The asshole next to Jamison's desk clapped a few times for effect, closed the briefcase and set it down next to my leg.

"Seems you understand all too well what we know around here, Mr. Darlington."

"What's that?" I asked him and, for the first time turned and addressing him directly.

"Money speaks. And a lot of money speaks loudly."

Two more seconds and I was bustin' down that door." Caleb was livid, but his sense of humor always coated the anger.

"They're amateurs, dude."

"You're an idiot."

Gave him a straight face, even though I wanted to smack him. "Why?"

"Remember, ask how, not why. And I'll tell you how you're an idiot: for one, idiot, these guys might be amateur killers in your eyes, but they know all the right bad guys to cut your head off in the same time it'd take to spank some fine ass. Two, you don't go into an office full of businessmen who do this shit for a living and try to make them nervous. Ain't gonna happen. These buttheads aren't smart enough to know when to be scared, 'cos they're blinded by their own arrogance, which makes them even dumber than you."

Caleb was dressed in a white polo shirt and hyper-colored Bermuda shorts.

"I'm getting a lecture from Bob Hope on how to do my job."

"Hey, bud, this Bob Hope has been on both sides of the tracks, theirs and ours. You've been on the wrong side all your miserable life, so you best wise up or you'll get me killed."

"What about me?" Popped a handful of chewable ice in my mouth, crunched as loud as I could.

He got up and pointed his beer at me, looked me dead in the eye: "You'll be the first casualty, son."

I should've been scared, but I wasn't. And that made me stupid. And dangerous.

The drive to Tampa was uneventful. Caleb didn't say a word,

neither did I. We'd discussed all the details of the mission, did it 'til we were sick of it, then did it some more.

Caleb had reminded me of something Sun Tzu said, "Know yourself and your enemy and you'll be victorious in every battle."

I reminded him of something more important than Sun Tzu: shit happens, regardless of what you know about anything. The Universe ensured this.

TPA was bustling as ever, with six freighters in the queue to offload cargo. All from China, bearing goods for Walmart, Costco and Sam's Club. With each offload, the American economy sunk a few more points into the red, but who was counting, let alone giving a damn? Ahhhh, the pandafication of America.

At eight p.m., we were already in place, and I was still wondering why we took this gig. Caleb was happy with the contents of the oversized case they'd handed me. All told, half a million dollars. Blood money, I'd said. And he reminded me that as long as it wasn't our own blood, it was righteous.

I thought otherwise: gradually, I had been selling out to BigMoney and it made me sick, even though I justified it best I could. I loved to kill bullies and take out the trash, clean up my town. Bottom line, I was too numb to care about the appearance of selling out to these moneyed assholes, because deep down I knew I wasn't.

The plan was to do overwatch of two shipment containers that were due in at 2100 from the same freighter, the *Sun Anne* from China by way of Singapore and Malaysia and other points we weren't concerned with. We both suspected what would be off-loaded but didn't speak its name.

Peter Jamison and his boss, Felix Something, made it clear that we were now part of their team, their well-oiled organization that had zero tolerance for hiccups. They had made it clear to me they suspected it was I who dropped their buddy Viktor, still no one seemed to want to kill me over it. Caleb said it was because they already had plans for Viktor and it wasn't to give him a gold-colored Timex.

By this time, I was spent. Rachel was always on my mind, fallout from the Viktor thing at the lake was right there, too, trying to bump aside thoughts of Rachel and how I would somehow make it right between us, and I was being bumped aside by SurferBoySlob who was probably taking full advantage of my dear love as I stood out here on this crappy op.

Tonight, none of that mattered a damn.

We would follow Caleb's plan because I was too sizzled to have organized it in my basket-case present, and because it was simply a sound plan.

The first freighter docked at 2110 and the large gantry crane began off-loading forty-foot containers onto the TPA docks. If all went well, we would be back home in a few hours, and Caleb would be convincing me that this was the right course of action: getting inside the camp of people who probably wanted us in the same boat as Donny.

As Caleb would say, pun intended.

I knew he was right, though: it was a precarious foot in the door to organized crime at a high level, and I thirsted for the action, and even more so wanted to know who was at the top of this organization. Thing is, I wasn't ready for it on any level, and I'd already shown this at the firefight in Tampa with that crazy woman and her crew when I'd seized up in a fit of anxiety and nearly walked into a moving locomotive. Doubtless, Felix and Jamison were certain it was Caleb and I who did the deed, but they only mentioned us loosely in conversation, in Jamison's office.

Again, this was a fucked-up cat-and-mouse game where both animals knew each other, their habits and behaviors, and they knew each other in an eerie Sun Tzu-kinda way.

Question was, when both parties were onto each other and there were no secrets, why not just come out and admit it, and then commence the fucking battle?

Because, Caleb explained, cat and mouse is more fun for both sides. If it wasn't a game, then why play?

In the middle of my reverie, the first explosion punched me in the chest and rocked the entire gantry crane, which called out in some horrible metallic wail, then bent over and fell into the drink just off the dock, carrying with it our second container. Workers screamed in tiny distant voices, some in English, some in Spanish, and they ran in every direction, even off the dock into the water to avoid the spreading gusher-flames.

Our first container had already been offloaded onto a big rig, which had rolled off soon as it had been properly cleared. It was probably out of the TPA area and onto I-275 heading north to deliver the package.

The second explosion tore into the side of the ship itself, sending dozens of containers overboard and into the deep channel below.

I swear I heard a hundred high-pitched screams, cries and wails from inside each container, but Caleb said it was just the flames licking the sides of the vessel, popping high-tension lines and cables, and renting and twisting tons of iron and steel.

He was wrong and I knew it.

Caleb knew it, too.

A thousand scenes ripped through my mind because I had done some very foolish things lately and now was in the crosshairs of men who traded more than just spice and tea.

Theirs was a modern-day Silk Road that moved and pushed human slaves, people who had no say whatsoever in how their lives would be played out. My worst fear at the moment, besides our current mission having been compromised, probably by the very people who hired us, was being caught in the deadlight of their powerful beam that bought and sold humans like cattle.

I'd grown up here in North Longboat Key and Sarasota, and felt the burning stares of BigMoney, who saw me as meat on the hoof. Unlike them, I was 100% debt free and swimming in cash millions, while they were all glued to the nearest stock ticker and any word by the Fed Chairman, and dying the slow death from ceaseless high anxiety.

With crispy new intel now in my box of tricks, I was determined to learn more about Felix and the Jamison brothers . . . but clearly not today.

Impatient as I had become, now wanting to know everything about these assholes and their operations, after tonight I would go back home and regroup. Maybe steal down to the Keys for a spell, get the hell away from this place and all in it.

Hell, I'd leave the pimps alone, too, although after what I did to Tyreese in the Newtown jungle, many of them were now thinking twice about setting up shop in my town. I'm sure Father Chappy and his congregation would also send around little advertisements to that effect, warning all the wannabes from outta state they'd get eaten alive if they set even one slicked-up, thousand-dollar boot in these parts.

As I sifted through all the rubble inside my contaminated mind, Caleb muttered something I could barely hear: "When your time's up, your time is up, Tommy, and the only thing you can do is put up a vain fight against the inevitable."

I wondered if he were talking about our life here in America or our current situation on the docks. Either way, it seemed we were, as Father Chappy liked to preach, "on a lonely road of the damned, no longer marching to a familiar voice."

The ghost of emptiness shot out of purgatory and found its way to the foot of my boots. Nodded its bony head, that familiar deadlight emanating from its eye sockets, sending me a clear message.

Thought about it a second, flipped off that ghost with two long middle fingers, then cocked my head toward Caleb. Outta the side of my mouth: "If I'm goin' down, I'm takin' warm bodies with me, motherfucker."

As I did that, some voice deep in my subconscious reminded me of something I had conveniently repressed: this day I would pay the butcher's bill.

REDWEED

Running would've done no good.

So we didn't bother.

Just stood there, mesmerized by the dancing inferno, a two-seat Burning Man without the dust, girl-groupies and medicinal smoke.

After the second explosion on the docks, the entire facility went into immediate lockdown, with Homeland Security roaches crawling out of every crack and orifice, and blocking all possible exits from the Tampa Port Authority area, even water exfil. Anyone would've been impressed: they shut down TPA in less than twenty minutes.

Twenty minutes.

To the naïve observer, this sounded most impressive and it made for historic international news, demonstrating the mastery and spunk of the United States' equivalent of the Gestapo against a terrorist bombing on the fatherland.

Normally it would've taken an entire US Army Airborne Ranger battalion hours to parachute in, seize the facilities and lock down and secure them. And that's twelve hours after they got the go-ahead to launch, loaded up the birds and went wheels-up to the target. In reality, it would've been a full twenty-four hours from soup to nuts.

Before that, Tampa Police and the Hillsborough County Sheriff's Office would've done overtime until the cavalry arrived to do a relief in place.

Even Rangers wouldn't have secured the facility 100%. Sure, they would've gotten all men in place, at least those who didn't break an ankle or leg on the drop, or failed to link up with their respective companies. Happened all the time, even with the best units and the best men. I called it LUC: the law of unintended consequences. And, as LUC would have it, things took a lot more time than we expected or planned for, and it also meant shit would happen regardless of how careful one's preparation was.

Everything's great 'til something goes wrong.

How these Homeland pukes got into position so quickly meant only one possibility: they had been in place long before Caleb and I even set up for the surveillance op that night. They'd probably known about it for a week and had several days to get staged, while we planned our little op in total secrecy over cases of Heineken, Stella and Peroni, hot buckets of extra-crispy KFC, and reruns of

Hawaii Five-O and "Danno, book 'em" spinning in the background.

Plain and simple, this was a shitty set-up and Caleb and I were the whipping boys who got plugged by a hundred bang-bangers. But why? Payback for my having killed the old man, Viktor? Payback for our having offed a few of the Jamison's sloppy killers in Tampa? No, it was more complicated than any of those. We were just the whipping boys who got the dubious credit.

Black-clad Homeland agents, coifed out in the latest go-to-war pajamas and lowest-bidder bling, had us surrounded just as we left our surveillance positions and tried to link up at our designated rally point, since Caleb and I got there via different routes. They must've been laughing at us as we found each other near the RP and made a hard right turn at a row of forty-foot containers, then ran right into the first few dozen of them, all standing around like cops at Dunkin Donuts.

A cartoon moment for fuck-certain. So much so that Caleb and I looked at each other and belly-laughed loud enough to rocket off the surrounding containers and roll over into the ghetto across the street, riling the inner-city natives who took up positions with their plastic pitchforks, cell phones and camcorders along the fence line, budding CNN reporters, all.

Caleb unloaded and safed his weapon, placed it at his feet, casually dropped all his gear on the concrete, took a knee and drank from his Camelbak. I pretty much did the same, except instead of taking a knee and hydrating, I lit up a cigarette from a fresh pack I'd bought hours earlier, my first in a long time. Caleb smirked at my choice of reunion smokes: Newport Menthol. I recall telling him, "If the cigarette companies are gonna kill me, it'll be at $4 a pack and not $8."

He replied, "Yeah, dumbass, but you only get three puffs off a four-dollar-a-pack dick-stick, so you're still paying the same."

"Hey, it's still a nice savings and I'm on a budget," laughing as I dragged hard on that cigarette, all the way down to the filter. Then I smoked that fucker, too, knowing I might not see another one for a long time.

This reasoning coming from a guy who had nearly four million dollars in cash stashed away in secret hiding holes around my home,

North Longboat Key, the top end of a nine-mile-long barrier island off Sarasota.

Although we provided comic relief, the actual arrest was still bothersome. It was also largely uneventful, and I'm sure the boys in black would've preferred at least a fistfight. As we were being escorted to vehicles in cuffs, some of the guys recognized us from Ranger Bat and started telling old war stories about Caleb and me, sending the entire arrest team into a laughing fit. The onsite agent in charge, who'd never put on the uniform like we had, wasn't too pleased to have his men laughing in front of news cameras, looking like a bunch of teenage sailors on R&R.

Their Public Affairs Officer ran the story through an industrial, high-speed spin cycle, but it still came out soggy and full of holes. Shame these people thought we were all so gullible.

Actually, most of us were.

Still, the unflattering news and PR were a small victory for us, even as they stripped us of all our Constitutional rights, and invoked the National Defense Authorization Act and the Patriot Act.

"And Act III of Hamlet," Caleb reminded me.

They transported us to a military holding facility at MacDill Air Force Base for processing. I honestly can't recall the last time I had been arrested by 500 smurfs in crisp, starched black BDUs, and bearing shiny new weapons. I seriously doubt bullets had zipped through any of the barrels of those assault rifles, even on a range. Some smelled fresh off an assembly line in Mexico or Bulgaria, just like their newly minted toy soldiers in black and bling.

A night to remember. . . .

Prison is pretty much the same anywhere you go in the US: claustrophobic cell, aging toilet, five walls and a heavily guarded lobby decorated in scary-industrial modern. An exception: in deepest Mississippi, prisons look the same today as they did in 1863, and guys still fell through fractures and fissures and got lodged down a deep crevice, ample food for whatever boogies lived at those depths.

In a few choice parts I know of in Venezuela, 25 guys were kipper-packed into a little 10' x 10' cage, no toilet except a shit-crusted hole in a dark corner, and it was 100% yoyo—you're on your own—and that was usually up against some pretty mean taco benders, chicofros and fajita-flippers who had no regard for human life simply 'cos those fuzzy brown stink-ass xenomorphs weren't from this galaxy.

Good thing I was there only twelve hours. Case of mistaken identity: they were looking for the guy who'd just shot and killed some government official and I just happened to match a description given by the man's wife who also swallowed one of my bullets.

Was too rushed to check to see if the bullet I had put through her neck had actually killed her, but I had just suffered a severe anxiety attack and had to do some on-the-fly, deep-breathing exercises in earnest and beat it out of there before I seized up like a statue of some hilarious Disney cartoon.

After joking it up with the prison guards, they figured I couldn't possibly be a killer and was, in fact, the computer nerd I'd first reported. It wasn't that they were gullible; I was just pretty good at what I did.

Except when I was being exceptionally stupid or came under direct attack from my own personal demons.

Special Operations Command or SOCOM had its own little version of a supermax prison, except for a few small details: you're in solitary confinement twenty-four hours a day, with only two meager meals every twenty-four hours. Just like in Mountains Phase of Ranger School during winter back in the day. The idea was to break you, starve you down to skin and bones, then get you to commit suicide so your next of kin couldn't capitalize on your misery, not that SOCOM desk-dicks gave a crap whether your next of kin collected on a death gratuity.

At the time of our arrest, Caleb and I were immediately separated and taken in different vehicles. As he was being pushed into a truck, he spun around to me and yelled, "Any backwater prison silverback takin' my white hiney for ass-pussy loses his Johnson at the root!"

That crack drew more than a laugh from Homeland Security hooligans.

I was blindfolded and shoved in the back of what felt like a panel van with benches. Just as I was getting comfortable on the bouncing metal corrugated floor, collecting more and more bruises on my face, a soft, slight hand shoved two little red pills in my mouth and held my nose so I swallowed them and, in what seemed like nanoseconds, I was swimming in a field of puke-green and pink tulips and purple marshmallows, nibbling on smoked baby alligator dipped in silver cheddar cheese. The little gator looked at me, then suddenly morphed into a giant crocodilian that swallowed me whole, tenderizing me as I slid down the length of its jaws and into the esophagus. As I passed down the massive gullet on my one-way trip to the boiling acid bath, saw a pocket-size room with a figure slumped over a toy Jeep. I waved at her for days and days, calling out and telling her not to drink the water, because I'd just seen what the gators did in it.

Rachel.

Over years and years, my sweet Rachel slowly faded from me, the dreaded vacuum between us pulling off the rest of my skin, much the way it had when SurferBoy had taken her from me on North Longboat Key.

Thoughts and dreams mixed in colorful confusion over the next few days, as the last dose of LSD finally ground down to a single nanoliter that crossed a synapse and landed smack on a lonely dendrite within my limbic bowels. Red and green tracers flew back and forth until my eyes popped open and I bolted upright and yelled her name.

Something I noticed: while those red pills were definitely LSD or LSD-like, there was something else, too, like additional artificial sweeteners that gave me the munchies, made me a tad paranoid, and gave me a bad case of voodoo doodoo.

Years back when I started out in corporate mercenary work, this guy at the company gave us all sorts of pharmaceuticals so we'd know what to expect on some mission if we accidentally ingested them or were forced. The point was to build a portfolio of sensations in response to the various drugs and stimuli. I'd volunteered for every drug known to mankind, mostly because I was a closet anxiety-depressive in desperate need of a cure, not to mention daily fixes, so I did it all. The sampling not only expanded my mind in creative and scary ways, but it also gave me an encyclopedia of the effects of all those drugs.

At one drug per page, my portfolio was more than 100 pages.

In the end I was disappointed when I discovered that the only thing that could relieve what ailed me was an ice-cold six of Peroni or Heineken or Stella. And if that didn't do it for me, I'd down another six and stare at the Gulf of Mexico until the sun came alive again and licked my face like my father's hundred-year-old bloodhound used to when I was a kid.

This time, I was definitely given a sideways martini of multiple gins that slowly transformed me into an alternate being, a complete psychedelic beast.

Normally in 100% darkness, the eyes get mischievous and invent colors and shapes and little creepy things yet to be defined taxonomically. That's what the childlike mind does when you don't pay attention to it. The first color I always saw was purple. It started as a tiny pinprick in the center of my field of view, and gradually expanded into a swirling cloud that danced in front of my eyes, even closed.

In time, the eyes got bored with purple and started ripping hues from the color wheel and spray-painting my universe in haphazard schemes that soon formed familiar shapes. As the shapes grew into human forms, the eyes once again got bored and added sound to the palette.

Pretty soon, you had an entire roomful of talking blob-heads that were all yelling at you in perfect asynchrony for not having enough food at the banquet in their honor. This certainly wasn't Darwin's theory of the evolution of humans by any stretch. It was my own psychedelic invention, fueled by a hyped-up, 21st-century variant of Dr. Albert Hofmann's Purple Mike, and I could no longer discern reality from—whatever this bizarre dimension was.

I thought the worst of it was that I was fucked up, but the worst part of it was that I knew I was fucked up and, as a captive audience, had to witness the whole chaotic scene from inside my own head. It was worse than pulling a groundhog day and watching *Lost in Space* over and over again.

Danger, Tommy Darlington!

An idle mind with a lot of time to play with and get tangled up in can easily venture off-map. In total darkness it is a demonic kitten with a gigantic ball of yarn, and no rules or reg's.

I had only been in solitary for three and a half weeks and had already begun to lose track of my six remaining marbles and all sense of who I truly was. On the street, I usually had anxiety issues once a day, and could deal with them with my stop-gap meditation or something in my tackle box of pharmaceuticals (read: a near-frozen six-pack of good beer). Funny how those two powerful treatments, *meditation* and *medication*, differed by only one letter, but they both had the same effect. Strangely, if you removed both letters, you were left with *mediation*. Definitely a cosmic connection in there.

In the joint, anxiety visited me every second and melted my constitution down to a puddle of Sex Wax. I could only imagine what happened to men who did this for months ... years, even. They called it "correctional," this modern form of torture that sought to rehabilitate. Yeah, right. Anyone who believed that was a fool who bought into the whole junior high school theatrics. Or a member of the sinister cabal that attempted to subjugate us all.

I simply called it infernal. . . .

The thought alone dumped a bucket of ice water on my shrunken head, inflating whatever gray matter I had left and brought me back to some semblance of life.

I yelled her name again.

"Rachelllll!"

A guard came to my heavy metal door, the one with a tiny window that couldn't have been less than a foot thick. He peered in, laughed at something, walked back to his station. I didn't care if they came in and beat the crap out of me, long as they sat down and visited, paid me some attention.

As a child I learned quickly that if you wanted attention from my old man, you needed to do something stupid to get it. And got it you did, usually a nice ass-kicking that ended up feeling so good you wanted another one. I swear it was better than a hug and a goodnight chocolate on my pillow.

There was nothing I could find to throw at the door to get the guard to come back, and I figured that later I might need my head for something more than a battering ram, so I sat there on the floor, naked and cold, in my own pee and poop. Didn't bother me a bit.

During my acid trip, I'd thought it was snow in my backyard on North Longboat Key so I did snow-angels all over my cell floor.

In piss and shit.

"Word just came down," said the supervisor of the guard detail. "Darlington's gonna be moved."

A junior guard asked, "Gettin' out?"

"Dunno, but he's leaving us in about an hour. Some private military types are going to pick him up, so you need to get him cleaned and dressed."

The junior guard was stunned.

He'd watched and laughed while I did the snow-angels for three days, then finger-painted the walls of my cell with the extras, occasionally licking my fingers like popsicles. Thought I heard him wretch at least once.

The hazardous funk gradually leaked out of my cell and into the common area where the guards' station was situated, raising the possible issue of gas masks. By the way, they committeed that option to death. As an alternative, they dropped wet towels at the bottom of my door. When that didn't work, they duct-taped the edges of my door frame.

Somehow, though, my stench was a platoon of acidic swords, cutting through all manner of metal and material in a frantic effort to spread the Gospel of Tommy. It was a fine stench, indeed.

Even unhinged, I kicked ass.

Felix Heydrich was officially measured at a millimeter under 5'9" but his self-importance easily stretched him well beyond. At parties, when someone asked how tall he was, his spring-loaded reaction was always "Six feet," less than a nanometer of space-time between spitting out the six and the feet.

Standing ramrod straight and wearing the slimmest suit they could hand-sew for him, he more resembled a *Vogue* model in the latest twig-skinny couture. He wore only two shades: black and dark gray, with the occasional charcoal silk scarf.

Everything was handmade for Felix, using only the finest ingredients from every choice market on the planet.

His gourmet girls and boys were no exception: only the sweetest and most delicious Latino and Eastern Euro children and teens for his twisted sexual pleasure.

Heydrich's thirteen-story downtown office tower on Sarasota's Tamiami Trail had magnificent 360-degree views of the town, the keys and the Gulf. He had only recently moved from Tampa into the penthouse office suite to better monitor his holdings in Sarasota and Bradenton, and to prepare for a new offensive in what he called his little satellite village across the bridge from grownup Tampa.

The penthouse suite now doubled as a second home and office, placing Heydrich above all others in Sarasota. Just the way he planned it. His minions, the Jamison brothers, sat several floors down, far enough not to infect him with whatever scheme they were into at the moment, and close enough to summon on a moment's notice. Heydrich had to admit, the Jamisons got things done, allowing him to pursue his pleasures all the more.

"In my office now, Peter." Heydrich pressed his favorite button on his phone, the one painted in red, severing the connection.

Minutes later, Peter Jamison was ushered into Heydrich's office by a slender suit of impeccable quality, and wearing very expensive and fashionable Lindberg glasses. Jamison thought his attire perhaps suited him in a busy office in the City of London, but he knew better: Heydrich's assistant was a former SAS door-kicker who hunted down persons of interest for the British government in the late 1990s. No one knew much more about him, and absolutely no one wished to know more about him. He frightened even the hardest of bodyguards who crossed Heydrich's threshold, that off-world predator chemistry of his.

Perhaps most unsettling of all was the man's seemingly polite nature: "G'day, Mr. Jamison. You're a minute and half late, according to my watch . . . Mr. Heydrich will see you presently. Oh, and lovely to see you once again." He opened the large heavy double doors for Jamison, who entered quickly, hoping not be get bitten on the ass by Heydrich's troll in bespoke threads.

"Punctuality is something we appreciate highly around here, Peter." Felix waved off any attempt to bullshit him.

Jamison got right to it: "As you ordered, Darlington and Gatewood have been transferred."

Small smile on Felix. "Good. Let's prepare them for the next assignment."

Jamison started to talk, got waved off dismissively.

"Pay them double for their efforts in Tampa. We appreciate their loyalty during their ordeal in custody, and not talking to anyone about us. And see to it Mr. Darlington gets his new house. I understand there's been some question about the validity of the deed, yes?"

"House?"

"It appears to me Mr. Darlington has a deed signed over by the late Mr. McCracken."

Jamison's face slid down his head half an inch. "Felix, that's absurd—"

Small wave of the hand. "He has the deed to the house on Bird Key—yes, I know it is your house, Peter, yours and that recluse brother of yours—but we're all a team here. You need to go along with this as I've explained to you—for the second time. Understood?"

Jamison nodded, a child accepting his Catholic scolding.

"One more thing, Peter: when you send out Mr. Darlington, leave off his assistant, will you, please? We have other ways of keeping tabs on his activities and whereabouts."

As Jamison was leaving, Felix added: "We're doing this for the good of the company. You realize this, don't you, Peter?"

Jamison sort of nodded.

"Good. I'm sure you and your brother will find a suitable home in the area. I can refer you to my real estate agent if you wish." He rose. "Good to speak with you again."

"Did a cog just slip outta your head, Ranger Darlington?"

Caleb was standing in the center of the condo on North Longboat, livid and still in his own personal pain from our prison stint. And wearing that old uniform: white polo shirt, hyper-colored Bermuda shorts and lime-green flips: Bob Hope, who forgot to take his psych meds this morning.

"Those assholes set us up. Again. And we're not gonna do anything about it? You kidding here, Caleb?"

We were actually playing a game to see who could be madder'n hell. I say I was winning.

He stabbed me with his beer: "Every time we go into the merge with the bad guys, we somehow get closer to them and deeper into their organization. You ever thought about that?"

I paused a sec, knowing there was a syllable of truth in there somewhere, but I wasn't in the mood to acknowledge it. "You mean, along with getting tortured and chopped up into McNuggets? Yeah, I've thought about it. And I've also thought about how we need to start offing some people right quick." In that moment, thought of the next few pimps I would cuddle up to and relocate to some Dumpster casket over in Manatee County.

That smile of his cracked me up even in my sorry state.

"Take a knee, face outward and hydrate."

We both went into the spacious kitchen, grabbed a six of Peroni and went onto the balcony. Damn, what a view. I only wish Rachel were—

Caleb turned to me, said, "You sure are a pain in my ass."

I met his gaze: "So's a tetanus shot, look what that does for you."

We were forging a team of two, something I had avoided like untreatable herpes all my professional life. Simple: I just didn't trust anyone. But more and more I felt like I needed a little help, as I saw my once-sharp edges start to soften and fray. Clearly I needed some kinda relief, other than Stella and Peroni, but I wasn't sure how or where to find it.

Clinked bottles, downed both of them in seconds, reached for two more.

It was like that for the rest of the evening: drinking good beer, watching the sun drop achingly slowly into the Gulf, hanging with Caleb, and not talking about the most important thing crawling all over each of our brains.

Sometime during the night, heard the slight creak of floorboard near the French door of my bedroom. In some eerie vision, saw my body pull up from the bed and walk to the doors, pushing them open. Tasted the mild ocean breeze, and saw her lying on the chaise.

Rachel.

Her robe was parted from chest to knees, and I felt her warm glow from across the balcony.

Reached out to her . . .

She called me . . .

Knelt at her side, put my hand between her soft, lovely thighs . . .

Kissed and nibbled on her tummy . . .

Several large waves ganged up and hit the beach in one CRASH.

Found myself kneeling over an empty chair, tears flooding my eyes, the world around me moving slowly, a merry-go-round knocked off its axle but still carrying on haphazardly.

The fucked-up part of the whole post-redweed REM nightmare was recalling her last sentiment: "Tom, I liked you better when I thought you were barely worth two figures and not some cashed-up millionaire taxi driver-cum-hitman in acid-hole jeans and calf-leather flips."

In the morning, Caleb made breakfast and left it on the balcony table for me before he headed out for errands. I got up later, looked at the plate of dessicated bacon and eggs, smirked, got a few beers instead. Six, to be accurate. After the crap we'd just gone through, I was ready for early retirement. South Africa came to mind, for some reason. The silly irony of such abnormal logic made me laugh and snort beer out my nose: leaving the most dangerous job in the world and retiring to the most dangerous country in the world.

Then again, I didn't do normal. Before I dropped that thought, Goodland came to mind as a healthy alternative. Wondered if I'd ever get down there.

Goodland. . . .

"Roger, he's in my sightbox." Caleb made the smallest of adjustments, correcting for a slight right-to-left eddy-current diffusing off the surface of the little lake.

CLICK!

The little missile launched out of the suppressed rifle, cut the humid air like an invisible spear, and found its target true.

Looking through some damned fine milspec opera glasses— Made in Japan optics, methinks—I saw the impact as clear as if it had been two feet away. Red matter and tissue erupted in a small volcano that shot off in all directions from the target.

I shivered involuntarily at the sight, though we were covered in a warm blanket of 88 Florida degrees and 99% relative humidity. If ever you wanted to melt down that '69 Mustang 350 engine block, today was the day for it.

"Too bad that was only a watermelon." Caleb smirked and looked just right of the rifle, as if he were casually observing a seniors' bowling match.

We'd perched a dozen red algae-filled watermelons atop tree stumps deep in the woods across I-75 off Fruitville Rd. Wrapped them heavily with 100-mile-an-hour tape, after compressing as much algae in it as we could inside each one. The greater the pressure inside the watermelon, after having sat in the sun for six hours, the bigger the boom. Caleb and I liked big booms.

The grisly scene was a giant spray of redweed that I strangely snapped a still image of and filed away in a dark recess of my dungeon-mind. I'd seen images like this before, but somehow this one stuck to my neural wall like spaghetti al dente in crimson.

"That algae was a good idea," he said, breaking down the rifle and bagging it for the trip back to the condo. "Next time, though, you get to collect it from the beach. Stuff stinks."

"Blame it on climate change. 'Sides, you're the one with the shovel and a bucket. Stop sniveling. Think we have enough firepower to take these guys on?" Dunno why I asked that. I knew we were woefully outgunned, outmanned and out[fill in the blank]. When I worked alone, I always had exactly what I needed. Working with someone else, I was questioning whether we had enough, knowing we didn't.

"Need to expand that brainpan, Tommy. We're going after people a helluva lot worse than that old man Viktor. He's peaches and cupcakes up against Felix and his crew."

"He was with Felix's crew. Not quite the Chairman of the Board like I thought, but important enough."

"I know, but he ran his own little operation out there in the woods, all those girls he imported. The discards from Felix's operations." Soon as it escaped his mouth, he stopped. "I'm sorry. I know Rachel was—"

Bristled at that comment. "Let's just get this done." I was still too exhausted to talk about Rachel. A few weeks in SOCOM's prison, courtesy of Felix Heydrich and company, did me in. They knew it, too. And that made me a vulnerable target.

The moment when we have to fight the hardest is usually the time when we're weakest and lacking everything we need for the battle. The worst of fights comes at the most inopportune times, when we're already down and hurting, totally unprepared, and completely unaware. That's when you figure out what you're made of: steel or putty.

Me? Right now, I was putty with a spray-on veneer of steel that melted at room temp.

Sometimes, the best of us succumbed even to the less-powerful force of another, and it was okay to get your ass whooped once in a while. Didn't matter how much training you had, how many times a week you went to the range or gym, whether you were jacked on steroids or human growth hormone.

Once in a while, you simply had your ass handed to you and there was nothing you could do except peel yourself off the pavement or get wheeled out on a Stryker Power-Pro by EMTs.

What mattered most, though, was what you did in those few sick seconds of combat that determined whether you lived to fight again. Or wound up fertilizer in some lonely field or patch of jungle.

Those thoughts were now with me constantly, especially in the wake of losing Rachel, being framed by my own boss for crimes they paid me to commit, being thrown into a hellish prison, if only for a few weeks. Truth? I was off my anxiety meds. Had been for months. I wanted to see if Rachel and I could make a go of it without my relying on pharmaceuticals to get through each day.

And it was kicking my ass.

The last thing Caleb needed to know was that he had a basket case for a partner, although I knew he was worried about some of my actions of late. I wondered how long my nanometer-thick steel jacket would hold up in the current climate. . . .

Like his boss, he was slender, barely able to reach 5'10" without the aid of generous boot elevation.

Today, his boots were black and made of synthetic rubber, with flexible canvas-like uppers pulled together with heavy laces. Further up, slightly loose khaki cargo pants and a web belt, a white cotton shirt, tucked in at bottom, opened at top.

Sarasota's forecast: miserably hot and sticky. But this didn't concern him.

The boss's order had been clear: shadow Tommy Darlington.

That was it: spy on me. So he shadowed me for two weeks, as Caleb and I tried to readjust to life beyond a painful stint in SOCOM's autoclave. Blinded by pain and fatigue, we both missed seeing this guy, even though he stood out fairly well.

Guys like him, even when they're out of uniform, were still in uniform. Rough edges everywhere you looked, no smile lines creasing their face, strong ropy muscles up and down their arms, especially the workhorse muscle, the brachioradialis. You had a little bit of that one and people in the know could see you've been in some shit. Funny thing, too: most professional badasses liked showing off that jutting muscle by rolling up their sleeves, wearing polo shirts or tight, long-sleeved t-shirts. It wasn't just some kind of combat decoration, that hunk of protein; it was a loaded bazooka in your face.

Located on the outside of each arm, from the elbow down to the upper forearm, the brachioradialis added a little oomph to an arm beefed up by weight training and heavy lifting. It ensured you could heft a machine gun on a twenty-six-mile forced march, keep a fully loaded .45 steady for an hour, or keep your fist in the hammer position long enough to cave in the roof of a very large man.

That's the first thing I noticed on a man: the brachioradialis. If he had a prominent one, I tried not to turn my back on him. I found it more intimidating than a high IQ on a hot chick with banana-blonde curls.

This guy's "brake" was impressive. And I still consciously missed him. Even though he passed right by me inside a bar at Phillippi Creek, where I sat trying to avoid Caleb for a few days and deal with a small anxiety issue.

I'd sat at the bar for forty-five minutes, my skin tightening up all over me like commercial-grade shrink-wrap, and my muscles shaking and sometimes seizing in small fits that came and went without formal announcement.

Didn't spot anyone paying me much mind, so I figured I had blended in well enough in this little jungle to stick around a few more hours. Got a booth in the back near the creek-side dock, saw a few boaters pull in, un-ass their twenty-foot center-consoles, walk inside to get drunk, then stumble outside to their waiting yachts, and off they went. I never bothered to read the news or obits on boating deaths in Sarasota. Like those pimps I put to rest on occasion, it wasn't as many as I would've liked.

Awash in visions of drowned sailors and sunken yachts, I downed a few Stellas and finally got the nerve to ask the bartender why Stella only poured 11.2 ounces into each bottle, while Heineken drove in a full 12. Stella poured less and cost more. What's up with that noise?

That's when he walked by me, turned his head slightly to take me in a little more, and went to the men's room down the hall. And I'd missed him completely.

Consciously, that is.

What my subconscious took in was scary, and it filed that intel away for another day, replete with an accurate physical description and short behavioral analysis of this guy.

Things were so much easier when I worked alone, doing odd jobs for clients, driving my tangerine TommyTaxi for a few fares a day, and going home to Rachel after a nice day at the office, dear. And when things got monotonous, I took out a pimp or two, stuffed them deep in a Dumpster.

In the year I'd been doing that, not a single notice of the killings appeared in the Sarasota or Bradenton rags or on tv. I guessed that local law enforcement secretly appreciated someone's community service and didn't look too hard to find the benefactor, not that anything would trace back to me.

What I hadn't counted on was all those wannabe pimpins flooding in from New Jersey to take up shop where the dead had once reigned. That worked well for them right up to the wee hours of that morning when I escorted Tyreese "DaddyBoy" Glover to a special part of hell reserved for assholes who murdered innocent women and girls. Thanks to me, that area was filling up fast. Wondered if Satan was gonna bring in his Chinese construction crew and push the walls back a coupla miles.

Wreckuva man I was, I still got things done.

Never even had to think about placing trust in someone else to watch my back, because I had eyes in the back of my head, keen sensors with a circular arc that swept over my WEZ, my weapons effectiveness zone. And beyond that, a long-range radar. Self-sufficient is what I was, something I had built up and honed over a dozen years, and I had done it all alone, except for my time in Ranger Battalion.

When a person has to rely only on himself, he develops an entirely different array of weapons, sensors, actions and reactions. As a member of a team, that same person must rely on others for certain aspects of the job. Even in Bat, I was never a good team player. Too busy learning new skills and how best to deploy them in the worst of times.

Didn't enjoy delegating tasks at Bat, because we also had to rely on Ranger privates who were dumb as dirt and just as dangerous, especially when wet and on a downhill slope. Being a team player was never for me, because I could never feel safe, relying on others to take my back. Besides, I never actually needed anyone to have my six. I needed and wanted someone to be right up there out front, deep in the thick of things. Forget my back. My back had my back.

Simply put, I was a one-man killing shop that purred like an Audi Formula One—when it wasn't up on blocks back in the yard. And I fought hard to stay that way. Outta the yard, that is.

That all changed when I invited Caleb into the picture for that op in Tampa. After that, I had to adjust my whole way of thinking each mission or gig I did. Had to place blind trust and faith in him, not knowing if he'd developed the same or better skills as I had over the years. My subconscious told me to go with it, so I did. And each time I did, I saw a strong, positive connection between us, with excellent timing and communication, and he saved my ass more than once. Plus, he was high comedy when I needed a shot of it.

So why was I so nervous about this partner thing?

And then it hit me: it wasn't Caleb I was worried about. He was world-class cool.

It was me.

Off-meds, anxiety-depressive Tommy.

My question to me: Tommy Darlington, what were you gonna do

about your being the weak link in your own chain?

Such an irony it was, my now being the one failure point in a machine I'd designed and built from scratch. Alone, I was great, all modesty aside. Very effective, on time and on target. Well, there was that time I didn't check that government official's wife I'd shot, then wound up in a South American prison for twelve hours. But hey, I was in the middle of an anxiety attack that had to be dealt with on the run. Literally.

"I don't suppose you want to tell me where you've been the past week?" Caleb sat there, staring at me like my high school principal.

My reverie broken, I managed, "Alone time."

"Sounds like a time-out to me. Other than that, pretty cryptic."

"Not meant to be." We both knew that was a lie. I'd just finished questioning my own competence and was now getting drilled by my new wife.

Big sigh. "Still up for this cat-and-mouse game with these assholes?" He popped an heirloom tomato in his mouth, pointed his face in my direction, bit down.

It squirted across the table, leaving a splatter-trail of blood-red juice aimed directly at me.

The effect was not lost on me. Caleb was good with special effects.

Jamison's call came at six a.m. and went to voicemail: "Tommy, we'd like to see you this morning at eleven in my office, please."

Caleb and I showed up fifteen minutes early, sat in the ten-seat reception area.

Looked at Caleb: "For a high-end PI firm, sure is pretty quiet in here."

"Like Madam Rezinka's Palm Reading: it's a money-laundering outfit. They probably own the two banks downstairs, too."

"Funny."

"It's true. This place is great. All the best amenities, location location location. Clearly, they don't need clients, though."

Smiles on both of us.

Eleven a.m. rolled around and time stopped just for John Jamison, who came out to greet us: "Gentlemen, please follow me."

Another walk down that looooong hallway, past empty offices and cubicles to Peter Jamison's corner office that faced the marina. And an impressive section of Sarasota Bay, the Gulf, South Longboat Key.

"How was your stay in Tampa?"

They'd kicked our asses and were now rubbing our noses in it. As I thought this, I looked up at that photograph of Rachel at one of her book signings, with Jamison standing behind her. This time, I saw more details: he had his hand on her shoulder, fingers squeezing her. You'd have to look really close to see it, but it was there. Felt the back of my neck getting warm and prickly. . . .

Caleb didn't sit down. "Fuck you, Jamison." He was often subtle.

A snort escaped Jamison as he attacked my hand once again, dropped it and threw himself into his chair, more to get as far away from Caleb as humanly possible without appearing mousy.

Looking up at the pictures high on Jamison's bookshelf, Caleb said, "Don't tell me you served."

Jamison looked up at the same picture I'd found so disturbing the first time I'd been in this office. "No. Actually, that was a weekend hunting function in South Africa with old friends."

Weekend hunting function. High tea in the African outback.

The only person smiling in the picture was Jamison. I take it the safari hadn't gone well for the others. They were all probably still in South Africa, their shitty remains scattered across the territory of a squad of lions.

Caleb's laugh was booming.

Thought Jamison would shit himself.

Talking through the ass end of his laugh, Caleb shot, "Man, you people crack me the fuck up. Buying your toy-warrior weekends on someone's ranch out in the bush, sending a little lead downrange and calling it combat. They give you a t-shirt, maybe some panties?"

Jamison found it hard to hide his embarrassment. Even with a dark tan, his blush warmed the room. "Ahhh, we were hunting Cape buffalo. It takes brass balls to go out in the bush and hunt those beasts." His resolve was clearly weakened by Caleb's shot to the face.

Caleb erupted again in a laughing fit. When he calmed down

again, said, "At your age, the only thing big balls are good for is a counter-weight to a fat ass."

Jamison looked straight ahead, had his hands steepled, rubbed his two forefingers together nervously, then turned to me as if seeing me for the first time. Or maybe he was looking for a kindred spirit: "Tommy, you and your friend here have just been given a taste of things to come." He paused, thinking his words would sting.

But Caleb cut that plan short, not missing a beat: "Then maybe we should just kill you now, throw you out that million-dollar view." He moved closer to Jamison.

The desk warrior held out a hand, said, "Things to come . . . if . . . you step out of line again."

"Didn't know there was a line. And, come to think of it, can't recall stepping over one."

"Tommy, when we took you on and agreed to provide assignments, there were some things that were simply understood and not stated explicitly."

"Like?" I interrupted Caleb from saying something very stupid, I was sure of it.

On my balcony, drinking beer. I was already four helpings into my medicinal six-pack. "You lecture me about how not-stupid these businessmen are, and don't piss 'em off or anything, then you stare down one of them, insult him up and down in his own office, and threaten to kill him in situ?"

"In his own office, yeah." Caleb was somber, not his usual bouncy self.

Got up, set down my beer and walked slowly and carefully over to him, dropped my hands to my knees, found a nice comfortable position, my face now in his face: "Are you fucking kidding me!?"

I'd never been slapped by another man before.

No, really.

It wasn't a hard slap, either, the kind that stunned or arrested you in position and morphed you into a marble statue. Nope, more like something a father would give his son when he was being especially obtuse, just firm enough to get his attention but not break his spirit. Too much.

"Now get outta my face, back the fuck up, sit down, and let's get drunk." Long pull on his Stella, then pointed a finger right at the tip of my nose, just brushing it: "And stop sniveling, Ranger. You're embarrassing me."

Drew back as ordered and stood there for a moment, saw the error of my ways, stumbled back to my seat, all quiet now.

"Yeah, you're right, I did say those things, and I meant 'em." For a guy who just gave me a good slapping, he was pretty calm. "But I also said when things aren't going your way, you sometimes have to stir the pot to force something to happen. And that something is usually not what they were planning on doing. That works in our favor."

He was looking right at me, but I felt too small to look back. Wasn't embarrassed or anything. Just . . . not sure who I was, where I was, what I was doing in that moment. No, not an anxiety issue; I was calm. Something else. Thinking back on all that great intel I'd learned about my reactions to all those cool pharmaceuticals, I now wished I had done the same experimental exercises with a wider range of human emotions and behaviors. Because right this second, on this very evening in my miserable life, I wasn't Tommy Darlington.

I was no one.

Who had just gotten slapped across the face by a man who sure as hell knew who he was.

It was like all that drama with Viktor and the Jamisons and Felix had never happened.

Caleb and I got a call a week later to do a small gig, so we sat around and planned it over our usual beer and extra-crispy KFC, and then took a long drive down to Osprey.

Nothing was said about the slap. Dunno why. Maybe it had been good for me, funny as it was to think about. There was no discomfort between us. Quite the opposite. It seemed like the slapping Felix had given us had the same effect, too: electroshocked us into some new positive reality.

Their reality. And ours.

Still, it was the eeriest thing, my not feeling bad or uncomfortable or murderous about any of this shit that'd gone down recently.

What was going on? Was I numb to it all? That could be a dangerous thing, not being able to feel when you had your hand on a hot burner.

Caleb drove with one hand on the wheel, the other perpetually wrapped around the knob of the gear stick, like he'd rip it off at any moment.

I pointed to a small store off south Tamiami Trail, about a quarter-mile from Osprey.

He slowed and pulled into the store's parking lot. Caleb pulled out the receiver and we listened in:

"*The Foundation cannot function without you, Christine.*"

"*It's time for me to retire and leave this business to a young 40-year-old dynamo.*"

"*If you leave, we'll never be able to raise the money you've gotten for us.*"

"*Honey, it's not I they give to, it's to the Foundation.*"

"*You're so wrong there, Christine. The wealthy people of this town respect you. They love you. And they give to you, because they trust you.*"

"Why the hell would these guys wanna kill off that sweetheart?" Caleb was genuinely angered.

Pulled out slowly from the parking lot and moseyed on down to Blackburn Point Road, hung a right and drove a mile across the inland waterway to Casey Key, a largely forgotten sliver of overpriced sand just south of Siesta Key.

The rotating bridge was a bit disconcerting for me in that moment, so I closed my eyes while we sat waiting for two sailing yachts to motor on by. Worse than watching slow-motion lawn bowling.

My little episode wasn't lost on Caleb. Looked over at me, tapped my arm: "You okay?"

"Dizzy." My right hand covered my eyes. Maybe it was the sunlight assaulting me through the windshield. The a/c was on high and blowing right in my face, so I should've felt okay.

But I wasn't okay. I thought about this lovely woman we had to visit. Thought about Rachel and that vivid wide-awake dream I'd had on my balcony—when was it? Even after seeing her leave with some other guy, why was I still thinking about her? I should've been happy that pain in the ass voluntarily marched outta my life.

But I wasn't happy.

I was anxious.

This target—this woman, Christine—was not in any way a bad guy. More I thought about it, I wanted to drive back to Sarasota and kill the asshole who'd sanctioned her death. Why was I questioning things now?

"Yeah, fine, just got light-headed there a sec. I'm fine. Don't sweat it."

He was still looking at me, doing a nine-line on my medical condition, gonna radio for a medevac any sec. After a long minute, turned his head to the bridge, which was just rotating back to the closed position, allowing us to cross.

"You don't wanna do this, Tommy, we go back home or I can get it done alone."

My not answering was my answer: it was a tacit consent to do harm with extreme cruelty. Gawd, I love Archilochus.

On the drive back to the North Longboat condo, I thought about the gig, how we had to visit an innocent woman, a lovely woman by anyone's standards. How she begged us not to do it killed me inside. She showed us pictures of her daughters and their children, and Caleb had to leave the room. I saw tears in his eyes, too.

All so sweet.

Such a waste of a life.

But that's what they paid us for: to erase a high-profile business executive in Sarasota so they could muscle their way into her foundation before she could exit. Her retiring would've complicated things, I gathered. Now the foundation was part of their network, another small yet significant part in a very large mechanism.

BigMoney did stuff like that, even in seemingly insignificant towns like Sarasota.

Making it look like a robbery was easy: we trashed the place. But not before I walked into every room in her home, vowing not to forget this special human being.

Sending this woman on her next journey was too easy. And it destroyed what Rachel had left of my heart. No, my own mother—or even Rachel—was nothing like this beautiful elegant lady. And she truly was a lady by all measures: sweet, kind, wonderful, well educated and read, beautiful inside and out, and gracious to all. And that's just what the newspapers said about her. That much, I remember from those local rags. The rest I got from my short interaction with her and later doing my walk-through of her living space.

How the heck I got this gig was beyond me. Couldn't they have assigned someone else?

She knew what was happening, pieced it all together as it unfolded slowly in front of her. Still begged me to spare her life, even knowing this was inevitable.

"Take whatever you want," she told me . . .

Laid her down on the kitchen floor . . .

Tears filled her eyes . . .

Whimpered at first . . .

Then a flood of tears and uncontrolled crying . . .

And when it was done, my own cries melded with her final tears.

Caleb had remained outside the house, but I knew he'd heard everything. . . .

As we crossed the Ringling Bridge, I took in the panorama: exclusive Golden Gate Point to our left, all those lonely high-rises, so isolated, one way in and one way out, such a kept mistress . . . to our right, shallow turquoise waters for miles, dotted with drunken sailors and jet-skiers killing time that wasn't theirs.

This should've been my paradise. How could I no longer appreciate this beauty?

Then I remembered: I hated BigMoney, the assholes who'd ruined this town. Those who referred to the huddled masses as useless fat and gristle. I hated this town now because all I could see was what I couldn't see in front of my face. Only what was indelibly painted on the inside of my skull, my little planetarium, a constellation of dots that proposed some grand conspiracy.

They'd ruined my town: BigMoney.

I struggled with so many conflicting feelings and impressions: how could I think such thoughts about what was once a paradise . . . and then erase an innocent victim of a good organization that actually helped people in this town?

I was as much a part of what I hated and despised as BigMoney was. . . .

Thumb-up-the-ass shoelace-gazing, right here inside the twisted theater of Tommy Darlington.

She'd left another voicemail. Only said she was sorry for everything . . . all was okay with her . . . she left SurferBoy weeks ago . . . oh, and she missed me. . . .

Rachel missed me.

Listened to it over and over as I paced the floor of the condo, one tile at a time, and when I'd run out of tiles for the 100th time, took a long drive and walked around the malls in town, hiding in company I didn't know, never would know.

By sunset, I'd wound up on Lido Key, one of my favorite spots for sunsets, a place where Rachel and I used to come. The small resort was a ten-story structure at the beach, with views of the Gulf and that's about it. The giant picture windows of the bar faced the beach. Who needed anything else in life?

I sat at the bar so I could take in an unobstructed view, not be seen by too many people except the bartender. She was efficient, not letting all the bottles of Stella collect in front of me like other amateur barkeeps often did, making me look like the town drunk or the recently divorced father of two who'd just lost the house, the kids, the Audi Q7. Everything.

No, this one was cool. Made an effort to come over and talk to me. She knew something was up, so kept a respectful distance. Bartenders, regardless of their upbringing and schooling, were a curious lot, and tuned in to people and their emotions and struggles.

Saw her looking at me. No, she was studying me. I wonder what she'd gleaned in the hour and ten minutes I'd been sitting here, downing five Stellas and a glass of ice water. Lost in thought, just stared out at the vast ocean, not really thinking about anything. My subconscious was doubtless doing all my thinking for me, so I merrily went along for the ride, every now and then reaching out in vain to grab any loose thoughts.

"You okay?" she asked, wiping up some invisible stain on the bar in front of me. Nice excuse the check on one of her patrons.

At first I didn't hear her, then a tiny voice inside me suggested I turn my head a teeny bit to my right.

"You okay? Want another round?" Her sun-kissed smile reminded me of someone. All those perfect white teeth, framed by full kissy-lips delineated by a rich vermilion line.

"Yeah. Yeah to both."

That smile of hers. Wow. So full of energy, strong and positive. What I'd give to bottle it, take it home with me, use it each morning to kickstart my day. Wow.

In that moment, I wished that Rachel would've had that effect on me ... with just a smile.

She returned with my double-barrel Stellas. One was never enough, being only 11.2 ounces, and I could never get a bartender's attention when I needed it, so I always ordered two at a time, sometimes three. That initial two-beer buzz. Nothing like it.

"Thanks." I looked at her this time. Wow. Dark turquoise eyes. Never seen such a green richness before. Wait a sec, yes I have: the Gulf of Mexico in the late afternoon.

Grabbed a handful of spicy peanuts, tossed 'em in my mouth. I'd consumed the entire bowl of appetizers, not once considering how many dirty fingers had been in the bowl before me. Just contributing further to my healthy immune system.

"You're an hors d'oeuvre-ivore, I see."

Cute. The girl and the line. Hors d'oeuvre-ivore. Someone else I knew made up funny words like that. Neologisms.

She found a few other little things to do at my end of the bar, wiping down all horizontal surfaces, cleaning the clean glassware for the third time, restacking napkins just so, building a little tiki hut with toothpicks and spit. So that's what they secretly did with bar toothpicks before they stabbed an olive or a cherry and fed it to you.

Something inside me stirred.

An itch that was neither comfortable nor uncomfy. Like when you have to pee really badly and your bladder starts to tingle, like a prerelease-kinda orgasm. Dunno how else to describe it.

Guy five seats down moved next to me, said, "What a looker, huh? Don't get that in Jersey City, know what I mean?"

I immediately turned away from the bar, from him, looked outside again, that itch getting bigger, louder, more annoying.

He tapped me on my knee this time: "So, bud, you gonna do her or what?"

She looked over at both of us, saw the coming storm, picked up her cell phone, unfolded it, her eyes not leaving Jersey or me.

"Hey, bud, I asked you a question. Guy asks you a question, you answer. What are you, stupid or what?" Smacked me on my shoulder. His was a bear paw. Viktor, when he slapped the wind out of me that day at his cabin.

In ten years I'd look back on this day as a truly sad one, not unlike the day I had killed sweet Christine and effectively handed her prized foundation over to Felix and his goons. I'll think about this day and try to figure out why I hadn't just . . . walked away.

How hard is it to just walk away?

When that certain mechanism inside the dark corner of your mind raises up and starts to turn, there is no going back. You're just along for the ride.

My first shot to his jaw knocked him back and into the bar, snapping his head in an audible CLICK!

The second blow went to the side of his neck, as close to the jawline as I could, which crushed his left carotid artery, thus shutting off half the normal flow of blood to his Jersey brain. It also had another effect: overstimulating his vagus nerve and sending him into cardiac arrest.

As I watched him descend slowly to the floor, my boot found a soft spot in the center of his sternum. Sounded like the snap of a one-inch green sapling.

By the second blink, she had speed-dialed her buddy at the Sheriff's Office, the alarm in her eyes tracking my every move.

Took a last look out at the Gulf, turned around and met the still-shocked face of KissyLips, someone who would forever see me as a cold-blooded predator.

Casually strolled into a stunning sunset, my pulse hovering at a cool 54 beats a minute. . . .

Lying low and being an absolute zero was easy for me.

Done it all my adult life, hiding in plain sight of whoever I was trying to avoid at the moment. It's easy: make sure no one knows where you are, keep quiet, don't use landlines or cell phones, steer clear of the internet, and never answer the door, not that anyone ever paid me an unannounced visit.

Those past two weeks had been a special kind of hell, though. We'd been out of prison for a few months, done a few crappy yet good-paying jobs for Felix and his crew, and I felt I'd returned to some template of normal.

Whatever normal for me was.

Caleb had practically busted down the front door and confronted me about what the hell I'd done to that poor man at the bar on Lido. This time when he got in my face, I took him to the floor and wound him up like a pretzel, threatening to choke him out if he pulled that slap-Tommy shit on me again. Ever.

Things had built up since we'd gotten out of SOCOM's cells, since we'd had our own little incident—the slap. I thought all that was behind us, but it appeared to fade into a repressed niche deep inside me . . . only to emerge recently. And in a more damaging and frightening state than before.

I was drunk off my ass by eight p.m., trying to sleep it off on the chaise on the balcony, the same one where I'd seen Rachel that one night. Thought I'd seen her.

Caleb had left and then returned with dinner, a real dinner. "Foodage?"

Pulled my two-ton head off the pillow, still hugging that vision of Rachel. "Not really."

"Get some of this up in you. Feel better."

So I sat up at the table with Caleb, ate in silence, pushing one little morsel at a time into my mouth, learning how to chew slowly, ever soooo slowly. Like those damn sailboats passing through the Casey Key bridge when I had to—

Poor Christine.

No, poor Tommy.

After a few minutes, the food lubed up the atmosphere a little.

"Cops found the guy," he said.

At first, I had no clue . . . then it came to me, slowly at first, then in a torrent. "Jesus, what happened?"

"You don't remember punching a civilian to death at a bar. You shittin' me?"

Punching a civilian to death at a bar.

The tapes replayed over and over: the bartender, lovely, sweet thing . . . her kind attentions . . . the loud Jersey guy, foul and stinking . . . the look on his goon face as he fell and his whole world went to gray . . . then black. . . .

"Comin' back to you?" He was concerned for me, yes, but also very angry.

"Sorta. What do you mean, they got the guy?"

"Felix is more powerful than I thought, Tommy. Sumbitch pulled a whole lotta strings."

All the headaches and all-body pains came back in a sudden WHOOSH! I was flooded with emotions and feelings that overwhelmed my circuit breaker. Blew a fuse just recalling all the details of the beating I'd given that poor asshole in the bar. And the sweet bartender: just when things were going so well with her, when I knew I'd ask her for a number and email address, and we'd have a nice eve on the town, forget about my shitty life for a night.

Just when things had been going okay for me. . . .

I could barely hold my head up, but I looked at him: "Strings."

"Said you were a government operative under the aegis of SOCOM, working on a sensitive assignment, so the locals handed you over to them."

"Okay, so the cops found the guy—"

He pushed a fresh beer in my face: "Now, asshole, we get you patched up so we can get back to work and make some big kunas. Lot's happened since you were passed out."

I recall being dragged to the bathroom . . .

Long shower . . .

Frozen needles all over my back and head . . .

No exit . . .

I screamed but no one was listening.

Except Caleb.

He was the one taking care of poor, pathetic Tommy.

No way in hell I'd ever go see a shrink. No way.

"So, Mr. Darlington, have you ever seen a licensed mental health professional before?" She leaned forward a little too eagerly.

I wasn't supposed to be there. Wasn't in my blood. Evidently, neither was being normal, so I guess I was supposed to be there. Someone told me that "therapists" don't shrink your head, they just neutralized whatever fetid soup you had between your ears and then screwed your head on tighter. And when the threads were stripped, they applied generous amounts of Lok-Tite.

Her office was located in West Bradenton, far enough away from the prying eyes of Sarasota, close enough to get to in half an hour.

Tall, slender, brown shoulder-length bob, pleasant and inviting looks, unassuming, non-threatening, understated sensuality, soft intelligent voice and thoughts.

Dayum, you'd think I was rattling off all the characteristics of my ideal woman.

"No."

"Okay, that's fine. Then we should begin with a questionnaire, a little history of who you are, where you came from, your parents, siblings. Sound okay?"

I wanted to kiss her, she was so sweet, so nurturing. Everything Rachel never was. "Okay."

Filled out a twenty-page drill, took a few tests in front of her, then sat back and wondered why the hell I was here in her care.

Under orders. Caleb's orders.

What the hell was I now, his sous chef?

He'd said, "We're gonna find you somebody to pick up your head and put it back on your shoulders all straight, then get some good stainless-steel screws, hold it in place all proper."

I'd argued that this was a lousy time, since we had several gigs to do locally and regionally. I'd made it sound like we were a two-man band, hitting all the honky-tonks under the Bible Belt. Maybe that was why he dismissed me so quickly.

"Don't worry about it, Tommy. Got it all covered."

That's what worried me the most: Caleb had it all covered. Without me. And this was my profession. My job. I'd invented this gig, designed and built it from scratch. And now it wasn't mine anymore.

"When would you like to return, Mr. Darlington?"

My mind was not in a good space, still daydreaming about how Caleb had it all covered, how I'd lost it all, how I'd killed an innocent man in my fave bar, how I'd murdered the sweet innocent woman that was Christine Lodge. And now I was here in this office of loose screws and Gorilla glue.

My Code of Deathics needed a slight edit and it made me sick to think about my descent into a AAA rating: Anyone. Anytime. Anywhere.

"Uh, how about now?"

She laughed. "Oookay, let me look at my schedule for this afternoon."

She leafed to a page in her calendar. I could see it was empty except a few phone calls to make, pick up groceries on way home this evening, call her mom.

"Looks like I may have to juggle things a bit, but I can squeeze you in, I think."

I didn't let on that I knew she was free all afternoon. She was so sweet and earnest. "Thank you."

She leaned forward, her elbows on her knees, smiled. "You're anxious."

Oh, shit, I'd been made. "Uhhh."

"To have our first session, I mean." What a smile on her.

Relief. My false front still intact. "Yup."

"Let me look through all your answers for a few minutes. Meantime, why don't you have a seat out in the lobby?"

"Lobby."

"Yes, where you came in a couple of hours ago." She pointed to her right in such a playful, theatrical way.

Left on my own in a big lobby, other customers for the dentist and a few attorneys moving around, mingling, reading the latest gossip glossies. All a swirl of noisy colors. The heat and humidity roared in my ears. The ghost of emptiness hovered in front of me. My head began to spin. No, that wasn't it. Everything in my world began to spin. My head wouldn't move at all. . . .

"Mr. Darlington!"

Heard a muffled voice outside. Waaaay off in the distance. Over the snow bank. Across the lake. Soft voice calling me: "Darling, dinner's ready!"

"Mr. Darlington!" Slapped my face, and I wondered why Caleb was smackin' me around. Again.

"Tommy! Can you hear me? Wake up, Tommy."

The blinding light of the snow grayed down to a small tunnel, a quantum of deadlight . . . walked down the path . . . as I got farther from the snow, the tunnel opened up slowly into a large cavern . . . more lights . . . lots of chairs.

Chairs?

"Tommy? Are you okay? Can you hear me?" Bent over me, she held my head in her lap, gently touching my face.

Rachel had never done that.

Mumbled a weak "Hi."

"You passed out."

"I'm sorry."

People were gathered around us, whispering things I didn't want to hear, little judgments and false accusations. Sounded false to me: I wasn't a drunk, not a druggie, sure as hell not an epileptic. Not in a lobby. Not today.

Sara helped me up and I was able to stand on my own in a few seconds. My world slowly returned to me as if nothing had happened. Nothing at all.

"How are you feeling, Tommy?"

"Fine, thanks. How are you?" I wanted to kiss her.

She was taken aback by my apparent sarcasm. "Do you want me to call someone for you?"

Yes, her name is Rachel and she ruined my life. "I'm fine. Can we talk now? I think I need help."

Smiled and took my arm and led me down a long, gray tunnel to her office.

I think I need help.

That was the point you usually got 5150'd or Baker-Acted, depending on which coast you were at the time, for seventy-two hours. Yes, like it or not. And if you looked worse after that, well, they might just hold on to you for a spell, feed you some yummy pharmaceuticals, poke you and prod you, do some tests to pass the time.

I hadn't just hit rock bottom, I crashed right through it and discovered a whole new kinda hell. . . .

"Control this mutt, Peter."

Felix Heydrich stood at the edge of his desk, his finger ready to hit the red button on his speakerphone.

"Felix, this may be good for us in the long run," Jamison said.

He sighed impatiently: "How?"

"Tommy Darlington and Caleb Gatewood work for us now. They were scared straight after their visit to the facility in Tampa. I doubt either wishes to return."

"Your point?" Felix's impatience was growing.

"We employ them on various assignments, the ones requiring extreme skill."

"There are others in our stable for this."

"Yes, sir, but these offer an additional bonus: they are expendable in place."

"Suicide bombers, so to speak."

"Yes, they conduct sensitive missions successfully on our behalf and, when the time presents itself, they do not have to return home."

"A divine wind."

"Kamikaze. Precisely."

"This Darlington fellow is unstable."

"He's being kept in check as we speak."

"How?"

"As you said before, we have other ways of keeping track of him. There is a woman who will guide him along as we wish."

"She's in our fold?"

"Soon, Felix. Soon."

Seeing her again was sweet 'n' sour.

There were no apologies for the past, awful as it had been near the end of the end.

We just said hello, hugged and looked at each other. Lots of smiles and some laughter thrown in, mostly for effect. One would've thought this was some reunion of old acquaintances from high school, people who were never really comfortable with each other on the best of days, just got together to talk about everyone else.

"I can't stay long. Work to do," she said. "Is everything okay with you?"

"Everything's fine." I lied. Truth? I was falling apart at the seams and, worse, disintegrating from the center out. The two destructive forces would soon meet in the middle . . . somewhere around my demise.

"You look great." Half-smile on her lovely face.

My dear Rachel never looked better. Maybe it was the time. Distance. That's it: the distance, our having been physically apart that had her radiating such beauty and confidence. Away from me, she had blossomed into something I'd never imagined. Didn't want to.

How could she have done it without me around?

"How's work?" I was still holding her hands.

"Writing's good. Better than ever, actually."

She laughed at the naked truth of it, doing more than she had when she was with me, and looked somewhat embarrassed. She'd been a demon on the computer, knocking out 5,000 words in a single day and sustaining it over weeks. A 400-page novel was only a three-week task for her.

"New book?"

"Several."

"Wow." Part of me truly was envious of her. She'd succeeded while I had failed. Apart, she'd gotten better in all respects. Had it been SurferBoy? I was too scared to ask. "Seeing anyone?"

Melancholy smile on her. "Tommy—" She squeezed my hands, pursed her lips. "I'm okay."

"That means what?"

"Look, Tommy, I don't want to argue. I answered your call and came by to say hi, see how you're doing. Let's not—"

Felt steam coming off my head. Tried to hold it together. My heart raced, thinking of Rachel with someone else, and now standing here with me. Jealous of SurferBoy and his golden locks and sparkling baby blues, because I had nothing on that laundry list of beauty aids.

So plain was I, the Ambassador of Meh.

I was holding the hands of a woman that had held some guy's face, his arms, stroked his hair, his—

"I should go."

"Wait." I was still holding on. Too tight.

That block of air between us now frozen once again.

She perked up: "Hey, I have an idea: why don't we have lunch tomorrow?"

Lunch.

The heat and humidity sounded in my ears, threatening meltdown. "Uh, okay. Where?"

"Fried Jack's on the beach. Noon sharp." She squeezed my hands again. "Don't be late."

Watched her walk across the room and depart silently, not even looking back at me. It's as if there really was no interest there. She was just feeling sorry for me. Poor Tommy, all wrecked and no one to reassemble him. If someone did, there would be a few parts left over. Grab a bucket of paint and slap on three coats of miracle and he'll be fine.

Something was odd about her visiting me like this. It nagged me for the rest of the afternoon, while I sat around waiting for my session with Sara. Eager to share this with her, I wanted answers. Why was Rachel so different? And what the hell was up with asking me out to lunch?

Rachel and I didn't do lunch.

In the late afternoon, I rode my bike over to Sara's for my session. Where did she get her energy? Always bouncy and smiling, offering a kind word to me, she was a rock where I was a soft, mushy thing. I wondered what would happen if I just blurted out to the world that I was this insecure, anxiety-depressive man who was great at killing assholes and bullies, but really bad at maintaining a close relationship.

Dismissed the thought as soon as it surfaced.

This time I actually paid attention to her office. It was spartan:

generic bookshelf with the usual graduate school texts and professional books, nondescript carpet, large brown fabric couch with half a dozen throw pillows and a blanket.

As I lay my head back on the couch, I wondered how many crying wimps had been right here, head thrown back, bawling their eyes out for an hour, then walking out with more than a new coat of paint. And I thought about just spilling everything to Sara, so I could walk out of here a changed—

"How was your week?" Eager for conversation, it seemed.

Sara, I'm a fucking basket case. "Great. Got a lot of work done."

"Any cool news to report?"

Oh, yeah, I beat a man to death. Hit him twice and kicked him once and he was out like a bad Christmas light. "Saw my . . . ex, I guess I should call her now."

"Really? That's great. How'd it go?"

Well, the first punch probably broke his neck, and the second one shredded his carotid. Felt it through my skin. Wow, what a sensation, turning off some asshole's electricity like that. First, he seized as his circuits crossed and hissed and fried, then everything just went black for him. "Fine."

Pouty look on her, very cute and effective.

After I ended this asshole's life, I just walked out into a peaceful sunset. "Okay, it was . . . strange."

She just listened.

My thoughts went back to the guy at the bar . . . in combat, it was usually a good idea not to double-check whether your bullet was effective, because that gave the bad guys a chance to regroup and shoot back if you had fucked up. I found it best to give my best performance at the start, so I didn't have to spot-check the accuracy and integrity of my work. And if, on occasion, I wasn't up to my usual standards, then at least I got away.

Snapped her fingers.

"I'm here. Everything's fine," I blurted out.

"Tommy, you couldn't be further away now. Why don't you close your eyes for a few minutes, let me do an exercise with you."

Without questioning her, I shut down and just listened, tried to take in all the sounds and smells and feel of the room:

A/C off to my right front a soft hummmm . . .

60-Hz bee-buzz from the ceiling lighting only a few feet above me . . .

Scent of industrial-grade lavender just behind me, diffusing off a warming dish. . . .

"Picture yourself in a bright, spacious meadow, flowing grass, wind whistling through the trees, a million multicolored flowers in full bloom."

The moment she said meadow and flowers and trees, I almost sneezed from an allergic reaction. But I held it in, trying to go along with her exercise.

"You're walking into the center of the meadow. . . ."

And getting attacked by a platoon of giant Asian hornets, but please continue.

"You sit down on the softest grass ever. . . ."

Right on a red-ant farm and they crawl all over me and— "Excuse me, Sara?"

"Hmmm?" Suddenly aroused from her own trance. The one supposed to heal me.

"I'm really sorry, but this isn't working. I'm going nuts here and all this talk about meadows and bees and ants is driving me bananas."

Her face wrinkled up a bit. "Bees? Ants? What are you talking about, Tommy?"

And then it dawned on me: she would soon discover just how fucked up I really was, make one phone call to the local padded-cell room, and have me locked up for life. Forget the Baker Act.

"I'm sorry, I felt dizzy there for a moment and started daydreaming." Liar liar, pants on fire.

She looked encouraged: "Hey, maybe it was working, just not quite the way I planned. Why don't we try again?"

I hoped the look on my face said yes, because nothing fell out of my mouth. And my pants were still burning. Those persistent Florida red ants.

Reminded me of something this guy gave me years ago, scrawled on a napkin. Dino Something. Met him in Central America. Probably CIA. It was his philosophy, he told me, how he got through each day of hell. Based on the behavior of red ants he'd observed on one kill mission, while he waited for his target to emerge from a bar.

While he lay in painful wait, the ants crawled all over and slowly ate him for breakfast, lunch and dinner. He'd sorta modeled it after the US Army's "nine-line," a detailed medevac request.

The irony was not lost on me.

The Red Ant Work Éthique

Never complain about anything.
Do whatever it takes.
Never quit.
Always protect your queen (precious cargo).
Build a water crossing with a thousand of your best buds.
Do battle only when necessary.
Be kind to your developing larvae (family, friends, colleagues).
Celebrate a good life with a good quick death.
Recycle your carcass.

There had been nothing in the papers about the beating death of the man from New Jersey, not even in his own hometown rag. Evidently, Felix and his connections really knew how to shut down a story. I called the bar and asked for KissyLips, and the manager said she hadn't shown up for work in a while.

Shit. They'd gotten her, too. An innocent and beautiful human being . . . like Christine . . . now both dead because of me.

I now wondered if they would do the same to Caleb and me when we'd reached the end of our shelf life.

Caleb had been doing surveillance on a pair of Bulgarian businessmen who'd ridden into town six months back, dumped a ton of cash into a local no-name bank, and then tried to muscle their way into the drug scene. Boris and Josef were now safely ensconced at a Holiday Inn Express near Siesta Key.

All those millions and they still did a ghetto Holiday Inn. East-bloc mentality. I gave them the benefit of my doubt: maybe they had never heard about the Hyatt or Ritz downtown.

Uh-huh.

"Been sitting on these two fungos for a week now. You okay?"

Looked over at me.

We were sitting in a white Lexus suv, something Caleb picked up at a DEA auction. What those drug-runners lacked in brains, they accidentally made up for in good taste. In high-end suvs, at least.

"Good. I'm good." Looked at the waveforms of voices on the cool, high-tech receiver between us.

"Red wave on top is Boris. Yellow on bottom is Josef."

"So what's the plan here?" Dunno why I asked. He briefed me hours earlier.

"Same as a few hours ago: wait 'til they take a late-night drive, follow 'em, find a nice stretch of road with no buildings, run up alongside their vehicle, shoot 'em through the brainpan."

I'd done something similar to a guy out near Arcadia months back. That was when I was working alone and things were—

"How's things with the shrink lady?"

"Don't ask." I was looking through a nice pair of night-vision binos.

"Why can't I ask?"

He knew I was on the edge, so I needed to reassure him that all was fine with me. "Like I said, don't ask. Everything's fine. I talk, she listens, I pay her a lot of money, she says thank you. Repeat as necessary like, once a week."

"Her job's to exorcise the crazy parts outta you, make you—"

Pulled my twisted face from the binos, looked at him: "What? Whole again?"

He looked at me, small frown: "Actually, I was gonna say . . . not hurt so much."

The two Bulgarians exited their room at six past one a.m.

"Fight's on," Caleb said, turning on his whisper-quiet ignition, putting the suv in gear, and pulling out from the parking lot and onto US 41.

"You know where they're going?" Guess he'd left that out of the briefing earlier.

"Been watching these guys a week now. Seen their patterns, their new haunts."

"Bingo night for these guys?"

"Cathouse night, my friend. Stick around, this will probably get interesting."

We drove for forty minutes up Tamiami Trail past SRQ, southeast Bradenton and into downtown, and pulled into a small motel on 53rd Avenue East. Dingy would've been a kind word for this place.

"And we're here because? Forgive me, but this wasn't in that outstanding seminar you presented."

Caleb turned to me, snorted it out: "This, my dear Ranger buddy, is a whorehouse."

A dirty look from me: "I don't do whorehouses and you know it."

"This one is special. Follow me in for a looksee." He hopped out like we were at Disney World.

Before I could un-ass the vehicle, he was already skipping to m'Lou up to the front entrance, signing up to be the first guy on Mickey and Minnie's Ferris wheel.

Walking across the sand and crushed-shell parking lot reminded me of Old Florida: sand and crushed-shell parking lots. The building looked like it was going to lean over and hit the ground in about five minutes, but I braved it and moseyed on inside.

Moly hoses.

If ever there were a really cool bait and switch, this was it: the interior was all five-star Las Vegas, with elegantly designed tropical décor from floor to ceiling, soft muted pastels on one wall, bright splashy colors on another. Soft, overstuffed lounge chairs and couches everywhere, and at least one beautiful young girl guarding each one, dressed in—well, put it this way, not a whole helluva lot.

Not that I was some Victorian prude or anything, but these kids were too young to be wearing nothing at all and parading—or sitting—around in nothing at all, doing nothing at all except looking very come-hitherly.

My mind was rambling on about the whole place, because I was completely overwhelmed. Caleb was at the far end of the main room, talking up some cutie brunette in spiky, fuck-me heels, a few slices of colored thread across her boobs and pussy. That's about it. She had this lazy, could-givea-shit smile on her flawless face, the kinda face you see on a fourteen-year-old girl whose bedroom mirror had never seen a pimple.

This one baby-faced girl came up to me, took my hand and placed it between her legs. Wouldn't have been too bad for me, except she had nothing on but exceptionally soft, tight skin down there and absolutely no pubic hair, probably because she hadn't yet entered puberty and not because she'd just gotten a Brazilian.

Pulled my hand back, checked it for damage. Looked around, hoping no one had caught the act. Just what I needed this stage of my illustrious career: Tommy the Pedophile on some #MeToo list.

Couldn't think of anything to say except hihowareya, but she didn't understand. Even if she'd not been high-high on some relaxer, she wouldn't have understood me. Definitely from down under, like Costa Rica or Dominican Republic or the Republic of Pussy. Choose one. She was a child prostitute, so it didn't matter where she was from.

If only twenty-nine-year-old women would look at me that way, I think I could be maybe sorta begin to become happy. . . .

"Hey, young man, check this out." Caleb tapped my shoulder, put his hands on the side of my head and redirected my syrupy gaze from the underage blow-up doll filling my line of sight. . . .

To our left was a small stage with what looked like an old hitching post. I secretly hoped this wouldn't be a south-of-the-border girl and pony show.

In seconds, a very beautiful young thing sauntered out, tall like model-tall, sexy like cheap Hollywood-glam sexy, and young like kid-sister-in-braces young.

She turned her back to us and placed both her hands on the hitching post, twerking that sweet tail end her mama gave her, and driving the growing crowd of men, women and girls into a slow-boiling fever.

The music amped up and an incessant BOOM! BOOM! BOOM! quickly filled the room, a giant set of hammers threatening to cave the roof in but no one cared because it was the beat-setting stimulus that drove all the lemmings in the room over the edge.

Caleb smiled like it was, well, Disney World on New Year's Day, when no one was there except him because everyone in America was at home watching the Super Bowl. Or at the Super Bowl watching the Super Bowl.

I nudged him. "Aren't we supposed to be watching those Bulgarians?"

He pointed to a dark corner over to the right, way past the Western Smut Show on the little stage, to an Arabian Nights alcove. The two Bulgarians were seated under a low-hung tent in separate purple lounge chairs, each with two young girls on either side of him, fondling and giggling like it was a Friday-night, junior-high make-out session at someone's parent's house in the 'burbs. Neither man had enough hands and fingers to test-drive the girls, but they seemed to make pretty good use of the ones Mother Nature had provided.

Boris and Josef were sampling morsels and tidbits of what the rest of the world called illegally trafficked, imported sex toys, and were feeling no pain 'cos of the little bright-red pills a hostess kept dropping into their wide open mouths, feeding her hatchlings a few milligrams of 100% euphoria, bliss and fuck everything else in the world 'cos mami gonna take good care of you, papi.

This went on for an hour before I got impatient and stepped outside for my first cigarette since the night we got nabbed at TPA by the entire Department of Homeland Security Marching Band. Going from the bright lights of Vegas Does the Caribbean to the reality of Bradenton, Florida was a culture shock, but I somehow survived walking outside and finding a little place to sit my ass down and enjoy a smoke.

When you've not smoked in a long time and your body craves it like water, the best thing to do is go just for it, light that fucker and suck in as much of those 4,000 carcinogens as you can, and not think about how a cig is like a sausage: all sorts of shit go into it, and you don't wanna know what the key ingredients are or what they can do to you in ten years. But, damn, it tastes ohhh, sooo good.

Instead of dragging on mine, I inhaled all I could, sending a huge bolus of chemical sausage right up into my amantadine-starved brain and all over my pleasure centers and joy divisions until I almost passed out from the buzzy-buzz.

Singing in the background.

Looked around and saw that same young girl from inside, now standing just behind me, looking quite different than the sultry and sensuous young girl-whore inside the golden playpen.

"Okay I sit you?"

"You want to sit with me?" I corrected, reminding myself not to say something sarcastic and suggestive that would turn her sex-motor on again.

Nodded her head yes.

Now looking like a young runaway in trouble, she sat next to me on the bench.

"Rosita."

"Tommy." I extended my hand, she took it.

She was shaking.

Now what the hell was I supposed to do? The right thing? What was the right thing here? Bust down the door to the whorehouse and play shoot-em-up with the owner-operator? Do the Lone Ranger bit and ride my horse into the burning breech and rescue all the girls at once?

Right.

Caleb had planned only to do a recon of the place, so I put all my thoughts about a daring rescue back in my pants and just sat there and listened to this child tell me about life in the tropics waaay down under where little girls trade their teen years for a trip up to sunny sexy Disney World.

Listened to her sad drippy monologue and chain-smoked a buncha cigarettes.

The longer I hung around her, listened to her, the more her initial sexitude and deliciousness wore off, right down to the nub where she became a frightened little kid, just wanting to go home and curl up around mommy and daddy's bunny slippers.

"Roxy!" A rotund, mean-looking greaser Latino stood at the entrance to the place, looking over at us.

Didn't matter. He was another nasty pimp I'd not gotten around to trashing just yet. After tonight, there would be ample time for this one. One quick calculation: I'd hafta dump him into one of those industrial-size Dumpsters, probably with a crane. Still be worth the effort.

"Get your ass in here now, and you best have something to show for this free time you give the gringo!"

I almost became unhinged right there, not so much for the gringo slam but he sooo looked like a greaser who needed to be tenderized and stuffed down a very deep hole.

Then I recalled some little incident at my fave bar on Lido Key recently.

Rosita stood nervously, and from behind handed me a folded piece of paper. I took it and lit up another cigarette, watched her walk back to purgatory, to the open arms of GreaserPimp, all those gold teeth and that 280-pound butterjacket.

Like this broke-tail alligator once advised me, "See you again asshole . . . see you again."

Minutes later, Caleb strolled out, grinning like he'd just ridden every single ride at Disney World and hadn't had to stand in a single line all night.

"Find anything?" I was trying not to sound too sarcastic.

"Tell you on the way home."

"Do I get to kill someone soon?"

Caleb pulled his head from the slow, early morning traffic, looked over at me. "Guy from Jersey not enough for ya?"

Silence.

"Oh, how I hate to see a grown man pout." He sorta grunted.

Then we both shared the first belly laugh in a long time. Felt good.

"That guy at the bar—" I started.

He was still catching his breath. "Hey, you were so stressed out about everything, you didn't know which end to screw your ass on."

Didn't know what to say.

"Anyway, those two Bulgarian blockheads are trying to take that little skin-biz from the TexMex guy you saw tonight. I watched Boris and Josef finger the hell out of a buncha girls without paying a good damn dime, but no one started any shit."

"GreaserPimp, the one you call TexMex, doesn't have the heat to fire up Boris and his boyfriend."

"I think you're right, which means our Eastern friends are fixin' to roll back into town right quick, steal this guy's girls, burn down his shack, and set up shop somewhere nearby. Now, I could be wrong. But probably not."

"Agreed ... I want the two Bulgarians." It wasn't a request.

"All right. No mess this time, 'cos I seriously doubt we have any more favors coming from Felix."

"Got it." Oh, how I got it. For the first time in ages, I felt decent, and wasn't shaking inside the way I usually was. Maybe I just needed to get out and work more.

No, that wasn't it. I needed to stop thinking about Rachel.

As Caleb would've said, "Tommy, you just need to kill you a coupla assholes once in a while, is all."

"When you think Boris and boyfriend will strike?" Hope I didn't sound too eager.

"I'll betcha they're still scoping the place out. Best guess? Couple weeks, tops. That way, they get the girls, the action and all the new headaches that'll come with their new business venture."

"Headaches." I had one at the moment.

"Felix owns this whorehouse, Tommy."

"I gathered."

He pulled into a 7Eleven, got some gas.

Stuck my head out the window: "The Bulgarians didn't just roll into town on their own. They were summoned."

The little metal flap that holds the gas handle open was broken, so he had to hold the handle down the whole time.

"Good point. Felix plays both sides in this town. He has little guys like Boris and Greaser opposing each other on the same turf, sees who wins. A game of scorpion versus spider in a jar."

"More than that, the ruse lets everyone else think it's a genuine turf war."

"That no one controls." He slammed the gas handle back into its cradle.

"Just add water, Darwin and some bullets."

"Dammit, this thing ate my receipt. Fuck—"

A barrage of little rockets struck all around Caleb, puncturing the gas pump stand.

A series of images in slow motion:

I threw open his door ...

He jumped inside ...

Slammed the suv in reverse and went to full military power on the throttle . . .

We clipped the right side of the little building, shearing off our left rear taillight and gouging the fender . . .

The gas pump exploded in a series of thumping waves that pulsed in and out, a giant dragon in a spastic coughing fit . . .

A series of fiery streaks shot off the concrete in front of us, as bullets walked their way to the suv . . .

Caleb slammed the Lexus into drive and lit the afterburners, rocketing us out of the parking lot and onto south Tamiami Trail. . . .

We didn't exhale until we reached the airport and saw a line of emergency vehicles coming from Sarasota.

Wiggled all my fingers and toes.

Check.

Looked inside my pants to see if my thang was still there.

Check.

Ten fingers, ten toes, one penis.

I was duty.

"Slow down, dude." I was gently holding his arm.

Caleb was hyperventilating. "I think I took a round."

Turned on the light, looked over and around Caleb's head, neck, shoulders, back and legs.

"Unless they shot you in the ass, I'd say the only thing that ails you is the big pile of shit in your drawers, and don't lie to me about it 'cos it's stinking something awful right about now and that's not something you're gonna be able to talk yourself out of."

I upped the a/c high as it would go, opened my window all the way, sat back again, my arm hanging out the window, playing up-and-down airplane with my hand in the fifty-knot breeze.

He shook his head a few times, looked askance at me. "Listen, what happens in Vegas, stays in Vegas."

An ear-to-ear grin on me. "Just one little problem with that one, C-man. . . this ain't Vegas."

These guys weren't too smart, the Bulgarians, but then again their Founding Fathers weren't known for blue-ribbon gray matter, either.

Trying to kill us in the open the other night was just plumb dumb, especially without knowing anything about us. Or so we assumed.

Could Felix or the Jamisons have ordered a hit on us, or was this an independent, spring-loaded, Bulgarian reaction to Caleb's presence?

Something didn't fit right but I was sure the explanation was more simple and less complicated. Some called that Occam's razor. I called it common sense, with a pinch of shit happens.

More likely, Boris and his boyfriend made Caleb sometime during his surveillance, and then were surprised to see him at the little cathouse in Bradenton, so they decided he was a possible threat and acted quickly.

"No way those idiots made me, Tommy. No way."

"They reacted pretty violently after they saw you at the cathouse."

"Look, these guys may've mistaken me for someone else. After all, I am handsome and have that suave look of a master spy. This town's full of 'em."

"You're just gay, is all. Sarasota's full of those, too."

Laughter is good, especially between friends who have shared difficult times. Reminded me of Rachel and how we used to laugh and giggle over the silliest things. Sometimes.

"I still don't like this approach, Tommy." Caleb checked his weapons.

"If we go in all cool and calm and try to reason with these guys right off, they'll go for the guns and start a firefight. So we have only one approach. It's the only way."

"Remind me not to listen to you again, Tommy. Ever."

Caleb tied up Josef and perched him up against the bathroom sink next to Boris, then sat back against the bureau, battered and exhausted from two minutes of no-holds-barred, close-quarters combat that dumped a quart of someone's blood all over the carpet.

Our guests were unconscious, having fought valiantly against Caleb and me, as we tried to reason with the two barbarians. It took two cartridges from each of our tasers to subdue them, even when we shot them in their chubby faces. Evidently, their brains were only loosely connected to their heads.

"Okay, so I gave them too much credit. Big deal. We're all here in the same room now, so no sweat." I secured an entire roll of hundred-mile-an-hour tape around each of their hands, legs and feet.

"So now what, Mister Tree-Hugger Negotiator?" Caleb paced around and looked for something to maim and kill. He was still bleeding and in a whole lotta pain only fentanyl could kill.

"We wait."

"For?" Caleb definitely not happy.

"For Conan and Sheena to wake up."

"Then what?" You could hear his knuckles cracking.

"Then, my dear Gatewood, we reason with them."

"Reason with a pair of scorpions. Okay, I gotta see this to believe it, so I'm just gonna go sit down over here, me and my two little pistols."

Meantime, I looked through all their goodie bags, found something interesting: two plastic quart-size boxes of the same red pills we'd seen the two men being fed at the cathouse, the same pills I was force-fed in the back of a panel van en route to SOCOM's prison. Tossed both boxes in my backpack, kept looking around, my own little rummage sale.

Caleb was still sacked out by the bureau in front of the tv when Boris's leg started twitching. Seconds later, he loosed a long sigh and it then became apparent why: the big man had just peed in his trousers and a caustic odor soon filled the room. Dunno what the hell these Bulgarians had eaten and drunk in the past twenty-four hours, but it smelled like a can of dog food way past the expiration date.

"That's just wonderful," Caleb said, waking up from his slumber, his eyes not yet open.

Boris roused himself and grunted, rolled over and loosed a long fart.

"You think he needs to do number two?" That smile back on Caleb.

When Caleb happy, Tommy happy.

We dragged BigBoris into the small bathroom, propped him up on the toilet.

Caleb spoke first: "Boris, I need you to understand something very clear now: you can go potty only if you promise not to do anything stupid."

Boris nodded obediently.

Soon as I loosened Boris's bindings, he broke free and slapped

Caleb across the face. Hard. Man, you could've heard that one across the parking lot. Next, the big man grabbed Caleb's collar and tried to yank him close enough so he could bite his face off.

"Step . . . in . . . here . . . anytime . . . Tommy," Caleb grunted in fits and spurts, all the while trying not to get dragged into the snapping jaws of Boris.

ZZZZZZZTTT!

In a millisecond, Boris was slumped over, sleeping soundly once again, his bowels dropping stunky stuff into the toilet.

"If you'd given me another minute, I coulda had him." Sweat and energy poured off Caleb's face, soaking his shirt.

I loaded a new cartridge in the taser and stuffed it in my cargo pocket, helped Caleb up from the floor.

"Remind me never to trust you and that Bulgarian warthog again. Ever."

After we cleaned him up and pulled on his gigantic underwear, we trussed up Boris like before, with maybe a little extra tape, and decided not to wait for him to wake up on his own. Caleb stuck his penknife into Boris's knee, just above the bony cap.

The big man yelled something that sounded funny as hell, probably in Bulgarian so I didn't care, and bolted upright.

"How the hell do you interpret, 'Ahzh shtay tay oobeeya! Rahzvoorzhi me sayga!'" I was really curious.

"He's saying two things here: one, he's gonna kill you. And two, untie him now or he's gonna kill you. Either way, he's gonna kill you."

I'd forgotten that Caleb was polyglot, having spent some time in Europe and the old East-bloc.

"Welcome back, homeboy Boris." I slapped his chubby face and waved my finger back and forth at his big red-veined nose, kinda like Caleb did to me that one time. "Now, lissen up, you fat fuck: I've been nice to you so far, and you're not showing me any love, so here's what's gonna happen."

Caleb and I tag-teamed Boris.

Sitting opposite me, Caleb smacked his face again, said, "Slushitay vnimatelno." *Listen carefully.*

Homeboy Boris was not in a cheerful mood, but at least he was tuned in to our broadcast.

I continued: "We would love to be good friends with you and Josef, understand?"

Boris nodded, his eyes rolling in different directions, clearly indicative of a mild Bulgarian stroke.

"Tell him we would like to work with him and Josef."

Caleb was having fun, playing United Nations go-between and all: "Bikhme iskali—"

The big man's face went into a rictus. He shook his head, trying to pull his eyes in synch again: "Your Bulgarian isn't that bad, Mr. Caleb, but you butcher our beautiful language so please shut up. You are hurting my ears. And would you please give me beer? I promise our days of war are over."

He seemed sincere, even with that knife sticking out of his knee.

Sometimes you just know. Besides, we needed a coupla double-agents. And if they got outta line again, I'd let Caleb kill them.

Caleb cut the tape over Boris's hands first, let that soak in a little: we were his friends, too, in this strained détente, long as he didn't try to snap our necks. So, for now, we were gonna leave on the leg and foot restraints, and we hope you didn't mind terribly, homeboy Boris.

"This okay by me, Mr. Tommy. Now, may I please have beer? Two is good."

Smiled at that one, grabbed my new friend Boris some ice-cold beers from the little reefer.

Caleb whispered, "At least we don't have to give these two knuckleheads your house."

My look said big whoop. The more I considered the place on Bird Key, among BigMoney and its minions, the more I wanted to leave this fucking place and find a new paradise. One all my own.

"In my country, I am very wanted by many people."

"So important people respect you and want to do business with you?" Smartass Tommy, playing along.

"No, no, you misunderstand, Mr. Tommy. I am wanted criminal. Everyone wants to kill Boris."

"On what grounds?" Caleb asked.

"On whatever grounds they can find me: outside my house, in a park, at a café. Does not matter, long as they kill Boris."

Handed everyone two beers each, the new double-barrel method of food delivery. "Why did they want to kill you, Boris?"

"How you say in this country? Guns, drugs and pussy."

That one was worth an uproarious toast that lasted the remainder of the evening, no real business getting done, but plenty of back-slapping and glad-handing around the condo. Something special, too: the boys from Bulgaria got to see their first western sunset. Détente, indeed.

By early morning, we had replenished the beer cooler on the balcony with two new cases of Stella, because we'd drunk the first batch last night, and done a few shots of some very expensive tequila Caleb had gotten on his last trip to Mexico.

It was readily apparent that Boris and his crew were runners of the top three commodities in the world: firearms, drugs, and humans. While a part of me wanted to drown him in the Jacuzzi, the better part prevailed and wanted to know him and his organization better. Sometimes, it was important to ally yourself with bad people, although I can't really say Boris was bad. He was a funny and entertaining big-hearted guy who did bad things to a lot of people. And those were mostly bad, I guessed, so we had a similar Code of Deathics: we both took out the trash, including the occasional good person.

Hey, no one's perfect.

The thought of sweet Christine jolted me back to a reality I didn't want to face, because the Universe would insist on reparation. Question was, exactly what, how and when?

Boris was now an ally, plain and simple. Even though that didn't work for me, I went with it. We learned that the two men were desperate for allies in town, which was unusual for their hyper-aggressive type. Most of these Eastern Euros were animals who took what they wanted and killed to get it. If one got caught, others were quickly imported to fill his place. Eastern European gangsters were as expendable as those red plastic cups at tailgate parties.

These guys, though? A whole different kind of chemistry.

Caleb started in: "You guys need to scare those Mexicans at the cathouse just enough to make them nervous so they go crying to their boss, that idiot Felix."

"This is what we plan all time, Mr. Caleb, to take business for ourselves." Boris had such a thick accent.

"But how did you come to be in Sarasota?" I couldn't imagine they came here by choice. I mean, who the hell would come to Sarasota of their own free will? Oh, maybe for the seasonal red tide and art festivals.

"Got call from man in Varna. Tells me some American wants jobs for us in America, so we come to this country . . . maybe six months past."

"Did you meet the American?"

"Yes, yes, we meet with him, he tells what he wants Boris to do."

"Can you describe him?"

"Dark hair, strong build like Olympic lifter, 90 kilos, maybe hundred eighty centimeters, professional businessman, driving in very nice Porsche."

Caleb and I looked at each other, sang it together: "John Jamison."

The meeting we had Boris arrange with John Jamison was set for this morning at 8:30 a.m. at the tiki restaurant in Sarasota Marina. On time and to spec was Jamison, who strolled over to a table in his crisp linen suit and matching cream-colored Cole-Haan slippers. He shook hands with Josef and sat down.

Listening in, Caleb and I shared a few McDonald's double quarter-pounders with cheese. Plain. He knew not to get me my burger with any red, yellow or green shit on it. McDonald's cheese was gold colored, I reminded him.

From a distance, we could easily see and hear the two:

"Your instructions were to take over the business at said location. Did you not understand this?" John Jamison raised a finger at the big man.

"No, no, understand okay. But why can't we just set up our own little business, we get the girls in from Czech and Albania and Estonia, wherever, and do things our way? Why we no can do this, Mr. Jamison?"

Jamison leaned forward: *"I'll repeat the instruction of my boss for you, but I will not be repeating them again, understood?"*

Josef nodded, lazily looked off in the distance, over where Caleb and I were staged, about 800 yards south, just off Bay Point Drive.

"Yes, I understand this, but I don't see why we can't do it so much quieter my way than your way, Mr. Jamison. You want us get caught and go to prison in your country?"

Jamison was getting hotter by the minute. He stood up and approached Josef: *"Either follow directions . . . or we find someone else to do it for you. Understand?"* He didn't wait for a reply, just marched back across the street to the office.

We all linked up back at the condo on North Longboat. Caleb and I discussed how much we should share with our fast friends, the highly expendable Bulgarians.

"Lemme put it this way," Caleb said. "I don't trust anyone much, so how much you think I'm gonna trust a pair of East-bloc vushkas?"

I knew vushka. It meant parasite.

We'd made it a ritual to watch the sunset over the Gulf. It appealed to Boris and Josef because their families had come from Varna, on the eastern edge of Bulgaria, where the sun rose over the Black Sea. They had never witnessed a sunset over water, so he enjoyed sitting on the balcony, and staring out over the water, watching the sun drift away. Rachel use to say the big orange ball was rolling west to melt down California.

"So you're being set up by the Jamisons to take the fall for the, well, fall of the little cathouse in Bradenton, but why close down such a lucrative operation?" Some things didn't just make sense to me.

Josef leaned in: "I seen this in Russia, in Yugoslavia, in my own country. Big man come in and set up shop to sell guns, drugs or putka. But not for long, because too many people find out about it and then bad things start happen, so they close down and go somewhere new start over and make money there."

Caleb was getting wound up: "So you think these guys just wanna shut down the cathouse and then build another one somewhere else, maybe Sarasota?"

"Sarasota's a little too uptight for that, and would attract unwanted attention. Better if they kept it in Bradenton, which is far enough from their clients' families in Sarasota, but not too far to drive for a nightcap." My hypothesis.

"But new drugs they give us to—how you say this?—dis-tri-bu-tion? They tell us we sell in this place here . . . in Sarasota."

Josef fumbled with his English, but we got the point: the little red pills were a new designer drug and they would be flight-tested right here in the Land of BigMoney.

The same little red pills that had me psycho-swimming with baby alligators and monsters for three and a half weeks up in Tampa.

That's not what bothered me.

Sarasota was about to lose her virginity to a septic varmint. And it was all by design. But who was ultimately behind it?

"Chervena treva," said Josef, trying to teach me how to inhale a Stella, Bulgarian style.

I tried it, opening my mouth full and tilting my head back completely, thus creating an open channel directly into my stomach. The key was to dry-swallow first to close the epiglottis and not choke to death.

On my first try, I choked to death.

After a minute of coughing, found my voice and said, "Meaning?"

He gently patted my back, and then used his fingers for each word, bouncing up and down as he said them: "Is means weed that is red."

"Redweed."

Dunno why, but it just hit me in the face. I'd recalled subliminal thoughts about it after Caleb and I had exploded the red algae-filled watermelons. Now it was here again. I'd always known that the Universe communicated to us in crazy ways, and that my subconscious was the receiver and transmitter on my behalf. What was the message about redweed? Explosive and dangerous? Sounded simplistic at first, but then it made sense. Question was, what could we possibly do about it?

When Boris and Josef had settled down for the night, Caleb and I sat on the balcony, watched the moon go up and down, and listened to the water gently massage the shore.

"Nothing you can do about it, Ranger," he said. "It's fate."

"So we just let them walk into an ambush?"

"Not really. They were already going to hell anyway, when they'd planned to take over GreaserPimp's function in Bradenton. That was a given. Jamisons woulda killed them soon after, moved the girls somewhere else, started up all over again. So there's nothing we can do for them."

"We could tell them what we know."

They weren't all that bad, only just a little. And they were funny about it, good to have around, socialize, drink like drunks, and chatter on 'til the wee hours of the morn. Besides, it was good to get the perspective on life from a career criminal like Boris. Made me think about stuff from another angle. Truth? These comic-book characters took my mind off Rachel. Distractions were important in life: they left you free to do stupid shit that didn't matter.

"Tommy, tell me something: do we really know who these guys are? I mean, look at things: I'm doing a little recon on them . . . they see us at the cathouse . . . later shoot the shit out of that gas station, just barely missing my melon . . . we raid their little paradise at Holiday Inn, truss 'em up like pigs . . . talk some sense into 'em, make 'em feel like we're all old buddies . . . then start hanging out like we're—"

"Yeah, it's surreal. And just plain stupid. If we told this story to anyone in specops, they'd laugh at us and you know it." All I could muster at the moment, but my mind raced for a solution. The inner kid in me, especially my intuition, told me that these Bulgarians were dangerous men, regardless of how funny and sociable they were with us.

And they were regular killers.

No getting around that sad fact.

Good times at the Bradenton cathouse the following night.

All doors were open, lights and music spilled out into the streets at the intersection. It was a relatively quiet section of east Bradenton, with few homes and more businesses, so no one was around to complain about a little noise. Or a whole lotta noise.

The parking lot was full of cars of all make and model, mostly brand-new pickups and suvs, some outta-town plates from Louisiana, Mississippi and Georgia, lonely old guys who'd heard about the big throw-down tonight.

A contact through the Jamisons had provided Boris and Josef with stolen plastic explosive, a mix of various types from civilian and military lots, all very generic and with a shady provenance. Blasting caps, too. And about a mile of det cord.

The crazy Bulgarians had surreptitiously wired the entire cathouse, even before we had met them, and were waiting for a certain designated date/time to blow it. Theoretically, if it all had detonated at once, it would've dropped those few city blocks of 3rd Avenue and 9th Street near Green Bridge into the bay and removed about an acre of real estate from the city of Bradenton.

The only problem with their plan was that they had been given hard-wired detonators, which meant they had to be tied to the whole scene at least for a few minutes while they set them off.

The Jamisons had parked six dark-colored panel vans just outside in the parking lot to bus the girls out of the cathouse. Drivers were standing by, engines running. No one paid them a second look, all that action going on inside, free drugs and free unlimited sexation.

Peter Jamison had been pacing in Felix Heydrich's office for more than an hour.

"If we introduce a new designer drug to the city of Sarasota, it will gain national attention almost immediately, sir." Jamison paced the floor of Heydrich's office.

Felix sat in the center of a wide, plush couch, arms stiff, hands on the cushions. "That's precisely the plan, Peter. We've been given this gift and the time to act is almost upon us. There is only one chance, and we will not miss it. I will not have failure."

"I don't understand why it has to be now, though. If we wait—"

"There will be no waiting! Our plans are drawn up by someone very powerful, Peter, someone about whom you know nothing. And it shall remain that way. Your anxiety is noted. It is my fault for not providing you more information about the grand plan, and that is all my doing. You have been very loyal and productive for many years, Peter."

Felix rose slowly, his hands trailing behind him.

"My wish was to keep you in the fold, train you for higher duty."

Long, slender fingers found the handle of the pistol, five

independent constrictors that locked the hand firmly into place.

"But your usefulness has run its course, I am sad to report."

Peter Jamison stopped pacing, stood in front of Felix's desk. "What are you telling me, Felix? I have been loyal to you, served you and that invisible Jesuit in Miami I know you talk to, the one who gives you direction. Yes, I know all about him, your overlord in the archdiocese. The Tico."

Felix moved in front of Jamison. "All the more reason, Peter. . . ."

Heydrich's hand slowly showed itself to Peter.

"Felix—"

A single .45-calibre bullet found its way into Jamison's chest, kicking him into the desk and dropping him to the tiled floor with a dull SMACK.

"My dear archbishop." Felix Heydrich was standing at the position of attention, his speaker phone on high volume.

"Brother Felix, you bring me much joy this evening."

"We have good news to report."

"Yes?" An expectant voice.

"Our grand release will commence tomorrow."

"And how is our child, dear brother Felix?"

"Sir, she is the most beautiful creation! Slight and soft as glass, magical in conjuring precious thoughts and desires, and as rich and deep a red as the archbishop's robe." Felix swelled with overflowing pride.

"And the other, uh, surprise you promised?"

"As soon as we clear up a small accounting issue in Bradenton parish, they will be on their way to meet you, dear archbishop. Traveling in a caravan of six."

Sharp intake of breath. Silence, then: "Behold, children are a heritage from the lord, the fruit of the womb a reward. Like arrows in the hand of a warrior are the children of one's youth. Blessed is the man who fills his quiver with them! He shall not be put to shame when he speaks with his enemies in the gate."

"Psalm 127, verses three to five." Heydrich melted into the man's words. . . .

"Our grand release will commence tomorrow."

"And how is our child, dear brother Felix?"

"Sir, she is the most beautiful creation! Slight and soft as glass, magical in conjuring precious thoughts and desires, and as rich and deep a red as the archbishop's robe."

"And the other, uh, surprise you promised?"

"As soon as we clear up a small accounting issue in Bradenton parish, they will be in their way to meet you, dear archbishop. Traveling in a caravan of six."

"Behold, children are a heritage from the lord, the fruit of the womb a reward. Like arrows in the hand of a warrior are the children of one's youth. Blessed is the man who fills his quiver with them! He shall not be put to shame when he speaks with his enemies in the gate."

"Psalm 127, verses three to five."

The unholy gospel filled the condo through the two speakers on the table, vibrated everything except the afternoon sky.

"Tommy, I dunno about you, but that man just scared the holy crap outta me."

"Yup." All I could muster, though I had evil thoughts on my twisted mind.

"Holy crap. Holy fuck. Moly fuckin' hoses. Now what?" Caleb was also overwhelmed by what we'd just heard on the recorder.

"Ticos have everything figured out. How the blazes do you fight an entire militant army of demons who run around dressed up all nice and pretty like Catholic schoolboys and hand out candy and party favors to all the gullibles?"

Citizens of northeast Bradenton were awakened Sunday morning by the Lord's wrath: a giant explosion and small earthquake that rocked an entire city block at the waterfront. Hundreds of people were caught in the inferno that, onlookers said, started in a small massage parlor and quickly spread to neighboring buildings and structures.

Screams and cries for help could be heard for a quarter-mile in all directions. First-responders and other rescue personnel could not reach the site until hours later, after firefighter crews had dumped thousands of gallons of water over the flames.

As time wore on in the early morning hours, no more screams could be heard and all cries for help fell to whimpers ... low whispers ... then only the cracking and popping sounds of the smoldering heap.

Reports over the next several weeks came in from Newtown of a new designer high-high making its rounds in the 'hood.

Little red pills they called redweed, a little something-somethin' to take you on a psychedelic trip to your preferred destination.

Local rags told of a pair of burly white men who cruised the 'hood, dispensing redweed free to all takers.

Those reports could not be confirmed at this time, and local law enforcement refused to comment. . . .

A few months ago, I thought I was happy. If happiness was a state of mind, then I was in the right state.

Even if it was a crumbling state of Florida.

Had a good-paying job as a gun for hire. A fun side-job as a taxi driver. And a girl named Rachel who loved me.

Or so I thought.

Somehow without even thinking, I ended up neck-deep inside an organization that ran drugs and humans into Tampa, and then on down to my town, Sarasota.

The more I stuck around and watched, listened, the more I learned. And the less I liked.

I hated to admit it, but it all scared me. And I hadn't been scared since I was a nine-year-old, cowering under my old man's iron fists.

Wasn't supposed to be this way. I should've been with Rachel all along. Taken care of her, seen to it she had a safe and comfortable home, a place to share with her man.

Thought that was me. It wasn't.

It wasn't SurferBoy, either, although she sampled him for a few months, then spat him out, too.

How was it supposed to be?

Didn't know anymore. My old friend Caleb fell into my life, helped me out here and there, saved my life more than once, and kept me on the moderately straight and narrow, helped me see that being a wreck wasn't so cool and that I didn't have to struggle all on my own. He'd found me a competent shrink who listened. Cared.

Still, I was in a world of shit and pain, and little to show for it, other than the shit and pain, plus four-plus million dollars that I'd probably never spend. My boss, Peter Jamison, was now likely spread out in bits and pieces over Sarasota Bay. His boss, Felix Heydrich, turned out to be quite the psychopath, as Caleb and I slowly figured out.

But he wasn't the ultimate boss.

Then there was the archbishop down south. Knowing what I knew of the Segreta Antico, the Ticos, he was far from being the boss. The more I uncovered, the more layers I peeled back, the worse it got, the more horrific the people were, although they were fewer as you got to the top. It's all a pyramid, this evil organization, a giant mass of redweed, not unlike the putrid spray that boomed out of those watermelons Caleb and I took apart one lazy afternoon weeks ago.

And just when I thought I was getting somewhere, exposing these assholes, more popped up in their place, and they were more evil than those on the lower stones of the pyramid. Kinda like those wannabe pimps who flooded in to replace the ones I sent to hell.

It's like all the new Hollywood movies these days: a darker *James Bond* . . . a darker *Spider Man* . . . a darker *Batman* . . . more and more good people getting sucked into the antiheroes . . . more vile and pathetic characters that nibbled at your soul, taking the last bit of humanity you had left.

That was the Tico way, and it dated back thousands of years.

Worse, they had made it my way, too, having me kill innocents, good people who did good things in the world. I was no better than the Ticos I despised.

Looked all around me and saw evil. No wonder I couldn't see Sarasota and its beauty for the paradise it was. Too caught up in all the truth I had learned and now held deep within me. How could you see beauty when you knew shit lurked all around it? Controlled it. Maintained it. All I saw was actually an illusion, a passion play of nefarious characters who could either kiss you sweetly or stab you in the face. Either way they had you.

In the end, I made a choice.

Regardless of the shit I knew about things, especially the Segreta Antico, I would make an effort to see the natural beauty around me, to experience it the best I could, and to share it with special people. Didn't mean I would ignore the nastiness I knew all too well and was learning more about every day.

It simply meant that I would put that shit in a deep hole, cover it with fresh dirt, add water and grow a few palm trees. Or maybe just sit down in front of an easel and paint something cool and mushy. Hadn't done that in ages.

Those things would have to wait for another day, hopefully soon.

That SAS khaki guy had been following me around for a few hours, as I walked around downtown Sarasota, over the Ringling Bridge all the way over to St. Armand's Circle three miles away. He hadn't tried to disguise himself in any way. Even smiled at me each time I turned around to check my six.

Took a right at Boulevard of the Presidents and jogged 500 yards near the last house on the right, took another hard right into the neighborhood, scaled an eight-foot-high estate wall. Wasn't sure what I was going to do so I just leaned against the wall and counted sheep, thought about Rachel, Caleb, Sara, and Christine, all the stupid things I'd done lately, the poor Jersey slob in the bar who didn't get to go home and see his wife and three kids.

The former SAS man did not disappoint: minutes later, he pulled himself up and over the wall, dropped to the ground and saw me.

I was now sitting on a few cinder blocks at the side of the house, chewing on a piece of grass. Don't recall exactly but I think I may have smiled. Wasn't a friendly one. Kinda like when a 400-pound bull shark opens its maw slightly and has that ugly grin stuffed with rows and rows of serrated knives, all freshly sharpened just for you, my dear.

Not hesitating a bit, he flexed those impressive brakes of his, came at me like he wanted to say heyhowareya, shake my hand, be my BFF, bestie and boo.

Whatever.

It didn't end with a handshake....

Shortly after I put Her Majesty's finest to rest, patched myself up and downed a double-barrel of Stellas. Took a long drive out in the sticks, mostly to get the hell away from the dead air I'd created in Sarasota, but also to feel Old Florida as I'd known it as a child: miserably hot and sticky wet, more mosquitoes than air molecules, and the biggest goddamn alligators outside of Jurassic Park.

Passed a small lake to my right, saw a stirring in the weeds just off the road. Stopped my TommyTaxi and walked around the front, pulling out a cigarette but not lighting it.

As I rounded the front bumper toward the passenger's side, I was greeted by a thunderous inhalation, followed by a deep throaty GRRRROWL!

Gave the growl a wide berth and walked farther ahead, wondering how long that fucker was. 'Bout fourteen feet, I guessed.

Inch by inch, it filled my field of view.

Something was oddly familiar about this one.

That broke-ass tail.

The beast seemed to regard me for a moment, flicked the tiny end of its tail, reminding me of his warning the last time we ran into each other, shortly after I'd run him over: "See you again, asshole."

The giant beast then lunged in one long movement that threw me off guard and made me spit out the cigarette.

Got that tail repaired, I see.

Stumbled over backward, landing on my ass but sitting upright, reached under my shirt, flashed my .45.

Aimed straight into an endless black hole that expanded with each passing millisecond.

Fucker swallowed six of my bullets and bellowed stink and thunder.

Coughed up a giant ball of redweed, remnants of its last murder. Then, like a fine Newtown-jungle pimp, went into a deep sleep.

For aye.

Pulled my carcass over to the side of the car, leaned against it. Looked over at the sleeping dinosaur, wondered how much the hide and meat would go for on the open market. Not nearly as much as one of Felix's Latino and Eastern Euro commodities.

Sat there for a coupla hours, dripping and sizzling like a

Thanksgiving turkey, donating beer-spiked blood and getting eaten alive by the bugs, and laughing at the absurdity of it all: somehow, I was still swimming in that SOCOM prison cell. . . .

TRAPHOUSE

"Goin' down, my ace boone coon?"

Bobby Rogers pulled up alongside his homeboy, DearChuckie, standing on the curb in front of Rogers' wooo-scary traphouse on Goodland Avenue in Newtown jungle.

DearChuckie reached in the passenger's window, dapped Rogers. "Something comin' in t'night, bossman. Real nervous 'round here, know I'm sayin'?"

A carbon-black, forty-pound low-rider pit bull, Ted Bundy, hunkered beside his supreme master DearChuckie, and foamed at the jaws. Even in the throes of deep sleep, Ted Bundy was veritable pissed-off thunder.

Rogers laughed, stuck his arm out the window, petted the dog, pulled his ears affectionately. It stopped growling a moment and licked the big man's hand and fingers, highly tuned gustatory receptors sensing the next best thing to garden-fresh Grade-A sirloin.

Rogers then stuck his head outside the window to get a face-lick from the animal.

In a vicious blur:

Ted Bundy lunged from the sidewalk, full body . . .

Snapped its massive jaws like a twelve-foot gator . . .

Just as Rogers jerked his head back inside the vehicle.

"Fuuuck!" Bobby Rogers leaped out from his old hammered Ford truck, threw himself over the hood, grabbed a shocked Ted Bundy by the lower collar, and cartoon-hammered the beast with a massive fist, killer shots to the head and body.

"Ohhhhhh, shiiiiiiit!" DearChuckie spun around and ran for the traphouse, not bothering to look back at the afternoon combat between his bossman and the best fighting dog he'd ever trained.

Long loud whines from the animal as it took blow after devastating blow from Rogers, who ripped off forty hammers in ten seconds, sending Ted Bundy and his dying thunder into spastic convulsions that soon gave way to a forty-pound sack of highway pizza and a farewell whimper.

The big man took both hands, wrapped his sausage fingers around two Dumbo-sized ears, and flung the bloody carcass across the street, scattering a hive of juvenile delinquents who screamed and shrieked and didn't stop running until they'd reached their mamas a hundred yards down the ghetto block.

Big man leaned up against the hood of his truck, said, "Hey, yo! Gimme a cigarette!" Rogers looked up at DearChuckie, standing at the left entrance to the duplex traphouse, his body shivering, head dropped to his chest, shaking, crying and mourning the loss of his beloved Ted Bundy, now fresh roadkill in the middle of Newtown jungle.

The beauty of Sarasota: evil lurking in tall towers . . . crime on the upswing . . . BigMoney fueling it all . . . Segreta Antico providing deep background cover . . . and I wanted to kill the demon-loving bastards.

Weeks had passed since we'd last seen the Bulgarians. Like an evil mist, they slipped in and out of Newtown jungle, Sarasota's blighted northern territory, and like that mist, left behind a thin acidic film of redweed destruction and loss across the entire area, infecting young and old alike with the new designer drug.

Traphouses had sprung up all over to keep up with the increasing demand for the unusual psychedelic buzz that lasted days on a single pill. The nation's opioid crisis was small news compared to redweed.

Law enforcement was at a total loss for how to handle new crimes. Sarasota County Sheriff Bill Kershaw was holed up in his air-conditioned office, not taking any calls. Hospitals were inundated with hundreds of new cases of a mysterious illness. Employers across the two counties, Manatee and Sarasota, complained of massive worker walk-outs that lasted days. The local economy was in shambles.

Caleb and I lay low for the time being, in the aftermath of Peter Jamison's murder by Felix Heydrich who, we assumed, was now our new boss. Reluctantly, we were climbing the ladder of success in a shady industry. The closer we got to the top, the hotter the flames.

"Maybe we should send him a Dean&Deluca fruit basket." I was sunning myself by the pool of my new digs on Bird Key, courtesy of Donny and the Jamisons.

Caleb had just pulled up from a brief errand and joined me outside. "Wait to be summoned."

"Sounds fine to me. This vacation lifestyle suits me well. Besides, North Longboat was growing moldy."

"BigMoney festering in its own juices." Caleb refilled the cooler with cases of Stella and Peroni.

"I was gonna say that," I said, taking a six and sinking it into the therapeutic ice bath next to my chair. "Stellabration time." Downed a double-barrel in thirteen seconds, a new world record.

Caleb looked over, smiled. "Let's let Heydrich do what Heydrich's gonna do, and we'll do what we're gonna do."

"You sound like a small-time lawyer." Loved the burn as the two beers scorched my throat going down.

"I was hoping he'd let us continue our little R&D project with his group."

I laughed. "Research and development or rust and dust?"

Caleb opened the newspaper. "Looks like Newtown's heating up."

That got my attention. "New drugs? Bulgarian philanthropy?"

"Little bit of both: says here they're fighting an outbreak of a new designer drug, redweed. You recall that one, yeah?"

Smiled at that, thinking back on my three and half weeks in SOCOM's prison. "After the Civil War, towns called Newtown sprung up all over the US, the promise of a new beginning."

Caleb looked over at me. "What are you talkin'? I'm trying to educate you here, and you're giving me a bum history lesson."

"Really. In Boston, like all the other cities and towns, Newtown turned into a ghetto, lots of crime, mostly drugs and prostitution."

He nodded politely, not really giving a damn. "Must be the Jesuit-fueled Irish."

"Cool thing, though, in Boston's Newtown, someone got the idea to change the name. Soon as they did, money and investments poured in, the place changed overnight."

"The new name?"

"Cambridge."

"As in MIT, Harvard, et cetera?"

"Yuuup."

"So you're proposing a name change for Sarasota's Newtown? Redweed City?" Caleb rubbed some sunblock on his nose. "I'd like to see that place renovated."

"Maybe I should spend some of that four mil on a private project—urban renewal of Newtown."

Looked over at me: "First, I want to kill those Bulgarians."

"Awww, and here I thought you and Boris were an item back in the day." A few more articles caught his attention. "People are losing faith in law enforcement. Guys killing innocents and no one's there to protect."

"Some crazy dudes shoot up Chicago, Washington Navy Yard, LAX and a dozen other places, and the government wants us to believe it was the work of lone gunmen. What crap. That's no different from all the other false-flag attacks by those idiots at the Tico-owned CIA."

"Don't talk too loud. Someone's always listening," Caleb reminded me.

"Don't even think it."

"What?"

"Felix Heydrich spying on us."

"You don't need to worry about him." His signature smile in full bloom.

"You're about to tell me something important and I'm sitting up straight, giving you my full attention." I sat up, turned to him. "Now you can start."

"Felix pulled his operations out of Sarasota, moved everything up to Tampa."

I wasn't sure whether to clock him or kiss him. "You know this how?"

He pulled out a greeting card, read it. "Gentlemen, I hope this missive finds you well. Please note we have moved our operations to Tampa, and will call on you shortly. All the best, Felix."

"Where the—"

"Check your mail once in a while," Caleb said. "We're still on his leash."

Took the card from Caleb, read it again, "Felix is playing both sides of this drag race, we already know that. He plays both sides of everything, because he has the cash and the resources and the connections to increase his wealth and power. It's the only thing that makes sense. He keeps it all heated up to just below boiling, so the players never stop moving, never feel comfortable, and when he needs to tilt the odds to one side, he adds a little bit of energy here and there and conjures up the outcome he wants. It's all so jesuitical."

"That's the way it is in almost every town, but no one knows about that hidden hand," he added.

I took a look at the envelope. It was addressed to me at the house on Bird Key. Why would a guy who hires killers to do his shit work send me a cheesy greeting card?

"He knows where we are. Likes to rub it in, in his own elegant, stylish way."

"Hell, C-man, he's known all along."

"Time to move on?"

"Where?"

"Maybe the Keys. There's this little place I used to rent down on Islamorada."

"He knows about that one, too, 'sides last hurricane destroyed the whole vibe," I reminded him.

"The bitch court-cool?" Rogers stood towering over DearChuckie, grinding him down to powder.

"C'mon, BigB, you know me like that. She street-cool, fresh out mama's oven."

"Here's a reminder, Chuckie: court-cool is eighteen and over, all legal. Street-cool is twelve and over. Don't be bringin' the street kids up in my traphouse, boy. I'll sculpt you a new jawline with a butter knife."

Skulking off, DearChuckie looked back at his bossman, nodded his head.

"Medic!" Rogers yelled to his top-ho and the traphouse's in-house doctor, NickyHeil. "Heil Hitler, bitch, where you been?"

NickyHeil slapped his arm. "Chuckie tried to bring in two girls last night, kept them both in his back room. I found them this morning, walked them both to the recreation center."

"I'ma kill that Chuckie. Homeboy just don't learn. Whaddup with the red, baby?"

She pulled out her notebook: "We have four, two-gallon bags of redweed pills left."

"Thousand reds left? That all?"

"Til Boris says otherwise."

"Where is that boy? He and Josef been gone too long. You call 'em?"

"Five times a day. No answer. Not even voicemail anymore. Their mailbox is full."

"How much earn we got from those two bags?"

"Thousand pills, $20 each, minus dealer cuts, expenses . . . $18,000 and change."

"Chargin' us how much a pill?"

"Boris said initially they would charge us $5 each." Rogers went ballistic, picked up the couch, threw it against the wall. The bas-relief installation gave the place a new look and feel.

NickyHeil said, "Correction: $18,000, minus one new couch and some Chinese drywall."

"Bitch, this my house. I wanna decorate it postmodern urban-edge Cubano, I do it."

"Yessir, bossman, and I'm the general manager, accountant, medic and—"

"My top-ho!"

As NickyHeil walked out the front door, she punched him in the stomach and he slapped her on that fine ass.

"Oooo! More like that, girl, I make you one of my soldiers!"

Rogers did a walk-through of the entire premises, waking up junkies who'd overstayed their welcome.

Looked down at one man, lying on the floor in a back bedroom. "Hey, blueface! Get the fuck outta my house!" Rogers kicked the man in the groin, then realized he was twenty-four hours deep into rigor.

Flipped open his cell phone, speed-dialed his traphouse medic. "NickyHeil, straight up: got a blueface on the floor here. Been gone twenty-four maybe. Get his ass gone from my place now."

When Rogers turned back to face the corpse, he bent down and sacked all the man's pockets and his bag, pulled out a nice lighter, some chewing gum, a small writing notebook. Stood up, popped in two sticks of gum, smacked loudly, leafed through the book. His eyes widened as he read the dead man's account of his time at the traphouse.

Word by word, line by line, it resembled a report he once saw on a man's desk . . . a police report on him as a juvenile, a laundry list of infractions that stretched two full pages.

"What the—who the fuck are you, man?" Rogers kicked the dead man's frozen blue face.

"If we're gonna dig deeper into Felix and his spreading business, we need to get tapped into the Newtown pulse, 'cos that's the proving ground for Felix's product. If it takes off there, he'll flood Sarasota." I pulled our gear together for a midnight op to Sarasota's northern territory.

"Already there."

"'Splain that one."

"Got an inside man."

"Where?"

"Been stationed inside this traphouse for weeks."

"How'd you find him?"

"Ex-cop."

"He have good intel?"

"So far, this redweed is being distro'd from the traphouse he's been shacking in. Guy they call Bobby Rogers, BigB, Bossman, whatever, runs the joint. He and his girl, NickyHeil something."

"And you've know this for how long and didn't tell me?"

Turned to face me. "Listen up, Tommy: I had a life long before I signed on with you."

Kept packing things into a small ruck, turned around. "Got it. Thing is, when you have intel that affects me and my business, I'd like to hear it, and not yesterday. You got that?"

"Point made. Will do. Now, you wanna hear more about this guy or not?"

No comment.

"He's an expert on redweed but been on the stuff for about a month, last he told me."

"Woh, wait a sec. Your man is hopped up on redweed and feeding you intel?"

"Don't worry, he's got it covered," he said as we walked out to the truck.

"Get that fuckin' cop outta my booty-Q now!" Rogers likened his operation to a fashionable *boutique*, a word he twisted to fit his own image.

The body of former police Sergeant Clarence Johnny Jones was dragged from the room where he overdosed, unceremoniously thrown onto a stack of wood and trash, and set afire. It burned throughout the day and into the next evening, occasionally sending a sweet aroma into the neighborhood air as the remains of Johnny melted ... evaporated ... and disappeared over tony Sarasota across the tracks.

Bobby Rogers was on fire, too. He'd gathered everyone at the traphouse into the large living room, sat them down on the old wooden floor, looked around at his little army of dealers, lieutenants, soldiers, homeboys and hos.

"This my house, you muthafuckas!" Beat his massive chest like a gorilla. "Nothin' gets done in my house 'less I say so! No one come in my house 'less I word that man, that girl. You muthafuckas don't do shit 'less BigB check the block. None a you fools got authority here."

NickyHeil bristled at that statement, said nothing, just stared at the dirty floor in front of her.

"Last night, gotta blueface on the floor, back bedroom, OD on my ass. He now a firestarter in the backyard. And none a y'all sayin' shit about it. Not ever!"

A few people mumbled, "Church" and "Word." The others squirmed on their asses on the floor, their eyes glued to the man BigB.

"Tonight, we gonna flood this town with the red! Y'all gonna go forth and fuckin' conquer, you hear me, you muthafuckas!?"

The room erupted in loud cheers, screams and fist-pumps into the sweet, damp air.

Rogers cleared the room after handing out assignments to his crew. To NickyHeil: "Bitch, we gotta find out who his contact is."

"TonyZ was a cop, huh? How am I supposed to find—"

Rogers had never slapped or punched his girl.

SLAP!

She backed away slowly, stunned by the blow and the fact her old man had hit her. Other men did it to their girls, but Bobby never had. He'd been good to her, respected her intelligence and managerial and medical skills.

But now.

Her only thought: *Ohhh, Bobby Rogers, what have you done?*

We cruised past 3636 Goodland Avenue, a run-down, bone-thin duplex with broken front doors, ripped screening, and multi-color exterior paint. A rotten Easter egg in the 'hood.

"This the place?" I was holding my nose, hoping my shots were up to date.

"Yeah. Not much to look at but it does some pretty business, even out of season." Caleb pulled up past the house half a block ahead, parked in front of an abandoned factory.

"Now you're gonna tell me your man wired A/V in the place."

"No. They would've found it. No place to put anything in a house like that, 'cos they've got no décor to speak of, except shitty old couches and mattresses on the floor. No lighting, no paintings on the wall. Most of the drywall's been punched through, so the place looks like a skeleton. Their soldiers go through it once a day, usually in the morning, and sweep for bugs. And I don't mean cockroaches, which are always welcome, something to snack on after a bender."

"They're more sophisticated than I thought."

"Hey, man, these guys might look dumb, they might not dress for success, but they're sure as shit tough as nails and they've got the latest in spy-tech and are funded by guys high up like Felix, so do not underestimate them."

"How does your guy get the intel to you?"

"Takes a walk coupla times a day, drops notes in a yard down the street. That's where we're headed next." He got out, started walking down Goodland Avenue.

And I eagerly followed.

Down near King, Caleb stopped short of a ratty unkempt yard. The chain-link fence had been flattened a hundred times by cars and trucks rolling over it. It was now a chain-link-fence walkway that led up to the abandoned house.

As we approached a door on the left side of the house, a dark presence diffused from the shadows, stopped.

Caleb whipped out a pistol. "Hands where I can see 'em," he told the big man.

"You be TonyZ's bossman," Bobby Rogers said, a huge gold-toothed smile greeting us. "Careful where you point that thing, white boy. This the 'hood all them nasty hurricanes come from."

At first, Caleb and I didn't say anything. The atmosphere felt off for some reason, although I had no idea what normal may have been for these parts.

"Boys pro'ly wonderin' who I be."

"Not really." Caleb was making friends fast. As usual. "Keep your hands where I can see 'em."

"Just want a cig, man. Okay w'choo?" Rogers didn't wait for a reply, reached inside his two-foot-deep cargo pocket, pulled out a pack of Camel raw, pitched out exactly one cigarette from the pack, popped it in his mouth, lit it with an invisible lighter.

How'd he do that?

"Okay, bossman, you lookin' for someone, eh?" Rogers loosed a cloud of blue-gray smoke in Caleb's direction, and gave me a sideways look of recognition.

In the still misery of the day, the cloud remained motionless, a barrier between us. Reminded me of the frozen air between Rachel and me.

"What makes you think—" Caleb started.

"Man, you white boys think we all obtuse and shit. Hurricane o' hate runnin' in your veins. Well, we ain't stupid like you thinks we is. Got no high-rise condo on Longboat or the Point, all those richies live. Got no house on Bird Key. Got no country-club membership. Nope."

He took a small step forward in Caleb's direction, licked his lips sideways like a gangsta-rapper. "But what we got is your attention, bleach-white. We got your eyes and ears on us 'cos we Cubanos and chicofros make you pilgrims nervous, so you keep them eyes and ears open at night, waitin' for some jungle demon to come round your place, steal your fine-ass daughters, rape your bitches, turn your sons into our little homeys, workin' the streets for five Benjamin a day. Shit, dude, tha's pro'ly more'n you make in a nine-to-five, huh?" His was a fine belly laugh, indeed.

"Tommy, you need a copy of *The Winchester Confessions* just to understand this punk." Caleb wasn't nervous, he was hot under the sun, pissed off that we had to leave the 68-degree a/c of the truck, pissed off at me because I wasn't reading his mind at the moment and dropping this smack-rap with a bullet to his fat head.

Rogers and I comically exchanged a glance, like, what the hell did that mean, *Winchester Confessions*?

"This boy TonyZ. He your man, cop." Rogers tossed a small notebook at Caleb, hit him in the chest with it.

"We're not cops," I said, pulling out a Newport Menthol, holding it a sec.

"Listen up, you fat brown ass, one way or the other, you're gonna give me answers or I'm shoving a stick very far up your migrant ass."

"Ah, dude, no need to get all racial on me."

"That ain't racial, asshole. It's called *color analysis*."

"Them's fightin' words, old man. Go straight to jail for that shit; forget GO." Rogers laughed so hard his belly shook. But deep underneath his butterjacket, heavy, solid muscle that did serious damage.

"Since you're not from my country, asshole, I'll learn ya a little: what I just said is protected under my First Amendment rights in my US *Constitution*."

Rogers got serious, lowered his grizzly-sized head, then aimed it at Caleb's face, fangs and all: "My turn now, old man." Small smile grew on his face. "Nineteen forty-two ... the Supreme Court of your country ruled in *Chaplinsky vs. New Hampshire* that fightin' words were not protected by your First Amendment." Rogers' smile split into a hundred harmonics of another hearty laugh.

Caleb was speechless.

Rogers had been watching me out of his right eye, which was yawed a few degrees outward.

Disconcerting to some. Not to me. This dude was a comic book.

He stuck out his oaken arm, offered me a light. I took it. Could hear Caleb now: "Ranger, what the fuck are you doing, messin' with my game plan?"

If this had been an actual conversation, I would've said, "What you should be doing, C-man: not antagonizing the very man who has intel we need. And since he knows the First Amendment better than you, maybe you should shut your hole and back down. That should be your only play in your one-page game book."

Wasn't that way, though.

Inhaled again and blew my own cloud . . . aimed it above the bushes, the trees, watched it ascend into the deadlight of the sky, all washed out from too much sunshine and scattered light-gray clouds that promised a cleansing rain but didn't step up. Held out my hand. "I'm Tommy. This is my pal George Washington, uh, I mean, Caleb."

Caleb flinched when I went off-map, introduced us like we were meeting old buddies at cocktail hour. My eyes weren't directly on him, but my guess is, he dropped a load in his pants. I could smell the pre-shit vapors.

Rogers could, too. He casually walked forward, shook my hand. From his looks, I would've guessed he could have crushed my hand. But he didn't.

It was a soft touch. Firm, but soft. And it surprised me, like Boris had after we'd spent some time drinking and unwinding. Something told me this man Bobby Rogers wasn't such a bad guy, but Caleb would never believe that one.

"Tell me something, Rogers," Caleb said. "What makes you think this man TonyZ is my guy?"

" 'Cos you askin' about him." Rogers lit up another cigarette, offered me one of his this time.

"Man, you need to measure off them Newports. Only get like three puffs off them things. Plus them filters poisonous, man."

"Measure off." Caleb looked over at me, smirked in Rogers' confirmation of the three-drag rule about Newports. "That a fancy way of saying quit, asshole?"

"Somethin' like that." Rogers fired up my Camel.

227

I inhaled sharply and deeply, threw myself over and coughed.

Rogers almost fell backward shaking his belly, laughing. "See, man, you gonna smoke, may as well be these expensive muthafuckas, not them little hollow twigs you got. Man, may as well smoke a straw."

Didn't know how to respond to that one, so I just laughed along and kept inhaling. Damn, this stuff was good. Went right to my brain. All the anxiety I felt before? Now gone. Caleb probably thought I was a traitor to the cause, smoking it up while he held a gun at Rogers, although now lowered toward the ground at big man's toes.

"All I sayin' is this, white rice: your man dead." He blew a series of smoke rings into the sky. From below, they resembled those silvery rings you blow underwater on scuba. Rogers' moving artwork climbed up into the air, getting wider and wider, like they'd all come together and swallow a cloud.

Caleb's gun came up to meet Rogers' face. "If you did this—"

"Hold on, man. I ain't done shit to your man. He die on my floor yesterday. OD from some primo psycho-tea. Redweed."

Could see Caleb's heart sink, his finger tighten around the trigger ever so slightly.

I asked, "Where is he now?"

"Ashes to ashes, dust to dust," the big man said, solemn like it was a funeral.

Caleb started to pull back on the trigger.

"Eh, yo, hold on now!" Rogers put his big paws in the air, bent an arm to pull the cig to his mouth, drag on it, then both arms back to the sky in Leonardo's Vetruvian Man. "We do things different up in Newtown, man. Dude die on me in my own house. Don't know shit about the man, so we get rid of the body. Dude dead so who give a shit anyway?"

"His wife and two little girls." Caleb shot Rogers in the left ear, tearing a hole right through it and leaving just enough behind.

"Awwww! Shit, man! You shot me, muthafucka!" Rogers held his ear with both hands, and for a moment dropped one to drag hard on that Camel. "Stupid muthafucka." His head was bent over, bleeding, and he looked over at Caleb, said some unintelligible things. He then stood up high and straight: "What part of your *Constitution* give you the right to shoot me?"

"Somewhere after where it says the right to bear arms, asshole."
Without further word, Caleb walked away from the mess, leaving
me behind.

"You got some fucked up friend there, man." Handed him my
bandana. He held it to his holey ear.

"That man you burned, regardless of how he came to be in your
house, was someone special to my friend. You should know that."
Turned to walk away, looked back. "Thanks for the cigarette, big
man."

Bobby Rogers thrust his chin up in a small motion, an
acknowledgment, small golden smile on his chico-brown face.

He was already sucking down a six of Stella. A six year old in
time-out.

Didn't acknowledge me when I walked in, sat down next to him.

"We're either on the same frequency . . . or we're not, Tommy." He
was staring out over a very big ocean.

Left me nowhere to go. "You know me, Gatewood, I like to
channel-hop, see what's up on other freq's, so stop whining and
relax." Clinked my bottle against his.

He didn't say anything at first, then: "All right, I see your point
with this guy, but he murdered a good friend of mine. And I can't let
that one go."

"Rogers didn't murder anyone and you know it, otherwise you'd
have already killed him. I'm really sorry for your loss, C-man, but
Jones OD'd in his house. Somehow, he got lost on the dark side,
couldn't find his way back. You know this."

"That's just second-hand smoke from a piece of fuckin' shit."
Caleb absently fingered Jones' little notebook Rogers had thrown at
him, ignored all the circumstantial evidence.

Didn't matter what I said now, 'cos Caleb was off on his own
mission. "Look, Tommy, you need to be on-map with me. We got
some fresh produce to skin up in Newtown and I need your A-game
buzzin' 24/7."

Set my beer on the little table between us, reminding myself not
to get in his face like last time and get slapped like a bad horse. "I

ain't your sous chef, C-man."

He wasn't listening.

"A teeny little reminder is indicated here: this was all my gig long before you came into the picture, so get off that high horse of yours and let's get back to work. Last thing we need is a spousal disagreement over a northern-territory taco bender. We need this guy."

Didn't budge a centimeter, so I left the house, took a long walk.

It'd been a long time since I'd had a fare, driven my tangerine TommyTaxi anywhere cool. I've never been one to question what I do, how I do it. Just go with the flow and let my subconscious sort it out. This current flow shoved me in the seat, ignited the motor, and ripped off three miles up the north Trail before I knew where the heck I was.

And then I was there: 3636 Goodland Avenue pulled me along some magnetic levitation track all the way to the traphouse. Hell, I didn't even have to burn any gas.

"You the man tore up Tyreese." Bobby Rogers dragged hard on his Camel. "Uh-huh, I knew it was you. Got that alien predator chemistry goin', don'tcha? Yeah, it was you." Pointed one huge finger at me.

"I'm here for Sergeant Jones' ashes," I said to him, standing at the right-hand door to his duplex traphouse.

Wuuut a flippin' dump.

"Man, whatever swag that flame didn't smoke is all shit-mixed with everything you 'magine."

"I want some ashes." My expression didn't change.

He motioned me to go around the side of the house. Didn't want me to see his elegant digs. Walked through six-foot-high elephant grass, bumped hard into the front fender of an old Lincoln Town Car. "Shit."

Found my way to the backyard, not at all prepared for the sight. What had obviously been a bonfire was now a four-foot-tall by ten-foot wide diameter of smoldering detritus. Smelled like the rectal terminus of a ruined zoo. They must've burned a lotta bodies back here over the weeks and months. A few ivory-white bones peeked out from the mound, and I was tempted to investigate but thought better of it. An infinity of bones in the middle of a ghetto, right next door to sweet Princess Sarasota.

"See what I mean now, TommyBoy?" Rogers and that laugh of his.

Almost threw up. Held it in long enough to scoop some of the ash into a paper bag I'd brought with me. No one except Bobby Rogers and I would ever know about this.

"This where we buried Tyreese after you smoked him. The parts you left."

Turned to him. "Thanks. Someone will appreciate this." Held Sergeant Jones's ashes as close to my heart as I could.

He didn't speak. Lotta class in his silence.

Still wasn't ready for home so I cruised around, wound up farther north at this cool little bar on Holmes Beach, Skinny's Place. No one outside, decided to sit and watch the tourons drive by, gaping at the sand-floored Old Florida bar, wondering if it was safe to go inside. Glad the place frightened those Canucks, Buckeyes and Hoosiers, and was grateful that Lewis and Clark were long gone. Finally, I would have some peace and calm in one of my haunts.

"Fuck you, Tommy."

She was right behind me, poking me on the shoulder. Felt her hot, shimmering electric field even before she spoke.

Lifted my leg outta the well of the park bench, swung around and stood before her. Rachel.

"What, you're mute now?" She ran a hand through my hair, held my cheek a sec.

"No, no, just . . . surprised to see you here."

"You never called me for lunch." Sat down across from me.

This was no coincidence. I didn't do coincidences. "We don't do lunch, Rach."

Her face: the most imperceptible twitch, but I caught it, filed it away. "Okay, so we don't do lunch. Then there's breakfast . . . or dinner . . . or. . . ." She tried to pull off an impish grin. Didn't work.

"Sorry I didn't call."

She laughed. "Got some nice jobs, do you?"

"Same old stuff."

"Killing people?" Forced laugh now.

Something was so off here. What was it? Hell, I was still unsettled over the odd atmosphere at that house where we first met Bobby Rogers. Maybe I was just seeing things where there was only a painful vacuum.

But I didn't normally just see things. I sensed things for a reason. When I felt something, it was because something was there to see, to feel.

"You don't seem yourself." Reached for her hand.

She pulled back, crossed her arms. "I'm fine. What do you mean?"

I know you, Rach. "Nothing." Looked at my imaginary watch. "Hey, gotta go, Rach. Been good seeing you."

Before she could say anything else, I was shifting into second gear in TommyTaxi, heading back to Sarasota, more edgy than ever.

Now I saw Rachel through a different lens: a withered abstract in a desaturated color palette. The thought was as nauseating as the dead ashes in Rogers' midden heap.

"I can't do this." Soon as she was forced down by a hidden hand behind her, she squirmed in her chair, clearly not used to be on the receiving end of an interrogation.

"You can. And you shall." Felix Heydrich sat in the center of the couch, his hands out at his sides on the rich leather, stroking it imperceptibly, his secret lover.

"You can't make me do this. I don't care how powerful you are." The more frightened she became, the more she melted into the chair.

Leaned forward, looked deep into her. "I can . . . and I shall."

"The only thing you can do is hurt me and my family." Fear gave way to false bravado.

"Isn't that enough?" Sat back again, fingering the soft calf leather.

"Didn't think you'd be coming back, Tommy," Sara said, clearly relieved to see me.

"I'm sorry. Been out of sorts lately." Let me show you my laundry list of things that ail me, Sara.

"That's okay. Tell me how things have been going." She looked uncomfortable, a forced smile.

That in itself made me feel uncomfortable, too. I came here to feel safe, get healed in some way. She was off and it was obvious. To me.

"Saw Rachel again."

Not much of a response from her.

Looked around the office: a few little things weren't put away in their proper spaces. The carpet had a small coffee stain on it. Her shirt was wrinkled, not the usual crisp, starched button-down she wore to look strong and impressive in a softened manly kinda way. Then she blurted it out, like she'd forgotten to ask me soon as I popped in the door: "What kind of work are you doing now, Tommy?"

"Huh?"

Embarrassed, she backpedaled: "I mean, driving your taxi around? Anything fun?"

Spying on this drug dealer and his crew up in Newtown. "Just the usual. Couple of fares a day, sit around and drink beer, take long drives around town. Nothing much." Lies and damned lies.

"How'd you run into Rachel?"

I didn't say I'd run into Rachel. I said I saw her again. "We met at one of our favorite haunts on Holmes Beach. Had a short chat. Nothing much to report. She looked great." That was a lie. She was as confused as you are now, Sara, and it made me wonder—

"So you're working more, huh?"

"Yeah, yeah. Little here and there. This depression sucks. I almost wish I were somewhere else now."

"Where else would you be?"

"I dunno. Maybe a place where the only news is the cool weather."

She tried to smile at that. Just couldn't quite recruit the minimum 12 muscles, though. "Homesick for a place you've never visited maybe?"

Didn't know what to say.

"Do you feel like you're gaining some ground, finding your feet?" On the edge of her chair.

I feel like I'm losing ground every step of the way. In the wars I fight, you never really win anything except the dubious right to fight another day. "All the time." What a lie.

She sat back a little, disappointed. "Well, that's great to hear, Tommy. I'm happy for you."

Tell me again how much I was paying for this?

Maybe I hadn't lied to Sara: had two last-minute fares this morning, both to SRQ, easy in and out, good tips.

Beer money.

Picked up a few cases of Peroni and headed back to the house. Once I stepped inside, I knew things would never be the same between Caleb and me.

"You've turned the place into a war room," I said, carrying the beer to the dedicated reefer in the oversized kitchen, filling it bottle by bottle, taking in the prep of combat, the art of war.

"This asshole's going to hell for what he did." He didn't stop moving, scribbling down notes on the dry-erase board, taping up Post-Its, rearranging pictures and little maps.

For just a moment, I wondered where the hell I was.

Then I snapped out of it for a moment, recalled that I was the one who was nutso with anxiety-depressive disorder, among things I had yet to discover.

And Caleb was the normal one.

Uh-huh.

That's what I stacattoed silently to myself 20 times, over and over 'til it eventually became the truth.

Without looking at me, he said, "I already know what you're gonna say, and the fact is, Bobby Rogers supplied the redweed to my friend." That's when he faced me directly. Even though there was 13 feet of space between us, he was right in my face. "I knew Jones was an addict from the start. That's what made him the perfect candidate for the job. He could blend in, become a user, snoop around, see under the hood."

"Why'd you make a big deal of Rogers being the bad guy the other day at the drop house?"

"Rogers needs to think I'm the asshole here, Tommy. He likes you or, in the least, wants to show me he likes you."

"Gave me a light and ignored you that day." I tried to play dumb.

"Exactly. He already sees a brother in you, 'cos you're schooled and calm and even keel to him. All the things he wishes he were."

If only they knew. . . .

"I agree with you, Tommy, he's not a bad guy. He's got a heart and I saw that. The more I stepped on him, the more he hated me, and that's the way I want it from here on. He knows we're both trying to find answers to Jones' death, maybe dig deeper into things, in general. I really think he wants out."

"Of the traphouse deal?"

"The entire operation."

"Felix wouldn't let that happen. He'd murder him the second he got wind."

"Even though he probably doesn't know exactly who pulls his strings, Rogers does know someone out there does."

"And you wanna do what?"

Looked at me dead on. "We turn Rogers."

All quiet at the traphouse: Bobby Rogers did his nightly walkthrough, kicking aside stray legs and arms, clearing his way to the back bedrooms, looking for another snitch.

"BigB, we all good here. Just thuggin' and all, y'know." Dear Chuckie whispered, nervous and flinching.

"Why you sweet-talkin' me, Chuckie?"

"No sweets, big man. Just layin' the news. Got the shipment in, high noon today."

Rogers perked up. "Redweed."

"You know it, bossman."

"How much?" Rogers was all ears.

DearChuckie fidgeted, lowered his head. "NickyHeil say cuppa thou."

"Two thousand pills is all?"

Nod from DearChuckie.

Rogers swung around, put his big fist through a wall. "Fuckin' Russian mutha—"

A voice behind him: "Bobby, you need to do something about these guys." NickyHeil stood akimbo, holding on to the two gallon-size ziplocks.

Big man made a move to slap his girl again, thought better of it.

He already messed up hitting her the first time.

She didn't budge. Held out the two bags of redweed. "You have to find them, Bobby. Take whatever business they have for yourself. They're diming you down to nothing. Pretty soon they'll be in here taking over your whole business. You've got to do something. We can't last another month with this piecemeal inventory."

The old couch was still embedded in the front room wall, broken in two and jammed between several rotting studs. Rogers cocked his big head sideways, aimed his good eye on it, studied it like it was something to figure out. His favorite couch from childhood, from his mother's old home, been everywhere with him, ending up as a permanent wall fixture in a dilapidated house of strung-out losers, illegal pharmaceuticals and sexual horrors.

He closed his eyes, turned and walked outside, lit up a smoke, imagined what it would be like to blow a 200-mile-an-hour smoke ring into a building. He'd heard about vapor bombs on some sci-fi tv show, wondered if it could work. Even if they were true, he couldn't afford it, not with only 2,000 redweed pills to distribute.

The thought brought him back to reality: the ratty porch of a shit house in a shit 'hood, surrounded by shit people. This is where he would die. Some voice inside him told him so. Did it all the time lately, it seemed.

More smoke rings into the dead-hot Florida sky. Dreams lost into the invisible future he knew he would never see . . . confirmed in stone by the sins of an inescapable past.

Over the next two weeks, while Caleb did his research and surveillance on Bobby Rogers, I tore apart my new Bird Key digs, top to bottom, and started afresh. Last thing I wanted to breath in my new home was the Jamison's sloughed-off skin cells and mouth exhaust from the walls, floors, ceilings, a/c and vent system. When I said I gutted the fucker, that's what I meant. With the help of a contractor friend and his sons, we tore the place down to studs and nails, concrete flooring, copper wires and pipes.

At the end of week two, I'd dismissed the crew for the weekend and sat back in my skeleton house. Nice breezes off the water. Almost wanted to leave it this way, but I'm sure the neighbors would've said something about it: "Mr. Darlington, we realize you're Old Florida white-trash cracker and all, but would you please do something about that shack of yours?"

Were my paranoid, insecure thoughts already starting to infect the new place?

Saturday morning: doorbell rang six times. Only the UPS guy rings six times on a Saturday morning at nine a.m.

The UPS guy.

The package was addressed to me, no return address. Opened it and pulled out an envelope with another card inside. Thought the last one from Felix was over the top, but this—

"Welcome to your new home, Mr. Darlington. Please call on me for anything you wish. —Felix Heydrich."

Neither time nor distance seemed to separate me from this guy. Caleb was right, as usual: we simply needed to deal with Felix sooner than later and put a THE END stamp on our relationship. Of course, Felix would have nothing of it. Soon as he got word of our plans to jump ship—or murder him—he'd have an army of bad guys chop us into munchable nuggets.

Question was, did we go after Felix first or close down Bobby Rogers' traphouse? Then what? Shut down all the other traphouses in Newtown? And after that? Move on to Bradenton and Tampa and close up shop on all those illegal drug houses, too?

And what about all the pimps in Sarasota? By the time I got around to taking them out, they'd be unionized and under the protective care of someone like Felix.

When did it end for me?

I was too wrapped up in the danger and intrigue to get out of this business, which was the one stimulus that made me anxious as hell. And the anxiety didn't subside until I got back into the action and tasted the promise of blood and violence. It was all a ball of fur and fury, my life. Only one way in, no way out. As I thought about it, my destiny was right in front of me, and I refused to believe it, accept what was written for me in my DNA by a special celestial alignment the moment I was conceived.

Tonight I lay out under a few hundred stars, trying to be in the now. The now meant this: gutted house to my rear . . . beautiful pool at my dirty feet . . . Sarasota Bay and the Gulf out front . . . and a dozen palm trees at my flanks. Beauty was my now. Peace and serenity were my now.

Now, all I had to do was accept it and, hopefully soon, learn to enjoy the now. Something told me that my job description would never let me.

"We need to find the Bulgarians." I was sitting on the balcony of the condo. Had gone back to get a few things I'd intentionally left behind; an excuse to bust down the door, maybe surprise him at zero-three some dark morning.

Caleb was all relaxed, expecting me. "Try to keep up here, Ranger. They're not far from here." For the first time in weeks, Caleb was actually sitting down in a comfortable seat, not fidgeting. Ice water in hand, he appeared his old calm self again.

"Newtown."

"Yup, the whole time. They rented a warehouse off Martin Luther King, Jr. Blvd. You believe that?"

"King," I whispered to myself, thinking of a time not too long ago when things were so simple.

"You talking to yourself again? Hey, how's that shrink working for you?"

Yeah, how about that shrink? "Fine. Same as always: I speak. She listens. I pay. Repeat once a week."

"Sounds like progress to me." He rolled his eyes, downed the beer.

Handed him another cold one. "What's your plan with Boris and Josef?"

"Well, it's obvious those two used us last time and probably won't be friendly next time around. We know they're careless. My thought is to use that carelessness against them, get them to screw up, at least in Felix's eyes, then maybe he'll off them for us."

"Just for us. You invoking Sun Tzu again?" Not that I cared. If Sun the man had been around, I would've schooled him on shit happens regardless of what you preach.

"Man, lemme tell you: Tzu and I are best buds. Pulled an all-nighter last night, figuring out how to fuck those crazy Bulgarians, came up with a working plan."

I was silent, just nodded, thinking further on what it was like last year to do those small jobs, drive around in my tangerine-colored taxi, live the good life. With Rachel. Wondered if I could somehow get back to that old life. Without Rachel this time.

The little food market was only a coupla blocks away, so when the sun wasn't directly overhead she walked it, rolling along a grocery cart ripped from Publix or some department store near downtown Sarasota. Near the corner, she looked in both directions, crossed in her usual purposeful way, heard a sudden SCREECH! behind her.

No time to scream or react, NickyHeil froze in place, watched in horror as the black suv skidded to a halt right next to her cart.

"You are Bobby's doxy, yes?" Boris said from the passenger side window.

Her heart dropping down an octave, she took several deep breaths. "Doxy?" She tried to smile politely.

"Yes, doxy. Is old gypsy word. In my country, doxy is, uhhh, like a girlfriend to a gangster. You don't know this word? Is good word to know." He looked her up and down, stopping at her impressive chest. "Doxy."

"Who are you and what do you want?"

"Nicky, Nicky. So impatient." Boris looked over at Josef in the driver's seat. "I am your papi's boss, yes?"

"You're asking me who you are?"

Boris looked at Josef. "Asking you? What this means? Turned back to Nicky. "No, no, I no ask you. I tell you something you wish to know."

Mind on the redweed, she moved in closer: "I'm listening."

"You ever need anything. Anything at all. You call me, okay?" Boris handed her a cell phone. "This very special phone. Between only you and me, yes?" Boris, for all his broken English, got the message across: "You and me, baby, we like another."

"We're alike, you mean," she corrected.

"Yes, yes. We are alike. You need help, I help you. I need something, I come to you. This is okay?" It wasn't really a question.

NickyHeil understood the new business arrangement.

"Man, these guys kill me." Caleb peered through his brand-new Nikon binos at the black suv with the two Bulgarians, accosting NickyHeil in plain daylight. "Doing their biz so openly on the street like this."

"It's not business," I said, pointing the parabolic receiver at NickyHeil.

"What're they saying?"

Held up a finger. "Hold on."

Switched to speaker and we both listened in:

"You ever need anything. Anything at all. You call me, okay? This very special phone. Between only you and me, yes?"

"We're alike, you mean?"

"Yes, yes. We are alike. You need help, I help you. I need something, I come to you. This is okay?"

Caleb turned down the volume. "NickyHeil just got promoted to the C-suite."

And Bobby Rogers lost his girl. Almost felt sorry for the man, despite his dealings and method of handling dead bodies. Rogers had what other criminals lacked: a heart that wanted out. Now the woman who had his back was about to stab him in it.

Soon as the Bulgarians pulled away from the curb, we followed loosely behind, shadowing them for several blocks until they turned onto 17th Street. We knew where their warehouse was, so we u-turned and headed back to Bird Key.

Or so I thought. "Where we going?"

"Pay an old friend a visit," Caleb said.

Drove in silence all the way up to Tampa, to Davis Islands, an exclusive enclave not unlike Bird Key. Built up from Tampa Bay mud in the 1920s, the original three-island archipelago had morphed down to two when the little airport was built, connecting the two largest isles. Like Bird Key, it attracted BigMoney. Unlike Bird Key, it hadn't been ruined by it.

The problems trying to work inside high-end communities weren't lost on us: driving around in a Lexus suv when everyone else drove a Rolls or Bentley or something exotic; dressed in touron threads when the locals were decked in upscale tropical casual; and simply two men in sunglasses, driving round and round a tiny island reserved just for those who artfully evaded the US personal income tax.

"I take it your in-depth research on Felix's whereabouts have brought us here today." I was tired of sitting down, needed some fresh air, and I don't mean stale-ass Tampa air.

He stopped in front of a gated manse, not less than 16,000 square feet. And that was just the structure, not the golf-course-size yard and mile-high estate wall that shut out the rest of the world.

"I don't do domestic burglaries." I said it while crossing my arms like a 12 year old.

"We're not here to burgle, Ranger. We're invited guests." He buzzed the tower and seconds later we were ushered onto the parade grounds belonging to Felix Heydrich.

We were escorted inside the mansion by several guards, none of whom appeared to be carrying weapons.

"They are not armed," Felix told us. "However, they are." He pointed to more than a dozen men in concealed spaces around the roof and grounds. "Please come in, gentlemen."

No, we weren't given the grand tour. Felix wasn't that pretentious. He took us directly to his covered outdoor library where we sat near a saltwater pool of bubbling water, a twenty-thousand-gallon Jacuzzi.

For a full minute, we all sat and just looked at each other. Felix smiled the whole time, like he had some big surprise to share with his best friends. "I'm glad you decided to accept my invitation to join me."

Invitation. When the hell did we receive an invitation to join him?

Caleb sensed my discomfort, said, "We thank you for the opportunity to meet with you. Now let's dispense with the fucking social bullshit and get down to it." Again, Caleb didn't do subtle.

Felix leaned forward, reached for cheese and crackers on the impressive spread in front of us. "Traditionally, we say hello . . . we drink wine and laugh in mirth . . . we share experiences and little joys of the day . . . we do this especially with our enemies because it softens the friction between us." He ate several snacks, pointed to the table, inviting us to sample his faux generosity.

I spoke up: "I'm sorry, Mr. Heydrich, but we don't do the veiled overture as well as you and your society friends."

"I can see this, Mr. Darlington. You know, there is some history with this 'veiled overture,' as you put it."

Caleb reached out for a snack. "It greases every interaction, especially with assholes."

Felix dropped his head to deflect the insult, looked at me, said, "We here have a mutual knowledge of actions done, so we can move on and work together in the future as one coherent group. I am willing to offer you complete transparency so you feel comfortable working with us."

"You know I killed Viktor." I just spat it out, and didn't bother to punctuate it by reaching for a cheese-and-cracker combo.

"Yes, Mr. Darlington, I do. You did us a favor, in fact, eliminating a very dangerous man."

"So why all the indirect posturing?" Time for that cheese and cracker.

"This is how we do business, Mr. Darlington: by the veiled proposition, be it a request or order or threat. Worldwide commerce functions on this. We all know what's going on. We all know the lay of the land, who the players are and what their game is. We all essentially know everything, but we hide what we know, even though we know that the other players all know." He laughed at the silliness. "It is confusing, isn't it?"

Caleb wasn't buying this crap. "Would you please fucking get to the point?"

"Yes, Mr. Gatewood. Of course." He scooped up a raw oyster, tipped his head back, downed it.

I couldn't resist: "You ever take parasitology?"

Heydrich, as if caught off guard by a spitball to his nose, said, "I'm sorry?"

Caleb finished my thought: "Because if you had, you'd know that oysters harbor nasty copepods and other shitty little critters that eat away at your muscles for the rest of your life, kinda like we're gonna do if you don't drop your high-falutin' circumlocution and get to the fuckin' point."

"Animosity among enemies makes for poor relations, Mr. Gatewood." Heydrich tried to smile.

"Animosity among enemies is what makes the game worth playing, you fucking asshole," Caleb shot back.

For the first time since our arrival, Felix Heydrich looked annoyed. "Gentlemen, I think we're nearing the end of this conversation. I shall get to the point of this meeting."

I could feel Caleb sigh a big one.

"There is a disruptive element in Newtown, caused by rival gangs and drug lords, so my aim is to introduce a new calming presence."

"Redweed." I said it like it had been Heydrich's guarded secret and now I knew.

He looked at me, his face growing cold. "Yes, redweed. It has proven to relax the mind and perhaps even expand it if used correctly."

Caleb laughed out loud. "You gotta be shittin' me, Heydrich. You sound like a rep for a pharmaceutical company, pawning off the latest designer weight-loss drug on an unsuspecting population. Not to mention, you think we're both stupid. Redweed is nothing more than 21st-century LSD. Not something we wanna see anywhere near Sarasota."

"All speculation aside, gentlemen, I wish to make you my partners in all this."

Another loud sigh from Caleb.

I just listened.

"The Bulgarians are crude, to say the least. I rely on them to distribute redweed to Newtown. We all know that this bad element of north Sarasota is in dire need of a makeover, and we are in a position to effect this. I propose to eliminate the middlemen, the Bulgarians, and emplace the two of you to fill the void. Your job will be to—"

"Fuck yourself." Caleb got up and started for the giant double doors. He looked over at me. "You comin' or what?"

The boom boom boom was nonstop, starting at midnight.

It was now one a.m.

Bobby Rogers silenced the crowd of fifty-plus hardcores with one hand in the air. Not even a cough from the audience.

"Welcome, my homeys, to another Bobby Rogers production of Traphouse Fight Night!"

The crowd of mostly young men, some with their women, erupted in screams.

"We got ten fights on the card tonight, so make sure y'all got them pits o' yours in first gear. Y'all knows the rules so I ain't goin' through that noise. Violate my rules, yo's, and you findin' yo'self on the street without your dog, homes. 'Cos the penalty is your dog in my firepit. Y'all dig me now?" He pumped a huge fist in the air several times.

The audience pumped back in acknowledgement.

"A'right, I knows y'all got the redweed up in you."

Screams and hell-yeahs.

"We runnin' a special this evenin': two for one. You buy two pills tonight, first one at thirty-five dolla. The second one is free—"

More cheers, fists to the sky.

Rogers held that hand up again, near silence. "But you gotta donate to my traphouse, yo's . . . thirty-five dolla."

People looked at each other, then yelled and screamed again, agreeing to Rogers' terms, most not comprehending the rip-off mathematics.

"A'ight, yo's, number one and two, get your dogs in the ring, leashes on 'til the whistle."

The dirt ring looked like an old swimming pool, lined with shallow cement walls and chain-link fencing around the perimeter. Each dog was placed at either end of the ring, and its leash run through the fence where the owner, standing outside the fence, could release his dog at the starting whistle.

Bets were still being placed, cash changing from one dirty hand to another, hundred dollar bills being tossed around like baseball cards. Dogs 1 and 2 jumped in place, trying to reach each other. Their owners held fast, letting out each leash just a little to antagonize and build up a bloodthirst. Worked better for the crowd, which threw down bets at fever pitch.

"Betting . . . STOP!" Rogers held out both oaken arms and the crowd slipped down to a simmer, anxiously awaiting the starting whistle.

Spectators snapped and growled at each other.

The two demons inside the ring foamed and roared, threatening to break their bonds and commence Newton's first world war.

The big man raised the whistle to his lips, loosed a shrill of a hundred humans in agony, and the two owners released their dogs. A ball of black and brown fur erupted in the center of the ring . . .

Morphed into flowing red and black . . .

Red and brown . . .

Blood spilled from both animals' necks and backs, each pit digging fangs deep into raw flesh, ripping and tearing down to the bone.

Yelps and cries from the animals were drowned by the frenzied mass, pulling and jerking on the fence, spitting obscenities at the dogs and their owners, slapping each other as blood flowed and spilled further around the two animals, now hopelessly locked in a death-grip on each other's jaws.

After the first full minute, both animals were nearing exhaustion and loosened their grips, then snapped their jaws like crocodiles at happy hour, still sinking into flesh and bone, screaming in their own agony and weariness.

It soon became a fight of attrition as the brown pit dropped its head just slightly, just enough for the black pit to get a grip on the back of its neck, driving its incisors deep in and severing the underdog's arteries, causing an almost immediate convulsion.

The black pit shook its head violently until it, too, spent of all energy, fell to the dirt, the loser's neck still clutched tightly in its massive jaws. The victor's breathing was loud and hoarse, spitting foamy blood with each exhalation.

"How long we gonna sit here and listen to a bunch of animals rip each other down to loose threads?" I lit up a cigarette, inhaling as much as I could in one gulp, releasing it slowly out the window.

"Long as it takes to see who files out after the party's over." Caleb was pissed off. "This kills me, too, hearing these dogs kill each other and having a bunch of lowlifes cheer it on. But I do know this, Tommy: we stick around a little longer, video the assholes coming out, and we have ourselves some good intel for future use."

Sounded to me like Caleb was preparing for a long, drawn-out siege of Newtown. I almost wanted to remind him something his buddy Sun Tzu wrote, something about how it's not a good idea—

ever—to lay siege to a city. Or anyplace. Your resources were slowly drained, your morale was slowly sunk, and you eventually lost in the end. No, I wasn't gonna tell him that, because I'd agreed to do this thing with him, and also fund it with some of my cash. I reminded myself not to do this again. Ever.

At four a.m., the last of the homeboys stumbled out of Rogers' traphouse, carrying his dead pit bull.

Looked over at him as he threw the animal into the bed of his truck, said to Caleb, "Last man out, bud."

"Got it on video?"

"Every single one of 'em. It's Miller Time." I popped the top on two Stellas, was about to down both at once.

Until he looked over at me.

Handed him one, popped the top on another. For me.

"Now this is what I love about Old Florida, Tommy: going out on a Friday night, seeing the fights, sitting around with my Ranger bud, and sharing a cold one after. Pure joy, you ask me."

Are you delusional? "Yeah, C-man. Good times."

The last image I would recall before falling into bed was that dead pit bull being thrown into the back of its owner's pickup, and the guy yelling what a piece of shit it was. Reminded me of Sarasota's BigMoney, all those wealthy assholes who saw my kind as meat on the hoof, soon to be tossed into the back of a pickup on my date of expiration and not one minute after.

I turned down six fares this morning so I could lie out at Turtle Beach on Siesta Key, up my production of vitamin D.

As soon as he called, my ears perked up. Scooped up as much D in my hands as I could, then hit the road.

Drove out toward the northern territory on Tamiami and picked him up at Popeye's. He came walking out with two buckets of fried chicken, dropped into the rear passenger's seat, the cab immediately filling up with the sweet, deadly aroma of commercially slaughtered deep-fried chicken.

"Eh, man. Mind if I eat this bird while we chat some?" Bobby Rogers had lost his signature smile of gold, didn't look happy. Bit into a breast like one of his pit bulls, ripped off all the meat, swallowed it without chewing.

"Where can I drop you?"

His mouth was full. "Drive, man, just drive."

And so I drove us out to the Van Wezel parking lot at the shoreline downtown, parked as close to the water as I could, turned up the a/c and let the car idle away. Pulled out a cigarette and Rogers immediately stuck his big hand out, offering me a Camel raw.

"Thanks," I said, lighting it and sucking it all in much as I could, this time not spitting it all out like the first time in front of Rogers.

"My man, finally got that Camel rhythm down." He started to laugh, then remembered he was depressed for some reason, stopped midstream. "Tommy, you an addict, plain and simple. Not like one of them dudes does it all the time, but you's a user, man. Got something back in your cave ailin' you?"

"We all have something going on." Turned around, slung an arm over the seat. "What's on your mind?"

He'd already gone through four breasts and thighs, cleaned each down to the bone. A bucket of hydrochloric acid couldn't have been more efficient. Wiped his mouth with a handful of napkins, looked up at me. "Want out."

Wasn't surprised.

"Serious, man. I want the fuck outta this racket. I stay in a month longer, I'ma blueface like that cop up in my place."

"Why?"

"Why what, white rice? Why I want out? Why only a month? Why I'ma dead man?"

"E, all the above." I hoped to diffuse the tension and anxiety. Lord knew I was full of both and needed a release.

"Dude, you got knots all up in your neck and head. See them things ripple when you think about shit. You need to unwind more'n I do." He managed a laugh, came up short again. "Look, Tommy, I know you know the man."

Felix.

"You and your friend didn't come round my traphouse for no reason. You's there 'cos you want me. That man, whoever he be, wants me. Them fuckin' Russian muthafuckas want me. All got one thing in common, too: they all want Bobby Rogers dead on a slab.

Licked his fingers, dug into the second bucket, pulled out a wing, sucked the meat off the bone like it was butter. "Man, this the best fried chicken I ever ate. My mama took me to Popeye's when I's like six. She say, 'Bobby, this the best doggone fried chicken in the universe. You ever need to feel good 'cos someone just beat yo' ass, you find you a Popeye's and they do you right.' My moms was some woman, dude." Another thigh gone in five seconds. Used his shirt as a napkin 'cos he'd wiped out the fifty they'd stuffed in a separate bag just for the big man, their regular customer.

Did I tell him about Felix and breach Caleb's trust? If I told Rogers who pulled his strings, what good would it have done? Caleb was a friend and colleague and mentor. If I lost his faith and confidence, I'd never get it back, and I'd be a lesser man for it.

"His name is Felix Heydrich."

"Like the cat," he said, his mouth full of delicious dead bird. "Heard about this dude from the Russians, man. Do 'preciate you lettin' me know." He upturned the mashed potatoes, swallowed the contents of the 32-ounce container in a few gulps, chased it with a pint of seasoned gravy.

"They're Bulgarians." I took a piece of chicken from the bucket.

"Man, I know they Bulgarians, but that's too much to say in one mouthful. 'Sides, they all Russians when you look up the skirt. All act like some kinda Ivan in one form or another."

"Yeah, Ivan." Looked at him dead on. "Why'd you say Ivan?" Took a piece of chicken from the bucket.

"Dude, an Ivan is a pop-up target we used to knock down back in the day."

My curiosity piqued: "Back in the day."

"Man, I was a clean US Marine for four years 'fore all this shit." That belly laugh came back and shook my TommyTaxi down to its rubber roots.

I stopped eating even though my mouth was still full.

"What do you really know about Bobby Rogers, C-man?"

He stood at the retaining wall overlooking the Bay and Gulf, sipping his ice water. "Why are you asking?"

"Just wondering." If he wanted water, fine. I was doing super-cold Stella.

It got quiet for a bit, both of us staring out over the water. Wondered how Rachel was doing ... whether I should make another appointment to see Sara sometime soon ... finish redoing my new home ... or just sell everything and move to Costa Rica.

He walked inside and made some notes on the large dry-erase board next to Rogers' pictures and other scribbles. "Hey, what else did you find out about Rogers?"

"Sure you wanna know?"

Lit up a cigarette, caught a quick buzz, and things loosened up a bit.

He just looked at me.

I pointed my beer at him: "Robert Anthony Rogers was a US Marine Corps sniper for four years, did six tours in Afghanistan from 2002 to 2006, wounded in combat, Purple Heart for that bad eye of his, plus a Silver Star with V device for something that's still classified, honorably discharged."

He threw an eraser against the board, turned and looked at me. "Are you fuckin' shitting me? You expect me to believe that pile of shit?"

I knew this would happen. And was prepared for it. Pulled out a large envelope, handed it to him.

Looking through the sheaf of papers, including Rogers' DD-214, knowing it was official as official got, he set them on the table, looked down at the floor. "This shit just gets better by the minute, doesn't it?"

Shrugged my shoulders, not knowing what to say to the man.

"And you want us to do what? Extend our honored colleague a professional courtesy of some kind?"

"Caleb, I have no idea why or how you got a bug up your ass about this man. Maybe I don't wanna know. But I do know this: Bobby Rogers, for all his bravado and big mouth, is not a bad guy. He's not the man who killed your friend."

"Yeah, then who is?"

I knew he wasn't prepared to hear it. Took a few steps back just in case. "You."

If ever a man looked at me with pure venom, it was right now and it broke my heart that it was Caleb Gatewood. The fact he didn't throw anything or shoot me was a testament to his believing me, hard as it was to accept.

"You always said accuracy was the best method to use. Well, I'm being accurate here. I know it hurts—"

"What fuckin' kills me, Tommy, is your going behind my back to get this intel."

"Woh, man, hold on there. Let's rewind the tapes back to the day when you told me you had a life and a job long before you met me. Remember that conversation? It was the night you were putting Tommy Darlington in his place, as I recall."

Caleb just looked at me.

"All this crap is tough to get through, Brother. It's been a bitch for me not to lose it every single fuckin' day since Rachel—"

The tears came on and there was nothing I could do to stop them, so I just let them rain down my cheeks as I thought about her and what I'd dragged her into down at the lake with Viktor. I knew what he'd done to her, even though she'd never shared it with me. It was just too painful and horrific.

And it was all my doing.

Caleb reached out and touched my shoulder at first, then hugged me so hard I couldn't sob or breathe. That was okay, because I wanted nothing more than to die a coward's death right then.

Nothing was said for the next few days about my crying jag. What could we say? Tommy had a breakdown? Tommy was at the end of his rope and fell into that deep inky abyss where all anxiety-depressives eventually wind up? Instead, I threw myself into my new house while Caleb continued his research on Felix, the Bulgarians, and planning for D-Day.

Sitting around one hot afternoon, the foreman of my construction crew said, out of the blue, "You ever thought about completely tearing this place up and doing up new concrete?"

"What? The foundation, you mean? Why?"

"Since we've been ripping this whole place apart, just thought you might wanna start from scratch." He stood up and pointed to a spot in a far corner of the house. "See over there in that far corner?"

Walked over to the spot he was pointing to. "Here?"

"Yeah, that's new foundation right there. Can't be more than ten years old." He tapped it with a crowbar. "Hear that? Not as deep and solid as the rest. I'd say you got some cavity down there, maybe a small sinkhole. Be good if we broke it up, refilled it. Could do the same with the other spots in the foundation, too."

"Wait, you mean there's more than one like this?" All my previous thoughts about the Jamisons flooded back to me . . . then thoughts of Donny McCracken . . . too much data for me to handle. My world started to spin and I got dizzy.

"Be right back," I said, walking on shaky legs to the bathroom where I splashed cold water on my face, hung my head under the running water for a minute.

He walked over to me. "You okay, Tommy?"

"Yeah, yeah, I'm fine. Too much sun today." A lie. "Hey, why don't we knock it off for the day?"

"Okay, lemme know what you want us to do. We'll be back on Friday. Got this other job we're doing downtown. That okay with you?"

"Yeah, that's cool." Stood up, toweled off. "Any way you can leave me one jackhammer?"

He thought on it, said, "Sure, but have to charge you for it for those two days. How 'bout you just pay my rental on it?"

Looked at him and nodded, walked to the edge of the wall at the water, my paradise starting to spin again.

Donny McCracken and his family were the original Old Florida Redneck Royalty.

And he had been a friend of mine.

His murder by Felix cut especially deep. When I'd learned that Donny and his family had been railroaded out of their own home, I wondered why Donny had been so laid back about it, as if it had happened to someone else.

At midnight on Wednesday, I began the slow, tedious process of breaking up the cement foundation in the areas pointed out to me by my contractor. Rather than use the jackhammer, which woulda raised the dead, I opted instead for a simpler solution: the dead drop.

Got a small Bobcat frontloader, picked up a hundred-pound dumbbell with the bucket, raised it up seven feet, and dropped it onto the desired spot.

Did this a few times for each spot without any of the neighbors coming over and shooting me in the face. The first hole was the thickest and took half an hour to break through, mostly reloading the Bobcat with the dumbbell. At first, the opening was only six inches, but with some chipping and more drops, I widened it to a couple of feet in diameter, easy enough to drop inside with a flashlight and take a peek down there.

Not many things in my adult life have shocked me. Not when I shot and killed my first target. Not when a target put his knife into my back. Not when—

Rachel was the exception. Seeing her after I thought she'd been torn to shreds and bloodsmoke by Viktor's gators was truly the shock of my life. Hearing her small cries for help, touching her frail body, and then crying together in a warm knot on Viktor's porch was something I'll never forget.

That kind of shock was something I hoped never to feel again.

Until I saw deep into the hole I'd broken open.

Donny had told me of booty his father and grandfather both had brought up from the plane wreck offshore, the killing site of all those children and teens. By Felix, I could only guess. Donny's father had hauled aboard ingots and bars that Donny said were pure gold, but I didn't believe him. Too far-fetched for my conservative mind. He'd grown up watching all those swashbuckler movies where the bad guys stole the gold and the good guys took it all back by THE END.

Why had Donny so easily given up the house that his grandfather and father fought so hard for and eventually lost to the Jamison family?

Squatting down in the hole, stared into it for long minutes.

Maybe it was because Donny knew that someday he would return to collect what had been stripped from his family decades ago. And the most secure place to hide it was underneath the foot of a very powerful organization.

Reached down and touched a shiny surface.

Or maybe because it was that big fuck-you Donny gave to the Jamisons and their bosses, to people who killed to find all that lost gold that Donny's father and grandfather had diligently salvaged from the sea.

Almost fell asleep right there, my hand caressing the topmost gold bar. Tried to pick it up with two fingers. No way. Must've been 25 pounds. So were all the other ones, each tucked neatly into treated wooden boxes lined with burlap.

Six hours later, I had used the Bobcat to pull up 200 gold bars and ingots. From the first little cavern. By Thursday's sunset, I had opened up all the holes and extracted 1,000 bars.

At today's gold-market price, nearly half a billion dollars of pure gold.

Subliminal flashes of Rachel passed in front of my eyes, as I tried to fathom the scene:

A bright moon rising over a beautiful deep-blue and violet sunset over the Gulf...

Stars like candle flickers overhead...

The gentle sounds of surf hitting the north perimeter wall of Bird Key...

The hot, moist air dissipating and giving rise to a fresh new air, cool to the touch...

And the delicious scent of Wendy's Baconators and Chanel No. 22.

Baconators?

Chanel?

"Rachel." I froze in place.

"Hello, Tommy. Thought I'd surprise you. I brought dinner." She held up the bag of Wendy's goodies.

Dressed in a sage sleeveless t-shirt, white gauzy shorts with no undies underneath, and a pair of my old distressed-leather flips she loved to wear.

First thoughts: what the hell was she doing here? After our last meet, I was surprised she'd try to find me, let alone come all the way here to see me. Had she noticed the tarp that now protected the twenty bins of gold? Did Caleb send her here to check up on me?

Did someone else?

"C'mon, Tommy, you didn't have much to say the last time we sat together." She pulled up a lounger next to me, opened the bag, handed me a Baconator.

In times like this, on the verge of an anxiety attack, it was sometimes best to swallow a burger. It was one of a few things that truly calmed me down, other than cold beer, Camel raws, and Rachel's gentle touch on my face.

"Whatcha doin'?" She looked around at the broken foundation, blue tarp, and the frame of my new house.

"Renovating."

"All by yourself? On a lovely moonlit night?"

"You know me, Rach, I work best alone."

She walked around behind me, stroked my neck. "Were you ever going to call me, Tommy?"

My next question was, how the heck would I get her to leave? "Rachel, I appreciate your coming here to see me, but this is not a good time."

"I wish you knew how hard this is for me, Tommy. How hard it's been for me not to think about what happened to me. To us. I think about you all the time." She stroked my face. "Wondering how you are, what you're doing, how you feel, are you doing good things for others as usual, stuff. All about you. I miss you, Tommy—"

Pulled away from her. "Rachel, this is not a good time. I'm sorry."

Didn't want to but I framed the look on her face in the shallowest part of my mind, where I'd have to see it every single day for a looong time.

"Do you want your Ranger jacket back?" She got up and looked down at me.

"I guess."

"When? I could drop it off tomorrow and pick up my blender and toaster oven."

"Or we could do a prisoner exchange at the border over the Ringling Bridge." It just fell out of my mouth.

"Fuck you, Tommy!" With that, she was off.

An afterthought, she ripped the Baconator outta my hand and took the rest with her.

How do you hide a load of gold bars and ingots?

I'd left the gold outside in the bins under the tarp all night, because there wasn't a damn thing else for me to do with it. Sometimes plain sight was the best protection. Like anonymity is the best defense against would-be attackers. I'd learned this over a baker's dozen years of special-operations work overseas in some pretty hostile and unforgiving territories, from a bevy of unsavory people who were good at killing others indiscriminately.

At six, I roused myself and casually walked outside. Everything was in the same position I'd left them in last night. Funny how I would get anxious over a meeting with someone, or going into a mission, but not being in possession of half a billion dollars in precious gold.

Seems the more outrageous a situation is, the better we're able to cope with it.

I thought my four million in untraceable cash dollars was outrageous, but this. . . .

Donny McCracken talked to me from the grave, said, "Tommy, I want you to fuck the Jamisons with this money. And fuck Felix, too."

The bad guys only muddied up an already difficult calculation, and Caleb had seen through it all along to its very core: the Jamisons and Felix Heydrich had to be eliminated from the equation to balance out everything else. What Caleb hadn't considered, though, is that the bad guys were working for a much more powerful organization. And it had a lot to do with that Segreta Antico cardinal down south.

How would we deal with that? Simply erase a few numbers, shuffle some variables?

Today, there were a few more pressing issues, like how to transport twelve tons of dense precious metal. It's not so much a challenge to move twelve tons, but when its mass is packed hard like gold, it tends to collapse normal flooring. You had to spread out the bars over a wide surface area.

It's silly even to think about such a thing, discovering gold under your own house. Only in Old Florida. What the hell would you do with it? Try to sell one bar at a time? And to who? Guys who'll follow you back home, murder you and steal the rest? While it's romantic to dream of windfalls and fast riches, the reality is far more complicated, because, as dear Donny McCracken told me more than once, "Big money, big responsibility."

A dozen times every second I lifted and hauled, bent down and dropped, sweated and bled, I wanted to call Caleb and fill him in on the shocker of a lifetime.

But I didn't.

It would've changed things. Again. We would've committeed it to death, over cases of Stella and buckets of KFC, figuring out what to do about Paul Jamison and Felix Heydrich, and agreed on doing nothing. After all, half a billion in gold buys a lot of doing nothing, except buying a fifty-foot Meridian motor yacht and cruising the Bahamas with two hotties who didn't speak English. Why complicate a fine adventure with conversation?

There was one thing half a billion in gold could not buy: peace of mind.

And that's the reason I didn't tell Caleb.

My cell rang, reluctantly picked it up. Rachel.

"You're a tease, leaving with my dinner the other night."

"You're an asshole, Tommy."

When Rachel came back the following week, I'd already stashed all the bars in a safe place, just I'd done with all my cash. In the end, it wasn't hard. Just hide things in plain sight, a space people won't get curious about.

Outta sight, outta mind. Outta mind, outta hand.

Soon as I left the hiding space, I'd shoved all thoughts about the booty deep into my subconscious. A bounty of precious metal that cost three generations of McCrackens their livelihood and ultimately each of their lives. Donny knew what he was doing when he left me the deed to his home, banking on my forcing it through Felix and the Jamisons. He knew I would make good on his wish to see these people die a horrible death. He was just a little oblique in his approach.

"Three Stellas, please," I said, sitting on one of the barstools at my fave beach bar on Holmes Beach. Rachel brought me here on our first date years back, and so I'd been sitting in the same space, give or take, for the past many years since we first met. Over the years, I burned a nice image of myself into the little corner at the bar, and reminded others that this was TommySpace.

Seconds later, ice-cold Stellas filled my field of view, and I downed each one quickly as I could, getting that anti-anxiety buzz going. After all the drugs and pharmaceuticals I'd tried over the years, I came to the inescapable conclusion that self-medicating with sufficient Stella or Peroni, backed by a pack of cigarettes, was the only way I was gonna feel any relief in my lifetime. Plain and simple. Pathetic as it was, I gave in to the sad fact that I was messed up in the head and there wasn't shit I could do about it.

Something I could never tell Sara. Or anyone else.

The only remedy: suck down some good beer at the bar, step out once in a bit for a smoke, come back in and get lost in the atmosphere that was Old Florida, a lost time and space I longed for. Old Florida was slowly being destroyed by BigMoney. They killed off anything good.

In all my travels over the world, I've seen that, wherever you find beauty, there will exist a conspiracy to control it, manipulate it, and ultimately destroy it.. They've done this in every part of the world, seeking to wrest beauty from Mother Nature herself, milk it for every coin, and turn it to ruins. In the same way most people turn good into shit.

Those thoughts quickly turned to Rachel. Why had she come by the other night? It wasn't like her to pursue me. We didn't do lunch, Rachel and I. Things didn't add up.

When things naturally don't make one and one equals two, I know there's a hidden hand in there somewhere, an external influence that seeks to control . . . and ultimately destroy.

So who was controlling Rachel? She knew Peter Jamison. I got this from that photograph of the two together at one of her book signings.

Another name came to mind: Felix Heydrich.

"Stop . . . the . . . presses," I said, walking into my home.

Caleb turned around after writing something on one of his gigantic dry-erase boards.

"You can stop planning D-Day, 'cos I have this all figured out."

257

"The hell you talkin'? You high on something funny?"

Okay, so I was drunk. Stumbled over the furniture, all pushed to the walls to make room for the war room, and fell into a lounger.

He walked over to me and sat down, patted my knee. "How are you doing, Tommy?"

"Peachy." Closed my eyes 'cos they wouldn't stay open. The room began to spin, an unceasing gyro lifting me into a cloud of nausea.

Worse, a heavy sound barrier positioned itself between us, like that block of frozen air that sometimes separated Rachel and me, nothing in sight to break through it.

"Tell you what: while you're riding on that 500-knot, merry-go-round buzz, I'll fill you in on the latest intel." He hopped up and went to one of the boards, pointed at things I couldn't see through Stella's brume. "Felix gets his shipments in from a lab in the Yucatan, come straight over to Tampa where they're offloaded onto big rigs, carted off to points unknown as of yet."

Fuzzy voice up a hill. Looked up and saw a P-47 Thunderbolt screaming into my face.

Did what any self-respecting drunk woulda done: SCREAMED.

"Woh, Ranger! Settle down now." Caleb had me by the shoulders, put me back down on the couch. "You seein' things?" He looked up at the ceiling fan directly overhead. "That, my friend, is an electric ceiling fan, invented about 130 years ago by a great American who understood the power of evaporative cooling."

I knew what he was trying to do: have me focus on something absurd, and hoping I'd come around. All I could spit out at the moment: " 'Vaporative . . . cool."

Looked up again, saw that Thunderbolt dive-bomb me again.

I think I threw up. . . .

"I'm just saying that you need to ride their ass to get more product, Bobby. If you're not forcing the issue, then they're going to think you're just weak." NickyHeil stood in the center of the ratty traphouse living room, if you could call it that.

Bobby Rogers held back another slap. This time, he listened to the one person in the world he knew he could count on.

"The Russians have plenty of redweed. I checked. They're

supplying two other traphouses in Newtown. So if you don't go over there to that warehouse and kick some ass, someone's going to roll over on you and all this—" She waved her hand around the dingy room. "This will be gone. No more parties. No more being the big man of the 'hood. No more—"

" 'Nuff o' this shit, Nicky!" Flicked a lit Camel into a dark corner.

"I'm glad to hear you say that, Bobby, because it's time you got a dose of reality and the reality is that we're in competition was some heavy people who want all the biz in Newtown, and they're going to do whatever it takes to get it."

Rogers was silent, flicked a hand out. "K. Now what?"

"The warehouse has a stash of redweed, enough for about a year. That's for one traphouse. We go in there, take over the place, guard it from the others—"

"You tellin' me to start a war with all the other playas in this 'hood?"

"If you don't, Bobby, they will. Guarantee it."

"Makes you think they come kill my ass?"

"I'm the one who does the books here, Bobby. I see everything from warehouse to product to dealer to user. All of it. You insulate yourself with your gansta fantasy world and false friends. How can you possibly see what I see?"

Silence. Another Camel magically appeared, lit itself, he dragged hard on it, blew smoke rings down the hall into the next room.

"I see it coming, Bobby, and it's coming fast. These Russians came into Newtown and flooded the market to get people high. They created a demand for a product that didn't even have an outlet yet. Then they found you and these two other gangstas, and leased out dealerships to you players."

"Leased out."

"Yeah, as in, you don't own shit. You just work for them."

"A'ight. So you want me to start this war that's comin' anyway."

"Bobby, you have the manpower, you have the money."

"Yeah, long as you here, we got the brains, too. That it, bitch?" He laughed.

"You're still the leader of this operation, Bobby. I'm just the accountant."

He grabbed her, pulled her into him, kissed her perfectly formed mouth deeply, pulled off her top and fondled every beautiful, delicious curves. "Girl, time to start this muthafuckin' war you preachin' to me 'bout."

Each day, I made a conscious effort to experience the beauty of Sarasota, all 97 degrees and 99% humidity of her.

The same thick, sticky air hung right over Newtown, a dirty old blanket that held down all the car and truck exhaust, smoke from outdoor fires, belches from fast-food joints, and residential bad breath that stank of stale wine, fried chicken and beatdowns.

The two other traphouses sat at opposite ends of 24th Street, bookending the bleak ribbon of northern territory's hardship: N. Orange Avenue to the west, 301 to the east. Further south, 301 grew and expanded on both sides, feeding off the bustling downtown as it wound its way into Sarasota, getting lost at US 41, Tamiami Trail. Promise lay only farther ahead. Seemingly so close to Newtown, yet well beyond its grasp. . . .

Rogers scoped out the Orange Avenue side first, watching the tide of dealers and users flow in and out of the more-upscale traphouse. He wondered why this one had a nicer lawn, all cut and trimmed up, the trees not rotting away or the front screens not broken and hanging like deadfall.

Memories of missions deep into the heartland of Afghanistan came flooding back in multiple flashes, seeing his targets move in and out of doorways, behind windows, across rooftops, somehow knowing they were his prey.

If only he still had his shooting eye to confirm it all. That was long gone, replaced in two surgeries at the Bay Pines VA with a delicately painted orb of glass that closely matched his other eye. Seeing everything now in his line of sight was a slight blur that dissipated only with long minutes of concentration, little muscle exercises the VA tech had taught him.

Stereo vision now gone but it didn't matter, viewing a target a hundred yards off through the scope. All he needed to see was his designated target, lock onto it with his sixth-sense radar, put it in his crosshairs, breathe just right, gently squeeze the trigger on his M24 rifle. The bullet did the rest.

Hours later, he moved down the street to the 301 traphouse, making little mental notes of the goings on, temperature of the wind, direction of little breezes that flowed with their own special patterns. Eyeing the asphalt road, he saw the nearly invisible Schlieren waves that swirled off the oven-baked surface, creating their own specific convection currents that acted like a distorted lens. Real or not, you could see whatever you wanted to see.

All these data he filed away.

People going in and out of both traphouses moved slowly, especially those on a redweed trip. At one point, a platoon of Mexicans came stumbling out en masse from the Orange Avenue house, a giant brown amoeba of giggles.

Rogers laughed: "Stackin' tacos for the dinner shift."

The bosses of each house moved a little faster when walking about, but stood around in one place for long seconds. Easy targets, all.

By early evening, Rogers had filled his neural data log with enough intel, headed back to 3636 Goodland, mumbling to himself the whole time, "How these muthafuckas get money for a clean traphouse? Dumbass yo's. Dontcha know Feds like shiny things? Ya'll like a big magnet, keepin' the Man offa my Cuban ass. Dumbass tacos up in that place. But who the hell threw Benjamins at that place?"

Only one answer came to mind: the Russians and that catman Felix.

"D-Day, two days. Woo-fuckin-hoo." Caleb sat with me inside the newly constructed frame of my Bird Key spread, admiring the excellent work we'd done.

"Time?" I asked.

"In place at 21, hit at 2300." He was nursing ice water again. "Sure you're up for this?"

Just looked at him.

"Good, 'cos I wouldn't wanna have all the fun to myself."

A moment of silence.

Even in times like these, we sat comfortably in the same space, sharing a beer, some conversation, a sunset. I never wanted to tell him anything about my anxiety issues. Never.

"I dunno what you're going through, other than with Rachel and her experience out in the bush with Viktor, but seems to me some of your . . . issues . . . run deeper than that. How am I tracking?"

Didn't wanna talk about it, but this was a come-to-Jesus moment I could no longer avoid. "Pretty close."

"How long?"

"Since birth, I imagine."

We sort of laughed, he clinked his glass on my Stella.

"Figured that. You can hide stuff like that only so long before people start to see things in you, your behaviors and actions, things you say and how you say them." Sipped his water. "Man, I swear you were born in a black hole."

Sometimes it was just best to shut the fuck up and let the wisdom flow over you.

"Look, Tommy, we all have issues we deal with every day. I know I have mine, although can't think of a single one at the moment." He nudged my arm. "Like at the Olympics, every athlete out there has practiced for years for this one event, and they have to be perfect only for that hundred-meter dash or mile or the two minutes on the balance beam. They can get drunk afterward and get hit by a train and it wouldn't matter, long as they got it right on game day."

Silence from me, conserving energy and heartbeats.

Turned to face me. "You've done this for a long-ass time, Tommy, and I know you've done it under the same shit that's ailed you since your mama first spanked you. I dunno, maybe she put an extra chromosome in your cereal. I can understand that. I respect it. Sure, you had your Kodak moments in training—we all did—but I've never seen you fuck up when the bullets were coming at us. You were always cool under fire, even enjoyed it. So did I."

He got a little closer. "But if you fuck this up, I will fuckin' cut you ear to ear with this little pen knife my daddy gave me when I was eight. I shit you not, Ranger. This is your Olympic games and you best be on you're A-game from the time we're on target to the second we exfil."

Caleb had done my thinking for me, said what needed to be said. It was his idea of a pep talk and it was effective.

Set my beer, only half finished, on the stool between us, dropped my Camel to the new cement foundation, ground it down to dust, looked at him with that knowing look we exchanged just before the bird lifted us into combat, added a little smile at the end to punctuate my conviction.

My commitment to the mission.

Our mission.

She was in Rogers' face again: "So what are you going to do about it, Bobby?"

Big smile on the big man. "Got it covered, girl. Dontcha worry 'bout a thing." With that, Bobby Rogers strolled outside, lit up a Camel, surveyed his neighborhood.

Seconds later, a black, late-model Mercedes rolled around the corner . . .

Just out of sight of his good eye . . .

Sprayed shots across Rogers' bow and his traphouse . . .

Nicky at the right-side door of the house . . .

Her mouth open in shock . . .

Designer basketball shoes welded to the concrete . . .

Two young girls next her . . .

Looking up at Nicky . . .

Smiling . . .

Tugging on her t-shirt . . .

One bullet surprise for each of the girls . . .

One found a forehead . . .

Other ripped into a tiny chest . . .

Rogers threw his bulk to the ground, just underneath his old truck . . .

Mercedes pulled up next to the truck . . .

Two black demons leaped out . . .

Each with an AK . . .

Emptied two clips into the house . . .

Achingly slow legato of bullets in microseconds . . .

Felt like an hour . . .

Rogers pulled two .45 pistols from holsters in his waistband . . .

Crawled underneath his truck, hands outstretched . . .

Inched sideways to the other side of the truck . . .

Aimed each pistol . . .

Some shithead's bare ankle . . .

An asshole's kneecap . . .

Calmly, purposefully tore off two bullets each into the assassins' tender joints . . .

Redirected his aim higher and to the left, 66 degrees . . .

Found the driver's fat head and wicked, gold-plated leer . . .

Two slugs from Rogers' left pistol . . .

Lead-infected blood and gold dust splattered the windshield . . .

Right pistol crawling along the ground, finding purchase . . .

Rogers rolling over to his left . . .

Spying passenger's long brown hair and perfect upturned nose, jamming to the bullet-beat like it was a rave . . .

A very special bullet for the dark princess . . .

SCREECHING MUSIC from the Mercedes . . .

Left pistol pulled up and slightly right, then down six degrees . . .

Single bullet to the dashboard . . .

Silence in the street, that eerie feeling after a devastating storm.

Blood covered Nicky . . .

All Rogers could see was blood . . .

On her face, arms, jeans, shoes . . .

Double-tapped each assassin on the road, in driver's seat . . .

Jerked up two men in street, one in each hand, like a limp Ted Bundy . . .

Threw them into backseat of the Mercedes . . .

Looked back at Nicky . . .

Not her blood, he just knew . . .

Nothing he could do for the little girls . . .

His girl would clean up, make it right . . .

Slammed his right arm into the driver's torso, just underneath his armpit, shoving him onto the passenger's bikini'd lap . . .

Car in drive . . .

Aimed wheels east . . .

Pulled away from his traphouse . . .

"Don't look back at Nicky," he said to himself. "Don't look back."

Slowly reached the end of Goodland Avenue . . .

Took a left heading up north a ways, about a mile . . .

Found the dilapidated fence . . .

Pulled into the warehouse parking lot . . .

Inside the massive structure . . .

Mercedes now quiet, not moving . . .

Opened twin cabinets along the west wall, a familiar hiding space for him . . .

Six, five-gallon containers of gas . . .

Washed down Mercedes . . .

All six cans now lonely . . .

Pulled out a Camel raw . . .

Lit up . . .

Looked around at his old playground . . .

Dragged hard on the cigarette . . .

Smoke rings into the twenty-foot ceiling, burning a skylight into it . . .

Looked up at the sky through his imaginary window to heaven, wished upon it . . .

Flicked the cigarette high in the air . . .

Ballistic spark found a soft spot on the roof . . .

Flames shot up fifteen feet, struggling to reach Rogers' faraway window . . .

Looked at the Mercedes . . .

Paint peeled off the body, bubbles popping, screaming in agony . . .

Softer bodies inside sizzled and boiled over . . .

Load moan from front passenger's seat . . .

Rogers with a small grin . . .

Then she SCREAMED something unholy that melted into the oxblood Nappa leather. . . .

Rogers already out the door.

" 'Nuff said, 'nuff done," he mumbled to himself.

Flipped open his cell phone, speed-dialed a number. "Traveler need a ride. You workin' or slummin'? Now be good, homes."

I took down his address. "Ten mikes. Keep your head down. Stand by." Put down my phone, looked over at Caleb, reassembling his sniper rifle.

"Some sexy rich lady off to SRQ?"

"Pretty close."

"Back when?"

Looked at my watch. "Hour."

"Wheels up at 21." I'd been a civilian too long, had to convert 2100 to real time: nine p.m. Just kidding.

Another driving adventure into the northern territory, home of crocodiles and other dinosaur creatures. Woo-fuckin-hoo.

Ten minutes went by at thirty-five miles an hour. Too slow for my taste today. Not into smelling the roses in this part of town. They were all black and decaying.

Rogers was leaning up against a building off 301, keeping it from falling down all around him. Soon as he saw TommyTaxi, pushed off and gave me a little wave, walked over and dropped into the back seat.

"Try not to bleed on my seat, big man," I said, looking at the spreading red blotch on his right stomach. Handed him a towel, a bottle of water.

"Six tours in the 'Stan, only lost an eye. Come home, take two rounds in my Goodyear."

I laughed. Couldn't help it. "Spare tire?"

"Yeah, man, saved by forty-five pounds of mama's homemade lard, dude. You believe that shit?" Took the towel, pressed it hard against the two bullet holes in his abdomen, looked up at me. "Well?"

"Destination?"

"Man, you gotta ask?"

"Sarasota Memorial?"

"Fuck, no, dude. Got my own medic, NickyHeil. Take me home, ambulance driver. Shiiit."

"Wanna tell me what happened?"

His mind was miles away. Came back a sec just for me. "Shit you don't wanna know, man."

I figured silence was good.

"Playas from other traphouse come a-gunnin' for me." Saw tears forming in his eyes. "Got two o' my little girls."

Didn't know what to say. "I'm sorry, Bobby."

"Shit, man, I want outta this shit so bad. You don't even know." Tears gave way to something else altogether.

Knew the feeling, when rocks of emotion came down with the flood, crashing and tearing up all barriers and obstacles that ordinarily dammed up the waters.

The big man cried into the towel, bloodying his face with the awful memory of the loss of the two little girls.

"FRAGO: We're hitting two other traphouses on 24th Street."

Caleb shook his head. "You're a turd, Tommy."

"Turn on local news."

In a few minutes, the news flash repeated: "Two children, victims of drive-by shooting in Newtown."

Caleb immediately recognized the address: 3636 Goodland Avenue. "Well, ain't this just the bee's knees."

"We're doing an op with a guest operator." I faced him directly, wanted to make sure he heard every molecule.

"What the—"

"Relax, he may be as good as you." Wondered if a smile would help. "Maybe."

"Robert Rogers? You fuckin' shittin' me or what?"

The temperature in the room jumped up ten degrees.

"Take a listen, C-man."

The heat in his ears expanded the ear canals, shutting down all forms of higher communication, so I tried another approach . . . I wrote it on one of his big boards: Bobby Rogers is an ex-sniper who has valuable intel for us. BREAK. We do him this favor and take out other two traphouse lords. BREAK. And he does us a little favor. OVER.

He sometimes came around when I shot his world full of humor.

"Favor. Kinda favor we talkin' here, Ranger?"

Felix Heydrich stood at the front of his massive desk in his home.

Paul Jamison sat in a wooden straight-back chair three feet in front of him.

"When we brought you aboard, Paul, we had plans from the beginning."

Heydrich looked down at the man, shook his head slightly, side to side. "Peter got out of line. He had to be dealt with swiftly."

"You could've relegated him to some office in Miami. Something!"

Held out a hand, stopping Jamison cold. "We're beyond that." Moved to the other side of the desk, sat down. "Our introduction of the new designer pharmaceutical is moving forward as planned, although there was a hiccup this afternoon. Minor, of course."

Jamison seethed, didn't say anything.

"We've established which of our dealerships will be the primary and which shall be the secondary, with the elimination of a third." Picked up a piece of paper, read it. "Rogers has been terminated."

That's when Jamison perked up. "Do you mean permanently or temporarily terminated, Felix?"

Heydrich flinched imperceptibly. "Your meaning?" he hissed.

"My sources tell me that Mr. Rogers survived the assassination attempt. Worse, he shot and killed—and burned, I might add—the team assigned to kill him. That tells me that Mr. Rogers is still in contention to be the pri—"

"Nonsense!" Heydrich was on his feet, pacing the room. "Where did this come from, this . . . report from your so-called sources?"

Again, Jamison smiled inwardly. "The fact is, Felix . . . I don't know. Sometimes I receive information from anonymous sources, whether via email, voicemail, or a couriered letter."

Felix Heydrich stared at the man, wanting to crush him. "Fine. Doesn't matter. The Bulgarian team will distribute redweed to the primary dealership this evening at approximately eleven p.m. I want you there to supervise."

Paul Jamison had never been outside the office on business, always relying on his brother Peter to take care of operations. His smile quickly dissipated.

Even with Rogers' makeshift surgery at the vet, who removed two big bullets, flattened by the big man's belly fat, we were staged by 10 p.m.

Caleb was shocked to see Rogers toting and emplacing his sniper rifle, an old M24 with the ancient Leupold Ultra M3A scope. The big man lay down on top of the building, approximately 420 yards from either traphouse on 24th Street.

Had to admit, Caleb did a beautiful job of planning this last-minute change that I thought would've had him in hissy fits all night.

The Orange Avenue traphouse was still a-buzz with activity, given they'd lost four of their made members earlier today. Soldiers and dealers were scampering in and out of the house, making it difficult to clearly locate and identify the new upper management, which was trying to consolidate and reorganize the sloppy leftovers.

But Bobby Rogers knew who they were. He whispered to Caleb, "Guy in red top, black b-ball shorts."

"Who's he?"

"He the man, dude." Tonight, I was bitchboy for both shooters, manning the spotting scopes. I had one Leupold Mk 4 positioned directly at the 301 traphouse, just off to our right, and the one I was on now, at the 24th Street house. Spotter scopes are bigger and easier to handle and look through, because they're self-contained units. My two were on small tripods with small bags of shot, all tethered, on each leg, giving me vibration-free sight to each target.

The second scope had a small video adapter attached to it, allowing me to monitor the field of view without having to switch to the other scope during the Orange Avenue traphouse shoot. The little three-inch monitor sat at my chest, two inches below my right eye. As I peered through the scope at the 24th Street target, I could glance down periodically at the monitor to see activity at the 301 house. Any movement would've immediately caught my attention.

Eleven p.m.

"There he go." Rogers had two bullet holes in his gut, and still maintained a cool air.

Looked through my scope and found him. He was about 6'6" and all mouth and muscle. Beautiful target. "Roger, got him. White skull cap, red jersey, black shorts."

"Confirmed," Rogers acknowledged. "Okay if I blast this muthafucka?"

"Cleared to fire." I just smiled.

The audible CLICK! could've been a Zippo striking up, it was so quiet and smooth.

One second, I was looking at a formidable animal, this man in red.

Split-second later, his hips and knees buckled and all 250 pounds of potatoes came a-tumblin' down onto the front porch, people looking down at the fallen timber in utter disbelief.

"Man, these dudes stupid." Rogers loosed another round. And another.

My field of view was just enough to catch two more traphouse soldiers fall under Rogers' lethal rounds. Caleb then opened up on the gathering crowd, dropping three more soldiers in quick succession.

When those men fell, the crowd got wind of what was up: they were making nice targets for some awesome snipers somewhere out there in the nasty darkness.

The Bogeyman had come to 24th Street and he was hungry. BOOOOOOOOO!

Movement on my little monitor. "Shooters, we've got movement on target two. Shift right," I whispered to Caleb and Bobby.

Both snipers changed positions, drew beads on the new targets at the 301 traphouse.

Caleb was up first. "Four deadheads out front. Can't tell who—"

"Guy in white. He the man. Guy in blue and white top, baseball cap turned backwards. His number two." Without word from me, Rogers dropped both men before anyone could react.

Caleb looked over at Rogers. "Now what kinda gentleman fires out of order?"

Saw him nudge Bobby in the arm. Both men exchanged a quick glance, recognition between brethren.

I'd switched the monitor to the scope on the 24th Street traphouse. Same deal as before. Scanned both sectors, saw only three more people, all women, exit the 301 house. No further activity at the 24th Street house.

"Pull up, boys. Time to cruise," Caleb whispered, picking up his gear and dropping over the building on the rope, sliding down to ground. Rogers followed. I double-checked both traphouses for activity, packed up shop and joined the two on the ground.

The old van I'd pinched earlier was parked on the south side of the street, no working streetlights illuminating our path. Just three amigos out for a midnight stroll.

Caleb stopped and did a double-take at the 24th Street house: "You gotta be shittin' me," Caleb said, running back to the building. "On me, Tommy."

Bobby was slowing down, but he kept up with me, not complaining about anything. All rights, he should've been in the ICU at Memorial.

Caleb had already scaled the building again, ran down to the area near our original firing position. He'd seen something. We followed.

Didn't bother asking what the hell was up. He'd fill us in a second before we were scheduled to lay rounds on target.

He was already in position, eyeing his target. "Spot me, Tommy."

Without thinking, without looking, I dropped down to the roof, my scope already out and ready to emplace. No tripods or shot bags to steady it, I placed it on the edge of the roofline, right next to Caleb. "Target?"

"You wouldn't believe me if I told you, Ranger."

"Okay, then don't tell me." Peering through the scope, which I yawed slowly left to right and back again, I then figured out what he was so excited about. "Those dumbasses."

Finger already pulling back in the trigger, he said, "G'night, Boris." CLICK.

"Sleep tight, Josef." CLICK.

"Just get me there. I do the rest." Bobby Rogers was pacing the hotel suite we'd gotten so we could decompress after the mission.

"We've already set up a meeting with him. You and Nicky will drive up in a truck Tommy'll get for you. Let her drive. The man has snipers positioned on the rooftops of all buildings in his compound, with roving sentries walking around 24/7. Last time we were there, they let us in. You won't be able to do that, so you'll drive in with us, tucked in the bed of the truck. They won't check it 'cos they think we're morons like last time. We'll try to park close to the front entrance as possible. There's no way to stay out there to see when the walkers will be near our car, so it's yoyo for you guys."

Rogers stiffened up, rubbed the bandages over his stomach. "Yoyo, huh? Fuck's that?"

Looked at him and said, "You're on your own."

"If I'da known I'm yoyo on this mission, I mighta kicked both your asses and said fuck them white boys."

Caleb and I looked at the wounds on the big man, shook our heads in disbelief.

NickyHeil stood behind the chair, hand on her man's shoulder, not saying a word, lifted his shirt to inspect the bandages.

There was a time back in the day when I would never have allowed someone like NickyHeil in an ops planning session. For some odd reason—and I think I knew what it was—I let this one play out, 'cos it probably didn't matter anyway.

Nearly midnight, we were ushered into the Davis Island compound by two walkers who spoke something into a handheld. Men on the roof shifted positions. Only two men out tonight?

"You guys on vacation or something?" I asked a walker.

"Boss gave most of us the night off. Celebrating something. I never hear anything, so don't ask."

"I know how it is, being in the dark and the last to know anything. Get it all the time." Pointed to Caleb.

Walker smiled, pointed the way.

Inside, we were asked to sit in the drawing room. Drawing room, huh? If I hadn't known better, would've said I didn't bring my crayons.

Rogers stirred a moment, pulling the canvas cover from his head. No movement on the roof, he eased over the side of the truck, pulling his rifle with him. NickyHeil didn't move.

"I'm told there was some trouble in Newtown recently." Felix Heydrich was seated in the center of his couch, facing us, both in high, straight-back chairs designed specifically for discomfort.

I looked at Caleb.

Caleb looked at me.

"No? You two don't keep up with the news?"

"You promised us there'd be movement on our next assignment. Haven't heard anything from you in weeks." Caleb was trying hard to be polite. Very hard.

Heydrich looked over at his desk, watching something on a bank of monitors. He paused a moment. "Gentlemen, will you excuse me?"

It wasn't a question. Soon as he exited the room, I jumped up and looked on at the monitors.

My heart rose up into my throat.

Shit.

"What is it, Pearson?" Heydrich asked his head of security, looking into the bed of the truck.

"I don't know, sir. Thought I saw something. Normally, I'd not be out here like this, but as you know, we're light-staffed this evening." Pearson wasn't happy being shorthanded.

Felix turned to him. "You're paid well enough to do the job on your own, Mr. Pearson, so I suggest you get to it.

Rogers and Nicky had crawled under a thick hedge to the left of the main entrance, and lay still in the bushes. As Felix and Pearson discussed the level of security, Rogers slowly and carefully lifted the rifle and pushed it ever so carefully into the giant hedge, positioned it just so. He then separated the thick branches and pushed his body well into the bushes, coming down just over his rifle, his good eye positioned over the breech of the rifle. Looked through the scope and lined up Felix Heydrich in his crosshairs, waited for the right breath, the minimum heart beat that slowed down to a pause.

Nicky raised the pistol to the back of Rogers' head.

BOOM!

Shots rang out immediately in front of the main door. I was already out the door, just behind Caleb, who was rotating his peach like a spinning top, trying to take in the situation.

"Sir! In the bushes! Left of door! Twenty feet!"

More shots into the bushes.

SCREAMS.

Heydrich had already run for the cover of the truck, which was only about fifteen feet from where he had been standing with Pearson.

Caleb and I looked on in terrible sadness as the two sentries dragged out the limp bodies of Bobby Rogers, face torn away and blood leaking from a massive head wound, and his girl NickyHeil, unrecognizable from the multiple gunshot wounds to her head and torso.

Our drive back to Sarasota was in silence.

I mourned the loss of the big man with the big heart, the man who tried to pull himself out of a bad situation, even though he knew there was no way out. In the end he sacrificed himself to ease the suffering of many people. And he let his own girl pull the trigger.

Caleb had done quick planning: he had spotted both rooftop snipers . . . retrieved Bobby Rogers' sniper rifle . . . slipped under the fountain in the center of the circular drive . . . drawn good aim on both men who were at opposite ends of the 200-foot-long roofline. And dropped each one with precision head shots.

Following his lead, I'd grabbed NickyHeil's pistol, the one she had used to murder her own husband minutes earlier, and put both sentries to the pavement with double-hits to the head and neck.

Felix Heydrich had cowered below me, begging me not to do it.

He spent long minutes explaining the outline of his business operations, from Hong Kong to California, Florida to London, he had it all covered. His ultimate Segreta Antico boss, thousands of miles away in Rome, would see to it we were safely escorted out of the country on a private flight to the destination of our choice. Anywhere you wish! Anytime! And we'll throw in $25 million cash! What employer in his right mind would do such a thing for his valued employees?

Yes, what employer would do such a thing?

Flashes of my prison time . . . the redweed high that gave me strokes and heart attacks just knowing I wasn't in any kind of reality at all, going on some grand adventure to the destination of my choice. I was in purgatory.

Tired of his pitch, I interrupted his narrative with two .45-cal bullets to his brainpan as he was explaining the weather in the Azores this time of year, and how the little girls there—those soft, delicious budding curves—were ripest in late August.

Along with the fruit on the vines. . . .

Rachel invaded my head the next morning, reminding what a fuck-up I was, how driving TommyTaxi was the lamest job in the world.

Her world.

Called her and said I wanted to do lunch.

We met at our favorite bar out on Holmes Beach and I told her about Felix Heydrich and she immediately broke down and told me he'd forced her to give him information, reveal things I wanted hidden from that bastard. From everyone.

Her words a blur.

"I'm sorry, Tommy!"

Empty and hollow to me.

"I love you, Tommy!"

My heart just not there, not in it.

"I want us to be together again!" she cried.

"Your heart's in the shade, Rachel," I said.

Enough was enough.

Trust had diffused away, dissipated into the afternoon sky, and disappeared altogether into some heaven I couldn't believe in, let alone see with my own eyes.

Didn't want to.

As I walked away from the love of my life, she shotgunned one plea after another, trying to get me to stay with her.

Shit, a guy needed an exit visa just to get away from this woman.

Saw Sara the next day. Things seemed better with her. I was able to relate on a different level, tell her about the things I'd wanted to share, to work on. Her family had seen two deaths over the past two months and she just wasn't herself, she'd said, apologizing profusely and telling me I could see her for free for a month, if I wanted.

Wanted to tell her about the now-deceased Bulgarians, thanks to Caleb's last-second marksmanship, Felix Heydrich and his worldwide business of trafficking in the human soul, the traphouses we'd shut down, and the brave man Bobby Rogers who wanted out so badly, and in the end gave his life for a righteous cause.

I wanted to share with Sara the pain of seeing warriors with a heart die in front of me, leaving behind the detritus of this world.

I was skilled at running fast and making sense out of chaos, having to decide who lives and dies, all in the narrow span of milliseconds. But I couldn't figure out how to repair myself.

Maybe I needed Sara to do all that for me. Or someone with gray-haired wisdom.

Most of all, I needed to hear her tell me my decision to leave Rachel altogether was a good decision and not one based on some spring-loaded emotion. God knows I could kill a man without putting any thought into it, but I was a wreck of a man when it came to the ultimate affair . . . a lifelong relationship with someone who truly mattered.

All my thoughts over the next two weeks focused on one grand theme: trust.

The only person I knew I could trust, thick or thin, was Caleb Gatewood, my old Ranger buddy. He'd been there when Rachel had blown me off, and gotten me into decent enough shape to continue on when I was falling apart in front of him.

His best advice to me: said I needed to cruise for a while, see the sweet parts of the world where bullets weren't flying in my direction. Said I should hop a sailboat as a crew member and head down to South America. Or was it South Africa? South Somewhere is all recall.

Yeah, South Africa.

So off I went, from the mean streets of Princess Sarasota and its anguished northern territory to the most dangerous country in the world, where bullets and spears flew every which way as casually as after-church chatter and homemade fried chicken.

And that is where I hoped I would find something I'd not felt in many years, if ever: some much-needed peace of mind.

The more I considered my wish, the more I sensed I'd wind up back here.

Magnetic pull of Old Florida, you know.

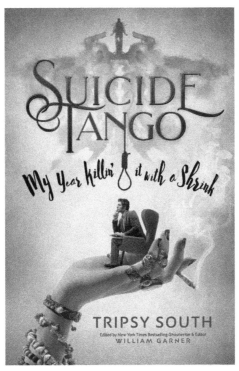

Suicide Tango
My Year Killin' It With A Shrink

"A challenging black comedy that aims to entertain and save lives."
—*Kirkus Reviews*

"Illuminating, gallows humor look at teen suicide . . . Full of wry observations, and justifiable outrage, *Suicide Tango* is a must-read for everyone." —*Seattle Book Review*

"An entertaining, edgy portrait of therapy." —*BlueInk Review*

"A well-written book that slaps the reader upside the head with the snark of a young woman." —*Chanticleer Reviews* (Best Book, 5-Star Review)

Paperback available from Amazon.com and other retail outlets.

Please visit AdagioPress.com for other esoteric reads.

The Prince

Niccolò Machiavelli's *The Prince* has become a classic over the centuries since it first appeared around 1510, not because of its elegance or style but because of its subversive content about the true nature of power. Mainstream historians and academics have labelled it a "political treatise," but this is only a small part of the picture.

The Prince isn't just for princes who thirst for, or are forcibly thrown into, advancement. It is a raw and bloody field manual for upper- and mid-level managers on predatorial ethics and power: what it is, how to obtain it, and what to do with it once you have found, stumbled across, or been granted it.

Paperback available from Amazon.com and other retail outlets.

Please visit AdagioPress.com for other esoteric reads.

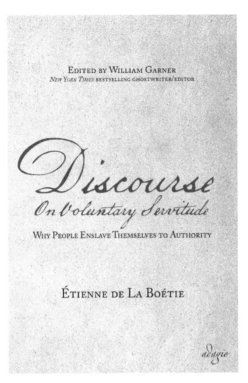

EDITED BY WILLIAM GARNER
New York Times BESTSELLING GHOSTWRITER/EDITOR

Discourse
On Voluntary Servitude
WHY PEOPLE ENSLAVE THEMSELVES TO AUTHORITY

ÉTIENNE DE LA BOÉTIE

adagio

Discourse On Voluntary Servitude
Why People Enslave Themselves to Authority

While short in words, William Garner's updated version for the 21st century speaks volumes to all those who value liberty on all levels, but who are currently trapped in the yoke of oppression by the many tyrants in every government and institution.

This book may be considered the flip-side to Machiavelli's *The Prince*, which teaches would-be dictators how to acquire and maintain power over people and institutions.

Paperback available from Amazon.com and other retail outlets.

Please visit AdagioPress.com for other esoteric reads.

Sun Tzu *The Art of War*
Ancient Wisdom . . . Modern Twist

The late *New York Times* bestselling author and ex-Delta commander Major Tom Greer, aka Dalton Fury:

"Dean Garner's version of *The Art of War* confirms for us that for the past 2,000 years the fundamental principles of special operations in battle have not only remained true, but they apply equally to today's boardrooms and bedrooms. When on the hunt or holding ground, success can only be had by the precise application of disguise, deception and diversion, and a genuine appreciation for angles, inches, and seconds. Ranger Garner masterfully shows us how."

Paperback available from Amazon.com and other retail outlets.

Please visit AdagioPress.com for other esoteric reads.

CPSIA information can be obtained
at www.ICGtesting.com
Printed in the USA
FSHW022010070819
60790FS